A GRAND THING

Sheila Norton

ABOUT THE AUTHOR

Sheila Norton lives near Chelmsford in Essex and has been writing avidly since childhood.

A GRAND THING is Sheila's fourteenth novel. She has been published by Little Brown/Piatkus (as Sheila Norton and as Olivia Ryan) and also enjoys a successful self-publishing career.

She also writes short stories and has had over 100 of these published in magazines including Woman's Weekly, Yours, The People's Friend, etc.

She worked for most of her life as a medical secretary, until retiring early to concentrate on her writing.

Sheila enjoys hearing from readers and can be contacted through her website: www.sheilanorton.com

Other books by Sheila Norton:

Romantic comedies:
The Trouble with Ally
Other People's Lives
Body & Soul
The Travel Bug
Sweet Nothings

'The Tales From' series (written as Olivia Ryan):
Tales from a Hen Weekend
Tales from a Wedding Day
Tales from a Honeymoon Hotel

'The Sisters' Series:
Sophie Being Single
Debra Being Divorced
Millie Being Married

Short story anthologies:
Travellers' Tales
Let's Get the Kettle On!

Novels set in the 1960s:
Yesterday
Ticket To Ride

**To find out more about the author and her books, or to
apply for email updates, visit : _www.sheilanorton.com_**

It's such a grand thing to be a mother of a mother –
that's why the world calls her
a grandmother. (*Unknown*).

KATE

Once Upon a Time

I got the call about the baby towards the end of a fairly normal kind of day with the twins. Alfie seemed to have eaten something that disagreed with him, resulting in several very unpleasant changes of nappy, and Amelia had fallen over outside and, despite the absence of any sign of bruise, bump or blood, was still snivelling and rubbing her knees self-pityingly two hours later. Only eighteen months old, and a drama queen already. By half past five, when I'd fed them both and got them tidied up ready for their dad to come and collect them, they were both happy to snuggle up with me on the sofa while I read them a story.

'Once upon a time ...' I suppressed a yawn, deciding I'd be going to bed early that night, 'a baker baked a gingerbread man.'

And then the phone rang.

'I won't be a minute,' I told the twins. I picked up the phone, half expecting it to be their dad – my son – warning me he was running late. Or their mum saying she'd come for them instead. But it wasn't. It was my son-in-law Ben, and he was shouting at the top of his voice before I'd even said hello.

'It's coming, Kate! It's coming already!'

'The baby?' I said, stupidly. What else? 'But there's still two weeks to go.'

'I know, I know, but I'm telling you, it's coming *now*. Steph's waters have gone, and she's getting contractions every five minutes.'

'*What*? Every five ...? When did it start, Ben?'

'Only an hour or so ago. Steph was going to call you later – we didn't expect things to progress so fast. It's coming really quickly! We need to get to the hospital.' He sounded panic-struck. 'Can you come round and stay with Izzie?'

'Um ... I can, of course I can, but I'm just waiting for Michael to collect the twins. He should be here in half an hour or so.'

'Half an hour? But ...'

'Unless I can get hold of him, or Jo, and see if they can get here sooner.'

'But then it'll take you another half an hour to get here, and we'll still have to get to the hospital, and ...' His voice was shaking. 'Can't you bring the twins with you?'

'Yes.' I was beginning to appreciate the scale of the urgency. 'Yes, right – of course. I'll be there as soon as I can. Don't panic,' I added, fighting to stay calm myself. 'Tell Steph to hang on!'

Five minutes later, the bewildered twins had been bundled into shoes and jackets and strapped into their car seats in the back of my car, and I was locking the front door while leaving a garbled message on their father's voicemail explaining where I'd gone – where he'd find his children. We hit the rush hour, of course, going through the town, and at every red light and roundabout I drummed my fingers on the wheel, muttering *Come on, come on!* like the kind of short-tempered impatient driver I normally hated.

When I finally pulled up outside my daughter's house, the front door was open and Ben was standing at the threshold, looking out for me.

'She's here!' he shouted, running back into the house as I unstrapped the twins and lifted them out of the car. He returned, far more slowly, with my daughter holding onto his arm, puffing and blowing as she walked. 'Thank God, Kate! I don't think we could've left it any longer,' he said.

'OK, just get going. Do you need help getting into the car?' I added to Stephanie as she gasped and clutched at her stomach.

'No, don't worry about *me,* you've obviously got your hands full already!' she snapped, nodding at the twins, who were both hanging onto me for dear life and shrinking away from their unusually stressed-looking aunt and uncle.

I didn't rise to the bait – the sarcasm, the implied criticism. She was anxious, frightened – understandably so, and anyway I was used to it. Today wasn't the day for having the same old arguments, dealing with the same old complaints.

'Where's Izzie?' I asked instead as Ben opened the passenger door of his car and helped Stephanie inside.

'Sitting in front of the TV,' he replied. 'I've put the *Frozen* DVD on so that she'd stay there. I didn't want her seeing her mummy like this. I kept Steph in the other room.'

'Come *on,* Ben, for God's sake!' she shouted. 'We've wasted enough time already waiting for Mum to get here. Do you want this baby to be born in the car?'

I touched my son-in-law's arm briefly as he turned to get into the driver's seat. 'Drive carefully,' I said. 'I hope it's all OK. Let me know.'

'Of course,' he said, and with a roar of the engine and a rattle of the exhaust, they were gone.

'Come on, you two,' I said brightly to the twins as we stared after their departing car. 'Let's go and find your cousin.'

'Mummy and Daddy had to go and get the new baby,' Izzie informed me without raising her eyes from the TV. 'But Mummy didn't say goodbye.'

'Oh, I'm sure she did, darling.' I bent to kiss the top of her head. 'You probably just didn't hear her.'

Amelia and Alfie sat down, one either side of her, giving her adoring looks. Izzie was three and a half, and as far as the twins were concerned she could do no wrong, even if occasionally she yelled at them and refused to share

7

her toys. I went into the kitchen and put the kettle on. I needed a good strong cup of tea. My hands were still shaking from the shock and the rush of getting round there so quickly and I needed to pull myself together.

'*Frozen*'s finished!' Izzie wailed in distress a little later. 'Can I watch it again, Nanny?'

Amelia and Alfie were rubbing their eyes with tiredness. It was half past six and I hadn't heard anything from their father yet.

'Why don't I get you all changed into your jamas, get you a nice drink of milk each and read you a story instead?' I suggested.

I'd picked up the Gingerbread Man book with the twins' things when I left home. Might as well carry on with that one.

'Once upon a time,' I began again as all three children had eventually finished their bedtime drinks and were settled next to me on the sofa, 'A baker baked a gingerbread man.'

'Why?' Izzie asked. Every three year-old's favourite word. 'Was the gingerbread man going to get gobbled up by a fox?' she added with a horrible smile.

Just as well the twins weren't old enough to be upset by her spoiling of the plot. I should have remembered that this particular story usually led, with Izzie, to a bloodthirsty conversation about body parts being bitten off. Before I had grandkids – to say nothing of my own kids, of course, (which sometimes felt like centuries ago), I might have thought the idea of the poor little gingerbread man being devoured by the wicked fox would frighten a child of such tender years. But then, there were a lot of things I might have thought. A lot of things I might have got wrong, once upon a time.

Once upon a time, I was Kate Freeman. Just Kate, not *Mum*, not *Nanny*, not one of that cross-section of the community who jump the minute they hear a child screaming because they assume it's one of theirs. As Kate Freeman I had a career, I had a tidy house – and I had a husband, as a matter of fact but that's another story. I used to wear high heels, straight skirts and smart jackets. My grocery shopping never included chocolate spread or biscuits shaped like animals. And then we had our first child, Danielle. Five years later we had Michael. And then, after another four years, our little after-thought, Stephanie. And just as Stephanie was coming up for seven, and teething babies and stroppy toddlers were becoming ever more distant memories, Danielle got pregnant at the age of sixteen and it started all over again.

Don't get me wrong – my children were all very much wanted and loved. I loved being a mummy, I made it my full-time career and threw myself into it totally, the way we did back then in the days before maternity leave was invented, when most mothers fully expected to stay at home with their babies. I did exactly that, with my first two, but after Stephanie was born I had to go back to work. Their father had been made redundant and my money was needed to support the family. And although Danielle's pregnancy was a shock (to put it mildly – she'd managed to hide not just the pregnancy until the fourth month, but the fact that she had a boyfriend at all), I did what mums do. I offered her nothing but unconditional love and support, and money for the pram, the cot and the babygros, and help with night feeds and dirty nappies and everything else a sixteen-year-old hasn't given a moment's thought to when she recklessly says yes to unprotected sex thinking she's in love and she *can't help it*.

Since then, Danielle had married a Frenchman and had two more children and was living an apparently idyllic life in rural Brittany, only coming home with her bilingual adolescent brood at Christmas and other family occasions. Her first son, Toby, was a strapping six-foot almost-twenty-year-old now. But I often had the younger two kids to stay for a couple of weeks in their summer holidays.

More to the point, I now had these other three gorgeous little grandchildren living much closer to home – actually feeling at times like they were all living in my house – and a fourth one literally on the way. And the soon-to-be Big Sister was staring up at me, waiting for the story to continue.

'Well anyway,' I said, turning the page to move quickly on with the tale rather than get into a full-blown discussion about serial killers of gingerbread men, 'When the baker's back was turned, the gingerbread man jumped out of the oven ...'

'Your phone's ringing, Nanny.'

'Yes.' I jumped up, handing the book to Izzie and telling her to show the twins the pictures until I got back.

'Is it my mummy?'

'I don't know.'

My heart was pounding with anxiety as I ran outside to the hall where I'd dumped my bag, and grabbed the phone. It was Ben, and he sounded slightly hysterical.

'We've got a little boy!'

'Already? Oh, Ben, that's wonderful! A boy! I hope you got to the hospital in time?' I added, my head suddenly filling with alarming images of Ben delivering the baby in the car.

'Only just!' He laughed. 'It was bedlam, Kate – as soon as we arrived they put Steph in a wheelchair and rushed us round to the labour ward. I heard him take a breath. 'I was scared it was too early, but they said everything would be fine ...'

'So *is* it fine?' I interrupted. 'Is the baby OK? Steph OK?'

'Yes! Yes, absolutely. Steph's over the moon, she can't believe how quick, how easy it was, you know, compared with last time.'

Izzie's birth had been the exact opposite. Nearly two weeks overdue, an agonisingly slow induced labour – agonising for me as well, waiting at home for news – Steph and Ben had both been exhausted. When I visited, with flowers and hugs and little pink outfits from Mothercare, Steph's face was still white with shock and tiredness. *You didn't tell me it was going to be so awful*, she hissed at me as if it was my fault.

'Well, thank God,' I said now. 'Thank God everything's all right. Congratulations to you both!'

'Thanks, Kate. And thanks for dashing round like that to look after Izzie. I'm sorry we were both kind of stressed. Is Izzie OK?'

'Of course. I was just reading them all a story, actually, so I'd better go and finish it.'

'The twins haven't been picked up yet, then?' he said, managing to sound critical despite everything.

'Not yet. I expect Michael will be here any time now. Then I'll get Izzie to bed.'

'Thanks. They're keeping Steph in here till the morning, but I'll come back later and get some sleep. Give Izzie a kiss from us. Will you tell her about Isaac?'

'Who?'

Ben laughed. 'Her baby brother. We're calling him Isaac.'

'Oh!' I felt stupid for not asking. *Isaac.* Well, I supposed I'd get used to it. 'Would you like me to? Or would you prefer to tell her yourself?'

'Um, yes, actually maybe that'd be better, Kate. Do you mind?'

'No. I agree, I'll leave it to you. Otherwise I'll never get her to sleep.'

'OK, I'll tell her in the morning, then I can take her with me to bring them home – Steph and Isaac. You can stay over, if you like, Kate, to save you waiting up for me? Then you can see the baby tomorrow.'

'I'd love to. But I'll have the twins again in the morning.'

'Oh yes.' There was that slight edge of disapproval to his tone again.

'I'll come round to see him as soon as I can, though. I can't wait!' The shock was beginning to wear off and the reality of the birth suddenly hit home, making me laugh out loud with relief. 'Give Steph my love, won't you. I'll see you later.'

'You were a *long* time, Nanny,' Izzie said accusingly when I returned to the lounge. All three children had gone to lie on the floor in front of the TV (which was now showing the News with the volume turned down), and they all looked on the point of dozing off. 'Was it my mummy?'

'No. Someone else,' I prevaricated – and luckily, before I could be interrogated any further, the doorbell rang, finally announcing the arrival of my son to collect the twins.

'You got the message then?' I asked him quietly as we helped them into their coats again. 'Sorry about the short notice, but ...'

'That's OK. It's good news, yeah?'

Ben had apparently called him already.

'Yes, brilliant news. Ben says they're both doing fine.'

'*Isaac*, though. Where the hell did they dig that one up from?'

'Well, it's their choice, Mike.'

'I know. But *Isabel and Isaac*. I suppose if they have another one it'll be Isaiah, or India, or ...'

'All right! For God's sake, it's their baby, their choice – what difference does it make to you?' I regretted it as soon as I'd said it, of course. 'Sorry. Didn't mean to snap. I'm tired.'

'Have the twins played you up today?'

'No.' I sighed. 'Of course not.' They were still babies, really, still too little to play anybody up, but they *were* hard work. Much harder work for an over-sixty-year-old, however much I hated to admit it, however much I enjoyed having them. 'But it's been a long day, and I suppose I was worried about Steph.'

'You worry too much, Mum.'

This time I managed to swallow back the irritation. Dearly though I loved him, my son sometimes exasperated me. OK, he was probably no different from most men of his age – the flippant comments that showed complete lack of understanding. Hopefully he'd improve as he got older. Some men did.

'Yes, well, it's my job to worry about you all. As I'm sure you know, now you're a parent yourself.'

'No point worrying, Mum. OK for tomorrow, usual time?'

I had the twins three days every week, and I tried to vary their activities. Tomorrow was Thursday and I usually took them to a Mini Music Makers' group. It was fun, but tonight my head was aching at the thought of it.

'Yes, of course,' I said, kissing the twins goodbye. 'See you then.'

It didn't take long to get Izzie into bed. She was half asleep already, and as I kissed her soft pink cheek and watched her eyes close, I wondered how this child – who I loved so much it actually hurt, sometimes, to look at her – was going to receive the news of a baby brother in the morning (*Isaac* – not sure about that). All she'd talked about ever since she'd been told about the baby in Mummy's tummy was a sister. Stephanie and Ben hadn't wanted to know the sex of the baby. *We like the idea of having a surprise.* It'd certainly be a surprise for Izzie.

I'd poured myself a tiny amount of wine, all I dared allow myself because of driving home later in my state of tiredness, and was halfway through a completely idiotic TV programme about people who ate like pigs and claimed they couldn't understand why they were overweight, when my phone rang again. This time it was Danielle calling from France.

'Lovely to hear from you!' As I didn't see Danielle or her family too often, I sometimes found myself imagining them all in a kind of rosy glow of sweetness and nostalgia. 'How are the kids?'

'Fine, fine.' Danielle brushed this aside. 'Just phoning about the new baby! Exciting, isn't it! Have you seen him yet? *Isaac?*'

'No, not yet – and don't say it like that. Isaac's a very nice name.'

'*Isabel and Isaac?*' she laughed. 'It's a bit *Jeremy and Jemima-ish*, isn't it?'

'Well, we'll soon get used to it – and it's their choice, at the end of the day.'

'Of course it is. I wonder what Izzie said? She wanted a little sister, didn't she?'

'She doesn't know yet. I'm at the house with her – she's asleep upstairs. But I'm sure she'll be thrilled with the baby.'

'Hmm. I wouldn't be too sure about that. They need to watch out for jealousy. I told Ben, they need to handle the situation carefully. I mean, I know Steph's been sending her round to you a lot while she's been pregnant, and with all due respect, Mum, it must feel to Izzie like she's being palmed off, you know? And if they keep doing it now the

14

new baby's here, she'll feel like she's being got out of the way, while he gets all the attention.'

'Danielle!' I felt close to snapping again. 'She's not *palmed off* with me. She enjoys spending time with me. It's not like she's being farmed out with a stranger!'

'All right, I know that, obviously, I was only saying ...'

'Well, don't. If you want to say something, say it to your sister. I don't want to be continually caught in the middle like this.'

'Sorry, Mum.' Danielle sounded offended. 'I wasn't having a go at you, or anything. What's the matter? Has someone upset you?'

'No. I'm tired, and a bit emotional. Emotional in a *good* way, you know? I'm just relieved and happy that everything's OK, so I don't want to hear anything negative. Izzie will be fine.'

'Of course she will.' Danielle's voice was more gentle. 'I'm sure she's always fine with you. All the children love being with you. You have Izzie far too much, though – *and* the twins. Don't let them start leaving the new baby with you all the time too. It's too much for you, Mum, at your age. They shouldn't be putting on you.'

'They're not. It isn't like that,' I said wearily. It wore me out, this constant nit-picking between my kids. In many ways, Danielle was the worst. She seemed to resent every favour I did for her brother and sister, although God knows I'd done enough to help *her* over the years, before she moved to France.

Jealousy, I told myself after we'd said goodbye. I drained the wine glass and shook my head. Danielle was jealous of my closer relationship with the other two. No wonder she thought it was her business to comment on Izzie's possible resentment of the new baby. I loved all my children equally, and all the grandchildren equally. Could I help it if some of them were in France, while others were ... let's face it, more often than not in my house? I was too happy about the new baby to give a damn what they called him. I didn't even mind how often I might be asked to look after him. I just couldn't bear it if his arrival caused even more tension between my own kids. It was time they all bloody well grew up and stopped their bickering!

KATE

The Old Woman Who Lived in a Shoe

'Can I drop Izzie off with you again, Mum? Only Isaac's not feeding well, I don't think I'm producing enough milk and the health visitor says I need to get more rest. It's impossible with a three-year-old to look after.'

'I know.' I did sometimes wonder whether my darling daughters forgot I actually brought up three children myself, back in the dim dark ages when nobody ever told me I needed to get more rest. 'Shouldn't she be at pre-school today though?'

'It's half-term.'

Already? The terms, and half-terms, seemed to pass so much more quickly these days. Were the holidays longer, or more frequent, or was I just getting older even faster than I realised? Already baby Isaac was two weeks old – how could that be?

'Right. Well, OK then, but you'll need to drop her round. You know I've got the twins today.'

'Oh yes.' Steph's voice sounded grim. 'As usual.'

'Yes. The same three days every week. It's what I agreed to do – there's no need to sound like that about it.'

'Well, honestly Mum, they're not really being fair. It's not as if you're a spring chicken.'

'Thank you, dear.'

'You know what I mean. You look worn out half the time. The twins are a handful.'

'No they're not. I enjoy having them, just like I enjoy having Izzie, and no doubt I'll enjoy having Isaac in due course. Michael and Jo both have to work, and you know how expensive the nursery is.'

'In that case …' Stephanie paused. 'Well, you know what I think.'

'Yes.' Steph's views on the subject were aired often enough, and I didn't want to hear them again. 'But you're fortunate, aren't you. Ben earns enough to support you all.'

'Only because we live within our means!'

It was a well-worn argument. 'OK,' I said with a sigh. 'Look, I'm just doing the twins' breakfast, and I'm taking them to Mini Music Makers today so if you bring Izzie round now, she can come too. It's no problem.'

No problem apart from the obvious one of managing all three of them single-handedly, but it'd be fun – wouldn't it?

'I really don't mind. She's not any trouble,' I told Bob later over coffee. 'But I do worry a bit that she might feel pushed out, you know? Now her mummy's got the new baby. My other daughter keeps on about that. '

'The daughter in France?' The poor man probably had a job keeping up.

'Yes. Danielle. She keeps on with all these dire warnings of gloom and doom about Izzie growing up to hate the baby. I tell her it's none of her business. My kids all seem to think it's OK to criticise each other's parenting. They disagree on virtually every aspect of it, from dummies to sleeping through the night, from weaning to schooling. It's bloody exhausting!'

Bob laughed. 'I can imagine. Poor you.'

'Well, as I say, normally I pretty much tell them all to shut up. But I'm a little bit concerned, now, that Danielle may have a point about Izzie.'

'Why? Has she been caught giving the baby a crafty pinch on the leg or something?'

'Oh God, no, nothing like that. She seems quite happy with him, to be honest. But they *are* getting her out of the way quite a lot since he was born. I know it's difficult coping with a newborn and a toddler, and of course, I enjoy having her, but …'

'I'm sure you're worrying unnecessarily. She seems perfectly happy. She loves coming to you anyway, doesn't she.'

'I hope you're right.'

We both turned to look at the kids. They were all playing in the café's toy corner – Izzie, the twins, and Bob's two-year-old grandson Freddie. Izzie was singing one of the songs that had featured in this morning's music session: *Incy Wincy Spider, climbed the water spout ...* and Freddie was trying to copy her actions, while the twins sat throwing things at each other. *Down came the rain and washed poor Incy out.* Give it a few more minutes and one or other of them would probably start whining, then they'd all drift back in our direction. A short play with the toys here, after already tiring themselves out at the Mini Music Makers' group, usually guaranteed that at least three out of the four would be ready for a nap when we got them home.

Sure enough, even as we were watching them, Amelia stood up and pushed her brother over, Alfie let out a wail, Freddie started to look upset, and Izzie turned to me, hands on hips, every inch the big grown-up cousin, announcing that the twins were being *very* naughty and Freddie was being silly.

'Bugger!' Bob said under his breath, giving me a grin. Our brief snatch of adult conversation was over for another week.

None of my children knew about Bob. Not that there was any *reason* to keep quiet about him. He was just a friend, just the only other grandparent who regularly came to the music group. So we'd naturally drifted into keeping each other company, being surrounded as we were by young mums and the occasional young dad, who thought nothing of squatting on the floor with their toddlers and throwing themselves around during the action songs.

'I'm afraid I'll need a chair,' Bob had said, the first time he turned up with little Freddie at the library where the group was held. 'If I sat down there, I'd never get up again.'

I felt much the same, but I usually stood at the back of the group because it was the only way I could keep an eye on both the twins and stop them from disappearing behind bookshelves.

'Nothing like having grandkids to make you aware of every joint in your body!' I'd sympathised with him, and just like that, we'd struck up a friendship. Within a couple of weeks we were stopping off at this terrible child-friendly café after the group finished at eleven o'clock, for a sustaining hot drink and usually a muffin too, and a chat. The chat, interrupted as it often was by the demands of one or other of the grandchildren, hadn't managed to progress much beyond sharing anecdotes about the kids and the reasons why we'd both ended up living alone.

I wasn't really sure whether I'd kept quiet about him because I was afraid my children might disapprove for some reason. Or, more likely, knowing them, they'd argue among themselves about it. Because let's face it, it wasn't just childcare they disagreed on – oh no – politics, religion, morality, nothing was too serious for my three offspring to take up arms with each other about. I sometimes wondered how, when I'd given birth to all three of them myself, they'd managed to grow up with apparently nothing whatsoever in common.

Or … perhaps I hadn't told them about Bob because I just didn't want to. I wanted to keep something, just this one little quite unimportant aspect of my life, to myself. It was nobody else's business, after all.

I was on my way home after saying goodbye to Bob when I bumped into Pam. She lived just along the road from me, but we didn't know each other very well. From my window I'd sometimes seen her going past with a little girl who looked about Izzie's age, and occasionally during the school holidays there was an older boy too. Today, though, she was on her own, walking slowly, her head down, looking so sad that it seemed churlish not to say anything.

'Hello. No grandkids today?'

She glanced up at me, looking surprised.

'Oh, hello.' She looked down at the twins in their double buggy, at Izzie trotting along next to it holding the handle, and seemed to decide to ignore the question. 'How are you?' she said instead.

'Oh, you know!' I laughed. 'Shattered, but that's what it's all about, isn't it – keeping them entertained, getting run off our feet …'

'Yes, I daresay.' She sighed, and as if making a supreme effort, went on, 'I see there's another new baby in your family.'

'That's right.' I smiled and nodded at Izzie. 'You've got a little brother now, haven't you, sweetheart.'

Izzie pulled a face. 'Yes. But he cries too much. And I don't know why they got a *boy*. I wanted them to get me a sister.'

'Oh dear, never mind,' Pam said. 'Little brothers can be good fun. You'll be able to boss him around.'

Izzie shrugged, and then started to whine about not wanting to walk any further.

'We're nearly home,' I told her. 'Why don't you go on your scooter? She insisted on bringing it,' I explained to Pam, 'but it lasted all of five minutes, now she's bored with it and I've got to carry it as well as pushing the buggy. Are you heading back? You're welcome to walk with us, unless you're in a hurry. We'll take all day at this rate.'

'I'm not in a hurry,' Pam said, and we matched our pace to Izzie's dawdle as we moved on. 'I've got all day. Nothing to rush for.'

'Wish I could say the same. Got to get lunch for these three when I get in. One likes ham, the other two like cheese but one will only eat it toasted, the other one likes sandwiches but pulls them apart and leaves the crusts ...'

'I can imagine,' she said, looking straight ahead. 'Must be difficult, with all those children.'

'Tell me about it!' I raised my eyes and laughed. 'It feels like dozens, but actually it's only these three, and now the baby, most of the time. But in the school holidays I get a couple of grumpy teenagers over from France too. I sometimes feel like the Old Woman Who Lived in a Shoe.'

She didn't respond. Just kept walking. I had a sudden very uneasy feeling that I was somehow putting my foot in it.

'How often do *you* look after the children?' I asked. Maybe I'd been going on too much about myself. Needed to turn the conversation round to her. 'I've noticed the little girl because she looks about the same age as Izzie.'

'Lily. She's four. And her brother's eight. George. But they don't come all that often.'

'Think yourself lucky!' I said, and laughed. And then stopped laughing very quickly.

Pam had stopped walking and turned to face me, looking upset and irritated.

'Actually,' she said, 'it's you that's lucky.'

'Oh. I know. I mean, I do know that really, of course!' I said quickly, but she was continuing, her voice tight with offence:

'You have *no idea*. Seeing your grandchildren every week – I know, I've seen them, always being dropped off at your house. Lily's got a little scooter too, just like that one. She brings it when she comes round. She was supposed to be with me today – and her brother, as it's half-term. I should have been walking home with them now, *looking forward* to making them lunch, not moaning about it. I've got everything ready at home. Chocolate spread – their favourite – and crisps, and biscuits, and orange-juice. I know they're not proper healthy food like they're supposed to have, but that's one of the pleasures of looking after the kids, if you ask me – giving them some special treats, things they're probably not allowed to have at home.'

'Yes, you're right, I ...'

'I buy them comics, too. Fun ones, not the educational ones. I'd already bought some for them today. They're lying on the kitchen table – *My Magic Pony* for her, and *Galaxy Raid!* for him. We were going to the park this afternoon. They were going to have fish fingers and baked beans for their dinner and play some games this evening.'

'That sounds lovely.'

'Yes! It all sounds very lovely, doesn't it, except that they haven't even come. It was cancelled again this morning, at the last minute, just as I was waiting for them to turn up. Not that it's anything unusual, but probably you can't understand it, can you, with your happy family, your hundreds of grandchildren, your lovely new baby. How can you *possibly* complain to me that you see them so often? *Think yourself lucky*? You must be joking!'

There was silence for a moment as she finally ran out of steam, and then her hand flew to her mouth and she gasped, 'Oh my God. I'm *so* sorry.'

'No,' I said, shaken but duly chastised. '*I'm* sorry. It was thoughtless of me, a thoughtless thing to say. Obviously I didn't mean it, but ...'

'Of course you didn't. I had no right to jump down your throat like that. What on earth must you think of me?'

'Don't worry, I understand,' I said, although to be honest, I didn't. I'd been too taken aback by her outburst to work out exactly what was going on with her family but it was pretty obvious she wasn't happy!

'Nanny,' Izzie said in a little voice. 'Can we go home now? I'm hungry.'

We started walking again, Pam stiff and silent beside me, looking straight ahead. I glanced at her and thought I could see tears in her eyes. When we reached my gate, we stopped to say an awkward goodbye.

'Hopefully you'll see your grandchildren again before too long,' I said gently, hoping it would be the right thing to say, rather than another red rag to the bull.

'I never said anything about them being my grandchildren,' she said. 'Did I?'

PAM

When she was Bad, she was Horrid

I banged the spray polish down on the kitchen worktop angrily, blinking back tears. Cleaning the house wasn't helping me to feel better. I knew I'd behaved horribly to that woman – Kate, from over the road. I wasn't normally such a bitch. But for God's sake, life was so ridiculously unfair. She had all those grandchildren, and that lovely new baby. I'd watched the daughter and son-in-law getting out of the car with him, wrapped in a fluffy white blanket, carrying him like he was made of china while the little blonde girl – Izzie – skipped up the path to meet her grandmother. Oh yes, I often spied on them, from across the road. Not that it made me feel any better. I only had George and Lily, but I hardly ever saw them.

I'd been so looking forward to having them that day. Russell and Tania had told me they were leaving them with me for the whole day while they went off on some mysterious errand that Russell didn't seem to want to tell me about. Well, he could be as secretive as he liked about it – I didn't care where they went, or how long they took about it. It gave me more time with the kids. Or so I thought.

I loved having them to myself for the day. I'd bake the gooiest chocolate cake possible, just to see their eyes, wide as saucers, and to hear George say, *'Wow! Mum would never let us have this!'* Their mum never let them watch cartoons on TV, apparently. Or take their shoes and socks off to paddle in the stream that ran through the park. Or climb trees, or roly-poly down sloping lawns, getting grass in their hair and making themselves almost sick with laughter.

I liked the fact that I was making them happy, but if I was honest I also liked the fact that I was being subversive. The kids would never tell Tania. They knew these little treats were our special secrets. What I really longed to do was to take them to the zoo, or to the seaside, or to one of those theme parks where everything is supposed to be horrendously expensive but children have the time of their lives (and I wouldn't care about the cost anyway. What else did I have to spend my money on?). But their parents wouldn't agree to it, and it'd be harder to keep a trip like that quiet, than the odd doughnut or chocolate ice-cream.

But that morning the phone had rung, just as I was getting everything ready.

'It's me,' said Russell, sounding as cold and distant as ever. Like I could possibly confuse him with anyone else. 'The children won't be coming today after all. Change of plan.'

'Oh.' I struggled to swallow back tears of disappointment. 'Is anything wrong?'

'No.' He sounded irritated at being asked. 'Everything's fine, we just don't need you today after all.'

We don't need you today. I'd stopped, long ago, imagining Russell or Tania sent the children to me because they thought I might enjoy it. I knew I was only ever being used as a childminder, and probably a last-resort one, at that. But it still hurt to have it spelt out so abruptly.

'So when will you?' I said, trying to keep the desperation out of my voice. 'When will you *need* me again?'

'Not sure. We'll let you know.'

No *thank you anyway.* No *sorry for letting you down. Sorry for inconveniencing you, sorry for letting you go out and buy lemonade and chocolate fingers and comics and sweets.* I'd long ago stopped expecting any of those niceties, too. Russell didn't like me, could scarcely bring himself to speak to me – I knew that. And Tania wasn't much better, although she was more polite about it (and sometimes I did catch a look in her eyes that was almost like an apology, like there might have actually been some understanding between the two of us if it hadn't been for her loyalty to Russell). I knew I was being used, but I put up with it, didn't complain about it because of course, I wanted to see the children more than I wanted to tell Russell what I thought of him (that he was an obnoxious, mean-spirited, rude and nasty little git whose father would have been ashamed of him).

Yes, *ashamed,* I thought now as I attacked the housework with a kind of demented fury, cross with myself for ruining any chance of a friendship with Kate-over-the-road by being such a ratty old cow. It was true, Colin would have turned in his grave if he could see how his son treated me now. *Colin.* Oh, if only he were still here with me. Nothing would ever be right now that he was gone.

Later, as I was watching the six o'clock news, sipping a cup of tea and still (I admit it) feeling sorry for myself, there was a ring at the door. For one completely daft moment my heart leapt at the thought that it could be Russell, turning up with the kids even at this late stage, just for the evening, no doubt looking reluctant and aggrieved that he'd had to bring them round after all.

But it was Kate from number forty-nine, holding a small bunch of flowers and looking like she wasn't sure whether I'd slam the door in her face.

'I just wanted to say sorry. I didn't mean to be nosy or unkind. I shouldn't have made assumptions when you were talking about the children.'

'Oh.' I felt myself go red. 'No, I ought to be apologising to *you.* I was very rude. I'm sorry. I was a bit upset.'

'Well, you didn't need me making things worse, did you. Here −' She held out the flowers. 'I bought you these.

They're only from my garden. The kids …' She swallowed, looking uncomfortably aware that she'd already mentioned her grandchildren again, then went on quickly, 'They helped me pick them. I thought perhaps they'd cheer you up.'

'That's very nice of you,' I said. 'They're lovely, but really there wasn't any need. Would you like to come in? I've just made a cup of tea.'

We both looked at each other for a moment. I could see her hesitating, probably thinking it was bad enough having to walk down the road with this madwoman, being subjected to my bad temper, without stepping into my lair and possibly getting it in the neck again every time she opened her mouth to mention her grandchildren.

'No, thank you,' she said. 'I really ought to go home and tidy up a bit. The kids have all just been picked up …' She tailed off again. 'Sorry,' she said again, awkwardly. 'I seem to keep doing it, don't I – putting my foot in it.'

'That's OK. I'm not normally such a crotchety old bat.' I smiled at her. 'If I had those delightful grandchildren of yours I expect I'd be talking about them all the time. And I'm sure you *do* know how lucky you are, so it was unforgiveable of me to take such a tone with you earlier. I'd been so looking forward to seeing George and Lily, you see. I'm afraid I was in a foul mood.'

'Don't worry, I quite understand. You must have been disappointed.'

She seemed so genuinely sympathetic, I suddenly felt sure that if I got to know her, I'd like her. I'd spent so long watching her from the window, counting the children coming and going, thinking how unfair it was, but of course, it was me being unfair. It wasn't her fault Russell was such an arse, and if she'd known what a paranoid old witch I was, she'd never have walked home with me earlier on, or come anywhere near me for that matter.

'Perhaps if you can't stop for tea today I can make up for it another time, to prove I'm not always so horrible? Do you have any free days, when you're not looking after any of them at all?'

We both managed to smile at this, and I felt like the ice between us had thawed a bit.

Kate gave a little apologetic shrug and admitted, 'Not often. But with a bit of luck, if Izzie's mum has enough rest this week, I might be free on Monday. How about you?'

'Monday? Yes, that'd be perfect. Come to me. Would the afternoon be better? Come about three, and we can have tea and cakes.'

'Great.' Kate smiled. 'I'll see you then.'

I watched her walk back down the path. She looked tired, which wasn't really surprising. I found myself thinking for the first time that maybe it wasn't all sweetness and light, having the grandchildren as often as she seemed to. There didn't seem to be any husband around to share the load. Well, we had that in common, at least, if nothing else. Perhaps we might be friends, after all. It was a strange idea to me. The friends I'd had before – if you could call them friends – had all disappeared long ago, turning their backs on me and Colin as soon as there was the first whiff of scandal about us. I always used to think friends would support you through thick and thin, but I couldn't have been more wrong. And now, now that I was on my own, I supposed ...

I was lonely.

The thought hit me like a blow to the heart, almost making me gasp. *Lonely.* I'd never allowed myself to think about it. I missed Colin, of course I did, every day, like an ache that never eased. But I'd fended off the realisation of loneliness, somehow, by getting on with things. Cleaning the house more than it ever needed. Baking cakes that (unless the children came) I ate all on my own. Going for walks to nowhere and back again. Listening to our old favourite songs on the radio. *Are you lonesome tonight? Do you miss me tonight?* Watching Kate and her family from the window. Feeling bitter and resentful.

Never mind being ashamed of his son. If Colin could see me now, he might have actually been ashamed of *me.*

KATE

Hide and Seek

Monday. I turned over in bed thankfully. No childminding today. Over the weekend I'd seen both Michael and Steph and their families (and spoken at length to the expat branch of the family in France), and today would be my chance to catch up on some household chores, get the washing done, maybe even tackle some of the weeds that were beginning to make the garden look like some kind of nature reserve. But not till I'd had a delicious extra half hour in bed. I closed my eyes, and the phone began to ring.

Damn. Why hadn't I ever learned to keep my mobile on the bedside table? How many times had this happened – a panic call at seven o'clock in the morning when one or other of the grandkids had been discovered, on waking, to have a rash or a temperature, diarrhoea and vomiting, or (on one unforgettable occasion) a piece of Lego stuck up his nose – any of which might call for my input either as an unqualified, and frankly outdated, expert on childhood malaises and misfortunes, or as an emergency carer/nurse/provider of transport to A&E – and I *still* didn't remember to keep the phone within reach at all times!

Not that I minded, I told myself as I staggered wearily out of bed. Not when I remembered how sad and upset Pam had been, about not seeing those children who (apparently) weren't even her grandchildren. I hadn't even dared ask her what the story was there, although maybe she'd tell me over Tea And Cakes this afternoon. No, I knew how lucky I was, having such a close relationship with all my grandchildren, and I was never going to complain, no matter how often ...

'Kate, it's Ben'.

'Oh. Hello Ben. What's up?' And why was *he* calling, instead of Steph?

'Steph's not too great. She had another bad asthma attack last night.'

'Oh no.' Steph's asthma seemed to get better while she was pregnant, but since Isaac was born she'd had a couple of quite severe attacks. 'Is she OK now?'

'Yes. But you know how she is afterwards – absolutely knackered – she's still in bed.'

'What started the attack off, Ben?'

Horrible memories were flooding my brain as we spoke. Memories of Stephanie as a toddler, turning blue, fighting for breath. Of myself, frantically calling an ambulance, screaming *asthma attack!* into the phone, almost passing out with fear as I listened to the rasp and wheeze of her breathing. Eggs, milk, nuts, chocolate, the list of potentially lethal triggers grew longer and longer, and my fear intensified that one day as she grew older and more independent she'd eat something, inadvertently, that might cause a bad attack, or that she'd forget to take her inhaler with her when she went out. The fear was that I wouldn't be with Steph when she needed me. Thank God, the asthma had got more manageable when she grew up, but there were still nasty moments occasionally. Like this.

'I don't know.' Ben sounded exhausted himself. 'But she's so tired all the time at the moment anyway, Kate, with the baby needing feeding every couple of hours, crying during the night. She thinks she might have forgotten to use her inhaler.'

'The preventer? That's not like her. She didn't take it at *all* yesterday?'

There was a silence.

'She doesn't remember taking it since Isaac was born.'

'*What?*' I nearly dropped the phone. 'That's nearly three weeks! Ben, she *must* have been taking it. She might have forgotten once or twice –' *That's bad enough.* 'But not every day. She'd be ...'

'In serious trouble. I know, that's what I've told her. But it was scary enough that she admitted she couldn't remember whether she'd taken it or not. She says she feels like day and night have all rolled into one, and ... and her life at the moment is just a constant round of breastfeeding and nappy changing.'

I swallowed. 'You don't think she's depressed, do you? After the birth?'

'No. She says she's OK. She's not tearful or anything like that. Just shattered.'

'What can I do to help?'

'Have Izzie again? I hate to ask, Kate. I know we *keep* asking, but I really think Steph needs to stay in bed today and get some sleep – as much as she can, in between feeds.'

'Yes. I agree.'

'I'd take the day off, but I've got a really important meeting this morning, and it's so soon after the paternity leave.'

'It's OK. I'll be round in twenty minutes – I'm just getting dressed. But I'll come to your place and look after Izzie there, Ben. I don't like the thought of Steph being on her own with the baby if she's still not feeling great. I'll let her sleep. It's a nice day, I can play with Izzie in the garden.'

While my own garden sprouted a few more dandelions, but what the hell? What did that matter, in the grand scheme of things?

'That'd be a weight off my mind. Thank you so much. I'll wait till you get here, then. Hopefully I can get home early.'

I left Izzie watching the morning cartoons while I went upstairs to see Steph. She was flat out under the duvet, her eyes half-closed, as if the effort of opening them was just too much, but she raised a hand to me in greeting.

'Hi, Mum,' she whispered. 'Thanks for coming round.'

I waved this aside. I glanced at the baby, tucked up asleep in his crib next to the bed. 'How long till he'll need feeding again?'

'God knows. Sometimes he's not even going two hours. I'm not sure if I'm producing enough milk, but the health visitor says I just need to keep feeding Isaac as frequently as possible.'

I bit my lip. I'd always been determined not to be the type of grandmother to give advice unless it was asked for. And of course, I was completely in agreement with the sentiments of the *breast is best* campaign. But sometimes I just wished people like health visitors and childcare advisors didn't have to be so bloody dogmatic and intransigent about everything. Feeding, potty-training, discipline, everything seemed to come with its own set of rules and regulations these days, and doing things your own way seemed to invoke stern disapproval all round. I didn't remember there being such strict childcare protocol when I was bringing up my own kids. I doubted I'd have survived.

'It's so much harder,' I told Steph gently, 'when you've already got an older child to look after.'

'I'm not giving up on him!' she exclaimed weakly, making it sound as if the (unspoken) suggestion of giving the baby a little top-up formula milk was tantamount to sending him to an orphanage.

'OK. But try to get some sleep now, while I'm here with Izzie. They both need their mummy to be fit and well.'

I didn't put any emphasis, or intend any hidden meaning, to the *both* – but Steph's eyes immediately filled up with tears.

'You think I'm neglecting her, don't you – neglecting Izzie because of Isaac. I'm not! I'm still giving her just as much attention, reading her stories, giving her lots of cuddles!'

'Ssh – of course you are! I know that. I don't think anything of the sort. You just need to recover from the asthma attack, today. Have you taken your inhaler this morning?'

'Yes. Ben pretty much stood over me and watched me do it. As if he hasn't got enough on his plate, now he's having to look after *me* because I can't even remember to look after myself!'

'Don't cry. I'm sure you have been remembering to take it. It's such an instinctive thing for you, you do it without even thinking about it.'

'I suppose so.'

'Don't give yourself such a hard time.' I smiled and bent to kiss her cheek. 'Now, get some sleep and when I hear Isaac wake up again I'll bring you a cup of tea.'

I went back downstairs. And Izzie had gone.

The TV was still on, showing a Peppa Pig cartoon. The child couldn't be far away – Peppa was her absolute favourite, or at least, it used to be before *Frozen* came into her life. I was *not* going to panic, but I also wasn't going to shout out Izzie's name and frighten the life out of Stephanie.

'Izzie?' I said softly, looking in the kitchen first. I'd never liked the combination of kitchens and children, ever since Michael, at the age of two and a half, had loaded the tumble dryer with crockery from the cupboard while my back was turned, and managed to switch it on. The noise was awful, and scared him so much he never did anything like it again. And surprisingly, only three cups got broken. Today, though, in Stephanie's kitchen, there was only the gentle hum of the washing machine doing what it was supposed to do, presumably set in motion by Ben before he went to work. No Izzie.

Bathroom. That was almost as fraught with nasty possibilities as the kitchen. I ran back upstairs as quietly as I could, peered cautiously into the bathroom – no taps running, nothing thrown into the toilet or the bath, *no Izzie.* Well, if she'd crept up to her own bedroom, all well and good. I was sure, as I pushed open the door with the pink *ISABEL'S ROOM* plaque, I'd find her sitting on the floor, looking at one of her favourite books. So sure, I actually checked behind the bed and even under it before accepting that she wasn't there. She wasn't in the little bedroom that had recently been prepared and painted blue for Isaac, either. I was starting to feel alarmed now. Back downstairs, checking the lounge again, checking the kitchen again. Surely she hadn't managed to get out of the house? The front and back doors were both shut and locked, the keys and bolts well out of a three-year-old's reach. But still, with a rising sense of panic, I opened them, one at a time, ran outside, looked all around, and finally – the risk of waking my daughter suddenly mattering a lot less than that of waiting a single minute longer before shouting my head off – I did exactly that, my voice quivering with fear, my throat hurting with the force of the yell: '*IZZIE!*'

Nothing. A neighbour's cat, making its way through the garden on its daily inspection of its territory, paused and stared, miaowing its disapproval. I ran back through the house, slamming the back door, opening the front door again, hollering into the street: '*IZZIE!*' My heart felt as if it was going to burst through my chest – I could hardly breathe. '*IZZIE!*' I tried again, beginning to feel real fear, starting to wonder about police, about search parties, about scenarios nobody, anywhere, ever wants to imagine, least of all a parent or a grandparent, least of all a grandparent left in sole charge of a precious, precious child I loved more than my own life.

'What?' came a sudden small voice from behind me – and, gasping with such deep grateful sobs that I could actually feel my diaphragm straining to cope – I swept Izzie into my arms and clung to her as if we were both drowning.

'What's the matter, Nanny?' Izzie asked curiously. 'You're squashing me.'

'Oh, Izzie. Didn't you hear me calling you? Where were you? I thought I'd lost you – I was so worried.'

'Don't worry, Nanny!' She smiled at me as I let her go and struggled to get my own breath back. 'I wasn't lost. I was being *helpful.*'

'Were you?' I took her hand and led her back into the house. 'Where, Izzie? *Where* were you being helpful?' *Just so I know for another time.*

'I was getting the hoover out. To clean up the crumbs, Nanny, only I couldn't, because it was too heavy and I *pulled* and *pulled*,' (she demonstrated the vigour of her pulling action, face contorted with the effort), 'but it wouldn't come out.'

The cupboard under the stairs. God almighty, the child must have been right inside it – how the hell had I run straight past its door without hearing her, seeing her, even thinking to look there? I'd panicked, that was how. I'd got through a myriad of similarly scary incidents when my own kids were little, some of them with less happy outcomes (like the time with the roller skates and the pond, but let's not dwell on that), without losing my cool. Three children – you learn to cope with all sorts – but a few minutes with a grandchild out of my sight, and I'd turned into a gibbering wreck.

'Was I a good girl, Nanny? I did *try* to get the hoover.' Izzie stopped, looked down at her feet. 'The crumbs ... they was the biscuit's fault, not mine.'

'Oh, I see!' I bent down and gave her a kiss. 'Never mind about the crumbs.' As we went back into the lounge,

I noticed the biscuit packet, lying open on the floor, several broken ones spilling out of the wrapping. How had I missed *that* before?

'I was *hungry*,' she said, her lower lip coming out in anticipation of a reprimand.

'All right. You were a good girl for *trying* to hoover up the crumbs, but let's leave that till later now. The noise might wake Mummy up.' (If my frantic shouting in the garden and in the street hadn't done that already.) 'How about you bring your doll's pram outside while I hang out Mummy's washing for her?'

'Yes!' Izzie ran to get the little pram from the hall, singing to herself as she went. I turned off the TV, which was now showing a slightly fearsome programme about pirates, and started pulling the washing out of the machine. I was calming down a bit now from the fright, and beginning to look forward to the rest of the day. It was starting to warm up – it was already the first week of June – and I thought happily about the long days of summer ahead, with all the nice things I could do with the children: the park, the paddling pool in the garden, maybe even a day at the seaside.

There was only one thing I wasn't thinking about, unfortunately. With everything else that had happened that morning, I'd completely forgotten about Pam's invitation to afternoon tea and cakes.

KATE

What are Little Boys Made of?

The next day it was pouring with rain. So much for summer arriving. I normally took the twins to a playgroup at the church hall on Tuesdays, but Alfie had a cold, Amelia was teething and I had a headache. None of us were really in the right frame of mind for joining battle with hordes of other toddlers over the Lego box or the House corner.

I was just dosing them both with Calpol when the phone rang. *Not another asthma attack?* I thought, but this time, to my surprise, it wasn't any of my brood asking for help. It was Bob. He'd never called me before, and sounded embarrassed about it.

'Kate. It's Bob here. From the children's group. The music thing.'

'Bob, hello!'

'I hope you don't mind. I found your number in the phone book.'

'Of course I don't mind. Are you all right?' He didn't sound it. And what an idiotic thing to ask. If he'd been fine, he wouldn't have been calling me. 'What's wrong?' I added.

'Well, actually, there's something …' He hesitated. 'I just wondered, well, I thought perhaps we could have a chat. If you're not busy, that is, but I expect you've got the grandchildren.'

'I have – just the twins. But …'

'Yes, sorry, of course you have. I forgot, you always have them on Tuesdays, don't you. Don't worry,' he said abruptly. 'Forget it. Sorry I bothered you, Kate.'

'No, wait, Bob, what is it? It's fine – I'd already decided not to bother with playgroup today. Of course we can chat. Did you want to meet up for a coffee or something?' I was quite worried. I'd never heard Bob sound quite so unsettled.

'No, really, don't worry,' he started to say again, but I decided to insist.

'I'll tell you what, the twins are a bit fractious, so I'm thinking of trying to get them down for an early nap. Why don't you come here instead of meeting me somewhere? If they go to sleep, we can talk quietly without them disturbing us.'

'Are you sure you're not too busy?'

'Of course I'm not. I'm number forty-nine, OK? Blue front door. Will you be all right to get here?' He lived closer to the town centre than me. It'd be quite a walk for him. 'Can you get the bus from where you are? It stops just round the corner from me.'

'Yes, I'll do that. Thanks, Kate.'

'Just give me half an hour to get these two settled, then, and I'll get the kettle on.'

The twins were both asleep by the time he arrived. I was quite shocked by his appearance. Although of course I knew about his arthritis, he'd always played it down, making a valiant effort to walk and talk in a sprightly fashion even when it was obvious he was in pain, always looking smart and ... I hated the word, really, but it kind-of summed him up: *dapper.* But now he looked tired, fraught, and almost like he'd just got up and slung on whatever clothes were lying on the floor. *Crumpled.* He looked crumpled, and weary, and *old.* I wondered what on earth could have happened to him.

'Sorry,' he said again, panting slightly as he settled himself in an armchair. 'I'm sorry to be such a nuisance.'

'You're not, at all. Look, just sit and get your breath back, then you can tell me what's wrong. Would you like tea or a coffee?'

We had our drinks in front of us before he eventually took a deep breath, let it all out again in a long, sad, sigh, and said, staring into his coffee, 'It's Craig. He called me this morning. It's a bolt out of the blue. He's splitting up with his partner.'

I knew Craig was his son – his only child – and Freddie was his only grandchild. Bob had told me once how sad he was that his wife, Shirley, didn't live to see Freddie, but he hadn't dwelt on the subject, moving on quickly with a shrug and a smile. *That's life. These things happen.* Let's face it, people of our age had all experienced loss, sadness, regrets – we didn't need to go on about it all the time.

'Oh dear. I'm sorry to hear that,' I said. 'Was it his decision, do you know? Or hers?'

Bob was silent for an unnaturally long time. I waited, not wanting to rush him, but wondering all the same why this news – not really so very unusual nowadays – seemed to have upset him quite so much.

'His partner isn't a woman. Craig's gay. He's been with Nathan for almost ten years.'

'Oh, I see.' I nodded, taking this in, and then, looking up at him with sudden realisation: 'So … Freddie …?'

The question hung in the air for a moment.

'They used a surrogate,' he said. 'IVF.'

'Of course.' My mind was rushing ahead. Custody disputes were enough of a worry when a couple split up, but in a case like this, I supposed it would depend … 'So, er, which of them is actually Freddie's father? Biological father?'

'We don't know.' He raised his eyes to mine now, and I could see the anxiety in them, and understood it only too well. 'They didn't want a situation where one of them felt less of a parent to Freddie than the other. So, well …' He dropped his gaze again, looking uncomfortable. 'Putting aside the actual physical process – suffice it to say, it could have been either of them.'

'I see,' I said again, feeling helpless and a little bit out of my depth. 'So what's your son going to do?'

'That's just it. He has no idea what to do. He sounded quite hysterical on the phone. The break-up's so sudden – they were so happy together, I never dreamt this would happen.'

'Are you sure it's not just an argument that's got out of hand? They might get back together again?'

Bob shook his head. 'Apparently it's more serious than that. A matter of infidelity.'

'Oh dear. '

'Nathan's moving out. And he wants to take Freddie with him.'

'But he can't, surely! I can't believe he'd have the right to do that. Especially if he's leaving to be with someone else?'

'He isn't.'

'You said … you mentioned infidelity.'

'Yes. But it's not Nathan being unfaithful – it's my son,' Bob said, shaking his head again. 'I don't understand what's got into him. He says he's fallen in love with someone else, that he *can't help it* – like he's a fifteen-year-old schoolgirl for heaven's sake, not a grown man with responsibilities!'

'I think it happens, Bob, unfortunately, whatever age, whatever sexual preference someone is.'

'Oh, I know. But for my own son to behave so badly, so stupidly, and then to scream and shout like a thwarted child because Nathan's threatening to take Freddie ...' He took a mouthful of his coffee and put the cup back down in its saucer with a clank. 'The flat belongs to Craig. Nathan just pays him rent, so he's leaving, and Craig wants to move this new guy in with him. Apparently he just expected to keep Freddie with him! I told him, he's an idiot! He should have known Nathan wasn't going to give him up, just like that. Why would he? I actually feel sorry for the bloke. He's losing Craig, being turfed out of the flat, and possibly losing the boy too.'

'So how's it going to be resolved? Do you know?'

'Yes. A DNA test.' Bob's eyes suddenly shone with tears. 'The thing is, Kate, I've always *known*, of course, that Freddie might not biologically be my grandson. But regardless of that, it's exactly what I've always felt him to be.'

I reached across the table and laid my hand over his.

'Of course you have. Your son and his partner have been together a long time, after all. It must have felt as stable as a marriage.'

'I wish they *had* got married. Or at least had one of those civil partnership ceremonies. Then, I don't know, it might have been different. But they never bothered. They always said they didn't think it was necessary, they were confident they'd always stay together.'

'Even in a marriage, we all know that doesn't always happen,' I said. Instinctively I rubbed my own naked ring finger.

'All right, I know a legal document wouldn't necessarily have stopped Craig from being unfaithful. But it might, perhaps, have given me some kind of right as Freddie's granddad. If ...' He swallowed hard and looked away. 'If it turns out Nathan is his biological father,' he finished quietly.

I nodded slowly. Poor Bob. How could he bear it, if the little boy he adored, whom he'd helped to care for on a regular basis, was suddenly declared to be absolutely nothing to do with him?

'I know I'm being selfish,' he said. 'I realise that.'

'Of course you're not!'

'Oh yes, I am. I should be more concerned about my son, about the fact that he might lose custody of Freddie himself. But I can't help it – I can't help thinking he's brought this all on himself. Do you know what he said to me on the phone? Crying, sobbing, as if it wasn't bad enough telling me about this – it was a complete shock to me, the whole thing! – *I'll kill him if he takes Freddie away from me.* Anyone would think it was Nathan who'd betrayed *him.*'

'Well, you know, there's always right and wrong on both sides. Perhaps there's more to it than meets the eye. They might have been unhappy for a long time, and Craig just didn't want to let you see it.'

'Perhaps.' Bob sighed. He looked shattered. 'All I know is, my son sounds very afraid that the DNA test might go against him, very afraid of what that might mean. But not afraid enough to give up this new man and give his relationship another try. So what does that say about him? How would a judge view that, in a custody case? He'd say Craig doesn't seem to love Freddie enough.'

'But *you* do.' I looked at him with sympathy. 'You're his granddad, whether it's a biological fact or not. They can't take that away from you.'

'Oh, I think they can, though, Kate. I think, if Nathan's his father and he wins custody, that's exactly what he'll do. I don't think I'd have any rights whatsoever.'

'Don't start thinking like that! Surely there's a fifty-fifty chance of Craig being his father?'

Bob put his empty cup to one side. 'I never thought about it too much before, you know. It didn't seem to matter. But you know how dark Freddie is? Those black curls, those big brown eyes? Craig's blond, pale, freckly.'

'But surely he could have inherited the surrogate's colouring.'

'Yes.' He shrugged slightly, as if it wasn't important, as if it wasn't weighing on him like a ton of bricks. 'Or Nathan's.'

I spent the rest of our time together doing my best to console him, trying to persuade him to try to think positively, to stay strong for Freddie's sake. The kid must have been unsettled enough already by whatever rows and angry scenes had been going on at home. Even at the age of two, I pointed out, such things couldn't help but have an effect on him, and Bob could be a stabilising influence for him at the moment.

'I know. You're right. It's just that today, it was such a shock. I really needed someone to talk to. You've been very kind – listening.'

'I wish I could do something to help.'

But what I was actually thinking was that I *might* be able to get him some help. I hadn't wanted to make any promises, but there was just a chance.

'Mum – hello. Is everything all right?'

Michael could be forgiven for sounding surprised. I hardly ever phoned him at work. I'd planned to wait until the evening, and call him at home, but I felt so upset about it, I just didn't want it to wait.

'I need your advice,' I told my son. 'It's for a friend.'

I explained the situation as briefly as I could.

'So who is this guy, exactly?' he asked when I'd finished. 'I don't think I've heard you mention him before.'

'I told you, just a friend. He takes his grandchild to the Mini Music Makers' group where I take the twins.'

'Or *not* his grandchild, as the case may be,' Michael observed.

'Don't say that.' I sighed. 'I feel so sorry for him. He's so worried he might lose access to Freddie if the other chap turns out to be the biological father.'

'So you meet up with this guy, then, do you? Apart from at the kids' group, I mean?'

'What?' I swallowed back my irritation. I might have guessed my son would be more interested in my friendship with Bob than in the situation I wanted his help with. 'No, not normally. He just came round today, because he was upset and wanted someone to talk to.'

'I think you should be careful, Mum. You hardly know him, by the sound of it, and he's already coming to your house, and playing on your sympathy. His family set-up sounds decidedly dodgy to me.'

'Michael!' I exclaimed. 'Can you help, or not?'

'Well, it's not my area of expertise, as you know, but I could talk to one of the partners.'

'I'd be very grateful. Thank you.'

'Don't sound so offended, then. I was only expressing concern. I don't like the idea of you adopting some guy's problems. He shouldn't be bothering you with all this, should he? He really needs to sort it out for himself.'

'Yes, perhaps,' I said. 'But he hasn't got a paralegal for a son.'

'More's the pity, by the sound of it. If he had, perhaps the son would have had a bit more bloody sense.'

Or be a bit more bloody arrogant and up-himself, like you, I thought as I hung up. How was it that Michael so often succeeded in annoying me? Why did I sometimes feel like I didn't much like the way he'd turned out? He was my son, I loved him, I'd jump in front of a bus for him – but when, and how, did he get to be such an *arse*?

I supposed he must take after his father. That'd be it.

BOB

There was a Crooked Man, and he Walked a Crooked Mile

I'd only just got out of bed that day, when I got the phone call from Craig. I'd had to get up slowly, because of my knees, and they were still giving me odd spasms of pain. I knew why. I knew I really shouldn't have got down on the floor with Freddie the day before, to play with his cars with him. But for God's sake, how was I supposed to entertain a toddler on my own, without using the bits of my body that were, sadly, long past their sell-by date? I was limping and wincing with every step as I made my way to the kitchen and sat gratefully on a stool to wait for the kettle to boil and the toast to pop out of the toaster. I decided I'd leave it till later to have a shower, or maybe a hot bath would help. I was just going to sit there for a bit with yesterday's paper (no time to read one on the days when Freddie was with me, and after he went home I was too shattered). But that day, and in fact every day when I didn't have Freddie, I didn't need to rush in the mornings. It wasn't like I could go to the allotment anymore – my back wouldn't stand for it, and my knees would probably give out completely as soon as I bent to pull out a weed, never mind contemplating anything strenuous like digging.

Arthritis, that's all it was, nothing to make a fuss about, and nothing anyone could do about it. There were painkillers, of course, and anti-inflammatories, but everything except for the mildest, least effective remedies came with dire warnings about what could happen to you (far worse things than a spot of arthritis) if you took them long-term. And let's face it, arthritis is nothing if not long-term. Still, there were lots of people much worse off than me – I knew that only too well – people who were ill the way my wife was ill. Cancer. Now that *would* be a depressing way to spend your retirement years.

Retirement. It was supposed to be the reward for all those years of hard graft, wasn't it. Actually I used to enjoy my working life, but I'd never been one of those people who dreaded retirement or wondered what the hell they were going to do with themselves. Shirley and I had made a lot of plans. We were going to travel, see as much of the world as we could manage before we got too decrepit to do it. In some ways, although I still missed her unbearably – missed her with a pain like a heart attack every morning when I woke up on my own in our bed – I liked to think Shirley would have been grateful she never had time to become old and decrepit. She'd been such a beautiful woman, proud of her appearance, and until her illness she'd always looked at least ten years younger than she was, even without any make-up.

Well, now I felt it was my *duty*, in a way – my duty as one of the lucky ones who'd survived to retirement age and beyond, you see? – to carry on cheerfully and gratefully, trying my best not to complain about trivial annoyances like a bit of arthritis or the odd touch of loneliness.

Most of the time I didn't find the loneliness so very hard to deal with. I'd take a stroll (or a hobble) to the shops, chat to the people I met in the street, sit on one of the benches in the square if the weather was nice enough, watch the world going by. Most lunchtimes when I wasn't looking after Freddie, I'd have a slow amble down to the Foresters' Arms and meet up with some of my cronies there – the other old geezers like me, all of us sitting on our designated bar stools with our pints, trying to put the world to rights. Sometimes I'd have my dinner there too. They did a nice steak and kidney pie, not as nice as Shirley used to make of course but it was tasty and filling and saved me the bother of cooking for myself.

And then, every Thursday, I met Kate. Bright spot of the week, that was, although I wasn't going to admit it, even to myself. A few weeks back, under the influence of perhaps a pint too many, I'd gone and mentioned her to my mate Jim in the pub.

'Seeing her every week, then, are you?' Jim said, giving me a bit of a look over his specs.

'Yes, we just have a cup of tea or whatever – you know, with the grandkids, after the music-and-movement thing at the library.' I noticed the smirk on Jim's face then, and added quickly, almost kind-of panic-struck: 'Nothing like that, mate! Bloody hell, she's got about six grandkids.'

'Glamorous granny, is she, then?'

'She's just a friend, right? Well, not even a friend really, just more like an acquaintance, just that we're the only two grandparents at this kids' thing.'

'So you get together for a cosy little drink every week? Nice!'

'We've got all the kids with us. It's just a cup of tea, for heaven's sake.'

'OK, calm down, I believe you.' Jim lifted his beer to his mouth. 'Thousands wouldn't,' he added wickedly as he took a mouthful.

'Think what you like, you daft old sod,' I told him. I knew it'd only add fuel to the gossip fire if I kept protesting too much.

But to be honest, it did make me think. Was I being entirely honest with myself? Didn't I actually enjoy my meetings with Kate a little bit more than I was pretending? A bit more than if she'd been, well, someone less interesting, less pleasant to talk to? Less attractive?

Even thinking this made me go hot with something like guilt. It felt disloyal to Shirley to be considering another woman pleasant and attractive. Actually Kate was just a nice, ordinary woman – not slim and beautiful like one of those catwalk models in the newspapers, but not sloppy or overweight either – just *normal,* in a comfortable, cheerful kind of way, with her jeans and bright coloured T-shirts, her no-nonsense flat sandals and short dark hair that occasionally showed some grey roots because she hadn't had time to get to the hairdressers. And *I* was seventy years old for Christ's sake, (probably a good ten years older than Kate, by the way, not that it mattered what age a *friend,* an *acquaintance* was, of course) – I wasn't some sex-starved boy in his thirties or forties embarking on one of those internet-dating things to find a woman. I wasn't interested in such things, hadn't ever contemplated looking for another woman to replace Shirley – as if I ever could. If I was going to start getting ridiculous ideas in my head about Kate being pleasant or attractive, I really ought to stop meeting up with her.

But needless to say, I hadn't stopped. I managed to convince myself, every Thursday, that we were just two grandparents keeping each other company. And to be fair, all we normally talked about was our families – our kids and the grandkids. She had a lot more to talk about than me in that respect, and I did enjoy hearing about them all – her son and her two daughters, the way they bickered with each other and tried to rope poor Kate into the arguments. I smiled to myself now, thinking about it. She often looked tired from all the childminding they asked her to do, but she was always bright and cheery, and always made me laugh with her stories about the family. Perhaps that was what I found so enjoyable (I was telling myself now as I buttered my toast) – the glimpse she gave me, for that half an hour every week, into the life of a proper family.

Proper family? I almost dropped the butter knife. What the hell made me think something like that? My own little family was, of course, just as *proper*, in its own way. I'd be mortified if my son knew I'd been thinking like that. I shook my head, dismayed at myself.

Didn't mean it like that, I muttered aloud to myself. Of course I didn't – I'd never been ignorant or bigoted in that way, not in *any* way, never had been, couldn't understand people like that. I was broadminded, pretty unshockable, *live and let live* was my motto. It was just that, well, Kate's family, with its sibling rivalries, its in-laws, its weddings and births and big rowdy family parties – that was how Shirley and I used to imagine our family life might be, long ago, when we first got married. We didn't *mind* that it all turned out differently. We might have only had the one son, but we loved him so much, it hadn't ever seemed to matter. It still didn't. Nothing mattered, as long as Craig was happy, and now there was little Freddie too, an unexpected blessing.

It's all good, I was telling myself that day, taking a bite of my toast. *I'm a lucky old git, I can't complain.*

And almost as if I'd cursed my luck, it was just at that very moment that the phone rang, and everything changed.

When Kate suggested I go round to see her, it was ten o'clock and I was still in my dressing-gown. The bath would have to wait. I threw on some clothes, hardly glancing at myself in the mirror, grabbed my jacket from the hook and set off to hobble the short walk to the town centre, where I then didn't even have the patience to wait for a bus but carried on hobbling, all the way to Kate's house. I wasn't ever going to admit it, but recently I'd sometimes daydreamed about the possibility of ringing Kate like this and suggesting we meet up in the middle of the week – between music group sessions – preferably just the two of us, without the children. I'd never even dared to contemplate going to see her at her own house. But now, this was different. All I cared about was that she'd understand. She was another grandparent. She'd know why I was so afraid my heart was going to break.

And of course, she listened, she understood and commiserated, she was kind and sympathetic just as I knew she would be. But what did I really expect her to do? What, at the end of the day, could anybody do to help me? What a silly old fool I'd been, living in my fool's paradise with my fool's dream of a happy family, never even anticipating something like this could happen one day. It was always a disaster waiting to happen – why didn't I see that? My own son, stupidly wrecking his own life and Freddie's into the bargain. And mine. For Christ's sake, mine too! Because in my heart of hearts, I was already halfway certain Craig wasn't Freddie's biological father. I wasn't his granddad. And without him, what exactly did I have left? A doddering old fool, full of aches and pains, smiling at strangers in the street and pretending I was perfectly happy?

By the time I got home from Kate's house I was already wishing I had the nerve to call her again, just to hear her tell me again that she understood how I felt. But she was far too busy with her family for me to bother her with my moans and groans. Actually, I wasn't even altogether sure now whether it had been Kate herself I'd been feeling so attracted to – or her life. Her family. Her busy, happy family. I'd probably have given anything to be a part of that.

KATE

Crosspatch, Draw the Latch

I couldn't stop thinking about poor Bob and his worries all the rest of the morning. I'd made him promise, before he left, that he'd call me again if he needed to talk. If only Michael could come up with something that might give him a bit of hope, but sadly I wasn't very optimistic about it. The twins woke up even more grumpy than before they went to sleep – Alfie's runny nose making him miserable, Amelia screaming – and my headache was worse too. I made them little sandwiches with the crusts cut off for lunch and sat them in their booster seats at the kitchen table.

'Come on, babies,' I pleaded as they both pushed their plates away and carried on crying. 'It's not that bad, is it?'

But maybe it was, to be fair – how would I know? None of us could claim to remember how it felt to be eighteen months old with a cold or a tooth coming through!

It was the doorbell that stopped them both crying for a moment. It played a stupid tune – I'm not even sure what it was but it sounded a bit like *Three Blind Mice*, one of their favourites. They both looked at me, mid wail, and Amelia proclaimed in a little voice made shaky from crying: *Daddy*!

'No,' I said. 'Not time for Daddy yet. I'll go and see who it is.'

It was Pam from down the road. And she wasn't happy.

'If you didn't want to come, you should have said so,' she said as soon as I'd opened the door. 'I mean, fair enough, I might not have blamed you, I probably scared you off last week, the way I spoke to you, but you could at least have said.'

'Oh, God! Pam, I'm *so* sorry.' *Yesterday! I'd completely forgotten. What an idiot.* 'It wasn't deliberate, honestly. I had a bit of an emergency – my daughter ...'

She nodded, looking almost satisfied. 'One of the grandchildren again, I suppose. And you couldn't even have knocked on my door and told me you couldn't make it?'

'As I said, it was an emergency. Steph – my daughter – she'd had an asthma attack, and I had to rush round there. I must admit, our date went completely out of my head.' I sighed. I was probably just making it worse. 'I'd been looking forward to it up till then, honestly. Look, why don't you come in – please, have a cup of tea or some lunch or something.'

I really didn't know how to make it up to her – she looked so cross – but I sure as hell didn't want her standing on the doorstep ranting at me, so I opened the door wider and stepped back, making it hard for her to refuse. I closed the door behind her and led the way to the kitchen.

'As if it wasn't bad enough being let down the other day by the children,' she muttered as she followed me down the hallway. 'It must be me! Everybody lets me down. I'd made a cake!'

'I really am so sorry. I was at my daughter's all day, you see, and I had a bit of an incident with Izzie. I thought I'd lost her. It made everything else go out of my mind.'

I was making excuses for myself, of course. It really was awful of me to forget – especially as she seemed so vulnerable and sad. We'd reached the kitchen now, and as soon as I went through the door I knew what a mistake it was to bring Pam in here. Both children were screaming again. Amelia had thrown her plate of sandwiches on the floor, and Alfie had knocked over my glass of orange-juice. Thank God it wasn't a cup of hot tea. The pool of sticky liquid was spreading across the table and dripping onto Amelia's lap.

I grabbed a cloth and threw it on the table, mopping up as much of the juice as I could before unstrapping Amelia from her seat and picking her up.

'Wet!' she screamed. I was actually quite impressed – it was a new word. But this wasn't the time for singing her praises. It wasn't really the time for telling her or her brother off, either, because it was completely my own fault for leaving them on their own, even for a minute, with food and drink. I pulled her little summer dress off over her head and sponged her down at the sink, taking off her nappy and muttering about giving her a bath in a minute. Meanwhile Alfie's nose was running right down to his chin, and he'd somehow got a piece of cheese stuck to his hair, so I got him out of his seat too and had barely turned my back to get a tissue to wipe his nose before he'd run at his sister and pushed her over. It might not have been deliberate. I would have liked to give him the benefit of the doubt. With both of them still yelling, my head pounding, and having now trodden on a squashed sandwich, what I actually felt like doing was going back to bed. It really hadn't been a good day.

'That child,' Pam said in the most disapproving tone imaginable, having watched the fiasco so far in stony silence, 'has just wet herself all over your floor.'

'*Shit!*' I said, before I could stop myself. If Amelia repeated *that* word at home, I'd be in trouble. Pam looked even more disapproving. I suddenly really wanted to shake her. OK, so I forgot to go and have cake with her. *Obviously* it wasn't deliberate. If she disliked me that much, why invite me in the first place? It wasn't my bloody fault her grandkids – or whoever's grandkids they were – hadn't turned up the other day, for God's sake!

'I'd better go,' she said now, turning on her heel with a last dismissive look at the chaos of my kitchen. 'You're obviously not coping.'

'*Pardon?*' I said, looking at her in disbelief. Was she seriously daring to criticise my childcare? Later, a lot later, I did see the funny side of it. To be honest, I'd have felt like criticising the childcare of anyone whose kitchen, whose grandkids, were in the state mine were in right then. But at that moment it really was not funny, and really was not what I needed to hear.

'I'm surprised your children actually *want* their kids to be left with you,' she said as she strode back down the hall, with me following her, gasping with indignation. Not to mention being trailed by one naked child dripping orange juice and urine, and one whose nose had now run onto his T-shirt and whose hair was smeared with cheese – both of them crying and trying to grab my skirt.

I'd only just about regained the power of speech by the time I was opening the front door to ... I'd like to say *throw her out*, but she was going anyway.

'I know you're upset,' I managed to say somehow, 'but I've said I'm sorry, and there was no need to be so rude and insulting. As you can see, I'm *very* busy, and unfortunately I do forget things.'

'It's strange, though, isn't it,' she said, turning back to face me, 'how you managed to find time to entertain your *gentleman friend* this morning. I don't suppose you forgot about *him* coming round.'

'You nosy cow!' I said, aghast – first at her, for actually spying on my house, and admitting it! – secondly at myself, for behaving like a fishwife on my own doorstep and in front of the twins. 'It's none of your business!'

'I bet your children don't know about *that*,' she said, her face smug with satisfaction. With which she marched off, her nose in the air.

'Stuff your stupid tea and cake, you nasty-minded old bat!' I muttered, hoping it was loud enough for her to hear but not loud enough to echo down the street.

Unbelievable! I'd had visions of making a new friend, and instead I'd made an enemy without even trying. Well, to hell with her. I wasn't going to let her get to me. I turned back to face the task of cleaning up the children, to say nothing of the kitchen, and discovered the reason they'd both now finally gone very quiet. Being freed from the constraints of a nappy had apparently encouraged Amelia to evacuate her bowels as well as her bladder. And both children had been investigating the resultant pile on the floor with their fingers.

I wanted to cry.

Of course, by the time Michael came to collect the twins, they were clean and sweet-smelling, fed, dosed with Calpol and a whole lot better-tempered. Fortunately they weren't old enough to take home tales of Mad Nanny's fight on the doorstep with the witch from down the road.

'I did try to ring you to say I was on my way,' he said. 'But you were engaged.'

'Was I?' I didn't remember talking to anyone. I checked the phone and found it half on, half off its base, making a silly noise to tell me it hadn't been hung up properly. 'The noise isn't loud enough,' I complained, putting it back firmly on the base. 'Not when there are two children in the house.'

'Have they been playing up?' he asked, looking at them suspiciously.

'No, they've been absolutely fine. They never *play up*. But Amelia is teething and Alfie's got a rotten cold – Jo warned me this morning. So they've both had Calpol.'

'OK, thanks. You do look a bit shattered, Mum. I hope you haven't been spending too much time trying to sort out other people's problems.'

'Other people?' I said, visions of Pam stomping off down the road instantly coming back to me.

'That guy you phoned about. The one with the gay son and the grandchild.'

'Oh, you mean Bob. No, of course I haven't. I had no idea *how* to help him. That's why I asked you,' I pointed out.

'Yes, well, I'll let you know when I've had a chance to talk to Clifford.'

Clifford, never *Cliff*, was the senior partner at his firm, and was generally spoken about in tones of awe as if he were God. I'd never met him, but if he could find out what I needed to know for Bob, I might even offer him a hymn of praise myself.

The twins were carried out to the car, and I waved my son goodbye. Hopefully tomorrow would be a bit less fraught.

'Mum!' It was Steph on the phone, just as I'd started cooking my dinner. 'Where have you been? I've been trying to call you all day.'

'Sorry. I haven't been out – the phone was off the hook. I didn't realise until Michael got here.'

'You've been at home? All day? Was your mobile turned off too?'

'No. Although ...' I glanced around me. 'I'm not too sure where I've left it, actually.'

'That's not like you. What's the matter?' She sounded worried. 'Have you had a bad day?'

And stupidly, because I was ridiculously grateful for the sympathy, I started to spill it all out. Not the whole story about Bob, but just the fact that a friend had been to see me and had a very upsetting problem. And how I'd had a tricky day with the twins because of Alfie's cold and Amelia's teething, and a little bit of spillage over the lunch table. And how I'd forgotten about having tea with another friend and she was annoyed with me. When I came to a stop, I thought for a minute Steph had hung up. She was silent for a whole minute before saying, in a very exasperated voice:

'Honestly, Mum, it's just not good enough.'

'Sorry? What isn't?'

'Mike and Jo expecting you to have the twins almost every bloody day, even when they're both obviously being difficult and having tantrums.'

I should have known, shouldn't I? Silly me for expecting some sympathy. I'd just gone and added to the heap of resentment building up between my children.

'They weren't having *tantrums.* They just both happened to be feeling horrible today. They couldn't help it, they're just babies, Steph, as you should know. Don't start!'

'Well, I'm sorry, but it's quite obvious the strain is getting to you. I mean, I'm sorry we had to call on you yesterday to help with Izzie ...'

'Don't be silly, it wasn't a problem! You know I'm always happy to help, and you weren't well yourself. Of course I wanted to come.'

'But Izzie said you lost her, and you were nearly crying.'

'What?' Well, I didn't see *that* coming.

'That's what I was trying to call you about, Mum. When I was putting her to bed, she told me she tried to get the hoover out of the cupboard and when she went to find you to help her, you were in the garden shouting for her. I mean, honestly, Mum, it's not a big house. How could you possibly think you'd lost her?'

'I didn't see her in the cupboard, that's all. She must have gone right in. It was only for a moment ... yes, I was worried ...'

'Well, now *I'm* worried. I think you're suffering from stress, to be quite honest, and it's not really surprising.'

'*What?*' I said again. This whole conversation had taken a very bizarre turn.

'What with all these *friends* giving you grief. As if you haven't got enough on your plate.'

'Hold on a minute!' I was getting irritated now. 'Are you saying I shouldn't have time for any friends? I should be giving up all my time to the family?'

'No, that's not what I'm saying at all! You know what I think about Michael's children – you have them far too often. But you can't start taking on everyone's problems, either. I don't know who this friend is who came round today telling you sob stories but it's hardly fair, expecting you to be agony aunt to her.'

'Him.'

'Sorry?'

'*Him.* He's a man. Bob. And he's not *expecting* anything – we're friends, so I've obviously listened to him because he was upset.'

'I see.' The tone spoke volumes. How did I manage to swap places with my kids as they grew up, so that I now felt like a troublesome teenager hiding secret boyfriends from her parents? 'And because of *him* being *upset*, you forgot to see your other friend, and upset *her.*'

'Stop talking to me as if I was about thirteen!' I said, trying to make a joke of it but apparently failing. 'If you must know, I was supposed to see the other *friend* yesterday. I forgot because of your asthma attack, which I thought was quite understandable. In fact I hardly know the woman, she's a neighbour rather than a friend, and from the way she reacted today, I don't *want* to know her, either.'

'Honestly, Mum!' I could almost hear her shaking her head at me. 'You seem to have got yourself mixed up with all sorts of strange people. I really think you've been taking on too much. Leaving the phone off the hook, losing Izzie, losing your mobile ...'

'I haven't lost it, I've just misplaced it.' I sighed. 'Look, I'm sorry if I frightened Izzie. I probably overreacted a bit when I couldn't find her, but she seemed absolutely fine about it at the time. And I'm absolutely fine too. So can we leave it at that?'

'If you say so,' she said, sounding completely unconvinced.

'And please don't start blabbing about all this to your brother, or your sister,' I added.

'Hmm,' was all she said.

Great. And even worse – I *couldn't* actually find the mobile phone anywhere. It seemed to have completely vanished.

KATE

I am the Music Man, I Come from Down your Way

I could tell from the look on Jo's face the next morning when she dropped the twins off, that things had been said. I wasn't quite sure which things, or by whom, and luckily the morning handover of the children tended to be a fairly hurried affair, with Jo checking her watch and muttering about parking and catching the train. So it was only the *look* that gave it away – and the way she asked whether I was *absolutely sure I'd be OK with them* (as Alfie still had his cold and Amelia was still teething. As if I hadn't dealt with such things more times than I cared to remember). I did wonder what she would have done, at that point, if I'd said that actually, no, I suddenly wasn't *absolutely sure* about it after all, so could she possibly take the twins away again? But I wasn't that mean, could never be that mean.

As it happened, we had a much better day. Well, it couldn't have been a lot worse. It was warm and sunny, but not hot enough to make the children fractious. We went to the park, and despite runny noses and painful gums, the distraction of the swings and the baby slide put them both in happier moods. Lunch went relatively smoothly, not much being eaten but not too much being thrown around either, and I then managed to settle both of them down for a nap at the same time (which believe me, is quite an art, and I often think there should be some kind of parenting or *grand*-parenting award based on it).

'You look less tired than yesterday,' Michael commented when he arrived to collect them, spoiling my cheerful, calm, *less tired* mood straight away.

'Well, thanks for nothing! Did I say I was tired yesterday?'

'No. You didn't have to. You looked totally shattered. Seriously Mum, Jo and I have been wondering whether we're doing the right thing, leaving the twins with you like this, especially when they're being difficult.'

'Why? Are you worried I might take them somewhere and forget about them?' I said facetiously. I really wasn't taking this seriously. After all, what the hell else would they do with the twins while they both went to work? They'd made it clear to the whole family that they couldn't afford double nursery fees (which always tended to make Stephanie snort through her nose and shake her head and raise her eyes to the heavens).

'That's not really very funny, is it – after what happened with Izzie.'

For a moment I couldn't even think what he meant. Then I just burst out laughing, which didn't seem to amuse him either.

'You *are* joking, I hope!' I said. 'Steph's obviously told you the story about Izzie and the cupboard?'

'Of course she has. Why wouldn't she?'

'For one thing, I asked her not to. Phoning round the family, making a mountain out of a molehill – for God's sake! And anyway, it was just a silly, momentary incident, nobody was hurt, I just panicked for a second because I couldn't see her straight away. Don't tell me you or Jo have never done anything like that!'

He shrugged. If he had, he obviously wasn't going to admit it. But on the other hand he probably didn't want to risk too much criticism of me, his sole provider of childcare, so he gave me a smile then, and said he understood I must find it very tiring looking after kids at my age (nice of him), and that he and Jo were of course very grateful, and by the way he'd now spoken *at some length* to Clifford about my *man friend's* problem – and unfortunately, the answer was probably not going to please me. Or my *man friend.*

'Bob,' I said. 'His name's Bob.'

'Bob, right.' Michael gave me a look over the top of his glasses, like he didn't think it was quite decent that I should refer to Bob by his name. 'Well, as you know, I asked Clifford about the law in relation to grandparents' rights. And basically, you don't have any.'

'Any what? Who doesn't have any what?'

'Grandparents. Any rights. None whatsoever, when it comes to access to the grandchildren. Not even if it's certain that the kids *are* biologically your flesh and blood, so to speak. So in *Bob's* case ...'

'If the DNA test proves his son isn't the natural father ...'

'I'm afraid the guy's going to be completely buggered,' he said, not looking particularly sympathetic. 'Sorry about that.'

I sat next to Bob at the back of the library the next day at Mini Music Makers.

'How are you?' I asked, as quietly as I could against the backdrop of *Twinkle Twinkle Little Star*.

'Oh, you know.' He smiled. 'Worried, obviously, but what can I do? Until I know more, at least.'

Now it had come to it, I didn't actually know how to tell him. I was slightly concerned he might – I don't know – break down and cry, or get really angry and upset. Perhaps I should have phoned him, rather than confront him with this information while he was in charge of Freddie. Although he'd always seemed a sensible, placid type of person, if I was honest I felt just a tiny bit uneasy about the fact that it was *me* he'd turned to when he'd had the shock of this news about his son. I liked him, of course I did – he was a nice guy, I enjoyed his company – but I was wondering whether he'd actually become slightly emotionally dependent on me. I mean, obviously I was glad I was there for him when he was so upset, and that he felt able to call on me. But on the other hand, I'd have thought there might have been other people he'd call, before me – a male friend, for instance, or someone he'd known a little longer. OK, we'd known each other for probably about a year now. But it could hardly be called a close friendship, could it? And if it could, was that, in fact, the most alarming thing about it?

I'd been divorced from Dennis for more than twenty years at this point. I'd made up my mind at the time that I wasn't going to get involved with another man – ever again, thanks very much – and I hadn't felt any need to change my mind since then. I was fine on my own. I actually enjoyed it, liked having my own space, not having to tidy up after anyone apart from myself, not having to compromise, or defer, or tiptoe around anyone's bad moods. The peace. The lack of arguments. And although it seemed to be unfashionable to say so these days, I didn't miss the sex either, not that there'd been much of that during the dying years of the marriage anyway. Oh, it had been good when we were younger, of course, when the blazing rows were followed by passionate make-up sex, and often followed by another blazing row, followed by ...

Just the thought of it made me feel weary now. Why would anyone want to be bothered with all that angst and aggravation, when you could go to bed on your own with a good book, turn off the light whenever it suited you, put on the radio if you couldn't sleep, take a cup of tea and a sandwich to bed if that was what you fancied?

Of course, men were OK as friends; I'd had plenty of those when I was at work, but I'd lost touch with most of them since I retired, and I suppose in my mind, Bob had just kind of slotted into the same category. I'd assumed he felt the same way. Well, hopefully he did, and hopefully I was worrying over nothing at all. My children *would* have a fit if they thought I was being looked upon as girlfriend material by somebody.

'Bob, I need to tell you something.' Now or never. 'I hope you don't mind, but I talked to someone. My son, actually. He works in a legal company, you see – well, I've probably told you that already – and I wondered if he might know anything about grandparents' rights. You know, in cases like yours. Rights to access, I mean, to the grandchildren, or ... children of the, um, partnership, in cases where there's a break-up.' I was gabbling, and it wasn't going to help. *Get to the point, Kate.* 'Well, he spoke to someone for me. One of the partners. And the bottom line is ...'

'I wouldn't have any rights.' He turned to face me, a pitiful sadness in his eyes. 'That's what you're trying to say, isn't it.'

'Yes. I'm sorry, Bob. And I'm sorry if I was interfering.'

'No, it was kind of you. I needed to know. To be honest, I'd guessed as much, already, but it's better to be aware of the facts.' He nodded. 'Thank you.'

'Believe it or not, *none* of us have any rights when it comes to our grandchildren, whether they're, um, actually our biological progeny, so to speak, or not. If we're not given access voluntarily, we'd need to go to court to fight for it.'

He raised his eyebrows at this and then turned his gaze to Freddie who was busy being a Dingle Dangle Scarecrow with all the other children and giggling away to himself. Bob didn't seem to trust himself to speak for a moment, and I felt awful for having given him such gloomy news.

'Let's look on the bright side,' I tried to encourage him. 'Let's hope, whatever happens, you don't *need* to fight for the right to see Freddie. Whichever of them wins custody, they'll surely want you to keep seeing him. It's in Freddie's best interests – he loves coming to you.'

'Let's hope so,' he agreed calmly, giving me a fleeting smile.

I decided it was best to change the subject. Glancing up, I noticed we had a newcomer in the group. She'd been dealing with the form-filling which was necessary on anyone's first occasion, and was now standing with a baby in her arms, staring wide-eyed at the throng of Dingle Dangle Scarecrows waving their arms and legs and making valiant and fairly tuneless attempts to sing along with the song.

'I think we've got another grandma to keep us company,' I commented to Bob.

'Are you sure?' He adjusted his glasses. 'I'd say she's just an older-than-average mum.'

'Maybe. But she looks ... a bit like I probably looked when I first came here. Horror-struck!'

'Let's be friendly, then. Poor soul! She's going to need to put that child down before she drops her.'

The baby girl, who looked about a year old, was wriggling in the woman's grasp and starting to protest. I got up and went over to her.

'Hi. I'm Kate. Is it your first time?'

'Oh, hi Kate. Jackie. Well, yes.' She laughed, and nearly let go of the child, who was still squirming to get down. 'But I don't think I'll stay. It doesn't seem to be exactly what I thought it was.'

'It's actually quite fun when you get used to the noise,' I told her. 'Come and sit at the back with us. They've only just started. What's your little one's name?'

'Autumn. She's my granddaughter. Don't ask me why, though.'

'Why she's your granddaughter?' I asked, a little confused.

'No.' She was following me to the chairs at the back of the room. 'I meant, why the hell did my daughter give her a name like that? Especially as she was born in the summer!'

'*Summer* is getting quite common,' I said, laughing. 'Maybe your daughter wanted a more unusual name. I still haven't quite got my head around my latest grandchild being *Isaac*.'

We sat down with Bob, and I introduced them.

'Autumn is Jackie's granddaughter,' I explained.

He smiled. 'You don't look old enough.'

'I don't feel old enough, either, but unfortunately it's true.'

She didn't sound like she was joking. Autumn was still wriggling furiously, and now started to squawk loudly with frustration.

'Why don't you put her down?' I suggested. 'She won't come to any harm. The floor's all carpeted.'

Jackie set her down somewhat nervously, and immediately the child, who had apparently achieved standing upright but not walking, sat down on the floor with a bump, letting go of her grandmother's hand, and began to crawl off towards the other children, laughing.

'Bugger,' Jackie said. 'There's no way I'll be able to get out of it and take her home now! Oh God, she's grabbing some kid's hair.' She jumped up and waded between the dancing toddlers, doing her best to separate Autumn's grasping fingers from another little girl's long curls.

'Poor cow, she looks frazzled,' Bob said in a whisper, making me smile as I watched her struggling. I suspected Jackie was someone who often made people smile. Slim and petite, she had sleek brown hair with red highlights, dangly silver earrings that I'd already noticed baby Autumn making a grab for, and was dressed in impossibly tight, bright green jeggings and a pink striped vest top.

'A reluctant grandma, I think,' I whispered back. Then I saw the look on Bob's face, and wished I hadn't said it. Reluctant grandparenthood was the last thing Bob could possibly sympathise with.

The reluctant grandma was meanwhile plonking herself back in the seat next to mine and sighing deeply.

'So this is your first time at the musical mayhem, then?' Bob asked her.

'Yes, and my last!' she said with feeling. 'How can you stand it? I can't *believe* they let the kids loose with bloody *percussion* instruments!'

'Oh, it's quite fun really,' he said, smiling. He was making an effort with the woman, anyway. Even if she did decide never to come again!

'Your idea of fun must be completely different from mine,' Jackie retorted. 'It's bad enough having to go all day without a fag. I mean, I know it's right, I know you shouldn't breathe smoke in their faces and all that, but seriously, when do *I* get any pleasure out of this?'

I wasn't sure whether or not she was joking. Bob looked away, watching Freddie shaking a tambourine, laughing with the twins.

'It's an enormous strain at times, I know,' I said, 'and really tiring, especially while they're at the crawling stage like your little one. Into everything!'

'Tell me about it! I daren't take my eyes off her! Trust me, I'd rather do a full day in the office.'

'Ah, well.' Bob smiled again. 'It's all right for us retirees, isn't it, Kate? We've got all the time in the world.'

'And it might be stressful sometimes, looking after them,' I said, 'but it *is* rewarding too.'

'Is it?' she said, looking at me as if I'd just spoken in tongues.

I decided to shut up.

Although Jackie was giving off such hostile vibes, I actually sympathised with her. I remembered how I felt myself, like a duck out of water, when I started looking after Izzie, having had a gap of ten years since my previous grandchild, Danielle's daughter Emilie. I'd never put a disposable nappy on a baby before, and hadn't realised how all the rules had changed – babies having to be laid on their backs instead of their sides or their tummies, not allowed in a car unless they were strapped into a child seat, and not given solid food until I felt like they were almost old enough to order a takeaway for themselves.

'Should we ask her to come to the café with us?' I suggested to Bob quietly when the session ended. 'She looks so fraught. She might appreciate a coffee and a bun!'

Bob glanced in Jackie's direction. She was struggling with the straps of her grandchild's pushchair at the same time as trying to quieten the child and remove a tambourine from her grasp. *No, you can't take it home. It stays here. Oh, don't scream – where's your dummy? What did I do with it?*

Bob smiled. 'Yes, ask her along. She's fun. We need cheering up, don't we, Kate.'

'We do,' I agreed, although actually I was thinking: *You* certainly do. And then I remembered the incident with Pam, the new friendship that seemed to have died a horrible death before it had even got started. And losing my mobile phone (where the hell *had* I left that?). And the way my kids had started to talk to me like I was losing the plot. And I amended my thoughts. We *both* needed cheering up!

'Come and have a cup of coffee and a cake with me and Bob, Jackie,' I suggested to our new friend. 'We can relax while the kids play with the toys there. I think it might do us all good.'

'You know what?' she said, turning to reappraise me. 'You're a life-saver, you are. That might just save my sanity.'

JACKIE

Boys and Girls Come Out to Play

When I first arrived at that kids' bloody musical thing at the library I wondered what on earth I was doing there. It was bedlam. Quite apart from the insane noise, I was terrified of letting go of the baby in case she crawled off, getting under people's feet, picking things up, putting things in her mouth. When I saw them getting out the percussion instruments I nearly turned round and walked out. *You have got to be joking!* I thought to myself. Personally I wouldn't have allowed a tambourine or a drum within a mile of any preschool child. And the way their parents and carers were singing along with those songs! Anyone would think they were enjoying themselves. They all had this kind of demented enthusiasm about them. It made me feel slightly faint.

I'd only gone there because I thought it was a playgroup, or rather, a crèche – you know, the type where you can leave the kids and ... well, I know how bad this sounds, but leave them and go home. Someone, some other well-meaning grandmother somewhere, had told me about these sessions held by the Children's Centre and I'd jumped to the wrong conclusion. To be perfectly honest, I'd leapt at the idea of being able to leave Autumn in the hands of some kind of professional carer for an hour or so and maybe get my hair done or go to the gym. I knew it couldn't be an actual nursery, of course. My daughter put Autumn in one of those on the other days she worked, and it cost her an arm and a leg. But when I turned up at the library, and the leader woman got me to fill in the registration document (with all its nosy and frankly unnecessary questions, considering the fact that I was expected to stay there with the baby anyway), and was then told it was *a social and learning opportunity for children, not a childcare facility*, I felt pretty silly, to say nothing of feeling disappointed and bloody irritated too.

And that was *before* I got subjected to the third degree by this Kate woman, who seemed to think she knew it all just because she was looking after twins. What was it with all these sanctimonious other grandparents I seemed to keep meeting – all at least a decade older than me – who seemed to be piously delighted to give up the freedom of their retirement years to devote themselves to kids for the second time in their lives? And why did they all seem to react with such shock and offence if I let slip that, as a relatively young working woman still in my forties, I felt less than enthralled about spending my day off every week, babysitting?

The thing was, I'd agreed in a moment of weakness. I was upset of course, sorry for my daughter – the pregnancy wasn't planned, and the father (the bastard) had stayed around just till it was too late for her to get an abortion, and then changed his mind and scarpered. I wasn't even particularly cut out for motherhood in the first place. Erin was my only child. Yes, obviously I loved her – if I'm honest, sometimes it took me by surprise how much I loved her. But I'd never been one of those traditional cuddly mummies. I went back to work as soon as I could, and I never had any desire to go through it all again. So I could only imagine Erin's situation with heartfelt horror. No man on the scene to share the burdens, no second salary to provide a few luxuries to cushion the blow of parenthood, no easy way to envisage a return to any kind of social life, or to any prospect of dating again. Poor cow. My poor daughter.

'I could look after her on Thursdays,' I offered without thinking it through, when Autumn was about four days old and Erin was crying her eyes out from tiredness, anxiety and raging hormones. I remember looking down at this softly sleeping new baby, and picturing myself with her on my day off – the baby always asleep, always somehow blending into the background of my life. I imagined taking her along to lunches with my friends, putting the car seat under the table in the nice restaurants we liked going to, getting on with things without too much change.

How the hell had I forgotten? The nappy changing, the feeding, the crying, the mess ... and now, at eleven months, the fact that the baby wouldn't even stay put anymore. What was I supposed to do with her?

I was so fed up about the music group not being a crèche, and being so awful, that when Kate started talking to me I was tempted at first to tell her to clear off and mind her own business. Telling me to put Autumn down on the floor! So much for that! Needless to say she crawled straight into the middle of everything, causing havoc, pulling one kid's hair and trying to grab another one's shaker, and I ended up having to wade in there and sort out the fracas. I was dreading her starting to really kick off, causing a scene among all those smug mummies singing their hearts out to *Twinkle Twinkle Little Star* and grinning at each other like they were proud of their ability to remember the words. And when I got back to my seat, Kate and her friend Bob were just smiling away, looking perfectly relaxed while their own demon toddlers were probably beating each other around the heads with drumsticks, and bleating on about how nice it was to be retired, having all the time in the world, and how rewarding it was to look after their grandkids. *Yuck.*

I sat there sighing to myself, watching Autumn anxiously in case she crawled off under a bookshelf or something. But to my surprise she just sat there on her padded bottom, shaking a set of sleigh-bells I'd handed her (in desperation) from the collection of instruments laid out in the middle of the floor, and grinning all around her, showing off her two teeth and making some of the young mums nudge each other and smile.

She's so perfect, I suddenly found myself thinking, as I did occasionally, giving myself a little thrill of a shock. And I suppose I started to relax a bit then, sitting there next to the woman with the twin grandkids – but I still didn't intend to stay. *I'll go when this song finishes*, I thought. I actually said it out loud to Kate, to emphasise the point.

'Oh, that's a shame,' she said. 'We always do *Ring-a-Ring-of-Roses* after the break.'

I'm overwhelmed with bloody excitement, I thought.

But somehow I was still there when everyone stopped for juice and biscuits. Well, I obviously wasn't going to be able to get my hair done now, so I supposed I might as well cut my losses and stay till the end of the session. When bloody *Ring-of-Roses* started, I even gave in to Kate's badgering to get up and join the circle of mothers and toddlers, feeling absolutely ridiculous holding Autumn in my arms and ducking down to the floor with her at *All Fall Down*. The twins, Amelia and Alfie, were giggling and falling around, while Kate looked on indulgently. A little dark-haired boy of about two, who apparently belonged to Bob, was hanging onto Kate's hand and singing '*Ring-a-Ring-a-Ring-a-Ring ...*' at the top of his voice, Every few minutes he'd turn and call out: *'Look, G'andad! Look me! Look me!'*

'Bob's arthritis is bad today,' Kate said. 'I told him to stay sitting down while I keep an eye on Freddie.'

As well as the twins? I thought. She must be some kind of superwoman. One of those earth-mother types who devote themselves to their families all their lives, never have a career, spend their whole time in the kitchen baking cakes and rolling out pastry.

Then, at the end, Kate and Bob asked me to go for a coffee with them, and I'd said yes before I could stop myself. The truth was, I wasn't in a rush to go home. Let's face it, an eleven-month-old isn't a lot of company. I'd got no idea what I was going to do for the rest of the day, apart from changing her nappy yet again, trying to get her to eat some lunch, and putting her down for a nap. But as we all headed out of the library pushing our buggies like a kind of convoy, I started to have second thoughts. The last thing I wanted was to become part of an unofficial grannies' group. Still, it was just a coffee – and I wouldn't be coming again.

'I'm glad you decided to stay for the whole session,' Kate was saying now. 'I'm sure Autumn enjoyed it. She's adorable, isn't she? My new one's a boy, Isaac. He's only three weeks old.'

'Oh. Congratulations.' I glanced from Kate to the twins and back again. 'You're surely not going to look after him as well?' The thought of having two children at the same time filled me with horror. How anyone could possibly manage three was beyond me.

Kate laughed. 'Probably, sooner or later! I often look after his big sister anyway – she's three, coming up for four. But the oldest three grandchildren live in France, so I don't often get called upon to do anything with them.'

Seven grandkids?

'You have my admiration,' I said. 'But it's as much as I can do to cope with this one – and that's only for one day a week.'

And to my own surprise, probably because I felt so starved of adult company, I started telling her and Bob how I commuted to London on the other days, to a job I loved, and that I sometimes wished I'd never taken Thursdays off because in fact, to be brutally honest, I'd rather be in my office surrounded by my colleagues, by the buzz of adult conversation, of frantically ringing phones, desperately urgent emails, deadlines, meetings, hurried lunches at my desk – than dealing with dirty nappies and mushy dinners dribbling down a baby's chin.

'Oh, I know how you feel, trust me,' Kate said. And it sounded so heartfelt, I started thinking maybe I'd misjudged her. Perhaps she wasn't quite such a smug nanny as she first seemed, with her beautiful blond twins, their angelic smiles and big blue eyes. 'It's hard with the first one. The more that come along, the more used to it you get.'

I shuddered. 'I doubt there'll be any more.'

'Never say never!' Kate said cheerfully.

We were at the café by now, and Bob, who'd been hobbling noticeably and pretty much leaning on his grandson's buggy as he pushed it along, commented that he couldn't wait to have a comfy chair and a nice hot drink.

'What do you do with the children while you're in here?' I said as I held the door open for him.

'Oh, there's a toddlers' play area – see? With some toys and books, some soft bricks and things to throw around. It always tires them out completely if the music session hasn't already done the job.'

'Great,' I said sarcastically. To be honest the last thing I felt like doing, after enduring that hell-on-earth of a nursery rhyme session, was spending more time with other people's kids bouncing off the walls and screaming. But on the other hand the idea of getting Autumn well and truly tired out was tempting. She'd started to cut out one of her daytime naps, and sometimes I found it frustratingly difficult to get her off to sleep for the remaining one. If she was absolutely exhausted, I could probably put her in the pushchair after half an hour here, and she'd go off to sleep for a good long time. Give me a chance to catch up with some emails when I got home.

In for a penny, in for a pound. It would only be a one-off, after all. There was no way I'd be coming again!

The talk over coffee was, inevitably, about grandchildren, grandchildren, and just to vary it a little bit, grandchildren.

'Sorry, Jackie,' Kate said eventually, seeing me starting to yawn. 'The children do tend to monopolise our conversations! I look after mine at least three days a week, you see, and Bob normally has Freddie twice a week.'

'Lucky you!' I said, with heavy sarcasm, and I saw Kate swallow, and then glance at Bob like she was worried he might be upset.

'Yes, we are lucky,' she said quietly. 'It's a privilege.'

'Sometimes,' Bob added, looking over at Freddie, 'you only realise what a privilege something is when you're in danger of losing it.'

They both went quiet, then, looking down and stirring their coffees.

'Oh shit,' I said. 'Have I put my foot in it?'

'No, it's just ...' Kate began, but Bob stopped her.

'It's my fault,' he said. 'I should have told you, but I didn't want you to feel awkward. I only found out last week. I won't bore you with the details. But there's a possibility I might not be allowed to see Freddie anymore if ... if things don't work out.'

'Oh God. I'm sorry.' Me and my stupid flippant remarks. What a stupid cow I am sometimes. 'I feel really bad now, for saying all that stuff. I don't really mean it.'

'I know. Don't feel bad.' Bob tried to smile, but I could see it was a struggle. 'We all complain about what hard work it is, looking after the kids – but as I say, if you're suddenly faced with the threat of never having them again ...'

We were all watching Freddie now. He was trying to build up a pile of coloured plastic bricks, which inevitably kept falling down again. Amazingly, Autumn was sitting there as good as gold, watching him.

'So ... I'm sorry, tell me to mind my own business, but you mean Freddie's parents might actually stop you seeing him at *all*?'

'It's rather a complicated situation,' Bob said. 'But basically, yes.'

'In *any* situation, the parents could stop us seeing our grandkids,' Kate said. 'We have no rights.' She glanced at Bob. 'And when it comes to break-ups of relationships, people can get very bitter. It's like they have to take out their hurt on someone.'

'Yes. The wrong person, it seems,' Bob said. He finished his coffee with a gulp. 'Sorry. I'm not being very good company. I'll leave you two to chat about more cheerful things.'

'No, please don't go,' I said, horrified to think I'd said anything to hurt this nice old chap. He'd needed me whingeing about looking after my grandchild, like he needed a hole in the head. 'I'm just flabbergasted. I didn't realise. I mean, I know I've been moaning about – ' I nodded in the direction of the toy corner, and then noticed that Autumn was now sitting there crying. I jumped up. 'Oh dear. All right, sweetheart, I'm coming.'

When I'd picked her up and brought her back, sitting her on my lap and kissing the top of her head, I said somewhat apologetically, 'It's not that I don't love her.'

'Of course. We know,' Kate said.

'It's just ...' I shrugged. 'I wasn't really ready for all this, you know? My daughter wasn't ready for it herself, but these things happen, and I had to help her out a bit. I don't mean to complain, it's just not what I envisaged at this stage of my life. But if anything happened, anything like *you're* saying, well, obviously I know my daughter would never stop me from seeing Autumn, but ...'

'It just makes you think, doesn't it,' Bob said.

'We get so attached to them,' Kate said. She paused, and then added, 'I thought I'd lost Isabel the other day. For a full three minutes, I swear my heart actually stopped beating. We were in her own house, for God's sake – how could I lose her? But I panicked, really panicked.' Her eyes filled with tears. 'It sounds so stupid.'

'No it doesn't,' I said, feeling a lot more sombre now and a lot more sympathetic to them both.

The three of us sat in silence. Autumn was already half-asleep now on my lap, one arm flung wide, the other curled against my neck. Then the twins both came trotting over, whining with tiredness, followed by Freddie, complaining of hunger and the need for *ham sanwidge and crisps.*

'Well,' I said as I lifted Autumn into her pushchair again, 'I suppose I *could* give it another try next week.'

'It's somewhere to take them,' Kate pointed out, smiling. 'And it does tire them out.'

'Hmm. OK, well, it's been nice to meet you both, and maybe I'll see you next Thursday.'

'We'll be there. We grandparents need to stick together,' Bob said with a shrug, and he and Kate looked at each other in surprise, like this had only just occurred to them.

'You're right,' Kate said. 'We need to support each other, don't we. Let's face it – no other bugger is going to!'

And I ended up, somehow, thinking I actually quite liked them both – even if they were a pair of daft old codgers.

KATE

Pat a Cake, Pat a Cake

The following Monday, I was working in the garden, trying to get a grip on the weeds so that I could actually see whether I had any plants left at all, when Steph turned up round the back way with Izzie and the baby.

'This is a surprise!' I said, rubbing some of the dirt off my hands and getting up from my knees with some difficulty.

'Well, as you know, we were busy at the weekend.' They'd gone to Ben's parents in Hampshire – not that she seemed to have enjoyed the experience, judging by the look on her face. 'So I thought I should come and see you today.'

'That's nice. You mustn't feel like you *have* to, though. I know how busy you are.'

She looked at me in surprise. 'Don't you *want* to see your grandchildren? Don't worry, I'm not leaving Izzie with you.'

Oh dear. Said the wrong thing again.

'Of course I want to see them – and you! How are you? Come into the kitchen while I put the kettle on. Do you want a biscuit, Izzie?'

Steph frowned. 'She really shouldn't be eating so much sugar, Mum.'

'Sorry.' Something told me my daughter was spoiling for a fight. I decided not to rise to the bait. 'I've got some cheese biscuits – she can have one of those. How's Isaac?'

'Still crying nearly all the time.' No wonder she was tetchy then, poor thing. 'The health visitor says it's colic. I've got some stuff for him, he's supposed to have it before every feed. The way he feeds, I'll get through the whole bottle within a couple of days.'

Isaac, in defiance of his mother's complaints, was lying fast asleep in his car seat, the picture of contentment.

'Sit down and put your feet up while you can, then,' I said. 'Maybe he'll stay asleep for a while now.'

'Can I help you make some cakes, Nanny?' Izzie asked, her mouth full of cheese biscuit.

'Well …' It was a lovely warm day. Baking was the last thing I'd planned to do. 'I don't think that's a very good idea, Izzie. You heard what Mummy said – cakes and biscuits are very bad for your teeth.'

'Oh, for God's sake,' Steph interrupted irritably, 'let her bake some cakes, Mum, if that's what she wants. She doesn't have to eat them all.'

'I think it's more of a *playing in the garden* day,' I tried to insist – but Izzie had already trotted off to the kitchen. So maybe I was a soft touch where my grandkids were concerned, or maybe I just didn't want to risk a confrontation that might wake up Isaac and cause Stephanie even more grief. With one last regretful look out of the window at my garden, I followed the child into the kitchen and got the mixing bowl out.

We were happily engrossed in breaking eggs into the mixture when the doorbell rang. I rushed to the door, hoping it wasn't going to wake up the baby, and was (not very pleasantly) surprised to see Pam standing there again.

'I was very rude to you last week,' she said, not meeting my eyes. 'I apologise.'

'Yes, well, OK, apology accepted,' I said stiffly.

I waited for her to walk away. I mean, there wasn't a lot more to be said, as far as I was concerned.

'I wondered if we could try again,' she said.

'Well, no, I don't think that would …'

'*Please.*'

She'd managed to face me now, and the look in her eyes made me blink with shock. It was almost *anguished.* Like it actually mattered whether I bothered to talk to her again. I'd already realised she was a pretty unhappy woman. Lonely. Perhaps she didn't have any friends – and no wonder, I found myself thinking a bit uncharitably, if she insulted everyone the way she'd insulted me.

'I *have* apologised,' she said, jutting out her chin like a sulky child. 'What else do you want me to say?' Her voice was becoming louder. I was either going to have to be firm – ruthless – and more or less shoo her away and shut the door, or else ...

I sighed. 'You'd better come in. My daughter's in the lounge with the baby – I don't want them disturbed. Come through to the kitchen.'

I wasn't planning to simply roll over, say everything was fine and we could be best buddies from now on. I wasn't *quite* that much of a soft touch. To be honest I wanted to sit her down and ask her exactly what her problem was. Was it the situation with the children, whoever's children they were, making her so unhappy? Was she such a miserable cow with everyone, or was it just me?

I walked ahead of her to the kitchen, but stopped still in the doorway as I surveyed the scene.

'Nanny,' said Izzie in a worried little voice. 'I did try to stir in the flour like you said.'

You know what happens if you tip a bag of flour straight into a cake mixture in a bowl – or if you don't know, you can probably imagine it. There was flour everywhere – white dollops like snowdrifts across the worktop, a fine dusting over most of the floor, and somehow, probably in trying to sweep some of the excess off the worktop, Izzie had got it all over herself too. It was over her face. It was in her hair. The stool she was perched on was covered – she was kneeling in it. And to make matters worse some of the butter-sugar-and-eggs mixture had slopped over the side of the mixing bowl upon impact with the flour, and Izzie had apparently tried to wipe that up with her fingers too.

'Oh, Izzie!' I grabbed her off the stool, and was immediately showered with flour myself. 'I didn't want *you* to stir in the flour. You should have waited. We were going to do it together.'

'I was trying to be *helpful*,' she protested, starting to cry. 'I didn't know the flour wanted to fly all round the room.'

'All right, all right, don't cry. Let's take your dress off. You've got eggy mixture in your hair, Izzie. I'm going to have to give you a bath.'

'Sorry, Nanny!' she sobbed. 'I wasn't being naughty.'

'I know you weren't, sweetheart. It's all right. I can clear up the kitchen later. Let's go and run the bath. I've got some bubbles.'

And as we turned towards the kitchen door, I realised Pam was still standing there.

'Hello,' Izzie said quietly, holding onto my hand.

'Sorry,' I said. 'As you can see, I've got my hands full right now. Perhaps some other time ...'

I knew how I sounded – like I couldn't really be bothered with her, one way or another – but I couldn't help it. The look on her face, the way she'd just stood there in the kitchen doorway staring at yet another example of chaos in my house without saying a word – it just infuriated me.

'It seems like you've *always* got your hands full,' she said loudly. 'Does your daughter realise what a mess you're making of everything?'

'Right, you'd better just go,' I said, my voice deceptively calm. If Izzie hadn't been there, I'd have told her to bugger off. I'd have called her a nasty vicious bitch and told her never to come back. *Try again*? Why bother?

It was pretty obvious by now that we'd never be friends –
that in fact, and for some reason I couldn't quite make out,
she seemed to dislike me, and the feeling was absolutely
mutual.

'What's going on, Mum?'

Needless to say, Steph had now come out of the lounge
and was looking from me to Pam and ... back again at me
and Izzie, a shocked expression on her face as she took in
the flour, the egg mixture in her daughter's hair, the dress
on the floor, the tears.

'It's OK. Everything's under control,' I started to say.

There was a snort of derisive laughter from Pam, and,
shaking her head, she marched to the front door and let
herself out.

'And bloody good riddance,' I said, not quite under my
breath.

'Why are you cross with that lady?' Izzie asked in a
whisper.

'Who was *that*?' Steph demanded. 'Is she a friend of
yours? Did *she* make all this mess?'

'No, of course not!' I managed, somehow, to laugh.
'No, she just she lives down the road and she ... oh, look,
never mind her. Izzie needs a bath, then I'll clear up in
here. Go back and rest while the baby's ...'

Not asleep any more. His wails started to fill the house.

'I'd better go and feed him. *Again*,' she said, looking at
me as if it was my fault.

I took Izzie upstairs and ran the bath, and we sang
songs about ducks together to cheer ourselves up.

With Izzie clean, the kitchen clean, Isaac fed and changed
and lunch prepared and served, everyone's mood seemed to
improve and Stephanie and I were having a nice relaxed
chat about the price of nappies over our cheese sandwiches
while Izzie watched something vaguely educational on the
TV.

Suddenly Steph put down her plate and turned to face me.

'Anyway, Mum, this isn't the reason I came round today.'

'I know. You said, you didn't have a chance to see me over the weekend, so ...'

'Well, that too, obviously. But I wanted to talk to you.'

It sounded ominous. 'What about?'

'Well, look.' She sounded shifty, uncomfortable. 'Don't take this the wrong way, but Ben and I have been talking.'

'About?' I prompted her, as she seemed reluctant to go on.

'About the amount of time you spend looking after the children. *Michael's* children,' she added pointedly. 'Don't shake your head at me like that, Mum! It's not right, and we think it's tiring you out. And if you're not prepared to say anything to him, we're going to.'

'Steph, we've been through this before. If I felt it was too much, I'd be quite capable of telling him that myself. And quite frankly, it's none of your business.'

'Well, that's nice, isn't it!' she exclaimed huffily. 'I'm only thinking of you, Mum! I've seen how tired you're getting, so don't try to deny it. The strain of having those twins every day is obviously starting to tell on you.'

'Three days a week. Not every day. And anyway, I sometimes look after Izzie almost as often as the twins.'

'What? Don't be ridiculous! Of course you don't! I hardly *ever* ask you to have Izzie. It's only been recently, because I've just had a new baby!'

'And before that, because you were pregnant,' I reminded her gently.

'Well, for God's sake, if you're not prepared to help me out when I'm pregnant, and when I've just given birth ...'

'That isn't what I said. You know I'm always happy to have Izzie. And the twins. Now, can we just drop this conversation, because it's simply a repeat of the same old thing, Steph, and to be honest I'm sick of it – you, Michael and Danielle squabbling between yourselves – can't you ever let up and just be grateful that I'm here for *all* of you?'

'*Squabbling?*' She stared at me, apparently stunned. 'We're not squabbling, we're just concerned about you. Whether you want to admit it or not, Mum, it's quite obvious to us that you're finding it hard to cope. Look at the mess you got into in the kitchen earlier on!'

'That was …'

'Because you were too busy arguing with some *friend* of yours to watch what Izzie was doing. And let's not forget how the other week at my house you actually thought you'd lost her. To say nothing of starting to lose *things* too. Have you found your phone yet?'

'No, I haven't, but I'm sure it'll turn up. You're making a mountain out of a molehill again. I'm absolutely fine. Apart from being pretty insulted that you think I can't cope with looking after the children anymore.'

She swallowed. 'Sorry. I didn't mean to insult you. And we *are* grateful, you know we are. I'm just worried about you.'

'Well, don't be.' I stood up and started to clear the lunch things. 'Subject closed.'

I was carrying the plates and cups out to the kitchen when the doorbell rang again. For a moment I stood stock still in the hallway, staring at the front door. Surely to God Pam hadn't come back again? I really couldn't face it. I considered pretending I wasn't at home – but Steph's car was on the driveway and all the windows were open.

'Are you all right?' Steph asked, following me out into the hallway and watching me looking at the door. 'Shall I get that for you, if your hands are full?'

'No. It's OK.' The doorbell rang again, and I quickly went to put the crockery in the kitchen before returning to open the door. If it was Pam, I'd just shut the door again. But it could be anyone, after all. The postman. The meter reader. Jehovah's Witnesses.

It was Bob. He was leaning against the wall, breathing hard, and he looked terrible.

'I'm so sorry to bother you,' he said, 'But have you got time for a little chat?'

KATE

Lucy Locket Lost her Pocket

I was alarmed to see Bob in such a state.

'Come in,' I said at once. 'Come and sit down. What on earth's happened?'

He followed me into the lounge, limping badly, and lowered himself slowly and awkwardly onto the sofa.

'Sorry. Knees are playing up today.'

'You shouldn't have walked all the way round here, then,' I admonished him. 'Why didn't you call me?'

'I tried. You were continually engaged.' He looked up and seemed to notice for the first time that he had an audience – Stephanie and Izzie, both staring at him openly.

'Hello,' he said, giving them a weak little smile. And then, turning to me, he went on, 'Sorry. I should have checked first whether you had company.'

'Don't be silly. It's just my daughter, Stephanie. Steph, this is my friend Bob. And Izzie you've met already,' I reminded him.

'I saw you at Music Makers,' Izzie said shyly. 'With Freddie.'

'My grandson.' Bob smiled at her, and then looked away, and added quietly, 'Or ... not, in fact.' He sighed and turned back to me. 'I've heard from my son.'

'About the paternity test? Have they got the result?'

'Yes. It's not good news.'

'Oh, Bob! I'm so sorry to hear that.' I wanted to do something – hug him or hold his hand – but I was conscious of Stephanie watching me. 'You must be devastated. Let me make you a cup of tea and then you can tell me more. You look all done in.'

'Thank you. I won't stay – you've got your daughter here. I'll just get my breath back ...'

'Nonsense. Stay and chat for a while. I'll drive you home. It's too far for you to walk.' I went out to put the kettle on, and at the same time, checked the phone. I knew I hadn't been talking on it continuously – and sure enough, I found that once again I hadn't put it back on its cradle properly. With so much going on, I hadn't even heard it making its warning noise.

'Sorry about the phone,' I called back. 'Left it off the hook again. Why didn't you try my mobile – I did give you the number, didn't I?'

'Yes. I did try it, but I just got your recorded message.'

'You said you'd lost it,' Stephanie reminded me, sounding exasperated. 'Have you forgotten already?'

'Oh yes.' I frowned to myself as I got out clean mugs and waited for the kettle to boil. Maybe I *was* losing my marbles. I really must try to find the damned phone when I had a moment.

With a mug of hot tea and a couple of chocolate biscuits to revive him, Bob began to look a little better.

'To be honest, you know, Kate, the DNA result isn't really a surprise,' he said. 'I'd been preparing myself for the worst.'

'Easier said than done, I'm sure,' I sympathised.

'Well, it *was* just a bit upsetting, getting the phone call today, you know, confirming it. But I've got to try to come to terms with it. It's no good keep getting myself in a state. It's not all about me, after all.'

'No, fair enough – but you must be worried now, about what might happen.'

'I'm trying not to look ahead too much. For the moment I'm still being allowed to have Freddie as usual, so I don't want to make any fuss and start upsetting the boy unnecessarily. There's been enough upheaval already.'

'That's true. It's obviously going to be better for Freddie, isn't it, if everybody stays calm around him.'

He nodded. 'If only. It's the state my son's got himself into that's upset me the most. He'd just been told the result when he called me this morning, and he was absolutely beside himself. He said he wishes he'd never found out.'

'But they only had to do this – go through this – because of him breaking up with ...'

'Yes, because of *his* infidelity! *His* stupidity! That's right!' Bob shook his head. 'Kate, I never thought I'd say this, but I'm so disappointed in my son. He's behaved like an idiot. Like a silly teenager. Nathan's a nice chap, but how can I blame him if he decides to make things difficult for Craig, with Freddie?'

'Can he actually do that? Aren't they both registered as Freddie's parents?'

'Yes, but now he's got proof that he's Freddie's biological father, he can apply for sole custody. If he gets it, he could take the boy away from Craig to live with him. Craig thinks that's what he'll do.'

'He only *thinks* it? Surely they should be talking about it! Whatever's happened between them, they ought to be putting Freddie's needs first.'

'Of course they should, and that's what I keep telling him. But you know what it's like when people break up, Kate. They're upset, they become irrational, they act like hurt children.'

'Yes.' I nodded. 'I do know.'

He considered me for a moment before going on. 'Sorry. I should have thought. Perhaps you had to go through something like this yourself, when your marriage broke up.'

'That was a long time ago,' I said, brushing it aside quickly. 'But yes, break-ups are always upsetting, of course.. And ...' I glanced at Stephanie, to see her staring back at me, her eyes wide. 'And it's always hard for the kids,' I added, meeting her gaze.

When I carried the tea things back to the kitchen, she followed me, pushing the kitchen door closed behind her.

'What's *that* all about?' she asked, nodding her head towards the lounge. 'Is he your *boyfriend* or something?'

I laughed. 'Oh, Steph, you should see your face! He's just a friend, but if he *was* my boyfriend I'd prefer you not to look so bloody disapproving about it!'

'Well, I'm sorry,' she said huffily. 'But honestly, Mum, I couldn't help listening to that conversation, and I really do wonder what the hell you're getting yourself mixed up in. Custody battles? Paternity tests?'

'Yes, his *son's* problems. His son's gay, and poor Bob's just discovered his grandson isn't actually biologically ... well, he's not actually his grandson.'

'I gathered it was something like that. It all sounds quite unsavoury and sordid, if you want my opinion.'

I turned round and stared at her. 'Well, I don't! And I can't quite believe you're referring to my friend's deeply painful family issues in those terms, either! *Unsavoury? Sordid?* The poor man's worried about his son, and the child. He just needs some sympathy.'

She shrugged. 'He shouldn't be inflicting all his troubles on *you*, that's all I'm saying. Stay out of it, Mum. You've got enough on your plate, without taking on other people's problems. What with that weird woman this morning – no wonder you're looking tired all the time, having these people to deal with.'

'An hour or so ago you were telling me it was having the twins that made me tired. Now it's my friends' fault.' I was too annoyed to realise I'd included Pam as a friend, when in fact she seemed to be exactly the opposite. 'I presume you don't *mind* me having a life of my own – a few friends of my own – in between looking after the grandchildren and listening to all your complaints about me?'

'Don't be silly,' she tried to soothe me now. 'I'm not complaining about you, I'm just concerned.'

'Well, don't be!' I snapped.

'You're on your own, that's all I'm saying, so you need to be careful. Having all these people in the house ... it's not like you've got Dad to look after you anymore.'

I put down the mug I was rinsing, so hard it chipped on the edge of the sink and I swore to myself.

'It's been twenty-two years,' I reminded her through my teeth, 'and he wasn't exactly looking after me when he *was* here, not that you probably remember. If you insist on bringing it up.'

'*You* brought it up. With him.' She nodded towards the lounge again. 'Saying all that stuff about it being hard for the children. You didn't worry about that when you divorced Dad!'

I kept my back to her, breathing hard, holding the chipped mug as if it mattered, as if it was the mug, the chip, making my eyes fill with tears. Sod this! I didn't need it! Not now, twenty-two years after the event, not now while I was trying, doing my best, to please everyone – the kids, the grandkids, Bob, even bloody Pam, not that it had done any good. I didn't need it being thrown back in my face by Steph, or anyone else – not now, and not bloody ever!

'We'll talk about this another time,' I said, trying to keep my voice level. I put the chipped cup down again. 'I'm going to take Bob home now.'

'Oh. OK, so I'll go, shall I?' she said, as if I was being unreasonable.

'It's up to you. You can stay here till I get back if you like.'

I wiped my hands on the tea-towel and marched out of the kitchen. I kissed Izzie, in case she'd been taken home by the time I returned, and helped Bob to his feet.

'I'll just get the car out,' I said, and went to get the car keys.

They weren't in the usual place on the hall table. Probably left them in my bag. I ran upstairs, picked up the bag and tipped it upside down on the bed. No keys.

'OK,' I called, running back downstairs. 'No panic, but I can't find the keys. They must be somewhere ...'

'I'll help you look,' Stephanie said a bit stiffly. 'Where did you last have them?'

If I remembered that, I'd find them, wouldn't I.

We searched the house. Even Izzie helped – she thought it was a game. Kitchen drawers, under cushions on the sofa, pockets of various clothes, dressing table, bedside table, by the sink in the bathroom. Went to the garage to check I hadn't dropped them on the floor out there or put them on the roof of the car while I unloaded shopping. It had been known.

'Not to worry,' I said, trying not to worry. 'I've got a spare key.'

'And do you know where that is?' Stephanie asked.

'Yes, I've already found it, in the drawer, thank you.'

'But what about your house keys? Are they on the same key ring as the car keys?'

'No. I carry them separately.'

'And you've got those, have you?'

I stared at her. 'There's no need to talk to me like I'm a special needs child.'

'Well, it *is* slightly worrying, isn't it. First the mobile phone, now the car keys. What next?'

'They've just gone astray – they'll turn up. Don't you ever mislay anything?'

'Not usually for longer than a few minutes.'

'Well, I'm pleased to hear it. Now then – OK, Bob, sorry about that. I'm ready now.'

'I really don't like putting you to all this trouble,' he said, looking slightly anxiously from me to Steph. 'I'm quite OK to walk home now I've had a rest.'

'Nonsense! It's no trouble at all.' I opened the front door and turned back to my daughter. 'I might see you later, then.'

'No.' She sighed, leaned forward and gave me a kiss on the cheek. 'We'll go now. I'm sorry, Mum. I hate it when we argue.'

There were a lot of things I wanted to say at that point. I wanted to make it clear that *I* hadn't initiated any argument, that it hadn't been my idea to discuss, yet again, how often I looked after her brother's children, or the fact that I (apparently) looked tired, was becoming senile, or had taken to fraternising with undesirable people during the time I (apparently) didn't have to spare. I wanted, above all, to remind her why her father and I had got divorced, to point out to her that as the youngest, she might not have quite appreciated at the time just how hard the whole thing had been on *me*, never mind them, the children. But the thought of doing so, of going into it all again, after all this time, of dragging up the memories, the hurt, the things that were said and done, made me feel so weary, so completely *knackered*, I just couldn't face it. I just couldn't bear it.

'I'm sorry too,' I said instead. 'But please, just stop worrying about me and trying to ... I don't know ... control my life for me!'

'We would *never* do that,' she retorted, looking injured. 'But if we worry about you, it's only because we love you.'

So what was I supposed to say to that?

'I love you too, silly. You know I do.' I kissed her back. 'Take care.'

'You too.' She looked pointedly at Bob, who was leaning against the car door, waiting. 'I'll just get the children ready and I'll be off.'

She was calling something else out to me as we started to drive away. I wound down the window. 'What?'

'Let me know about the car keys. And the phone. I'll be relieved when you find them.'

Hmm. Me too.

PAM

Rain, Rain, Go Away

Dear Kate

I chewed the top of my pen. I'd been thinking about this for a couple of days now – writing Kate a letter to apologise. Apologise *again.* I knew it was probably pointless. Kate wouldn't forgive me, and I couldn't really blame her. *Twice* I'd gone to see her, and both times I'd been rude and insulting to her. And the stupid thing was, I really wanted to be friends with her. To be brutally honest I needed a friend, and despite how it was beginning to look, I actually really liked Kate and thought we could enjoy each other's company. If only I could get past my horrible, vicious, jealousy that was filling me with rage and taking control of me like a live, wild creature every time I saw her with her grandchildren.

Well, she might never forgive me, but I still wanted to try, even if I couldn't manage to do it in person. And it was a miserable day, pouring with rain, making me feel worse every time I looked out of the window, so I might as well just get on with this now, in the hope it might make me feel marginally better.

Dear Kate

I'm writing you this letter because I obviously can't come to talk to you again. I doubt whether you'd open the door to me, and I don't blame you. When I came to see you the other day I intended, sincerely, to apologise for my behaviour and offer to be your friend. This must sound pretty ridiculous to you now and I expect you're going to feel like screwing this up and throwing it in the bin. The things I've said to you were unforgiveable. I can't make any excuses for myself. But I'd like to try to explain, even though I can't expect you to understand.

You ... how can I put this? You've got the life I should have had. You are the person I wanted to be. When I used to see you around with your children and grandchildren, I guessed I'd like you if I got to know you. You're obviously such a lovely mother and grandmother, with such a lovely family. Now it sounds like I'm just trying to ingratiate myself, but the other side of the coin is that I can't help envying you. I admit it, I envy you terribly. I thought I had it under control. I was so pleased when we started to talk to each other, I thought we could be friends. I thought, even if I couldn't have your life, I might be able to share in it a little bit – get to know your family, maybe help you with the grandchildren sometimes, if you'd let me.

But I've messed it up. It's not going to happen, because I haven't been able to cope with seeing you, so happy, so completely involved with the children, so cheerfully unconcerned by the mess and the mishaps and all the general chaos that goes with having a family. I couldn't bear it, because I want that – all of it, yes, even the mess, the sick and the poo and the crying. I want it, but I can't have it. Instead of being warm and noisy and cluttered like a proper home should be, my house is quiet, and tidy, and lonely. I clean rooms that don't need cleaning, make cakes nobody's going to eat. I look out of my sparkling clean windows and watch everyone with their families, and I try to feel happy for them – for you – but sometimes it just intensifies my own loneliness.

So there you have it – I'm lonely, I'm miserable, and of course it's my own fault because nobody wants to be friends with someone so eaten up with resentment that they lose control of themselves and call people names just because they envy them. I wish I hadn't been so awful to you. I wish I'd been kind, laughed with you about the mess you were in when I called, maybe helped you clear it up and made you a cup of tea. That's what I want to be like but instead I seem to become this raging monster. I'm sorry, really sorry, and all I can say is, if there's ever any way I can make it up to you, please let me try.

Hoping I haven't made things any worse by writing to you. I will understand if you don't reply.

Sincerely –

Pam

It took me a long time to write, and when I'd finished I read it through two or three times before finally folding it up and putting it in an envelope. I doubted Kate would even get to the end of it. Even to me, it just seemed like a long spiel of self-pity. I shook my head, annoyed with myself, and the thought came to me suddenly: *What would Colin think of me.*

He'd have been telling me to pull myself together, that's what. He'd have said I needed to get out more, to stop sitting around feeling sorry for myself. And he'd have been right, of course, as usual. Colin had always been good for me. *Too Mrs-Bouquet*, he used to tease me if I spent too long keeping the house clean and tidy, arranging the cushions neatly, straightening the pictures, putting out fancy cakes on a china cake-stand. He'd never been one for frills and fancies. He'd always brought me down to earth a bit. So had the children. I managed to smile to myself now as I thought about them – George with his funny hairstyle, his baggy cut-off jeans that never looked short enough to be shorts, or long enough not to be. The way he did that new dance – *Gangman* or something, wasn't it? – showing off his routine to me, proud of behaving almost like a teenager at the age of eight. And little Lily, such a *girly* little girl with her love of everything pink despite her mother's refusal to pander to it, (she seemed to believe it was some kind of subversive plot on the part of the children's clothing and toy manufacturers to stop girls from becoming fully functioning members of society). Well, Lily looked just as cute in blue anyway.

'Get over it, Nanny Pam!' George laughed at me last time I saw them. I'd been fretting over something trivial – the windowsills needing dusting or the fact that I'd run out of butter. *'It doesn't matter, Nanny Pam. We can just have chocolate spread sandwiches with no butter.'*

I'd learnt a lot from the kids, a lot about what didn't matter in the slightest. And a lot about what did. The things that mattered so much, I ached and ached to have them for myself.

It was still raining, but full of a new determination, I put on my mac and went straight over to Kate's house to pop the letter through her door, and then on for a walk round the block. I walked fast, swinging my arms, ignoring the rain dripping off my hair and down the back of my neck. *It doesn't matter, Nanny Pam.* It was hard not to think about the children again, hard not to think about them constantly. I loved them so much, saw them so infrequently, was so often let down and disappointed. And even at the best of times, I knew I was only being used as that last-resort childminder, the one the children's parents only called on when there was no other option, expecting me then to drop everything. And of course, I did just that. I made myself available, obviously, at the drop of a hat, not that I ever had anything else to cancel.

But I lived in constant fear of them suddenly saying *that's it – no more.* Although it was a kind of wicked bit of fun to let the kids do things their parents might not like, at the same time I knew that, if I put a foot wrong – got found out doing something they *really* disapproved of – they'd just stop the children from ever coming again. And then ...

My steps faltered for a moment as I turned the corner back into my road, facing into the rain. I knew it was an awful thing to say, so I'd never said it out loud, not to anyone, but I often found myself thinking it anyway.

If that happened, then I'd have absolutely nothing left to live for.

KATE

I Sent a Letter to My Love

Isabel *and* the twins were with me that Thursday. Steph had a doctor's appointment so I'd offered to have Izzie to make it easier for her. She'd accepted so gratefully that I decided she must have forgotten that only a few days previously she'd virtually told me I couldn't cope with having the kids. I took them all to Mini Music Makers and was pleased that Bob seemed in better spirits.

'I have to make the most of it,' he said, smiling as little Freddie toddled off to join in the performance of *Heads, Shoulders, Knees and Toes.* 'And anyway, you're right, it might not work out so badly. Nathan's been in touch with me. He's obviously upset with Craig – really hurt by him – but he says he doesn't want to fall out with me.'

'Or stop you seeing Freddie?'

'I hope not. But it might not be so easy, of course, or so often.'

'Well, whatever compromise you can work out between you, it'll be worth it for Freddie's sake, as well as yours, if you can still see him.'

'Yes, exactly. And as for Craig, I don't even *want* to see him, at the moment. I'm too mad at him.'

I didn't say anything. But I was hoping he'd change his mind once the dust had settled and everyone was a bit less angry. It would be so sad for him to fall out with his only son, however stupid he'd been.

The music group had been fun for the past couple of weeks, and that was mostly because of Jackie. To everyone's surprise (especially hers) she'd not only come back, but she actually seemed to be enjoying it. Not that she admitted it. She made us all laugh, the way she moaned about the noise, the loss of her dignity as she jumped around with the children like the rest of us, and the *sheer bloody stupidity*, as she put it, of allowing the children loose with percussion instruments. Yes, she did a lot of moaning, but she still gave in with a good grace, and laughed at herself too. Everybody liked her.

That morning, it was starting to rain again, and Bob decided he was going to miss out on our usual stop for coffee and head straight home before the threatened heavier downpour came.

'Probably a good idea,' I agreed as he went off with Freddie in the pushchair. But Jackie looked a bit disappointed.

'I've got the car,' she said. 'But I can't offer you a lift, unfortunately. I've only got one child seat.'

'You'd never get all my lot in the car anyway,' I laughed. 'But you could come back to my place for a coffee instead? I'm not far.'

'Oh, OK, if you're sure.'

She looked touchingly pleased. I gave her directions and by the time I'd panted up the road, pushing the pushchair and guiding Izzie on her scooter, she was waiting for me in her car outside the house.

We had our coffee and chatted, the children played nicely together, getting absolutely everything out of my toy box in the spare bedroom, and before we knew it, it was nearly one o'clock.

'You might as well stay for lunch,' I said. I'd been enjoying her company so much, and the rain was now pouring down outside. I made a plate of sandwiches, poured out drinks for the children and more coffee for us, and we settled down to talk some more about Jackie's daughter, her bastard ex-boyfriend, my own children and their eternal squabbling. And it was while we were laughing together about the fact that we'd both become grandmothers because of our daughters' inability to say 'No' and mean it – that Pam put her note through the door.

How the hell did she have the cheek? Posting it through my door and scurrying away – I saw her! – like she couldn't face me. Well, I supposed I could understand *that*. Bad enough that she'd been so bloody rude to me, twice, in my own house, without then expecting me to read all that self-centred, self-pitying drivel. I *did* read it all though, of course – curiosity got the better of me, although it made me so angry I wanted to tear it up into little pieces. And then – I couldn't help myself – I showed it to Jackie. She'd been watching me reading it, shaking my head, gasping with annoyance, swearing under my breath so the kids couldn't hear me. I couldn't *not* share it with her.

'A friend of yours?' she asked sarcastically when she'd got to the end of it.

'Huh! A neighbour. I *thought* we might have been friends, but not since she came round here *twice* and insulted me. What does she expect me to do? Forgive her, now she's written that load of rubbish? Be best buddies for the rest of our lives? Huh! On your bike, mate!'

'She seems to be admitting she's jealous of you. Because of your grandchildren.'

'Well, that's been pretty obvious. She hasn't got any of her own, but she occasionally has these two kids to stay. They must be some relation, I think. She got really upset because she was let down last time, the kids didn't come, so I felt sorry for her. But I wish I'd never got involved now.'

'She seems a bit mixed up,' Jackie said, looking through the letter again.

'That's putting it mildly! All that stuff about wanting to be more like me, with all my mess and chaos – is that meant to be a compliment?! She hasn't even attempted to explain why she's been such a poisonous cow.'

'She's obviously miserable about not seeing the children.'

'Well, I'm sorry, but it's no wonder, if she's half as difficult and bad-tempered with them, or their parents – whoever they are – as she's been with me. Honestly, you wouldn't believe how rude she was to me.'

'She sounds like she needs a friend, though.'

'Well, it's not going to be me. She's had plenty of opportunities in the past to knock and try to be friendly, but no, never a word, until the day we got chatting in the street and now suddenly she's started coming to my house acting like a madwoman. And now she gives me all this nonsense about wanting my life, wanting to share my family. It's *creepy*, Jackie.'

'So you won't be replying to the letter?' she said, laughing.

'Absolutely no way. In fact it's going in the shredder.'

'What's that, Nanny?' Izzie, who'd got bored with her sandwich, put down her plate and came over to have a look.

'Oh, just a bit of rubbish. Junk mail,' I said, sliding the letter out of sight under the clock on the fireplace for the time being.

'That's a funny place to put rubbish!' Izzie said. Kids never miss a trick, do they? 'Mummy says you always put things in the wrong place.'

'Does she?'

'Yes. Mummy says you lose things.'

Well, I couldn't really deny that. The damned phone still hadn't turned up, and nor had the car keys. I was tempted to have another game of *Let's search the house for Nanny's phone and keys* with Izzie, but I didn't want to add fuel to the fire of my new reputation as a scatterbrain.

'I know.' I smiled at her. 'I do lose things sometimes. But I'm sure I'll soon find them again.'

'I'd better make a move,' Jackie said. 'Autumn's falling asleep.'

She got up and gave me a quick kiss on the cheek. It suddenly felt like we'd been friends for years. 'Thanks so much for the lunch, and the chat. Do you know what? I've actually started to look forward to Thursdays now. I've enjoyed today almost as much as a day in the office.'

'Now that *is* a compliment,' I said, laughing.

I walked to the door with her, and just as she was strapping Autumn into the car, Stephanie pulled up.

'I'll leave the car on the road, shall I?' she called to me as she opened the driver's door. She looked pointedly at Jackie's car on the drive.

'You're all right – I'm just going,' Jackie told her. 'See you next week, Kate!'

She jumped into her car, put it in reverse and screeched out onto the road, winding down the window to wave to me again and beeping her horn twice as she disappeared round the corner.

'Who was *that*?' Steph asked after she'd driven onto the drive and got baby Isaac's car seat out.

'A friend from the music group.'

'Another one?' She looked at me slightly disapprovingly. Anyone would think I had rave parties for hundreds of drunken revellers at my house on a regular basis. 'What on *earth* was she wearing?'

'Fashionable clothes. She's not much older than you,' I added, wanting wickedly to see her reaction, 'but she's a grandma.'

'Blimey,' she muttered. 'A grandma in purple leggings. I've seen it all now. I just hope *you* don't follow suit.'

'I was thinking of getting some gold sparkly ones,' I said with a shrug, grinning as she shook her head at me. 'Come in out of the rain. Have you got time for a cup of tea? I was just about to try and get the twins down for a nap, and Izzie can watch some TV or do some colouring for a little while. How did you get on at the doctor's?'

'Fine.' She followed me into the kitchen. 'I had my postnatal check and my asthma check so that's all out of the way. I've got to take him – ' She indicated baby Isaac, asleep in his car seat by the door, 'for his check-up next week. Could you possibly have Izzie again? It's on the Friday. Would that be OK?' She looked at me expectantly, and I looked back at her, trying to think. Trying to imagine the following week's page in my diary.

'Yes, I'm pretty sure that's fine,' I said.

'Do you want to have a quick look in your diary, to make sure?'

'Yes. Yes, I will.'

'Thanks, Mum. I'll be putting the kettle on, then, while you take the twins up for their nap. Is your diary upstairs?'

Bugger it. I watched her filling up the kettle. 'I actually meant I'll check the diary when I can lay my hands on it,' I admitted.

'You've lost that too?' Steph was looking at me now like I'd grown an extra head.

'Well, not *lost* it, exactly. I just can't think where I've put it, that's all. It'll turn up.'

'That's what you said about the phone and the car keys, and they still haven't *turned up*, have they?'

'No, but obviously they will. They must do.'

'Have you tried ringing your phone?' she asked, her hands on her hips. If she'd worn glasses, she'd have been looking at me over the top of them.

'Of course I have. I just got my own voicemail. And last time, nothing. The battery's probably dead now.'

Steph carried on switching on the kettle, getting out the mugs and tea-bags, looking serious. I didn't like that serious look.

'Mum.' She turned back to face me. 'Are you sure you haven't left them all – the phone, the car keys, your diary –

together in a handbag, and lost the bag somewhere? I mean, for God's sake, your purse, and all your cards, could be in it.'

'No, of course not. I've been using my purse, and my cards. I used them today. I use the same bag every time I go out. I haven't got time to mess around changing handbags to match my clothes, like some people!'

I was being flippant, but really I was trying to hide the fact that these mysterious disappearances were starting to worry me too. Losing one thing was just a nuisance. Two things were a coincidence. Three things ... I felt uncomfortably like there was something going on here. Something like – either I'd gone into a sudden mental decline, or ...

'I'm wondering whether they've all been stolen, Mum,' Stephanie said in a disapproving tone, like it was inevitable, if they had, that I'd brought it on myself.

'Yes. I suppose I've started to wonder that myself.' It was a horrible thought, but, 'Do you think someone might've gone down my bag while I've been out?'

'No. I don't. They'd have taken your purse, for sure. And anyway, if you'd been out, with your car keys in the bag, how would you have driven home?'

'Good thinking, Sherlock Holmes.'

'Mum! This is serious!'

'Sorry. But you're right, they can't have been pinched out of my bag, can they. So they must be somewhere in the house, and I've just got to keep looking.'

'But ...' She turned away, poured boiling water into the mugs, looking like she wasn't quite sure how to go on. 'There's another possibility,' she said finally as I passed her the milk from the fridge.

'I put them out with the rubbish by mistake? I've thought of that, but ...'

'Someone's stolen them from *here*. From the house,' she said in little more than a whisper, making me most inappropriately want to go *Dah da da DAH*! right in her face to make her jump.

'No,' I said instead. 'How ridiculous would that be – to break in, not once but three times, stealing just one thing each time?'

'It didn't have to be three times. They could all have gone at once, and you didn't notice at first.'

'But they'd have taken something more valuable than my stupid diary! And if they took the car keys, they'd have taken the car!' I laughed. 'Let's not get carried away and melodramatic about this. I'll probably find them tomorrow.'

'They might be coming back for the car. At night, or when you're not here. And they've taken the diary to check when you're going to be out.'

'Oh, for God's sake!' I was still laughing. 'You've been watching too many police dramas. Nobody's broken in, all right? I'd have known.'

'Then perhaps it's someone who's been to the house. Someone you *let* come in.'

'Stop it. Now you're really spooking me!' I protested, taking a sip of my tea.

'Well, sorry, but it has to be said.' She watched me for a moment, holding her own mug to her lips but not drinking. 'You *have* been asking some strange people into your house, Mother.'

If there was one thing I hated even more than having my friends – well, my visitors, whether they were friends or not – discussed as if they were suspected criminals, it was being addressed as *Mother*, especially in that patronising tone.

'I do *not* have *strange people* in my house,' I said crossly. 'Unless you mean yourself and your brother.'

She ignored this. 'I *mean* the strange man who wanted to bend your ear about his family problems, and the strange woman who came and shouted at you in your own kitchen. To say nothing of that person in purple leggings today.'

'What are you most upset about? The fact that she might be stealing my possessions from under my nose, or the colour of her leggings?'

'Don't joke about it, Mum. Seriously, what do you actually know about these people? Because it strikes me you're inviting all sorts of weirdos into your life. And it seems quite likely to me that one of them is a kleptomaniac.'

KATE

Happy Birthday to You

It was bad enough being accused by my daughter of inviting strange people, *weirdos*, kleptomaniacs, into my home, without having the niggling feeling (however much I denied it) that she might have a point. Not about Bob – I was most indignant that Steph had included him in the list of weirdos. I'd known Bob for long enough now to feel confident about his lack of weirdness and absence of kleptomaniacal urges, even if *she* hadn't been aware of his existence until very recently. And not about Jackie – I was sure of that. OK, I'd known her only a short time, but she was so nice, so down-to-earth and normal, that the idea of her being involved in any phone/key/diary burglary was absolutely ridiculous. Whereas Pam; well, that was a different matter, and although I didn't particularly like myself for the way my mind was working, I actually found myself trying to decide whether any of the missing items might have been lying somewhere in the kitchen or the hall, in plain sight and asking to be stolen, on those occasions when she'd been in the house. I couldn't imagine why she'd want to take anything from me, but then again, I couldn't understand why she'd been so bloody offensive to me, either, so maybe Steph was right; perhaps Pam was just weird.

But I had other things to think about. The school summer holidays were about to start, and in France they'd started two weeks earlier. I knew this, because Danielle had been sounding me out about the possibility of sending her younger two children over, as usual. Clément was nearly fifteen now, and Emilie was thirteen, and although I loved seeing them, it was becoming harder and harder to keep them occupied for a week or two. It was also more and more likely that I was going to run into the sort of teenage behaviour – arguments and sulks about going out late/coming back late/buying inappropriate clothes and fraternising inappropriately with girls/boys – that I'd endured with my own kids years back and didn't relish going through again, thanks very much.

'Why don't you come over with them?' I suggested. 'It'd be lovely to see you. It's been ages since you came over.'

'I can't, Mum. It's impossible for me to take time off during the summer break. All the people with younger children book their holidays then.'

She pronounced *impossible* the French way. Sometimes she spoke a mixture of both languages without even realising she was doing it. If only she'd been that good at French while she was at school – she hadn't even got her GCSE.

'Why don't *you* come down to *us*?' she added when I didn't reply. 'You never come.'

'I never have time. Anyway, I thought you wanted me to have the children.'

'You could have them for two weeks, and then come back *with* them and stay for another two weeks.' *Four weeks*? I felt faint just thinking about it. 'Why do you never have time? You're retired! You can please yourself what you do with your time!'

I had to bite my tongue to stop myself from saying *Yes, exactly, and it doesn't please me – ça ne me plaît pas – to spend four weeks arguing in French with two grumpy teenagers, when I could be enjoying the summer in my garden, having coffee with friends, or even staying in bed with a book if I feel like it.*

'I do have other commitments, you know,' I said lightly. I was actually thinking (crazy though it sounds) of the Mini Music Makers sessions – not so much the jumping around, singing and clapping part of it but the chats with Bob and Jackie that had become such a pleasant part of my routine.

'Oh yes. Silly me.' Danielle's tone had changed. 'I forgot you have to be on constant call for childcare duty for Michael and Stephanie. As if you don't do enough for them! Can't they let you have a break for a couple of weeks in the summer? Aren't *you* entitled to a holiday?'

'A holiday?' I couldn't manage to bite my tongue this time. 'Looking after Clément and Emilie? Not that I don't want to,' I added quickly. 'You know that. I'd be more than happy to have them here for a week, like last year. I just thought it'd be even nicer if you could come too.'

'I know.' She sounded slightly mollified. 'I wish I could, too. I haven't seen the others for ages, either. How are all the kids? How's little Isaiah?'

'Isaac. You *know* it's Isaac. He's lovely. He smiles and makes all these goo-goo sounds already …'

'Yes, well, they all do that, don't they,' Danielle said dismissively. 'How about the twins? Still running you ragged?'

'They don't. They're fine!'

'Michael and Jo should have put them in a nursery by now. It'd be better all round, for everyone. I know it's expensive, but if you want to work, you just have to accept the cost of it. I keep telling him.'

'Well, I keep telling *you* – I wish you wouldn't interfere. We're fine.'

'And *he* says you have Izzie all the time now too. What's that all about, Mum? Can't Steph cope with the two of them? Honestly, when my kids were little, I had to …'

'When your *first* child was little, Dannie, if you care to remember, *I* had to look after him, while you went back to school and got on with your life.'

There was a gasp of French profanity.

112

'Why are you bringing *that* up? After all this time – God, are you going to hold that against me forever? I was only a child myself! What was I supposed to do?'

Help with the bottles and the nappies once in a while? Put him to bed in the evening occasionally instead of going out with your friends as if nothing had happened?

'Of course I don't hold it against you.' I was getting tired of this conversation. It made me sad that I spent so much of my time longing to speak to my elder daughter, and then when we did talk, it so often ended up like this. 'I did it because you were my daughter and I loved you. Because I loved Toby too. But it *was* a sacrifice, at the time.'

'It was a sacrifice for me! Having a baby at sixteen! It ruined my life!'

'Hardly, Dannie. Your life isn't ruined. And I only mentioned it because you need to remember that I've been happy to help *all* of you with your children. Let me know when you want to send Clem and Em over.'

'I'll discuss it with Clément and Emilie,' she said, deliberately ignoring the gesture of affection I'd offered by using their childhood abbreviations. 'They'll need to schedule it into their social calendars. You know what teenagers are like.'

'Yes, I do. I remember it well.'

Twenty years ago. Could it really have been so long? Danielle had been on a school trip to France, ironically, when it happened. She'd been home for a couple of months before she told me anything was wrong. How the hell had I not noticed? Was I really that blind?

'I haven't been getting my periods,' she'd said, going red and looking down at her feet. 'Do you think maybe it was going abroad that's done it?'

'What do you mean?' I asked her sharply.

'Gina at school says travelling can mess up your cycle.' She looked up at me, and I suddenly saw the fear in her eyes. 'Do you think that's true?'

'That's only if you've flown all round the world, I think,' I said quietly. 'Not when you've just crossed the English Channel on a ferry.'

'Oh.'

We looked at each other.

'What happened in France, Dannie?' I said, still very quietly.

She shrugged. 'Nothing.'

'*Nothing* doesn't stop your periods. I need you to be honest with me. Did something happen over there – with a boy?'

She nodded, her eyes filling up with tears.

'Don't be mad at me, Mum! I couldn't help it – I love him!'

I sighed, feeling for a chair behind me, and sat down heavily like I was the pregnant one, the one carrying the result of a *couldn't-help-it* baby and crying with fear about it. *Don't be mad at me, Mum.* No, I wasn't mad. I couldn't be. I understood only too well how it could happen, how you could be so *in love* you really believed you couldn't help it. I had been young myself, once, after all. But I was furious with fate, with God, for allowing this to happen. For messing up Danielle's life. Messing up *my* life! It wasn't fair that I was going to have to help her with this baby, this *accident*, when I'd only just started getting *my* life back from looking after my own babies. More to the point, I'd only just got my life back after the divorce.

Now, looking back, it seemed unbelievably selfish that I was thinking about myself, when my daughter was in such trouble. But we were only just about managing, our new little single-parent family – only just managing financially and emotionally to hold it together. If Danielle was going to finish her schooling, I'd have to stay at home with the baby for the few remaining months until she'd taken her GCSEs. I wasn't very gracious about it though, trust me. I did love baby Toby, but I never stopped letting Danielle know how fed up I was about the sacrifices I'd felt forced to make. No wonder she went off to live in France eventually.

As for Toby's father, he was a skinny seventeen-year-old called Ollie who never managed to look me in the eyes or talk to me without shuffling his feet. Their short-lived romance, begun at school and consummated in the girls' dorm of the hostel in Saint-Omer, was over almost as quickly as it took her to get pregnant. After he'd held the baby for the first time and experienced the sensation of vomit landing on his chest, we never saw him again. Danielle got over it sooner than I did.

The whole thing didn't appear to put her off France. She met Marcel – her husband – on a trip to Paris with a girlfriend five years later. She might have been twenty-one by then, but it was the same thing all over again. *I love him, I can't help it ...*'

Ah, well. *C'est l'amour!* Tell me about it.

Within a couple of days, Danielle had called me back to confirm Clément and Emilie would be *delighted* to come and stay with me the following week. I had my doubts about their delight, but nevertheless I was looking forward to seeing them, and the date was approaching fast by the time the last Friday of the English school term came around – which happened to be Izzie's birthday.

'I'm *four* now!' she shouted at me, running up the path to meet me when I called at their house on the day.

'I know! You're a *very* big girl now. Here you are – Happy Birthday!' I handed her the present she'd been eyeing excitedly from the moment she saw me getting out of my car, and she ran indoors with it, tearing at the paper as she went.

'Are you sure you don't mind?' Stephanie asked me. She was sitting in the lounge, with Isaac in her arms. He was crying plaintively and kept spitting out his dummy. 'You know I wanted to do it myself …'

'No. It's too much for you, in the circumstances.'

'But I *was* at least planning to come with her! Bad enough that you're doing her party, now I can't even come!' She looked close to tears.

'Steph,' I said quietly but firmly, 'you really ought to be in bed – you look awful.' She'd phoned me the previous day to say she'd come down with a horrible cold and her breathing was bad again. She'd made an emergency appointment at the doctor's and was now taking steroids to sort out the asthma, but she really wasn't well. 'Izzie's fine about it,' I reassured her. 'She's just excited about the idea of a party. She's too young to worry about anything else. Next year, when Isaac's getting out of the baby stage, you'll be able to have a proper party for her. She'll have been at school for a year then, and all her little friends will come.'

'Oh, stop it!' Steph wiped away a tear. She was far too tired – it worried me how easily she cried. 'I can't bear to think of it: my babies both growing up!'

'Well, not quite yet, they're not. Come on, Birthday Girl, we're going back to my house for your party.'

'Look!' Izzie screamed in response, jumping up and down and waving the present I'd bought her – a dress like her favourite character in *Frozen* – in Stephanie's face. She was already overexcited – I wondered whether she'd last the whole afternoon. 'I've got an *Elsa* dress!'

'That's lovely, darling.' Steph glanced at me. 'I hope you didn't spend too much.'

'Of course not. It was what she wanted, wasn't it.'

'Can I wear it to your house, Nanny? Can I wear it for my party?'

'No, let's leave it here for when you come home, Izzie, in case you spoil it by spilling anything down it – we're having jelly and ice-cream.'

'Can we have *birthday cake*?'

I smiled. 'Well, I'll see what I can do.'

'Oh, Mum! *I* should have made a cake!' Stephanie looked like she was going to cry again. 'I've just been so busy ... so tired ...'

'Don't worry.' I winked at her. 'Tesco's do a very nice *Frozen* one.'

'*Frozen* cake?' yelled Izzie. 'Are we having *Frozen* cake?'

'I'd better go,' I said, laughing, 'Or she'll make herself sick before she's even eaten anything.'

I'd been a little bit devious. Steph knew I'd have the twins with me for our little tea party – it wasn't one of their usual days, but she agreed it would be nice for Izzie to have her cousins there. And we were also picking up a little friend of Izzie's who went to her preschool. What Steph *didn't* know was that I'd now invited friends of my own too. Bob was coming, with Freddie, and Jackie was bringing Autumn; she'd actually taken a day off work for the occasion, and was having Autumn for an extra day that week. This was probably the greatest compliment she could have paid me (and Izzie) – I knew what a strain she found her grandmother duties at the best of times. I'd decided it would be fun to have my friends at the party. I'd been expecting to have the whole *weirdos and purple leggings* conversation all over again with Steph, but now she couldn't come, I'd decided what she didn't know wouldn't hurt her. I could always pretend afterwards that they'd just happened to drop in.

'Here's *Freddie*!' Izzie shrieked when Bob arrived. She grabbed hold of the poor child and hugged him. 'It's my

117

birthday, Freddie! I'm four now! I'm a big girl now! I'm going to school soon!'

'Sorry!' I told Bob. 'She's so excited, I can't get her to stop shouting.'

Bob laughed and hugged Izzie and gave her a present, which she ran off with into the garden to unwrap. It was a warm, sunny day, thank goodness, and the twins were already out there, with Jackie (wide-eyed with the horror of coping with more than one child at a time) trying to supervise their attempts to jump in and out of the paddling pool, while holding onto Autumn.

I got Bob seated in a chair next to Jackie and left them all to it while I went into the kitchen to start preparing tea. The jelly seemed to have set OK, the little sandwiches with their crusts cut off looked reasonably appetising, the sausages were nicely cooked, the birthday cake with its four candles was hidden under tea-towels waiting for its moment centre-stage.

'Let's give them another half an hour to run around and get tired out,' I suggested when I went back into the garden. 'Amelia, Alfie, let the other children have a turn in the paddling pool, please. Izzie, do you want your swimming costume on? How about Freddie – would he like a splash in the pool, Bob?'

Bob didn't answer. We all looked around for him. His chair was empty.

'Bob?' I said again. Had he gone inside, to the toilet perhaps? And then, with sudden anxiety, I called, more loudly: 'Freddie?'

'I'm here,' said a little voice from behind me. 'Where's G'anddad gone?'

I left poor Jackie with all the children while I searched the house. Searched the garden again – not that it was big enough for anyone to get lost in. Searched the house again. Looked up and down the street. It made no sense whatsoever. Somehow, within only fifteen minutes or so of arriving, Bob had managed to disappear. And not only had he disappeared, but he'd left Freddie, the most precious person in his life, behind.

BOB

Run, Run, as Fast as You Can

I hated doing it, obviously. I didn't know whether Kate would ever forgive me, or whether Freddie would ever get over it. At the last minute, as I was sneaking out of the side gate while Freddie was occupied playing with Izzie and the twins, Kate was in the kitchen and Jackie was busy with Autumn – the perfect moment for me to go – I looked back at Freddie and nearly lost my nerve. I hated leaving him. But it was no good, I had to do it. It was the only way I'd been able to think of.

That was what made it worse: I'd planned it, you see. It wasn't a spur of the minute thing. I'd been mulling it over for a while, and when Kate asked me and Freddie to go and join them for Izzie's birthday tea, I realised that it would be the ideal opportunity. Freddie would be with Kate, and the children. I knew she'd keep him there and look after him. I couldn't think of anyone who would look after him better than Kate, and I knew he'd be happy with her. I'd had to wait for an opportunity like this, on one of the days he spent with me, because I didn't want him to be there, in Ipswich, when I got there. And I didn't want to take him with me.

I'd asked for the taxi to wait over the road, just a few houses down from Kate's, in case she saw it pull up. It would have taken me too long to walk to the station. I was actually mopping my brow with my handkerchief when I got into the cab – it was a warm day anyway, and the exertion of getting away as fast as I could hobble, together with feeling nervous and upset, were taking it out of me.

'You all right, mate?' the taxi driver asked, looking at me over his shoulder. 'Where to?'

'The station, please. Thank you. I'm fine, just a little warm.'

I slammed the door shut and he pulled away, as I sat back, trying to calm myself down.

I'd forgotten about the road works on the main road heading towards the station. So had the taxi-driver, apparently, or else he didn't think they'd hold us up too much. I should have asked him to go by the back roads, it would have been a lot quicker. The queue at the temporary traffic lights was unbelievable.

'Sorry, mate. Probably should've taken the back roads,' he said as the lights turned red for the second time. 'Hope you're not in a hurry.'

I didn't bother to reply. I'd missed the train I'd been hoping to catch by then, and there wasn't another one to Ipswich for half an hour. I'd have liked to have been on the train, well out of town and on my way, before anyone started looking for me with any degree of seriousness.

Not that they'd have any idea where I'd gone. Or why.

When we finally got to the station, there was such a queue at the ticket desk that I started to wonder if I was going to miss the next train too. Anxiety was making me sweat and tremble, and standing in the queue was playing havoc with my knees. I really needed to sit down.

'Are you feeling OK?' The lady behind me in the queue was looking at me carefully. I must have looked even worse than I thought.

'Yes, thank you, just a little shaky. I'll be all right when I can sit down again.'

'You do look quite pale. Look, there's a seat over there. Why don't you sit down and let me get your ticket for you?'

I hesitated. There were still three people in front of me in the queue, and the one currently at the window seemed to be taking all day about it. It was possible I'd actually fall down if I had to wait much longer, but should I risk giving the money for my fare to a complete stranger? You heard all sorts of stories about people taking advantage of the elderly, tricking them into thinking they were being helpful and making off with their cash.

'I'll tell you what,' she suggested, obviously guessing the way my mind was working, 'I'll pay for your ticket on my credit card, and you can give me the money when I've got it for you.'

'Oh, I don't want to put you out!' I said, feeling awkward now but nevertheless tempted by the offer.

'It's fine. You're right to be careful with your money. Where are you travelling to?'

'Ipswich,' I said quietly, not exactly wanting to announce it to the world.

'Return?'

'Um, yes. Thank you, it's very kind of you.'

I went to sit down on the bench, mopped my brow again and breathed a sigh of relief. Ten minutes till the next train. Hopefully I'd still make it.

I wasn't sure exactly how much the ticket was going to cost, so I had my wallet out ready when the lady came over to me. She showed me her credit card receipt to prove how much she'd spent, and luckily I had the right money, so despite my usual fumbling because of the stupid arthritis in my hands, we'd finished the transaction in time for me to hobble up the steps to the platform and catch the train.

'You've been most kind,' I told her again. 'Thank you so much.'

'You're welcome. I'm going the other way, up to London, but I could help you to your platform first?'

'Oh no, really, you've done quite enough. I can hang onto the handrail to get up the steps.'

'Well, you take care, and have a good journey,' she said. 'Are you going to visit family?'

It was a natural enough thing to ask. She was just being friendly, and after all, she'd been so good to me, a pleasant response was the least she deserved. But I'm afraid at that point I just turned away from her, trying to pretend I hadn't heard. Friendly and pleasant or not, I didn't want to start getting into conversations with her, or anyone else, about why I was going to Ipswich.

I was glad now that I'd never given in and got a mobile phone. I'd never wanted one, however much Craig had nagged me about it in recent years.

'It's a safety issue, Dad, that's all,' he said last Christmas when he was proposing buying me one as a present. 'If you're out somewhere, and you get yourself into some sort of difficulty, you could phone for help.'

'What sort of difficulty?'

'Well, if you fell over, for instance, and hurt yourself, God forbid.'

'And who would I phone for help?'

'Me, of course!' He sounded hurt. 'That's why I want you to have one.'

'But by the time you'd driven all the way here, I'd already have been picked up, dusted down, and if, God forbid, as you say, I'd broken any bones or knocked my brains out, I'd have been carted off to hospital long before you arrived, and I'd have got the nurses to phone you. That's what they do – ask for the next-of-kin, someone they can phone for you. I've seen it on *Holby.*'

'OK. But what if I just needed to contact you for some reason, and you're out of the house? Say when you have Freddie, and you go off on your little jaunts to those music classes with him?'

'You'd leave a message on the phone at home, wouldn't you. I'm never out for long. Why does everyone nowadays think they have to be contactable twenty-four hours a day? For goodness sake, when you're out, you're away from the phone, simple as that!'

He shook his head at me, probably thinking I was a stubborn old dinosaur, frightened of technology, which was perhaps true. But now, of course, I was grateful there was no way anybody could try to contact me. Nobody knew where I was, or where I was going. It would give me the advantage of surprise when I arrived in Ipswich.

I sat back, watched the countryside speeding past the window, closed my eyes and tried not to think about Freddie. I had to believe he'd be OK. It wouldn't be for very long. Kate wouldn't let me down. I had a momentary pang of guilt that I hadn't confided in her – but she'd probably have tried to talk me out of it. Kate, dear Kate, she'd have been worried about me, told me it was a silly thing to do. No, this was something I needed to do on my own. Sort it out, get it over with, get back to Freddie. The train rattled on, the sun through the window made me drowsy, I closed my eyes and allowed myself to daydream about Kate.

KATE

Peek-a-Boo, Where are You?

It wasn't very often that I actually had no idea whatsoever what to do, but this was one of those occasions.

'It doesn't make sense,' I kept saying to Jackie. Whispering, because of course, we didn't want the children getting upset. Especially not Freddie, who (once I'd fobbed him off with a little white lie about Granddad having had to pop home for something) seemed perfectly happy playing with the others. We'd tried phoning Bob's home number, of course – three or four times. No reply. And unfortunately he didn't possess a mobile.

We didn't want the birthday girl upset either, of course, so we had to carry on with the jelly and ice-cream, the cake, blowing out the candles and singing *Happy Birthday*. We had to dole out little party bags with balloons and pots of bubbles and chocolate buttons. And all the while, we were looking at each other anxiously and whispering to each other, whenever none of the kids seemed to be watching, about what the hell could have happened to Bob.

'He wouldn't have just gone off, not without Freddie!' I kept repeating.

'Well, let's face it, he *has* done,' Jackie said. 'You don't think he's kind of suddenly forgotten where he was, and just wandered off?'

'Bob? Never. He might be a bit disabled physically, but mentally he's as sharp as a knife.'

'But he's been a bit upset recently, hasn't he, about his son, and the DNA results. Perhaps he's had some kind of a breakdown?'

'Actually, I think he's taken the news about the DNA surprisingly well. He was prepared for the worst all along,

125

and apart from being gutted when he first heard the result, he's seemed pretty philosophical about it.'

'Or he's just been putting on a brave face for your benefit?'

'I don't think so. He's really been sounding quite positive, apart from the fact that he's cross with his son. He blames him for causing the whole situation. But Nathan's been in touch with Bob, and it sounds hopeful that he'll still be allowed to see Freddie.'

'Then I'm sorry to worry you, Kate, but we need to consider whether he's been taken ill.'

'But he was sitting right there in the garden, looking absolutely fine!'

'I know. But could he have suffered some kind of … I don't know, dizzy spell or attack of some sort? He might have got up quickly without us noticing, and rushed out.'

'Why? If he'd just stayed where he was, we could have helped him. Oh, God, what are we going to do?' I whispered, glancing around at the children again. 'I'm really worried about him. I can't imagine how he managed to disappear so fast – let alone why.'

'Well, if he hasn't come back soon we're going to need to call the police,' she warned me.

I nodded, but I was thinking that actually, that was the last thing we should do. If we called the police, and told them he'd gone off, God alone knew where or why, without telling us, and leaving Freddie behind, I knew exactly what would happen. They'd get Social Services involved and unless there turned out to be a very acceptable reason for Bob's disappearance, it was going to do serious damage to his chances of looking after Freddie in the future. Nathan wasn't going to be very impressed, for a start. And at what point should I be contemplating trying to contact Craig to tell him his father had gone AWOL?

I was on the phone yet again, hanging on hoping for a response from Bob's number, when Stephanie arrived.

'Mummy, Mummy, we had a *Frozen* birthday cake with candles and I blewed them all out with one big puff, and we've got party bags, and I've eaten all my chocolate buttons!' Izzie was red in the face and jumping up and down with excitement. 'Can we stay a bit longer? It's not fair, Amelia and Alfie aren't going home yet and Freddie's not going home yet and Autumn …'

'Well, yes, we can stay for a little while if it's all right with Nanny.'

I hung up the phone. 'Of course it is. You're early!' I gave Steph a kiss on the cheek and baby Isaac one on his head. 'I didn't expect you back yet.'

I'd expected, of course, that Jackie and Bob and their children would have left before she arrived. Steph was giving Jackie a critical look as she leaned over the table to help clear some of the teatime detritus.

'Those shorts are *far* too short,' she muttered. 'Especially for a *grandmother*, whatever age she is.'

'Jackie offered to come and help,' I said. 'It was good of her.'

'Fair enough, I suppose. Is that little boy hers too?'

'No. That's Bob's grandson, Freddie.' I could hear the wobble of unease in my voice. 'Izzie knows Freddie, and Jackie's granddaughter, little Autumn, from when I've taken her to the music group. So we thought it'd be nice for her to see them today.'

'Bob?' Steph was looking around. 'He's the one who came to see you the other week, isn't he? Didn't he come *with* his grandson? That child looks a bit young to have just been *left* with you.'

'Oh, well, he had to go back home. He was expecting someone … a delivery,' I fabricated quickly. Why did I have to do that? Surely I should have been able to share this problem, this worry, with my daughter of all people?

What was I doing – trying to protect her from being involved in something that didn't concern her, or … trying to protect myself from her disapproval? And anyway why *did* I feel, recently, as if my whole family disapproved of me? It was ridiculous! I wasn't going to duck and dive, making excuses for myself or my friends, for another moment! I opened my mouth to correct myself, to tell her that actually, Bob hadn't gone home for a delivery, he'd vanished, and I had no idea what to do about it, when Freddie pre-empted me by tugging at my hem and asking again, plaintively:

'Where's my G'anddad gone?'

'He had to go home for something, sweetheart,' I said with more confidence than I felt. 'But don't worry, Nanny Kate is going to look after you here till he gets back.'

He nodded, apparently satisfied for now, and ran back off to play with the other children again.

'Actually,' I admitted very quietly to Stephanie, 'I don't know where he is.'

'What?' She looked at me in astonishment. 'He's *not* at home?'

'Not really. I've just said that for Freddie's benefit. He was here at the start, and somehow, while Jackie and I were occupied with the children, he … just went.'

'That was rude of him, wasn't it? To just clear off without saying goodbye?'

'No, he wouldn't have done that. He was supposed to be staying for the whole afternoon. And we looked up and down the street straight away – he can't walk very fast, and he can't drive, but he wasn't anywhere in sight.'

She looked sceptical, as well she might. 'Well, he couldn't have just vanished into thin air, Mum. He *must* have gone home, somehow, for some reason. Have you tried calling him?'

'Of course we have. Loads of times. No reply.'

'Well, I know what *I'd* do. You can't be expected to keep the child here until his grandfather deigns to come back for him. Put him in your car, Mum, and take him home.'

'And if Bob's not there?'

'No, I mean take him *home*. To his actual parents.' She hesitated, obviously remembering the conversation she'd overheard before. 'Or whoever it is that looks after the poor kid.'

'He's not a poor kid, he's a lovely little boy, and I know Bob would never deliberately abandon him. That's why I'm worried.'

'Well, then, that's why you should take the child back to his … parent.'

'But it's not that easy,' I began, starting to wish I *hadn't* bothered to confide in her. I was interrupted by a shout of *Hello! Where's the birthday girl?* from the side gate – and there was another flurry of excitement as Izzie treated her Uncle Michael to another screech of excitement about the cake, the candles, the party bags and the chocolate buttons.

'I thought I'd make the effort to get round here early for the twins,' he told me when he managed to get a word in edgeways.

'That's nice. I was expecting Jo to pick them up.' She didn't work on Fridays – she'd delivered the twins to me earlier, but apparently Michael had decided to come back for them so that he could see Izzie on her birthday.

'Hi Michael. Mum's worrying about one of her friends. He's *disappeared*.' Steph said it in a ghostly sort of voice, making a joke out of it.

'I'm sure there must be an explanation,' I said, sighing. 'But it is a bit worrying. He brought his grandson here, and then just … vanished.'

Michael laughed. 'So, first you started losing keys and mobile phones, now you've graduated to losing *people*.

129

You must have a black hole somewhere here, Mum, that everything drops into!'

'It's not funny, Mike,' I said. 'He's got very bad arthritis, so he can't have gone far.'

'Actually, I don't know why we're laughing,' Steph agreed. 'It really *isn't* funny. I've already said, Mum – ' She looked around her and dropped her voice, ' – that you seem to be getting mixed up with some odd people. Has anything *else* gone missing? Since the diary?'

'Diary?' Michael frowned. 'I didn't know about the diary. Haven't you found the phone yet, or the keys?'

'No, I haven't, but I haven't really had much time to look for them.' I didn't want to talk about missing diaries, missing phones – I wanted to find out where Bob had gone. And quite frankly, I'd wasted enough time already. 'Anyway, it was lovely to see you both, but if you don't mind, I'm going to go round to Bob's house now and see if he's there. I'll drop off Izzie's little friend Grace on the way. So unless you want to offer to stay here and look after Freddie while I'm gone …'

'I'd better get going, thanks,' Michael said at once. 'Come on, Alfie. Amelia – let's get your shoes on.'

'Me too – it'll take me ages to calm Madam down enough for bedtime.' Steph got up and called to Izzie to collect up her presents and things. 'Can't you take the little boy *with* you to Bob's house? Chances are, he'll be sitting there with his feet up waiting for him.'

'No. *If* he's there, I'm concerned that he might not be well. I expect Jackie will be kind enough to wait here with him.'

Even if my own family won't help. The thought shocked me, but I didn't have time to dwell on it. I kissed everyone goodbye, saw them out, waved them goodbye, and as I'd guessed she would, Jackie offered to wait at the house with Freddie and Autumn while I drove over to Bob's place.

She looked absolutely shattered, bless her, but insisted she'd stay for as long as necessary.

'I can phone my daughter to pick Autumn up from here if necessary. She won't mind. But what about Freddie – won't his dad be expecting to pick him up from Bob's house?'

'No. When Bob has Freddie on a Friday, he keeps him overnight and they pick him up the next day.'

'So the parents – the father – won't even realise if there *is* anything wrong.'

'No. Not unless we have to tell them,' I said – and immediately wished I hadn't said it. The idea of having to get hold of Craig somehow and tell him his father had gone missing wasn't the most appealing thought of the day.

I'd never been inside Bob's house before, but I knew where he lived. Riverview Close was a road of perhaps just a couple of dozen identical semi-detached bungalows, all with neat paved front gardens and handrails beside the front doorsteps. A community of elderly people. His was number thirteen. I always remembered because he joked about it being unlucky.

I parked outside, walked up the path and rang the doorbell. In the sudden silence after the chimes of the doorbell died away, I looked anxiously at the windows. There were no lights on, no curtains drawn, but I wouldn't have expected that, at six o'clock on a fine day in July. I tried the bell again, just in case he was asleep in a chair. Again, the sound of the chimes inside the house. Again the silence.

I stepped across to the front window of the bungalow. The front room was a lounge, and from what I could see, everything looked tidy – newspaper folded on the coffee table, nothing lying around on the floor or obviously out of place. I went back to the front door and peered through the frosted glass, but it was impossible to see anything other than a vague shape that might have been a coat stand. Taking a deep breath, I lifted the letterbox and called through it: 'HELLO! Bob, are you there?'

'He's not home, love!' The next door neighbour, evidently alerted by my shout, had opened her own door and was standing on the step, watching me. 'I saw him go out, with the little boy in the pushchair. About two o'clock, it was, and he's not back yet.'

'Are you sure?' I supposed nosy neighbours had their uses, after all.

'Positive.' She laughed. 'I always hear him coming home. He struggles a bit with the lock, you see, because of his arthritis. Takes him a few times trying to turn the key, and then the door generally flies open and bangs against the wall. And he'd have turned the TV on by now if he was in. Always does, regular as clockwork, to watch the six o'clock news. Can't help hearing it, you see, love – the walls in these places are so thin. It's criminal really, the way they were built – just slung up, they were. And you know what we paid for them?'

'No, I don't. Sorry, you've been very helpful, but if you're sure he's not here, I'd better …' I hesitated, about to turn back to my car. 'Actually, could I ask you a favour? If I leave you my phone number, could you call me if you see Bob come back home? Or hear him?'

'Course I will, love. Worried about him, are you? He's not as young as he used to be, what with his arthritis. But then, I suppose none of us are, are we.'

I wrote my mobile number on a torn receipt I found in my bag, and handed it to her, thanking her again. I was on my way home before I remembered I'd lost the mobile.

By the time I arrived home, Jackie had already phoned her daughter, who'd now been round and collected Autumn on her way home from work. Jackie was sitting with Freddie on her lap, reading him a story.

'No luck at his house,' I said, suddenly feeling exhausted and slightly tearful. What the hell were we going to do?

Jackie looked up at me, raising her eyebrows.

'I've made a discovery here, though,' she said. 'While Freddie and I were trying to tidy up a bit for you.'

'My *Bob the Builder* bag!' Freddie told me, jumping off Jackie's lap and running to show me the little red rucksack.

'It was in the back room where the toys go,' Jackie said. 'He'd just left it there, as if …'

'As if he knew we'd find it when we were clearing up,' I finished for her. 'Have you looked inside, Jackie? What's in there?'

She passed me the bag, giving me a warning nod in Freddie's direction and keeping her tone light.

'Freddie had it opened before I could even get to it.'

'It's my jamas,' the child said, surprisingly matter-of-factly. 'And my toothbrush. Am I going to go to bed in your house, Nanny Kate?'

KATE

Good Night, Sleep Tight

Jackie was an absolute treasure. While I took Freddie upstairs, bathed him and put him to bed in one of the two cots I kept in my spare room for the twins, she found some eggs in the fridge and made us both omelettes, with plenty of cheese and a side of baked beans. It was just what I needed. The little boy, tired out by the excitement of the birthday party and apparently quite happy about the fact that his granddad had arranged for him to stay with me for the night, had gone almost straight to sleep, and Jackie and I ate together in the kitchen in an anxious silence.

'You need to get home,' I told her wearily when we'd both finished. 'You've got work in the morning.'

'No I haven't. It's Saturday tomorrow, remember? Anyway, I need to show you something first.'

She looked serious. Oh God, could it get any worse? She got up, and extracted a folded piece of paper from the pocket of her bright red denim shorts – the shorts being so tight, standing up was a pre-requisite for getting into the pocket.

'I didn't want to give you this until Freddie was asleep,' she said, handing it to me. 'It was in his bag, folded up with his pyjamas. He asked me what it was, and I told him it was a note from his granddad, saying goodnight.'

That wasn't a lie. But there was a bit more than *Goodnight* in the note from Bob. I read it with an increasing feeling of disquiet. His vanishing act from my garden had obviously been meticulously planned.

Dear Kate

You can probably imagine how much I hate to do this. Leaving Freddie without any explanation, and without saying goodbye to him – I feel quite sick at the thought of it. But you're the only person I could trust to leave him with. I know he'll be in safe hands, and that if he asks for me, you'll tell him something that won't worry him.

I'm sorry I haven't told you where I'm going. You'd have tried to talk me out of it, and I suppose I know you might have succeeded. But I don't want to be dissuaded.

Don't worry about me – I'll be leaving by taxi and I'll be perfectly fine. By the time you read this I'll probably be on my way back anyway. I've taken the liberty of sending Freddie's night things. I hope to be back before midnight but I don't want you to wait up for me so I'll go home, and come back for Freddie in the morning. Kiss him goodnight for me.

I know this is the most dreadful imposition, and I won't blame you if you're furious with me and can't forgive me – but I hope not. Your friendship is very important to me and I hope I can make it up to you somehow.

With enormous gratitude –
Bob

'Did you read it?' I asked Jackie when I'd finished.

'Yes. Sorry, but I thought I'd better, in case he was telling us where he'd gone – and you weren't here.'

'Of course.' We looked at each other in silence, and I glanced back at the note. 'He must have taken ages writing this.'

'With his poor hands.'

'Yes.' The writing was spidery and uneven. But more to the point, he'd obviously thought carefully about what he wanted to say – the phrasing, the tone of it. This was no hastily scribbled note of apology and thanks. It had been written well in advance of his departure – hours, or possibly even days previously. 'Oh, God, Jackie.' I ran my hands across my face. 'What *is* he up to? Why the big secret?'

'It'll be something to do with his son, I bet.'

'Yes, I'm sure you're right. But what could he have been planning, that I might have tried to talk him out of?'

'I don't know. But at least he's expecting to be back soon. And if he's gone by taxi, I doubt he'd have gone very far.'

'That's true. Yes, that's a relief. Then he couldn't have gone to see Craig – he lives too far away for a taxi ride there and back.'

'Well, look, Kate, you can't do any more. I don't think there's any real need to worry. He obviously knew exactly what he was doing, it's not like he's just got lost somehow.'

'No. Although he *has* given us both a lot of worry, and I'm bloody well angry with him!' Ridiculously, tears sprang to my eyes again. Now that I knew he was presumably safe, not missing or taken ill but just off on some random secret mission, taking advantage of my friendship and hospitality, I was suddenly really upset, as well as being furious.

'Yeah. He's got a cheek, if you ask me. Make sure you give him a right mouthful about it when he comes back for the kid.' Jackie picked up her bag and looked at me a little uncertainly. 'Will you be all right?'

'Yes, I'm fine. Just tired and emotional. I'll probably go straight to bed.'

'Good idea. Give me a ring tomorrow, won't you. I want to know what happens.'

'Sure. And Jackie – thanks so much for everything. You've been such a help. I don't think I'd have coped …'

'Course you would. You're a champion coper, you are.' She hesitated, and then bent to give me a quick hug and a kiss on the cheek. 'Take care.'

I made myself a cup of hot chocolate and took it upstairs with me – but I fell asleep without drinking it.

Freddie was apparently a good sleeper. The first sound I heard from his room was a rendition of *Baa Baa Black Sheep* at about seven o'clock. I'd slept well too, and felt a lot better. It seemed a bit silly now, in the morning light, to have been quite so alarmed about Bob's disappearance. He'd obviously just turned out to be one of those people who thought it was OK to take liberties. It was disappointing, because he'd never seemed the type before, but maybe I didn't know him as well as I thought I did. Maybe Stephanie and Michael were right – I should be wary of thinking people were my friends when perhaps I didn't know them properly.

Feeling chastened by this thought, I got myself up and dressed Freddie. There was a clean T-shirt in his little rucksack, and a couple of nappies, although if I ran out, I had some in the drawer for the twins, which would probably be the same size.

'Ready for breakfast?' I asked him, deliberately being as cheerful as I could about it – although thankfully he still seemed surprisingly unconcerned. 'Weetabix or Shreddies?'

'I like Weet-ie-bix, Nanny Kate,' he said, following me down the stairs on his bottom.

Despite myself, I smiled at the *Nanny Kate*. Bloody hell. Overnight I'd acquired yet another grandchild.

We ate our breakfast, I cleared up while Freddie played with the Lego from my toy cupboard, we looked at some books together, did some jigsaws, sung some of our favourite songs from the music group, and finally I settled him down with some crayons and big sheets of paper while I got our mid-morning drinks. I didn't want to go out, or even into the garden, in case we missed Bob coming back.

But by twelve o'clock there was still no sign of him, Freddie was getting bored, and my anxiety was starting to build again. I'd just put down the phone from dialling his home number for the third time – with no reply – when the doorbell rang. Thank God.

'G'anddad!' Freddie shouted, dropping the crayons on the table and struggling to get down from his chair.

'It *might* be,' I warned him. 'Or it might be someone else. Wait there.'

As soon as I opened the door, I was glad I'd stopped Freddie from rushing out. I actually tried to shut the door again.

'Wait,' said Pam, holding the door to stop me. 'Please, it's important.'

'I don't want to talk to you.'

'I know. I wouldn't have come if it wasn't important. I need to tell you – '

'Look, I'm busy, I haven't got time for this, I don't care what it is.'

She was still holding onto the door. I tried again to push it shut, but she said, desperately, just as the gap between us was closing:

'Were you looking for someone? Because I think I know where he's gone.'

Reluctantly, I let her come in. To be fair, she seemed almost as apprehensive about it as I was. Even as she crossed the threshold, she was explaining, talking very fast and keeping her eyes on the floor, that she was sorry, she'd been watching from the window, she couldn't help it, she often sat in that chair by the window, it helped to pass the time …

'So what did you see?' I interrupted. 'And how did you know it had anything to do with me?'

'Well, first of all I saw you come home with the little girl – your granddaughter – and her friend in the car. They were in their party dresses and the other one was holding a present so I guessed it was a birthday party.'

Nosy bloody cow.

'Then I saw your son's wife bringing the twins, and your friends – that one with the funny hair and the strange clothes with her baby, and the older man who can't walk very well – he came with the little boy.' She looked up at the sound of footsteps padding down the hallway behind me and nodded. '*That* little boy. Hello!' she added quite pleasantly to Freddie.

'Where's my g'anddad?' he said.

'It wasn't your granddad at the door – it was this lady,' I told him gently. 'I won't be a minute, Freddie. We'll get the train set out when I've finished talking, shall we?'

I turned back to Pam. 'You must spend all day every day looking out of your window. Do you take notes, or something?'

She managed a tight smile. 'If you were as bored as I am, you'd understand. I know you're angry with me, and yes, if you like, I was being nosy. But if you're wondering about the little boy's granddad ...'

'I am,' I admitted. 'Go on. What else did you see?'

'He came back out of your side way, on his own. I particularly noticed, because he'd only been there a little while, so I guessed he'd probably just dropped the child off with you and was going home. He'd left the pushchair.'

'So you didn't think it was unusual.'

'Not particularly, no, although I was a bit surprised he got into the taxi that had been parked right outside *my* house.'

If I'd been giving her a rather grudging degree of my attention up till now, suddenly I was all ears.

'He'd had the taxi *waiting* for him?'

'So it seemed. And I did wonder why it was down the road a bit, like that. Not outside your house.'

Hmm. Just so that I wouldn't notice it, presumably.

'But still,' she went on, 'I didn't think it was *particularly* odd, not till you and the other woman came running out into the street calling *Bob?* and looking agitated, staring up and down the road, running back into the house. I started wondering whether he'd walked out on you – had an argument or something. But then I didn't think he'd have left the child.'

'You should work for the bloody CID,' I muttered.

'As I said, I'm afraid I don't have much to fill my days.'

If she thought I was in the mood to feel sorry for her, she had another think coming.

'Well, thank you for letting me know,' I said, not very graciously. I went to open the front door again, but she put a hand on my arm to stop me.

'I haven't told you the rest.'

'Well, I presumed that was it. I suppose you saw the taxi drive off, with him in it.'

'Yes.' She nodded, meeting my gaze now and beginning to look quite enthusiastic. 'But *just by coincidence*, I was going out yesterday afternoon. I had … an appointment. And it was just as I was getting into my car that I saw you and your friend come out to the street looking for the gentleman.'

'I wish you'd told us then, that you'd seen him!'

She gave me a look. 'I thought you'd probably just tell me to mind my own business. But in light of what happened afterwards – well, I've slept on it, and I thought, if you *are* still wondering where he went, you can say I'm being nosy if you like, but I should probably come and tell you.'

'Tell me what?' I was getting impatient. '*What* happened afterwards?'

'I drove to the station to get my train to London. That's where my appointment was,' she added unnecessarily. 'I went round the back roads to avoid the road works, you know, on the main road …'

All right, all right, I don't need every single detail of your afternoon out!

I sighed with exasperation as I looked back round the lounge door to make sure Freddie was OK.

'… and when I got to the station, there was such a long queue at the ticket office. And there he was, at the end of the queue – I'd had to park the car and everything, but he must have still only just got there before me.'

'Bob?' She had my attention now. 'At the station? Are you sure?'

'Of course I'm sure. I saw him getting in the taxi only a little while earlier, didn't I. I reckon his taxi driver got held up in the road works – they should know better! If I'd been your friend, I wouldn't have given him a tip, I can tell you that.'

'But …' I stared at her. I'd felt reassured by the mention of a taxi in Bob's note. As Jackie had said the previous evening, he wouldn't have gone far, not by taxi. It hadn't crossed either of our minds that the taxi ride wasn't the end of his journey. 'Where on earth was he going?'

'Ipswich,' she said, looking thoroughly pleased with herself. 'He was going to Ipswich – I know that for sure. I got his ticket for him.'

'*What*? Why?'

'Well, he didn't look at all well. I thought he was about to collapse, if you must know. Besides …' She gave me a satisfied smile. 'I thought it would help, you see? If you were wondering where he went.'

Ipswich. I had a horrible, sinking feeling in my heart. Something was definitely not right about this. Ipswich was where Bob's son lived. I couldn't imagine why he had to make such a cloak-and-dagger incident out of a visit to his son, especially as he'd told me he was too angry to even speak to Craig at the moment. And why wouldn't he take

141

Freddie with him? And more to the point, he should have been back by now. According to his own reckoning, he should have been back at least twelve hours ago!

'What on earth is he playing at?' I muttered to myself, forgetting Pam was still standing there next to me, smiling like she'd just cheered me up with some great news and henceforth we'd be best buddies for evermore.

'Shall I make you a cup of tea, dear?' she said.

JACKIE

Polly Put the Kettle On

I was up early that Saturday and by midday, the suspense was killing me. Kate had promised to call me about Bob, but I couldn't wait any longer – I gave her a ring instead, and a strange woman answered.

'Kate's phone,' she announced, sounding like one of the secretaries in my office.

'Is Kate there, please?'

'Who's calling?'

'Jackie.'

I waited to be handed over, and asked Kate straight away: 'Who was that?'

'Pam.' Kate sounded weary. 'She's … a neighbour.'

'Has Bob come back yet?'

'No. Pam came to tell me she saw him yesterday. He was getting on a train to Ipswich.'

'*Ipswich*?'

'Yes. It's where Craig lives.'

'Oh.' I bit my lip. Gone to see his son, left Freddie behind, and not come back yet. I didn't know what to make of that, and I was sure Kate didn't either. 'Are you OK? Shall I come round?'

'Um, only if you're free,' she said. I could tell by the tone of her voice she was glad of the offer. Perhaps Pam the Neighbour wasn't doing much to help, even if she had become Kate's telephone answering service.

'Where are you off to?' I'd almost forgotten about my husband, Keith. I tend to do that quite a lot. He looked up at me from his paper, trying to look interested. 'Shopping?'

'No. Seeing a friend. See you later.'

He nodded and went back to his paper. I sometimes wondered why we bothered, any of us, to have anything to do with men – after all, they're usually either a pain in the neck or a waste of space, and they're always the reason we find ourselves in the predicaments we do (having kids, grandkids, and all the other inconveniences of life). Unfortunately, I still quite fancied mine and there were times I found it difficult to keep my hands off him. I tried not to let it happen too often, though. Most of the time, it was like today – a nod, a couple of words, a passing of each other in the hall as we went about our lives. And I was quite happy with that.

The strange woman – the neighbour – opened the door to me.

'I'm Pam,' she said, sounding pretty pleased about it. 'Kate's sitting down having a rest. I insisted on it.'

'Is she ill?' I asked, feeling slightly alarmed.

'No. But she's had a lot of worry and stress, and with the little boy to look after as well – I told her, if she's not careful she'll wear herself out. So I've taken charge.'

'I see.' I peered into the lounge, where Kate was indeed sitting on the sofa with her feet up. 'Are you OK?' I asked her.

'Absolutely fine.' She pulled a face at Pam's back as the other woman went out to the kitchen. 'Can we get rid of her?' she whispered.

'I'll see what I can do. Where's Freddie?'

'She's given him lunch and put him upstairs for a sleep.'

'Oh! Well, at least she's …'

'*Taken over*,' Kate whispered. She beckoned me closer. 'I don't like her. I didn't *ask* her to help with Freddie – she just came to tell me about Bob, now she seems to think I need her here. I was just about to tell her to clear off when you phoned. I'm really glad to see you.'

I didn't know what the problem was with Pam. I presumed she was just being neighbourly and trying to help, although I could see it might be irritating if she was being too interfering.

'Leave it to me,' I said, turning back to the kitchen. With my usual tact and diplomacy, I'd tell her that now I was there, we didn't need to detain her any longer. And if that didn't do the trick, I could always just tell her to piss off.

'Tea or coffee?' she said without looking round, as soon as I got to the kitchen door. 'I've got the kettle on again, and I'm making some sandwiches. She needs to keep her strength up.'

'Oh. Well, that's … good of you.' What was I supposed to say? There she was, washing up cups and spooning out coffee, buttering bread and slicing cheese.

'I'll pop out and get her some shopping in while you're both eating,' she went on, still not looking at me. 'I don't suppose she's had time, what with the party yesterday and all this trouble with the gentleman.'

'Actually, I think Kate will be fine now,' I said as firmly as I could. 'If she needs anything, I'm sure I can give her a hand. You've been very helpful, but …'

'I think it's up to Kate to let me know when she's ready for me to go, don't you?' she replied. 'I'll stay as long as she needs me.'

'Yes, well, that's the point – I think, from what she's just told me, she's quite happy for you to leave, thank you, now that I'm here.'

'And you are … ?' She turned to face me, with a look that could freeze the tits off a tart, and suddenly I realised exactly who she was. The nasty neighbour! The one who'd walked in here and insulted her, twice, and then sent her that terrible letter saying how much she liked her and wanted to be her friend! *That* Pam!

'I'm Kate's best friend,' I told her, instantly and unilaterally promoting myself to that position, and at the same time muscling in to remove the butter knife from her hand. 'And *I'm* making the sandwiches now, OK? Thanks for your help, but we'll be fine from here.'

'I'll see what *Kate* has to say about that,' she said, red with annoyance, and huffed off in the direction of the lounge before I could stop her.

Oh well. I'd done my best. Hopefully now Kate could get rid of her. I finished buttering the bread and making up the sandwiches, listening to the murmur of voices coming from the lounge. I carried the plate of sandwiches in and put them down on the coffee table beside Kate.

'Thanks.' She gave me a wink. 'I've just asked Pam to put the TV on for us before she leaves.'

'All right.' Pam glared at me. 'I'll be off, then, as Kate seems to think you'll be able to manage without me. Now that I've done everything.'

'Wait!' Kate had suddenly swung her legs off the sofa and jumped up, almost knocking the plate of sandwiches off the table. 'It's the phone!'

Pam and I stood in silence, waiting, as Kate rushed out to the hallway to grab the phone before it stopped ringing.

'Hello?' we heard her say. 'Bob? Yes! Thank God you've phoned. Where are you? What the hell are you doing?'

I raised my eyebrows at Pam, who'd apparently decided to delay her departure until she'd eavesdropped this conversation. I was too relieved to care. At least Bob had finally got in touch, whatever he'd been up to, and whatever had held him up.

'What?' Kate was saying now. 'Bob, slow down, you're not making any sense. OK, right – before your money *does* run out, tell me quickly: *which one?* And why? What's wrong?'

There was a pause, during which I could hear Kate muttering about picking up a pen to write something down, and then, almost immediately, she exclaimed: '*Bugger*. His money's run out.'

I went out to the hall and looked at what she'd written down on the edge of a magazine that had been lying under the phone table. *Ipswich Hospital.*

'He's in *hospital*?' I said.

'Yes. Apparently.' She turned to look at me, frowning with anxiety. 'He didn't get a chance to tell me exactly what was wrong, but he was saying something about feeling ill on the train yesterday.'

'I told you, didn't I!' Pam had followed us out to the hall and was looking very smug. 'I said he didn't look at all well when I saw him at the station. I said he'd better sit down. He looked very pale. He was shaking.'

'I hope he's OK,' I said. 'Did he say how long he'll be in the hospital?'

'No.' Kate ran a hand through her hair. 'He just said he needed my help.'

'What sort of help?' I couldn't help feeling a bit irritated. I mean, obviously I didn't want the poor guy to be ill, in hospital, but hadn't Kate done enough already? What the hell else was he going to ask of her?

'He didn't have a chance to say – all he kept on about was that he'd only got a few minutes as his money was going to run out – and then it did. But he sounded very worried. I'm just dialling 1471 to get the number and call him back.'

We all waited. Watched as Kate wrote down a number, redialled, held on to the phone.

'No answer,' she said eventually.

'It might have been a pay phone,' I pointed out. 'If he's on a hospital ward.'

'Yes, of course, you're right. OK, I'll phone the hospital.'

'I'll find you the number,' Pam said immediately. 'Have you got a phone book, Kate?'

'Not for that area, she hasn't,' I said. I was already on the internet on my phone, looking for *Ipswich Hospital.* 'Here's the number for the main switchboard,' I told Kate. She wrote it down as I called out the digits, and immediately started dialling again.

'They're putting me through to some patient information person,' she said after what seemed like an eternity of waiting to be connected, followed by another eternity of Kate trying to explain who she was looking for, and that she had no idea which specialty he might be under. And then, after waiting yet again for a connection and yet again for Kate to go through her query, she turned to us and announced: 'Apparently he's on ward twenty-one. But they're not allowed to tell me what's wrong with him. This is so frustrating!'

'He'll surely get some more change and call you back, Kate, won't he,' I tried to soothe her.

'Maybe. But he sounded so shaky and upset – I'm not hanging around waiting. Where are my shoes?'

'Why? Where are you going?' I said, watching her picking things up – her handbag, her jacket, her door keys.

'Where do you think?' she said, and it was the calmness of her voice that unnerved me. 'I'm going to Ipswich, obviously. To the hospital, to see Bob.'

'Kate …' I began, but she cut me short.

'Whatever's happened, he's in some sort of a fix and he needs someone there with him, to help him.'

'His *son* lives in Ipswich, Kate, for God's sake,' I pointed out. 'If anyone ought to be helping Bob, surely it's him!'

'So why did he phone me, and not his son?' she retorted. 'Perhaps his son's not there. I can't just sit around here doing nothing, Jackie, when he's asking for my help.'

'You might not even be allowed to see him,' Pam pointed out. Somehow we seemed to have forgotten we were trying to get rid of her. 'You don't know what's wrong with him.'

'Well, the least I can do is try,' she retorted.

'He must have other friends he could have called on,' I tried to point out, gently.

'Yes – other elderly men he chats to in the pub. He's told me about them. None of them sound like they're particularly close friends, or like they're any fitter than he is. I'm going, Jackie, and that's the end of it.'

'In that case I'll come with you,' I said.

Pam coughed. 'Isn't there something you're both overlooking?'

As if on cue, Freddie, probably woken up by the noise we were making, started crying upstairs.

'Oh, damn, yes – what about Freddie? Nathan will be coming to pick him back up today – from Bob's place. He'll be worried sick about him, won't he, when he gets there and finds nobody at home. He won't have a clue where he is.'

'I don't suppose you know how to contact him?'

'No. And it's not like we can take Freddie home – I don't even know where Nathan lives now that he's not with Craig.'

Pam was looking from one of us to the other. I gauged that she wouldn't know about the background to this situation, or even who Nathan was. But nevertheless, she offered:

'I'd be happy to look after him. If you're both going to Ipswich.'

Kate hesitated. It was obvious she didn't want to agree to this. I knew she didn't even like the woman. How could she leave Freddie with her? The child didn't even know her.

'Or maybe it would be better,' I said quickly, 'if we take him with us, and I stay with Freddie in the car, or take him to a park or something – while you go to the hospital?'

'Thank you.' Kate gave me a ghost of a smile. 'I think that would be better – Freddie would be happier coming with us. And anyway, it might solve the problem. We can ask Bob how to get hold of Nathan or where he lives, and maybe we can take him home.'

'Well, I *did* offer,' Pam said huffily. We both ignored her.

'I'll get him up and change his nappy,' Kate said. 'Thanks for your help, Pam,' she added stiffly. 'We'll be OK now.'

I saw her to the front door. I supposed she *had* been helpful, and I could only think she was trying to make amends for the way she'd spoken to Kate previously. But I guessed it would take more than that for Kate to warm to her.

While Kate was upstairs, I checked the internet again to find the postcode for the hospital.

'I'll drive,' I told her firmly when she came back down. Freddie can use Autumn's car seat, and I've got a full tank of petrol and a Sat Nav.'

She didn't argue. 'OK. Thank you, Jackie. I really appreciate it.'

'Can I go home now?' Freddie said, rubbing the sleep out of his eyes. 'Where's G'anddad gone? Where's my daddy?'

Some questions, unfortunately, are just too hard to answer.

KATE

The Doctor Came with his Bag and his Hat

The journey seemed to take forever. At first, Jackie and I talked ourselves round and round in circles, trying to make sense of the situation, but it was obvious we weren't going to arrive at any answers, at least not until we'd managed to speak to Bob, so eventually we gave up, and apart from singing nursery rhymes to Freddie to keep him amused, we spent the rest of the time in silence with our own thoughts. Jackie's Sat Nav got us to the hospital without any difficulty, and once we were parked, we both turned to look at Freddie, wondering what to tell him.

'Where's my daddy?' he asked, looking out of the window. 'Want to go home now.'

'Soon,' I prevaricated. 'But first, Auntie Jackie's going take you to a café for a nice drink while Nanny Kate goes to see someone. Will you be a good boy for us?'

'Juice?' he asked eagerly.

'Oh, I should think so.' I smiled at him. 'And perhaps something to eat.'

'Cake?'

'We'll have to see what they've got in the café,' Jackie said. 'But I'm sure there'll be something yummy. A cake, or a biscuit, perhaps.'

'Chocolate?' Freddie was looking ever more hopeful.

'Why don't you take him to the café here, at the hospital?' I suggested to Jackie. 'Give me time to find out where Bob is, see whether I can talk to him at least. I'll come and find you once I know what's going on.'

'Good idea.'

We walked into the main entrance of the hospital together and parted company in the foyer, where Jackie headed off in the direction of a food outlet. I went to a reception desk to ask for help in finding ward twenty-one.

My heart was thumping as I headed for the lift. I had no idea what I was going to find out about Bob's condition and why he was there. Some of the scenarios I'd been imagining weren't the least bit comforting. By the time I reached the door of ward twenty-one I was almost dreading seeing him. I buzzed the intercom and told the nurse who answered it that I was there to see Robert Tattersall.

'Are you a relative?' she asked.

'No. A close friend. I heard he was in here ...'

'Right. Well, I'm afraid you won't be able to see him, but I'll try to find someone who can talk to you.'

She'd pressed the button to open the door before I had a chance to say any more. I went in and walked down the ward, looking at each four-bedded bay as I passed, hoping to catch a glimpse of Bob.

'Excuse me. Are you the lady who was asking for Mr Tattersall?' A disturbingly handsome and very young-looking man approached me, smiling and holding out his hand. I had to presume he was a doctor because of the stethoscope hanging round his neck and the fact that his ID badge insisted he was. 'I'm Doctor Agrawal,' he confirmed. 'Would you like to come into the office where we can talk more privately?'

'Why?' I stayed where I was, looking at him with suspicion. 'Why can't I see Bob ... Mr Tattersall?'

'Please, come with me, and I'll explain, Mrs ... ?' He waited for me to introduce myself, and it seemed rude to refuse.

'Freeman. Kate Freeman. Bob and I are good friends, doctor, and I've come all the way from Witham in Essex to see him, because I don't think he's got anyone else, you see, apart from his son, and ...'

I was trotting after the doctor as he walked down the ward, all the while nodding at me as if he completely understood but he wasn't going to say another word until he'd got me safely into the office. And once in there, with the door closed, and he'd indicated a chair for me, and sat down opposite me, he leaned forward so that his stethoscope drooped in a rather attractive fashion onto his knees and said in a very sincere tone:

'I'm so sorry that you've had a wasted journey, Mrs Freeman, but I'm afraid it isn't going to be possible for you to see Mr Tattersall.'

'Why not?' I had a sudden, terrifying thought that made me gasp out loud and almost fall off my chair with fright. 'He's not ... he hasn't ... please don't tell me ...'

'Don't be alarmed.' He gave me a smile. 'Your friend has not expired.'

Expired? For God's sake, what did he think Bob was – a parking ticket? An overdue library book?

'Well, I'm relieved to hear that. But what exactly *is* wrong with him?'

'I'm afraid Mr Tattersall was the victim of an accident.'

'Oh my God! Is he all right?'

'Well, he's suffering from multiple injuries, unfortunately. We've actually been trying to contact his son. His name and phone number were in Mr Tattersall's wallet, but there's no reply. I suppose you wouldn't happen to know if he – the son – has a mobile number?'

'No. I'm sorry, I've no idea. But can't Bob tell you himself? I mean, I'm sure he would have called Craig, anyway, if ...'

'No, that's not possible. I should have explained – Mr Tattersall hasn't woken up yet.'

'Hasn't woken up?' I stared at him. 'You mean he's unconscious? But he phoned me! He phoned me from here – the hospital – and asked me to come! I don't understand – you mean he's had an accident since he's been here? What's happened to him?'

Doctor Agrawal was frowning at me. 'He called you himself? But he was brought in by ambulance. Poor chap was hit by a car as he was crossing the road.'

'Oh, God!' I said again. 'Poor Bob!'

'Perhaps he called you *before* he had the accident,' Doctor Agrawal suggested. 'Perhaps he said he was *on his way* to the hospital, and you misunderstood him?'

I thought back to the phone call. It had been so rushed, and Bob had been so worried about running out of money, I had to admit it was quite possible I'd got the wrong end of the stick.

'I suppose so,' I said. 'But I have no idea why he would have been coming here.'

'To visit someone, perhaps?'

'Not unless his son's in here for some reason,' I said. That would explain a lot.

'Good point. I'll find out whether anybody's checked that.' He looked at me sympathetically. 'I'm sorry, this must have been quite a shock for you. Would you like someone to get you a cup of tea?'

'No! I just want to see Bob!' I said, crossly. 'I've come all this way ...'

'I'm sorry, Mrs Freeman, but as I said before, that's not possible.'

'Why? OK, I understand that he's unconscious, but can't I go and sit with him, try and talk to him or something? It might jog him out of his coma, or whatever it is, mightn't it?'

I'd watched enough episodes of *Holby* to know about this stuff. People were always waking up because a relative or friend started talking to them about their favourite football team or rock band. I could talk to Bob about the Mini Music Makers. Maybe sing *The Wheels on the Bus* to him. That'd do it.

'He's not in a coma,' the doctor said, gently. 'He was unconsciousness when he was brought in, but since then he's been sedated because of the pain. When he's a little more stable he's going to need surgery.'

'Surgery? Oh no!' I felt like crying. 'Is he going to be OK?'

'He should be fine,' he said, 'but it could be a long haul. He's sustained fractures of both legs, unfortunately, as well as a fractured collar bone and several other less serious injuries. It's going to mean a long spell in hospital, and a series of operations, to say nothing of the rehabilitation afterwards.'

'I see.' I blew my nose. 'Oh dear, I can't take this in. Who'd have thought – I mean, I was only talking to him a couple of hours ago!'

'A couple of hours?' Doctor Agrawal said. He looked puzzled, but didn't say anything. 'Well, look, the best thing I can suggest is that you go and get yourself a cup of tea ...'

'I don't want a cup of tea!' I said, more impatiently than I intended. 'Sorry, but I just want to see Bob. I realise he's not going to wake up, but please, at least let me just *see* him, to put my mind at rest that he's going to be OK. I promise not to scream or shout or go hysterical or anything. And I won't try to wake him up. I won't even speak. Or sing,' I added, although I didn't see the point of mentioning *The Wheels on the Bus* specifically. 'I just need to see him. I've been so worried.'

'Well.' He hesitated for a moment, looking at me carefully like he was weighing up whether I was dangerous. 'I suppose that wouldn't hurt, would it. Please, come with me.'

Doctor Agrawal might have only looked like a teenager, but he obviously knew his stuff. He should have had a part on *Holby*. He led me through the ward to a room at the far end. A nurse was just going into the room, and he held the door open for her and spoke to her as she smiled at him flirtatiously.

'Emma, this lady's name is Mrs Freeman,' he told her, 'She's travelled from Wickham in Essex to see...'

'Witham,' I corrected him, and then thought maybe I should have kept quiet, as they both turned to look at me like I was being difficult.

'From Witham in Essex,' the doctor went on, 'to see Mr Tattersall. She appears to be his only friend. As you are aware, we haven't been able to trace his son.'

'I know. Sister told me.'

'I'd like you to check with Sister, please, whether anyone has thought to make sure the son isn't also a patient here. It seems Mr Tattersall may have been on his way here to visit someone when he was involved in the accident.'

'Certainly, Doctor Agrawal.' Another flirtatious smile. I bet if he'd asked her to walk barefoot to the moon and back she'd have said yes. 'I've just got to do the patient's obs.'

'Good. Well, perhaps you'd be so kind as to allow Mrs Freeman to come in with you.'

'Sister said he can't have any visitors,' she said, the smile disappearing. 'He's sedated, doctor.'

'I know. Don't worry, Emma,' Doctor Agrawal said, 'I'll explain to Sister. As you can imagine, Mrs Freeman is very concerned about her friend. She merely wants to reassure herself that he has, in fact, not sustained any life-threatening injuries or indeed even expired. In the circumstances I've agreed to allow her to see the patient very briefly.'

'Well, as long as I don't get a telling-off from Sister,' the little nurse said doubtfully.

'Thank you, Emma, I'll make sure you don't.' Doctor Agrawal gave her a smile that made her blush to the roots of her hair.

And so, having been granted the permission of both the doctor and the nurse, I braced myself mentally for what I was about to see – poor Bob unconscious, broken, bandaged, bloodied, probably attached to tubes, wires, monitors, etc – and followed them into the room.

And after all that, as I stared at the poor unconscious figure on the bed there was only one thing I could manage to say.

'That's not Bob.'

KATE

Oh Dear, What Can the Matter Be?

Anyone would have thought I'd sworn in church. The doctor just gaped at me, and the nurse looked like she was about to faint.

'I'm sorry,' I said, as no-one else seemed to be speaking, 'but it's not – it's definitely not him. And to be honest, does this man even *look* seventy?'

The relief, on seeing him – this well-built middle-aged man, with a full head of hair and absolutely no sign of knobbly arthritic joints – was so intense, I would have burst out laughing if it wasn't so obviously inappropriate. I mean, I did feel sorry for him. But whoever he was, he wasn't Bob. And that was all I could bring myself to care about for the moment.

'Are you sure?' Doctor Agrawal said, looking from the patient to me and back at him again, like he expected the poor chap to sit up in bed and make some sort of protest about his identity.

'Of course I'm sure! I don't understand – why did anybody think it *was* Bob?'

'I ... think we need to ask Sister to look into this,' he stuttered, apparently overwhelmed by this turn of events.

Within minutes I'd been hustled back out of the room, led once again to the office, where Doctor Agrawal, this time, very apologetically asked me to wait, as he had other patients to take care of. After a few minutes I was brought a cup of tea (whether I wanted it or not) by another young nurse, who looked at me with such open curiosity I could only think she was somehow under the impression I was some sort of celebrity. And about ten minutes later a quite large lady wearing a different uniform and a no-nonsense air of authority arrived in the office, closing the door firmly behind her and sitting down to face me.

'I'm Sister Jackson, and I'm so sorry about all this, Mrs Freeman. It looks as though you really have had a wasted journey,' she said.

'What's happened? Has there been some kind of mix-up? The wrong records, or something? Where *is* Bob – in another ward?'

She shook her head. 'He's not here.'

'But ...' I began to protest, but she forestalled me.

'He's not here *now*. I've just checked the computer records. He was brought into A&E yesterday, admitted to the Assessment Unit overnight for observation, and discharged this morning.'

'Discharged? But he called me ...' I hesitated. If this was true, Bob must have called me *after* he'd been discharged from hospital. But anyway – I shook my head at myself impatiently – this was beside the point! The point was ...

'What *was* wrong with him, then? Did he even have a road accident, or is that all a mix-up too?'

'I'm afraid it seems to have been a *complete* mix-up, yes,' she said, looking so annoyed about it that I almost recoiled. '*Our* patient was brought up in a serious condition from A&E, where *somebody* had apparently seen the name Robert Tattersall was already on the system and presumed it was the same one.'

'You're surely not telling me there are *two* Robert Tattersalls and they've both been admitted here within hours of each other?' I said. 'It's not exactly the most common name in the world, is it?'

'No. We actually don't have any idea who our patient is, if he's not your Robert Tattersall.'

'He's not! He's nothing like him! I can't understand why anybody thought it was him.'

'He had a wallet in his pocket,' she said, 'with a debit card and senior railcard in the name of Robert Tattersall, and a return train ticket to Witham.'

'Oh.' I slumped back in my chair, almost unable to take this in. 'He must have stolen Bob's wallet.'

'It's beginning to look like that. Unfortunately he's not in a position to be questioned about it just yet, but as soon as he recovers consciousness ...'

'You'll have to call the police in!' I said indignantly. 'And we need to get Bob's wallet back to him! How's he going to get home – he won't have any money, or his rail ticket, or ...' I stopped, a glimmer of understanding flickering in my tired brain. 'That's probably why he phoned me for help. He must have discovered his wallet had been stolen, after he'd been discharged.' I sat up again, realising I still didn't know: 'What *was* wrong with Bob, then? Why *was* he brought here, if it wasn't a road accident?'

'I'm afraid I can't go into details about his condition, Mrs Freeman,' she said calmly, 'as you're not a relative.'

'But I don't know where his relative – his son – is! And I *need* to know! We've got Bob's grandson with us in the café downstairs and nobody knows why!'

I felt like crying. I was getting tired, and now I'd got over the shock, and the relief that it wasn't Bob unconscious in that bed, I just wanted to get back to Jackie and Freddie in the restaurant, and try to work out where Bob *had* gone. To say nothing of reuniting the poor child with his father, or at least his ex-other-father, or whoever the hell was supposed to be taking care of him.

'I'm sorry, Mrs Freeman,' Sister said a little more gently. 'Our first concern here will be to try to find out the correct identity of our patient in the room there, and obviously if there *has* been a crime committed, the police will have to be informed. It will then be their responsibility to return Mr Tattersall's property to him, so I can only suggest we take your contact details and keep you informed.'

I sighed. 'I haven't even got a phone on me at the moment – I've lost it. I'll give you my home number, but I think I'd better stay around here until we know what's happening. I mean, I might need to speak to the police. I want them to find Bob!'

'It must be a very difficult situation for you,' she said sympathetically. 'I'm sorry I can't do anything else to help. I presume Mr Tattersall won't even be able to contact you, if you've lost your phone.'

'He's probably ringing my home number,' I said. 'Perhaps it was stupid to rush up here like this, but I was so worried about him.' The Sister glanced at her watch and I got to my feet, apologising. 'Sorry, I'm keeping you from your work. I'd better go and see how my friend's coping with the little boy down in the restaurant.'

She held out her hand to me and wished me luck. I somehow felt like I was going to need it.

By the time I found my way back to the restaurant, where poor Jackie was now desperately trying to calm down a very hyped-up Freddie, I'd nearly lost the will to live.

'I've got no idea what to do next,' I admitted when I'd come to the end of the explanation about the man in the bed who wasn't Bob, and the wallet, and everything. 'What on *earth's* got into Freddie?' I added as we both tried to stop him from running amok around the tables. 'I thought he'd be getting tired by now.'

'I think I gave him too much orange juice. And sugary treats. I didn't know how else to keep him occupied. I'm not very good at this,' she added apologetically. 'Autumn hasn't got to this stage yet.'

'Not your fault – he must have been bored. Sorry I was so long.' I rested my head in my hands.

'So what now? Should we just take Freddie home with us again?'

'I don't know, Jackie. It's quite a worry. His father will be looking for him. He's going to think Bob's run off with him!'

'Oh God, yes, he will, won't he.' She frowned. 'Look, Bob's bound to try and call you again, isn't he? He'll surely have got some more change, and … oh, of course. He won't have any money on him!'

'Exactly. I wonder what he would have done, when he realised he had no more money? If he couldn't get hold of his son?'

'Gone to the police?' she suggested.

'Maybe, yes. The Sister said she'll have to tell them, anyway, about the wallet, and then the police will try to track Bob down themselves – or they'll call me, if they can't find him. But I could only give her my home number because I haven't even got a mobile at the moment. What a mess!'

'You could have given mine.'

I smiled at her. 'I don't even know it.'

'Well, here it is, and feel free to use it, Kate, while we're waiting. Sorry, I forgot you'd lost yours. Why didn't you say? You probably need to let your family know where you are, don't you?'

'Oh, bugger!' I took a deep breath. 'I hate to say it, but I hadn't even thought of that. I'm far more worried about Bob. We still don't even know why he was in hospital.'

'Or why he made this secret trip to Ipswich in the first place,' Jackie reminded me.

'No. Well, I suppose I'd better just give one of my kids a quick call,' I said, accepting the phone from her, 'before we decide what to do next.'

Jackie arm-wrestled poor little Freddie onto her lap and tried to calm him down by telling him a story, while I called Stephanie's home number. Without my own phone, I didn't know her mobile number.

'Not answering,' I muttered. 'Steph!' I spoke urgently into her voice mail. 'It's Mum – I'm just ringing in case you've tried to get hold of me. In case you're wondering where I am. I've had to go to Ipswich. I'll explain when I see you, OK? Don't worry, I'll be back soon.'

I couldn't think of anything else to say.

'I'm not sure that's exactly going to reassure her,' Jackie said, laughing as I hung up.

'No. I'd better try my son.' But there was no reply there either. 'Saturday tea-time,' I commented, checking my watch as I listened to the ringing tone. 'I'd have expected them to be at home, really.'

'Maybe they're all out looking for you,' she joked.

'Not funny. They already seem to think I'm losing my marbles.'

I didn't bother to leave a message this time. It was impossible to explain the situation properly in a short message and as Jackie said, if I couldn't explain, what was the point? I was probably just making them worry about me even more, and it was bad enough already.

'Speaking of the time,' Jackie said, suddenly looking concerned, 'isn't it getting a bit late for Freddie?'

The little boy was finally rubbing his eyes and looking sleepy.

'Well, if we have to take him home again, he'll fall asleep in the car. But I'm thinking maybe before we do that, we should see if we can get hold of Craig – Bob's son. I don't know whereabouts in Ipswich he lives, but surely there can't be too many Tattersalls in the phone book.'

'Yes, good idea, but we don't need a phone book – I'll get it from directory enquiries. Oh, hang on – is that nurse looking for us?'

It was Sister Jackson, and she was heading our way, looking relieved.

'I'm glad you're still here, Mrs Freeman,' she said, sitting down opposite us and sounding out of breath. 'I'm pleased to say our patient has regained consciousness already, and we've been able to talk to him now.'

'Good. Has he admitted it? Stealing the wallet from Bob? Are the police coming?'

'I have asked the police to send someone in, yes. But Mr Dutton – that's the patient's name – has told us a completely different story.'

'He's lying, then!' I exclaimed crossly. 'If he's got Bob's wallet …'

'He says he found it. On the pavement outside the station, apparently. He says he was on his way to the police station to hand it in when he was involved in the accident.'

'Well, he *would* say that, wouldn't he!'

'I think, having checked out the circumstances of Mr Tattersall's admission, he could be telling the truth, actually,' she said.

'But you won't tell me the circumstances!'

'I *can* tell you he was brought in by ambulance from Ipswich station. So it's perfectly possible that his wallet fell out of his pocket at the time.'

'I see.' The frustration was killing me. What was wrong with Bob? Why had he been brought here by ambulance? Where *was* he?

'I've passed your phone number to the police, and they're going to contact you.'

'Please could you give them my mobile number too?' Jackie said, hurriedly writing it down on a serviette. 'We're going to try to track down Mr Tattersall's son. Otherwise it looks like we'll be taking his grandson back home with us.'

Sister Jackson glanced at Freddie for the first time, with a frown.

'Perhaps we should be contacting Social Services about the child,' she said. I sat up straight in my chair, my heart racing with alarm.

'No! Absolutely no need for that! Bob knows we've got him with us, and I'm perfectly happy to keep him, if we can't find Bob or his son.'

'OK.' She gave me a look that made me feel as if I was being assessed for my suitability. 'If the arrangement was already in place, before Mr Tattersall was admitted to hospital, and you're happy to continue with that?'

'Definitely,' Jackie joined in, and I nodded, grateful that there were two of us, presenting a united front on the issue.

'Good luck with tracking down the son, then, and I hope everything turns out all right,' she said, getting up to leave.

'She might have reacted differently,' Jackie said quietly to me as we watched her go, 'if she knew Craig isn't even Freddie's father, and isn't supposed to be the one looking after him.'

'I know. But if we can find him,' I said, 'he'll do.'

Unfortunately, luck still seemed to be against us. Jackie shook her head at me as she listened to the response from the directory enquiries number she'd called.

'Nobody listed by that name in Ipswich,' she said. 'Damn. He probably just uses a mobile.'

'I wonder if we can try getting the address off the internet instead, and just go round there on the off-chance?'

Jackie glanced at Freddie, who'd wriggled off her lap again and was sitting on the floor, grizzling to himself.

'I don't think we're being very fair,' she whispered. 'He's so tired, Kate. And it might take ages to find the place even if we can get the address, and we don't even know whether Craig will be there, or what sort of reception we'd get.'

'No. You're right,' I agreed, feeling guilty now for even suggesting it. 'Come on – decision made. Let's go home.'

The silly thing was, there might even have been a message from Bob on the phone at home, while we'd been wasting time up there in Ipswich visiting a guy in a hospital bed who just happened to have had his wallet.

I gathered little Freddie up in my arms and together we carried him out to the car park. Poor little lad. I had no idea what I was going to say to him. His granddad had disappeared, nobody knew where or why, and we had no idea how to contact either of his dads. I could hardly believe this was all happening, it seemed so ridiculous. But one thing I was now absolutely sure about. I'd look after him for as long as I needed to. At least until Bob turned up, and I could only hope that was going to be soon. I'd had enough worry for one day, and Jackie had done more than enough babysitting!

PAM

Frère Jacques

I'd been a bit upset about the way they pushed me out. OK, I knew it was going to take time for Kate to start trusting me again, despite the fact that I'd been such a help to her – finding out where her friend Bob had gone to, and then staying with her to give her a break, making her lunch and helping look after the little boy. It was all fine until the other one – Jackie – turned up. Her with the sticky-up red hair and the ridiculous shoes. I could tell straight away she was going to take over and wanted me out of the way. Calling herself Kate's best friend! Who did she think she was?

All right, I admit it, I was jealous – could you blame me? I'd been trying so hard to make it up to Kate for the way I'd behaved. I had far more in common with her than that skinny minx did, and I'd happily have looked after that little boy. Let's face it, I was used to looking after other people's children. But there wasn't a lot I could do. They insisted on going to Ipswich together and taking the poor child with them. After getting the phone call from Bob, Kate seemed to be so anxious about him, she just gave in and let Jackie take control.

I went home feeling unsettled and I suppose, kind of left out. I knew the situation sounded a bit worrying, but it was quite exciting too, and I'd have liked to have been involved in some way, to have been able to help. I made myself another cup of tea and sat in my usual chair by the window to read the paper. It must have been a couple of hours later – I think I'd dozed off for a while – when I glanced out of the window and saw three young people hovering around Kate's front door. It took me a minute to recognise them. They'd all grown so much taller since the last time I'd seen them here, and the oldest boy, well, he wasn't a boy at all, he was a young man, probably about nineteen or twenty. They were Kate's other grandchildren. The ones who lived in France. What on earth were they doing there?

I stood up to get a better look, and as I watched, the older one stepped away from the door, and began looking through the front room window. There were two large rucksacks on the ground, and the other boy was squatting on one of them while he made a call on his mobile phone. Well, obviously I had to do something.

'Were you looking for your nan?' I called to them as I crossed the road. Stupid question.

They all turned to stare at me. The oldest one muttered something in French to the other two. My French wasn't brilliant, but I could manage the basics, and I caught the word *voisin*. Neighbour.

'*Oui*,' I attempted. '*Je suis un voisin.*'

'It's OK,' the young man said, 'We speak English.'

I didn't like the way they were all still staring at me. But I supposed the younger two were both at that age – surly teenagers. I had enough of that when I was teaching. Hopefully their older brother would be a little more polite.

'I just happened to notice you ringing your grandmother's doorbell,' I said. 'So I thought I should come and tell you she's not here.'

'So it seems,' said the older one. Then, as if he'd finally remembered his manners, 'Sorry. My name's Toby and this is my brother Clément and my sister Emilie. Do you happen to know where my grandmother's gone?'

'Yes, as a matter of fact, I do. She's gone to Ipswich.'

'*Ipswich?*' His eyes widened. 'But her car's here.'

'Yes. Someone else drove her.'

'Oh. Will she be back soon, do you know?'

'I actually have no idea. She went off in something of a hurry, you see. She'd just heard her friend's in hospital there.'

'Oh, I see.' He glanced at his brother and sister, and reverting to French again, asked the boy, Clément, whether he'd spoken to *Tante Stephanie* yet. The lad shook his head and said there'd been no response.

'Try Uncle Michael, then,' he suggested. Turning to me, he added: 'I don't suppose you have a key for my grandmother's house?'

'I'm afraid not. Was she expecting you?'

'Yes. My brother and sister have come to stay for a week. I've just brought them over – I'm going back tomorrow.' He scratched his head. 'We got a taxi from the station. Perhaps I shouldn't have let it go until we'd checked whether Grand-maman was here. I'm just a little surprised, because she knew we were coming, and she hasn't contacted us to say there was a change of plan.'

'It was something of an emergency,' I said. 'She probably hasn't had a chance to call you yet.'

Privately, I thought this was pretty typical of Kate, and the chaotic way she seemed to live her life. However much she'd been caught up with Bob's problems, you'd have thought she'd remember that her own grandchildren were coming to stay! But I'd learnt my lesson; I was going to keep my feelings about her shortcomings to myself. Nobody was perfect, after all, and if she was always such a disaster as a grandmother it was all the more reason she needed someone like me in her life to help her out.

'Well, thank you for letting us know,' Toby said.

'What are you going to do? While you wait to hear from her?'

'We're trying to contact someone from our family to come and pick us up. We can wait with them until she comes back.'

I noticed Clément putting his phone back in his pocket and shaking his head at his brother.

'You're welcome to wait in my house until you manage to contact someone,' I said. I smiled at the younger two. 'I've got some cans of Coke and some crisps.'

I always kept a supply of things like that, obviously. Just in case.

Clément and Emilie looked at their brother hopefully. Well, it was surely a better option than hanging about in the street with their luggage.

'OK. Thank you,' he said, and finally even the two surly teenagers gave me a smile of thanks.

The day was turning out to be a lot more interesting after all. Kate was certainly going to be grateful to me now.

I'd made a fruit cake the previous day, so I sliced some of that up and put it on a plate, with a few chocolate biscuits for good measure. Then I tipped a family-sized packet of crisps into a bowl, and took it all into the lounge, along with three cans of Coke.

'Help yourselves,' I said. 'There are glasses here if you want them.'

I didn't pour their drinks out for them, as I knew that most teenagers preferred to drink straight from the can. I wanted them to see that I was perfectly used to dealing with young people.

'Thank you. It's kind of you,' the girl, Emilie, said as she dipped into the bowl of crisps.

So she did have some manners after all. Good.

'Could I please use the toilet?' Clément asked, blushing.

'Of course. Upstairs, first on the left.'

I turned to Toby. 'You all speak very good English.'

'I'm actually English,' he said. 'Mum and I moved to France when I was five. Clément and Emilie were born in France but we all grew up bilingual.'

'I see. You're very fortunate. It's so useful to be able to speak more than one language, in today's world.'

'I speak Spanish and Italian too,' he said with a shrug, 'Clément and Emilie have to learn other languages at school as well. We're all Europeans now, aren't we.'

I couldn't help thinking how different this attitude was from that of the kids I used to teach. French, like most other lessons, like my own maths lessons of course, was deemed *boring* to the majority of them. And sadly, the few who really wanted to learn were called geeks by the others and didn't have many friends. I sighed. Sometimes I thought I missed my working days. And then I remembered what it was like at the end. Unbearable.

'Eat up,' I encouraged them. 'You must be hungry after your journey. Have you tried calling your aunt or uncle again?'

'Yes. Clément's left messages for them both. I've been trying to get hold of Grand-maman but her phone seems to be switched off.'

'That's unfortunate. Well, you're very welcome to stay here for as long as necessary.'

In fact, now they seemed to have got used to me and stopped that typically teenage rude staring, I was enjoying their company. We watched some TV together, finished off the crisps and most of the cake, and I was beginning to contemplate the idea that they might be forced to stay with me for the whole evening. I could cook them a meal. I had some mince in the fridge that I'd been planning to make into a large Shepherd's pie to last me for two or three days. It'd be nice to share it with these kids instead. We could watch TV together, and if the worst came to it, they'd have to stay the night. I'd make the spare bed up ready, just in case, and the two younger ones could have pillows and duvets on the sofas.

I went out to the kitchen to start chopping onions and peeling potatoes. It'd be best to start getting everything ready now. If by any chance Kate did come back any time soon, I'd invite her to join us. She'd be too tired to cook, to say nothing of being shocked and upset that she'd forgotten about her grandchildren arriving. I'd make sure there was enough food to go round. I might even have an apple tart in the freezer. I could get that out too.

I was humming a little tune to myself – I think it was actually *Frère Jacques* – as I chopped the potatoes and put them into a large saucepan of water ready to cook. And it was just at that moment that Toby appeared in the kitchen doorway and said:

'We'll be OK now, thank you. My Uncle Michael's on his way.'

And this might sound ridiculous, but it felt just like it did when I wasn't allowed to have George and Lily. I was so disappointed I could have cried.

KATE

Home Again, Home Again, Jiggedy-Jig

We were on the way home, somewhere around Colchester, when Jackie's phone started ringing.

'Could you get that for me, please, Kate?' she said. 'It might be Keith. Tell him I'm driving and I'll call him back. He does panic when I'm out for longer than five minutes.'

To be fair, the poor guy had no idea she'd gone to Ipswich or what she was doing.

'Hello?' I said. And it wasn't her Keith. It was my son Michael, and he sounded absolutely furious.

'Mum? What the hell's going on? Where are you? Whose phone is this you've been calling from? What was that message all about, that you left on Steph's phone? What the hell did you have to go to Ipswich for?'

I just stopped myself from asking him which question he wanted me to answer first.

'I'll explain later,' I said. 'I'm on my way home now.'

'Never mind about explaining later.' His tone was severe. I felt like I was in trouble. When did my children start acting like my parents? 'You were supposed to be *here.*'

I suddenly felt a shiver of apprehension. What had I forgotten? I'd done Izzie's birthday party, hadn't I. Did I promise to babysit for one of them? Bugger. I'd been too worried about Bob, to check my diary before we rushed out. Come to think of it, the bloody diary had disappeared anyway, hadn't it. Along with everything else.

'Sorry,' I said. 'This was an emergency, Mike. I had a call from one of my friends. He'd been taken to hospital, and …'

'One of your friends. The one who walked out of Izzie's party yesterday, by any chance?'

'Yes – Bob. I've been looking after his grandson, and he phoned to say he needed my help.'

Michael sighed. 'Look, Mum, it's good that you've got some friends, but since when did you put them before your *family*?'

'Since never!' I snapped, stung. 'In case you hadn't noticed, Mike, I give up most of my time for my family – not that I mind – but I don't think either you or Stephanie can ever lay that accusation on me.'

'What about Danielle?'

'What about her?' But even as the words were leaving my mouth, I remembered. 'Oh, shit. The kids. Was it this weekend?'

'Yes. It was today. They're here. They spent twenty minutes hanging around outside your house, and for the last couple of hours they've been shacked up with your neighbour. I've just got their message and been to pick them up. Jo and I had been swimming with the twins so we didn't have our phones on us. We don't like leaving them in the lockers at the pool.'

I ignored this. I was far less bothered about the lockers at the swimming pool than I was by …

'Which neighbour?'

'Number forty-four. Posh woman with permed hair and grey tights. Seemed put-out that I'd turned up to collect them.'

That'd be Pam, all right. Was she going to worm her way into every corner of my life? But albeit grudgingly, I had to accept that I was grateful she'd been there, nosing out of her window as usual.

'I'm so sorry, Mike. Thanks so much for picking them up. Look, I'll be home before long but I've still got Freddie – Bob's little grandson – with me, he's going to need putting to bed. Could you possibly drop the others round to me in a couple of hours?'

'For God's sake, Mum, *why* have you got someone else's child?'

'It's only temporary.' I sighed. 'Look, this is Jackie's phone, I'd better go, but please say sorry to Clem and Em. They weren't on their own, were they?'

'No. Luckily Toby's come with them. Who's Jackie?'

'My friend who's given me a lift. I'll explain later.' If I had to tell him the whole story right now, Jackie's battery would probably run out.

'So you still haven't found your own phone?'

'No, not yet. It's probably somewhere at home, if I could just get around to searching the house properly.'

'I'm worried about you, Mum. You haven't been yourself lately.'

'I'm absolutely fine, I keep telling you. Anyway, why didn't Steph call me back, if she got the message?'

'Oh, no reason.' There *was* a reason, I could tell that straight away. The tone of his voice had changed and he was trying to bring the conversation to a close. 'It was just easier for me to pick the kids up. Look, we'll catch up later, OK?'

'Is she all right?' I persisted.

'Yes. See you later, Mum, and for God's sake don't go off anywhere else looking after everyone else's kids until you've come home to your grandchildren.'

'Bloody cheek!' I fumed to Jackie as I handed her phone back. 'Honestly, my son either talks to me as if I'm the hired help, or treats me like an idiot who can't find her own way home.' I paused and sighed. 'But then again, I have really dropped a clanger this time.'

'You forgot someone was coming today?' She couldn't have helped hearing my end of the conversation.

'My grandchildren from France. Danielle's kids. They're only thirteen and fifteen, but luckily their older brother brought them over. I do feel dreadful about it. What a terrible thing to forget.'

'You'd have remembered if it wasn't for all this happening with Bob.'

'I know. But my son's right – I've put all this before my family. No wonder he's cross.'

'That's crap, Kate! You do everything for your family – you *always* put them first. You're entitled to worry about a friend who's in trouble too.'

'Maybe. But not to forget two youngsters coming over from France and being stranded on my doorstep.'

'Leave off with the guilt trip. It's all turned out OK, hasn't it? Do I gather that a neighbour took them in? That wouldn't have been your favourite person from over the road, would it?'

'Who else!' I raised my eyebrows. 'But to be honest, thank God she was there, being a nosy bloody cow as usual. I suppose I'll have to thank her.' I stared out of the window. 'Now I'm just a bit concerned about Stephanie.'

'Why? What did your son say?'

'Nothing. He was very obviously avoiding discussing her. But something's definitely up. She got my message but passed it on to Michael. She'd normally have rushed round to my place herself to sort out Danielle's kids.'

'Well, she has got the baby, and Izzie, hasn't she. She was probably just busy doing their tea, or something, and maybe her husband was out.'

'I suppose so.'

But you know that thing called mother's instinct. It was working on overdrive. And I didn't like what it was conjuring up.

Freddie was sound asleep in the back of the car when we got home, and didn't even stir when I lifted him out of the car seat to carry him indoors.

'I'd better get home, if you don't mind,' Jackie said apologetically. 'Are you sure you'll be OK?'

'Of course. Thanks so much for everything.'

'Give me a ring tomorrow and let me know if I can do anything else to help.'

She drove off and I let myself into the house, laid Freddie down on the settee and found his pyjamas in his little bag. Thank goodness Bob had left some things with us, although if Freddie was still with me the next day I'd be running out of clean clothes for him. The poor kid hardly stirred as I changed him and carried him upstairs. I'd just put him in the cot and closed the bedroom door when the phone started ringing. I nearly fell downstairs in my haste to pick it up before it woke Freddie.

'Ah, so you're back now.' Danielle sounded grim rather than worried. 'Where on earth have you been?'

'Dannie, I'm *so, so,* sorry. I ...'

'I wouldn't mind, Mum, but I'd only texted you yesterday to remind you the kids were coming.'

'I didn't get the message. I've lost my phone.'

'So it seems. When you didn't reply, I tried calling you – first the mobile – switched off. Or lost. Whatever. Then the home phone – no reply.'

'I must have left by then, to go to Ipswich. I'm really sorry.'

'Clément and Emilie were already on their way, but I wasn't worried, because we'd already agreed the date. I couldn't believe my ears when I heard they'd been left stranded in the street with their suitcases.'

'All right, look, I've said I'm sorry – it was inexcusable of me to forget, but don't make it sound like they're poor little orphans lost in the depths of the jungle. They've been looked after.'

'Yes, taken in by some *neighbour*. Honestly, Mum, she could have been anyone! I don't even know the woman. Pat, Pam, Paula or something? Apparently she didn't like it when Michael turned up to pick them up – she told him she'd been making them shepherd's pie and making up beds for them for the night. Michael said it was spooky, like she wanted to keep them there. What is she, some kind of nutter?'

'Don't be ridiculous,' I said, although actually I agreed with the diagnosis. 'It was very good of her. And anyway, they're not exactly babies, and they had Toby with them.' I sighed. 'Look, I don't blame you for being upset, but they obviously had the sense to call Michael, and they're with him now, so it's all fine.'

'They're still with Michael? You haven't picked them up yet?'

'No, Michael's going to bring them round in a little while. I had something I had to do first,' I said evasively.

'Oh, of course. Sorry, Mum. How is she?'

'Who?' My thoughts, still mainly with little Freddie upstairs in the cot, whizzed around inside my head in a whirl of confusion. 'How is who?'

'Stephanie, of course. I take it you've been to see her?'

'What?' Damn it. I *knew* there was something going on about Steph. 'Why? What do you mean? What's happened? Oh, bugger it – hang on a minute, Dannie, that's the door bell. I'll have to get it, in case it wakes Freddie up.'

Not that she had a clue who Freddie was. I threw down the phone and ran to the door, cursing Michael (if it was him already) for not having the bloody sense to tap gently on the door instead, knowing there was a little one asleep upstairs.

'Hang on, hang on,' I said, unlocking the door as the bell rang again more insistently. 'All right – come on in, keep the noise down, can you, I've got a child asleep upstairs. I'm just on the phone ...'

But it wasn't Michael. It was Pam, looking self-satisfied and superior and carrying a casserole dish covered with foil.

'Shepherd's pie,' she said, taking herself through to the kitchen and plonking the dish down on the counter. 'I thought you might appreciate it, after being out all day. Those French children didn't stay long enough to eat any. There's an apple tart in my oven for afterwards.'

'Wait,' I told her, sharply. 'I'm on the phone.' I shut the door and ran back to pick up the receiver. 'Dannie? What were you saying about Steph?'

But somehow, due either to the vagaries of cross-channel phone connections or to Danielle's impatience and general annoyance with me, the line had gone dead.

'Bugger! Sorry, I can't talk to you now,' I said to Pam without even so much as a nod in the direction of the shepherd's pie. 'I've got to call my daughter back. It could be urgent.'

'Your other daughter's in hospital,' she said calmly, 'if that's what you were needing to know.'

'*What*?'

'It's all right, don't panic. She'll be fine, she's in the best place. Shall I put the kettle on and make you a nice cup of tea?'

'*What*?' I said again. I could feel myself starting to lose control. 'No! No, I don't want a bloody cup of tea – I want to know what's wrong with Steph, and how the hell you came to know about it before *I* did! Which hospital? Why? What's happened?'

'Ssh, don't get upset,' she tried to soothe me, which only succeeded in making me feel completely bloody hysterical. 'She had a bad asthma attack. Your son told me, when he came for the children. Well, he didn't *exactly* tell me – he told Toby. Nice young man, that one, isn't he? Very sensible.'

'Which hospital?' I demanded again, the fear and the fury making my voice shake. Fear for Stephanie, fury with Michael for not telling me when we spoke earlier on the phone, fury with this nosy parker of a woman who knew more about my family than I did, who made shepherd's pies for my grandchildren and thought Toby was sensible, who seemed to be squirming her way into my life when I didn't even like her! I looked around for my handbag, my shoes. To be honest the last thing I felt like doing right now, after the ridiculous scenario at the bedside of the guy in Ipswich today, was visiting another hospital! But I couldn't even think about that. 'Quick – which hospital, since you seem to know everything? I need to see her.'

'You can't.'

'Can't what?' I snapped. I was close to tears. It had been a tough day, what with Bob and Ipswich, and the man in the bed who wasn't Bob, and Freddie, and forgetting my grandkids.

'You can't go to the hospital. Not right now. You've got the little lad asleep upstairs, haven't you, and your son's supposed to be bringing the others round.'

'Damn!' I sat down on the stairs with a bump, trying to work it out. I really needed to see Steph. I couldn't believe she was lying in hospital, ill, fighting for breath, needing me, and nobody had even bothered to let me know. I'd have to find a way. Maybe as Toby was apparently so sensible he wouldn't mind having the responsibility of a toddler he didn't even know? Or maybe Michael could be persuaded to stay here and babysit the whole lot of them, including Freddie, while I went to the hospital? 'I've got to see her,' I repeated out loud.

'So isn't it lucky that I'm here?' Pam said, and there was no mistaking the smugness in her voice. 'Off you go, then. The little lad will probably sleep right through, and the French children already know me.' She smiled, and despite the seriousness of everything that had happened that day, it was disturbing to see the way her eyes had lit up. 'Don't you worry about a thing, Kate, dear. Just leave it all to me.'

KATE

Who's Been Sleeping in My Bed?

I was so tired and so stressed, I didn't even realise I'd jumped a red light on the way to the hospital until I got honked at loudly by a taxi.

'I'm looking for my daughter,' I told the guy at the main reception desk, giving him Steph's name. 'She was brought in earlier today.'

I watched, my heart pounding uncomfortably, as he scanned his computer screen, scrolling down and back up again maddeningly slowly, staring intently at whatever data he had there until finally he looked back up at me and said:

'No. Sorry.'

'What do you mean, *No*?'

Don't tell me bloody Pam had sent me to the wrong hospital.

'I mean, no, sorry, she's not here anymore.'

'She's been transferred?' Oh my God, please don't say it was so serious she's been taken to some – I don't know – more serious hospital in London or somewhere. 'Where?' I'd go there, obviously. Right now. Anywhere. Even back to Ipswich if necessary, and wouldn't *that* be a farce.

'To her home,' he said, giving me a slightly puzzled look. 'Discharged home at seven-twenty this evening.'

'What! And nobody thought to tell me?' I demanded, and then remembering that I hadn't even known she was there in the first place, added only slightly less belligerently, 'What sort of time is that to discharge somebody? Halfway through the evening? What if she'd been a little old lady living on her own, with no food in the house?'

'I thought you said she was your daughter?' he said, his frown deepening.

'Yes, but even so, the ward sister, or whoever, really ought to be told ...' I don't know why I was being so difficult. I couldn't seem to help myself. I just felt so ... so generally *pissed off.*

'She wasn't even admitted to a ward,' the poor man said.

What? My poor daughter, fighting for her life, left lying on a trolley in a corridor somewhere? So it was all true what they said about the NHS. People could die waiting to see a bloody doctor. Well, I wasn't going to let this go. I'd be writing to my MP. I'd get the local paper on the case. I'd ...

'It says here she was treated in A&E,' he went on, 'Admission not necessary, discharged home.'

'Oh.' I suddenly felt a huge bubble of relief rising up in me, swallowing up all the annoyance and anxiety and irritation of the day. 'So she's OK? You're saying she's gone home because she's OK?'

'That's the way it looks to me. Perhaps you could talk to her and find out for yourself?'

Cheeky young man. But still, I was smiling as I walked away. Thank God. Thank God she was obviously OK enough to be sent home. The irony wasn't lost on me either – first Bob, and now Steph, rushed into hospital but discharged by the time I got there to see them! It was becoming something of a habit.

I looked at my watch. Nine-fifteen. I'd go round to see her now – that's what I'd do – while bloody Pam was holding the fort at home. If I didn't see her with my own eyes, I'd never be able to sleep tonight for worrying that the young man on reception had got it round his neck and Steph was in fact still lying, forgotten and struggling to breathe, somewhere in some dusty corner of the hospital where they kept the dirty linen and washed the urine bottles. You hear about these things all the time.

It took me less than fifteen minutes to get to their house. Ben answered the door.

'Kate!' he said, looking surprised. 'Are you all right?'

'Me?' I retorted. 'I'm fine. It's Steph I'm worried about.'

'Ah.' He held the door open for me to walk in. 'You've heard.'

'Yes. *Finally.*'

'Not my fault, Kate. I tried to call you. We all did. You need to do something about your mobile being lost.'

'Life did go on before mobile phones were invented, you know, *and* people seemed to be able to cope with emergencies,' I said.

'Yes, I'm aware of that. We tried your home number too, but you were out.'

'Oh, yes. Sorry. It was ...' An emergency. Point made.

'And when Mike finally spoke to you, you were up in Ipswich or somewhere, on some kind of mercy mission for a friend, and he thought it would only worry the life out of you if he told you Steph was ill. There was nothing you could have done, not from Ipswich.'

He said *Ipswich* as if it was somewhere in the Arctic Circle, rather than a forty minute drive away up the A12.

'So I was left to find out about it from my nosy neighbour, who's taking great delight in being more up to date on issues relating to my own family, than I am.'

'Look, Kate,' he said, with a perceptible sigh, 'Come in and sit down. I'm sorry if you feel offended, but at the time all that mattered was that Steph was in trouble, and we needed to get her to hospital.'

'Of course,' I said at once, feeling ridiculous. 'I'm sorry. I've just been really worried. How is she?'

'Fine. Well, she was tired, of course. You know how it leaves her, after an attack. It was pretty bad, but they put her on the nebuliser and gave her some steroids and she was perfectly OK to come home. She's asleep now. She went to bed as soon as we got back.'

'You stayed with her? In A&E?'

'Of course I did. We had to take the children – there was no time to think. If you'd been here ...'

'I'd have come and collected them. I'm sorry,' I said again, shaking my head. 'I wish I'd been here to help.'

'Well, never mind. Do you want a drink of anything, now you're here? You look pretty shaken.'

'No, I'd better get back. I've got ...'

'Danielle's kids!' He looked up at me suddenly, remembering. 'Are they OK? I heard some story from Mike about them being left on the doorstep.'

'That's an exaggeration. They were perfectly fine. Toby was with them, and my neighbour took them in. She's with them now, as a matter of fact.'

I decided it wouldn't serve any purpose to mention Freddie.

'Well, it sounds like you've got a good neighbour, at least,' he said, smiling like he thought that was a comfort.

'Mm.' I turned back to the front door. 'Sorry again for not being here, Ben. I feel really bad about it. Everything just seemed to happen at once.'

'OK. Don't worry. I'll tell Steph you called round.'

I drove home with the distinct feeling that I was being patronised. Treated like a poor old dear who needed help. When I got home and looked in the hall mirror, I couldn't say I was really surprised. My eyes were dark with tiredness, my hair tangled and standing on end, and worst of all, I'd put a cardigan on in a hurry before I'd gone out, not noticing it was inside-out. No wonder the young man at the hospital had been looking at me so warily. I was lucky not to have been sent straight to the mental health unit.

'There you are,' said Pam, walking down the hall towards me, wearing my slippers and one of my aprons. 'How is your daughter?' She helped me off with the inside-out cardigan (maybe I really had become senile) and hung it up, and without waiting for an answer, turned back to the kitchen, calling back over her shoulder that the shepherd's pie was all nice and hot, and she'd found some beans in my fridge to cook with it, and how about a nice glass of wine?

'Wine?' I said, wearily. 'That sounds nice.' I was just too damned tired to argue anymore. If she insisted on bringing me shepherd's pies and bottles of wine, so be it.

'Good. I chose a nice Merlot from your wine rack. The table's all set. Come and sit down. Everyone else has eaten.'

Everyone else? 'Oh! Toby and Clément and Emilie! They're here?'

'Yes, all present and correct,' she said, lifting the casserole dish out of my oven and starting to dish up huge spoonfuls of meat and potato onto one of my best dinner plates. 'Michael was very grateful to find me here, of course, as you'd had to go out again.'

'You did explain that I'd gone to the hospital, didn't you?'

'Well, there didn't seem a lot of point, after he'd told me your daughter wasn't there anymore. I guessed you'd probably go round to see her at home, though.'

'But you didn't tell him that's where I'd gone?' I persisted.

'Well, I couldn't be sure, could I? I mean, to be fair, you might have gone on anywhere.'

'What?' I stared at her. Was she deliberately trying to wind me up? 'So now my son's probably even more annoyed with me – thinking I just buggered off out, leaving you in charge again!'

'Oh, not at all, dear. Don't worry about Michael. He knows me now, of course, and I think he was just pleased to find someone reliable here, looking after things.'

If I wasn't too exhausted by now, I'd probably have picked her up bodily and thrown her out, shepherd's pie and all.

'Actually I don't really want anything to eat,' I said abruptly. 'I feel a bit sick.'

'That'll be the shock,' she said, smiling at me sadly. 'Well, never mind, you can let this cool down again and keep it in the fridge for tomorrow.'

'You can flush it down the loo for all I care!' I said. 'I'm fed up with the sight of it. Take it away – please.'

'All right, dear. I know you're feeling stressed. Shall we just have a little glass of wine together before I go? To calm you down?'

'No! I'll have a little glass of wine on my own, thank you very much.' I closed my eyes and made an effort. 'Thank you for your help tonight. I'm going to bed now.'

But when I went upstairs, sipping my wine and hoping it wasn't going to make my headache any worse, I discovered there wasn't even a bed for me. Whether at Pam's suggestion, or just taking it for granted, I couldn't tell – but Emilie was sound asleep on the camp-bed I kept in the little box room. And in my own bedroom, a suitcase was open just inside the doorway with T-shirts, jeans and shorts spewing out of it. On the floor next to the bed was my duvet in its clean white duvet cover, half buried by a heap of screwed-up clothes and two pairs of huge black boots. And on top of the bed, Toby and Clément were both sprawled on their backs in their boxer shorts, snoring gently.

It seemed just too much effort to wake them up and move them. I checked on Freddie, then went back downstairs with my wine to sleep on the sofa.

BOB

Jack Fell Down and Broke his Crown

It was all a bit of a nightmare. My trip to Ipswich hadn't exactly gone to plan.

For a start, I'd been feeling ill. I was hoping it was just the stress of the whole thing, and it'd wear off once I got on the train, sat down and relaxed, but at some point I must have passed out. I came round, lying on the hard floor, feeling sick and dizzy and with no idea where I was. There was a man standing over me, a large florid man in a uniform who was talking into a mobile phone or walkie-talkie or some similar contraption.

'Hang on,' he said. 'I think he's coming round.'

I tried to sit up, but my head spun. I started muttering, trying to ask where I was, and he put down his phone and tried to soothe me.

'It's OK, sir. Take it easy. There's an ambulance on its way.'

'Ambulance?' I was still looking around me, confused. I was on a train. I was on the floor of a train carriage. What the hell was I doing there? 'I don't need an ambulance. I haven't broken anything, have I?'

Hard to know, when I had no idea what had happened to me.

'Just a precaution, sir, as we found you unconscious here. We don't know how long you've been out, you see?' He was talking to me in a loud voice as if I was deaf or stupid or both. 'How are you feeling now?'

'Woozy. Like I've been bumped over the head.' I shook my head and it spun again. 'Not sure I can manage to get up.'

'Here.' He held out his arm and I grasped it and managed to get to my feet, grateful, with his help, to plonk myself down on a seat.

'Thank you. Must have passed out for some reason … silly old fool. Can't even remember what I'm doing here.' I looked around me, out of the train window. The train wasn't moving, and there didn't seem to be anyone else in my carriage. 'Where are we?'

'Ipswich, sir. Train arrived here a few minutes ago. A passenger found you in here on the floor when he was getting on. Looks like you've had some sort of a collapse, haven't you, sir, and it's best to be safe rather than sorry. Get you to hospital and get you checked over, right?'

'Well, I don't know. If I just sit here for a bit, maybe I'll be all right.'

I was beginning to remember. Ipswich – yes, of course, I'd been going to Ipswich. I'd been in a bit of a state. That awful business of leaving Freddie with Kate, without telling her I was going. I'd hated doing it, but it seemed the only way. The taxi had got held up in the road works, and then there was that queue at the ticket office. That woman had got my ticket for me. I'd felt a bit under the weather even then, but I'd presumed it was just the rush and the panic. Not used to it.

'Can't leave you here in the train, sir,' the chap in the uniform was saying. I suppose he was some kind of guard or station manager. 'The train needs to move on, see? People are waiting – we've had to stop the train while we … Oh, here are the paramedics now. Here he is, gents. He's passed out or had some sort of collapse, see? He was on the floor. I reckon he needs checking over. I mean, it could be his heart, and I wouldn't want to be responsible, know what I mean?'

The paramedics – there were two of them, both very young – checked my blood pressure and pulse and all those other medical things, and asked me a lot of silly questions about my name and age and whether I could remember who the queen and the prime minister were.

'OK, Robert,' one of them said eventually, without asking if I minded him using my Christian name, 'I don't think you're in any immediate danger, but we do certainly need to take you to hospital to do a few more checks.'

'But I'm feeling better now,' I protested, although to be honest, I still felt pretty sick and dizzy.

'It's the head injury we're a little concerned about,' he said, pressing the back of my head just to prove it, which made me gasp and close my eyes. 'See? You've got a nasty bump there. You must have hit your head when you fell on the floor.'

'And you seem to be suffering a certain amount of memory loss,' his pal added, kindly. That was actually because I'd pretended I still couldn't remember why I'd come to Ipswich. Well, I didn't want them knowing all my business. Nothing to do with them. 'So it's probable that you've suffered a slight concussion.'

So despite my protests, I was put in a wheelchair, (which was most humiliating, with everyone on the platform staring rudely, as if I was being arrested rather than being taken to hospital), taken out onto the platform, into a lift up to the station, and then into the ambulance that was waiting outside. When we got to the accident and emergency department, the nice paramedics handed me over to a doctor there, who looked even younger, and who went through much the same questions all over again and ended up saying I needed to be admitted to some kind of assessment unit for some tests.

'No,' I said. 'I'm fine now.'

'Well.' The doctor looked doubtful. She kept poking around at the bump on my head – I wished she wouldn't. 'I don't think you've done any real damage here, although I suspect you'll have a bit of a headache for a day or two. But I'm more concerned about why you passed out in the first place. I'm sorry, Robert, but we do need to keep an eye on you overnight and make sure there's nothing serious going on with you.'

I felt too weak to argue. It was true I didn't feel great, but I was worried about Freddie. I obviously wasn't going to get back for him tonight now. I knew Kate would look after him, but I'd have to call her in the morning and ask her if she could hang onto him a bit longer. It was a terrible cheek, but what else could I do?

I hardly got any sleep that night. By the time they'd finally found me a bed in this other unit, and the nurses there had gone through all the questions for a third time, and hooked me up to some kind of monitor, and done all the blood pressure and pulse checks and everything all over again, it was the middle of the night. The bed was hard, the room was too hot, and there were people coming and going all night. I found myself feeling grateful I'd never had to spend too much time in hospital before.

By the morning, apart from being shattered, I was feeling much better.

'OK, Mr Tattersall, it doesn't look like your collapse was the result of anything serious,' another doctor told me when he finally arrived to see me. It was nearly lunchtime and I was beginning to panic about whether I'd ever get out of there. 'I think we'll just assume you came over a little bit funny for some reason, shall we?'

Eighteen hours in hospital and the only diagnosis they could come up with was *you came over a little bit funny.* Still, I wasn't about to disagree.

'Yes. I was feeling a bit stressed about the journey. I'm sure that was all it was.'

'Right. And how's the headache now?'

'Better, thank you.'

'Good, good. So how about we get someone to come and pick you up and take you home? You've given your son as your next of kin, but there's no phone number here?' he added, looking at the notes he was holding.

'No. He's … not on the phone. But it's OK. I was on my way to his house when all this happened, so I'll just make my way there now.'

'We'd prefer it if he could come and pick you up,' the doctor said. 'Are you sure he's going to be at home? Hasn't he got a mobile number?'

I shook my head. Even if I'd been able to remember the number, I wasn't going to tell anyone. If Craig wasn't at home, I had a key for his house and I was going to let myself in and wait for him. He wasn't expecting me. My visit was supposed to be a surprise.

'It's fine.' I gave him what I hoped was a reassuring smile. 'I can get a taxi there.'

'Right. Give me the address then,' the doctor said, getting a pen out of his pocket and preparing to write it down on my paperwork. 'I'll get someone to organise you a taxi.'

Twenty minutes later, after only a short wait for the taxi, we were pulling up outside Craig's house.

'That'll be six pounds thirty, please, mate,' the cabbie said.

I felt like telling him I wasn't his mate, but I let it go. I felt in my jacket pocket – and that was when I realised my wallet had gone.

First I tried Craig's doorbell. Once he'd got over the surprise of seeing me there, he'd have to pay for the cab. But there was no reply. I debated asking the cabbie to take me back to the hospital, or even to the station, to see if I'd dropped the wallet anywhere there. But realistically, wherever I'd lost it, the chances were that someone would have picked it up by now and everything in it would have been stolen. I'd have to go to the police, but the thought of doing it then, on top of everything else, was just too much.

I had another search of my pockets, patting them all and pulling them inside out, and although I definitely didn't have the wallet, I did manage to scrape together two pounds ninety-three pence in change.

'I really am terribly sorry,' I told the cabbie. 'But I'm afraid this is all I have. I passed out, you see, on the train yesterday, and got taken to hospital, and my wallet seems to have gone.'

'Not having a very good day, are you, mate,' he said, looking at me with what appeared to be real sympathy. 'Don't worry about it. Have it on me. Hang onto that bit of change. Sounds like you might need it.'

'Oh no, please take it! I insist. My son will help me out, when he gets home, and then I'll be able to send you the rest. Shall I give you my name and phone number so that you know I'm genuine?'

'Forget it, mate. For Christ's sake, if I can't help out a poor old bugger like you, it don't say much for me, does it? You take care of yourself, now. Will you be all right? Sure? Can you let yourself in?'

'Yes. Thank you, you've been very kind.' Even if I did, privately, object to being called a poor old bugger even more than I objected to being his mate.

I watched him pull away. And that was when I realised the second thing: the key to Craig's house had been in my wallet.

I hobbled to the phone box at the end of the road. Craig's mobile number had been in the wallet too, of course, but luckily there was one phone number I was able to dial from memory – Kate's. Not because I'd consciously learnt it off by heart of course, but because it was a Witham number like my own and was a fairly easy sequence of digits. With the few suitable coins I had, I managed to call her, but I was so upset, and so worried about trying to tell her what I needed to, before the money ran out, that I couldn't

193

manage to string two sensible words together. I think I managed to tell her that I'd been taken to hospital, and was trying to explain that I needed her to help me by keeping Freddie for the rest of the day, when we got cut off. I stared in dismay at the few useless coins that were all I had left with me, and just prayed that Kate would have understood.

I wondered about going to look for the police station, but I had no idea where it was, so I decided to wait for Craig to come home. Being a Saturday, I was hoping he wouldn't have gone far. I walked back up the road and, finding the side gate to his house unlocked, went round to the garden and sat down on his back doorstep to wait. It wasn't very comfortable. But I leant back against the door and somehow, I must have dozed off. And that's where my son found me when he came home – I actually fell into the door when he opened it to put some rubbish outside.

Well, I'd intended to surprise him. But I think I scared him half to death. And that was before I'd even told him why I'd come.

KATE

When she got there, the cupboard was bare

I woke up with a stiff neck from falling asleep with my head on the arm of the sofa. To my horror, it was twenty past nine, the sun already hot through the lounge window, and I could hear the sound of laughter, and what seemed like a toddler squealing, coming from the kitchen. I sat up, the shock of suddenly remembering – of having forgotten – making me feel sick. *Freddie.* How was he up already – out of the cot? In the kitchen? And then there was the laughter again, and it all came back to me. Toby, Clément and Emilie were here. Presumably one of them had got Freddie up. He must have been awake, crying, wondering where he was – and he didn't even know them. How had I slept so late? How had I forgotten?

I got up, rubbing my neck, shock hitting me again as I realised I'd fallen asleep in my clothes.

'Hello everyone!' I said, as I rushed into the kitchen. 'It's lovely to see you, and I'm *so* sorry about yesterday. I had a bit of a problem, but – I hope you're all OK? You should have woken me up. Oh ....' I tailed off.

Toby and the two younger ones were sitting at the kitchen table, plates of bacon and eggs in front of them. Freddie had somehow been jammed into the highchair (which he was really far too big for), and with Weetabix round his mouth, was banging a spoon on the tray and singing his repertoire of half-learnt nursery rhymes, much to the apparent delight and amusement of the teenagers who were encouraging him. And standing at the cooker, frying pan sizzling, spatula in hand, was Pam.

'*There* you are,' she said, a look of satisfaction on her face. 'Come on, come and sit down, I've got more bacon frying.'

'What are you doing?' I stood in the doorway, staring at her. If she thought I was going to sit down and let her serve me, let her treat me like a guest in my own home, she was very much mistaken. 'How did you even get in?'

'Toby let me in, of course.' She smiled at him. 'He asked me to come in quietly because you were still asleep. Sorry if we woke you. We were *trying* to keep the noise down.'

'Yes, pardon, Mémée,' Emilie said, purposely using her babyhood word for *Nanny*. 'We've been too noisy, laughing at the little Freddie. He is so cute.'

'He's a *cool dude*,' Clément said, glancing at Toby for approval of his colloquial English.

'You should have woken me up,' I repeated, going to wipe the breakfast off Freddie's face. '*I* should have got him up – I'm really sorry ...'

'Don't worry,' Pam sang out cheerfully as she plonked another fried egg on Toby's plate. '*I* got him up – didn't I, sweetheart?' She took the wet-wipe out of my hand – actually snatched it from me! – and proceeded to wipe Freddie's mouth, while much to my annoyance the child smiled at her happily. 'He's used to me now, aren't you, little man? I've changed his nappy, so you don't need to worry about that, and I would have dressed him but there were no clean clothes left in his little bag, so I've put yesterday's ones in the wash. They should be ready soon.'

'Pam's put our things in the wash too,' Emilie said, smiling at Pam.

I wanted to strangle her. What was she even doing here? Who the hell did she think she was, coming in here, taking over? I felt a quiver of something actually close to fear. *Taking over*. I could almost feel it happening.

'I thought we should let you sleep,' she said, smugly. 'You were obviously exhausted. And the kids were hungry, so ...'

'The *kids* could have got their own breakfast.' I glanced at Toby. 'You shouldn't have let my neighbour wait on you like this!'

'She insisted!' he protested, while the other two looked at me with a kind of irritation. Make their own breakfast? When someone was offering to cook them eggs and bacon? Why would they do that?

'I brought the food in,' Pam went on, piling another plate full with eggs, bacon and tomatoes and pushing it towards me. 'That's why I came over. I guessed you might not have had time yesterday to do any shopping – what with rushing up to Ipswich and back, and then going to see your daughter.'

'It was kind of you,' Toby said. He gave me a look. The look said: *Even if you can't be polite and grateful to this wonderful neighbour of yours, I will.*

'Come on, sit down, eat up,' she said calmly. 'I'll put the kettle on for some more tea.'

'I'm not hungry.' I knew I must sound like a truculent child in front of these kids, but I couldn't help it. What I really wanted to do was to yell at her to get out of my house and stay out of my bloody life, so I think, in the circumstances, I was being remarkably restrained.

'I'll have it, then!' Clément said, reaching for the plate.

'Share it with the others, please, Clem,' Pam said. She smiled at me and added, 'If you're sure you don't want anything, why don't you go and have a shower or whatever you need to do. We're fine here.'

It was the use of Clément's shortened name that did it – so casually dropped in, as if she was their lifelong friend. I wasn't having it. I *would not* allow this woman to become some sort of proxy extra grandmother to my family, dismissing me like I was an unwanted servant in my own house. My house where she'd previously ranted at me, insulted me, virtually called me an incapable slut!

'I'll have a shower when, and if, I want one, thank you very much,' I snapped. 'And meanwhile, you can take your eggs and bacon and ...'

Perhaps fortunately, in view of the horrified looks on the faces of my grandchildren, the doorbell rang at that moment. I stalked out of the kitchen to answer it, conscious of the hush behind me and even more infuriated by hearing, from Pam: 'She's a bit overwrought. It's understandable.'

'Sorry,' said Jackie when I opened the door. 'I probably should have phoned first.'

'No, you shouldn't. Come in. I'm glad to see you.' I nodded towards the kitchen and added in a whisper. *'She's here.'*

I didn't need to explain who. Jackie grimaced and nodded.

'We'll see what we can do about that,' she whispered back, and added as I led her through to the kitchen, 'I just had to come and find out if there was any news about Bob. And whether you needed any help with Freddie. Oh!'

She stopped in surprise in the kitchen doorway, and I realised she hadn't met Danielle's kids yet.

'My grandchildren from France,' I reminded her, introducing them one by one. 'This is my friend Jackie,' I added to the children, emphasising the word *friend* for Pam's benefit. Freddie, gratifyingly, shouted out *Ackie! Hello Ackie!* as soon as he saw her, and held up his arms to her, which in turn delighted Jackie. At the same time as calling out a cheerful and badly accented *Bonjour!* to the three still scoffing their eggs and bacon, she lifted Freddie out of the highchair, gave him a cuddle, and raised her eyebrows at me behind his head.

'Still heard nothing?' she asked quietly.

I shook my head, and then, suddenly having a horrible thought, turned to Pam and demanded: 'There weren't any phone calls while I was still asleep, were there?'

'Of course not,' she said, looking offended. 'I'd have told you. Why? Who are you expecting a call from?'

'Nobody,' I replied, illogically. I wasn't giving *her* the satisfaction of knowing that I was half expecting to hear from the police!

'Nosy cow,' Jackie mouthed at me, making me smile. It was so good to have her here, in her too-short skirt and lurid turquoise top, trying out her terrible French on the teenagers, making them snigger.

'I like your earrings,' Emilie said, looking at her shyly. 'And your shoes.'

'Here, try them on,' Jackie said, kicking off her bright green ballet pumps and sliding them across the floor to Emilie.

Pam was scowling as she cleared the table. All that cooking and nappy-changing, only to be outdone in popularity by a pair of green shoes.

'Leave that,' I told her sharply. 'We'll do it. I'll see you out.' Again, the looks of surprise from the grandchildren. Nanny being rude to a neighbour – unbelievable. 'Thanks for your help,' I added grudgingly, only for their sakes.

'Well, I was going to stay and prepare some lunch for you all,' she said, in a tone of high offence. 'But if that's how you feel ...'

'She can stay for lunch, can't she, Grand-maman?' Clément asked, looking a bit anxious. Maybe he thought there wouldn't be any food unless she were there to provide it, and he might not have been far wrong.

'It's OK,' Jackie told him. 'I'll help your grandmère with anything she needs doing. Ça va?'

Again, the giggling at her pronunciation. Again her apologetic shrug that made them forgive her and seem to warm to her. And another scowl from Pam. I was almost starting to enjoy the show. Pam wiped her hands on my tea-towel and took off my apron, and I think she was just on the point of marching out of the house when – yet again – the doorbell rang. The kids stared at me, probably wondering whether it was always like this – a constant stream of visitors (some of them uninvited and unwanted).

But this time it was Stephanie and Ben, with Izzie, and baby Isaac asleep in his car seat.

'Hello.' Steph kissed me and walked straight in, followed by Izzie who was already telling me a complicated story about Princess Sofia.

'Here you go,' said Ben amiably, handing me a bottle of wine. I looked at it, bemused.

'Thank you. What have I done to deserve this?'

Everyone stopped in their tracks and looked at me. Even Izzie paused midway through what appeared to be the most exciting part of her story.

'You've forgotten, haven't you,' said Steph.

'You invited us round for the day,' Ben said.

'Because it's Clem's and Em's first day here,' added Steph.

'Oh, bugger,' I mouthed at her silently. 'I did, didn't I.'

It was supposed to be a lovely family day. We were going to have lunch in the garden – a barbecue, as long as the weather was fine. I'd been planning to make desserts, an apple crumble, and maybe chocolate mousse for the children. Everyone was coming ...

'I asked Michael and Jo, too, didn't I,' I said quietly. What the hell had I been thinking? Why? Why did I think it was always my responsibility to do these things – host the entire family, cook for them all, wait on them all – as if it wasn't enough that I'd got Clem and Em to stay for a week, as if I hadn't done enough by hosting Izzie's birthday party, as if I didn't actually *always* do more than enough for them all?

But of course, I'd planned it – offered it, invited them to it – before everything had kicked off. Before Bob disappeared, before Freddie became an impromptu part of my family, before the dash to Ipswich and the man in the bed who wasn't Bob and before I forgot about Danielle's children coming. Before I chased across town to the hospital to see a daughter who wasn't there anymore. Before Pam took over my family. Despite everything, I had a sudden urge to laugh at the thought that perhaps I should just go away somewhere, somewhere quiet and peaceful where solitude was guaranteed, and leave Pam to cater for the lot of them. See if she still wanted my life so much after that.

'Mum?'

I jumped, realising Steph had been talking to me.

'Mum, are you all right? I said, you didn't *really* forget, did you?'

I could have lied. I could have said *no, of course I didn't forget, I was just teasing you,* and then everyone would have been happy. Everyone would have come in, and sat down, and chatted amongst themselves as usual while I flew around preparing food, entertaining children with one hand and making cups of tea with the other (metaphorically speaking). But something stopped me. Something, perhaps, to do with the fact that actually I didn't even have any food to prepare. No sausages, burgers, chicken wings for the barbecue, no fresh salad to go with it, and certainly no home-made apple crumble or chocolate mousse. Something, maybe, to do with the looks on their faces: looks of total disbelief that I could possibly have had other things to consider, things that might have made this event slip my mind. To be fair, even Steph's asthma attack and hospital admission, once I'd found out about it, would have been enough to make me forget I was hosting a family party the next day, never mind all the other things they didn't know about.

And most of all, it was probably something to do with the way Izzie, who'd now abandoned her Princess Sofia story and had raced ahead down the hallway to the kitchen, was standing, dumbstruck, in the doorway staring at the unlikely gathering in there.

'Hello, Izzie,' Jackie said.

'Izzie!' shouted Freddie, running to throw himself at her.

'Hey!' said Clément, which he obviously thought was a cool English greeting, and the other two cousins on the French side looked up and smiled hello.

Pam, alone, said nothing, having been on the point of being thrown out.

Izzie, with Freddie clinging to her arms, turned back to face us.

'Mummy,' she said, 'there are a *lot* of people in Nanny's house today.'

'And you wonder why I forgot?' I said, just as the doorbell signalled the arrival of the other branch of the family. 'Let them in, can you, Ben? Take them all out in the garden. Do something with the kids. Make everyone a cup of coffee. Write me a shopping list and we'll go to Tesco's later. I'm going upstairs – I haven't had a shower yet, and I slept all night in these clothes, on the sofa.'

Ben opened the door, silently, and ushered Mike, Jo and the twins straight through into the lounge.

'Hello!' I called out after them. 'Sorry I forgot you were coming. Please sort yourself out with drinks. Toby and Clem and Em are in the kitchen. My friend Jackie's here too, but Pam's just going. Be with you in a while.'

I started up the stairs. Steph, alone, was still standing in the hall, watching me.

'Why?' she asked quietly. '*Why* did you sleep in your clothes? Why did you forget we were coming? What's going on, Mum – what's wrong with you? I'm *worried* about you.'

'Me?' I laughed. 'I'm not the one who has asthma attacks, who gets taken to A&E by ambulance, without me even being told about it.'

'I'm fine now.' She shakes her head impatiently. 'But you ... you're not. You're not yourself. You've always been so calm, Mum! So sensible and capable and ... and reliable.' Her eyes filled up with tears. 'We all rely on you.'

I felt a dull thud of pain in my heart. My family – all relying on me. Steph was right. What *was* the matter with me? I was letting everyone down. Forgetting things, losing things, not making puddings. What next? Would I start dropping babies, feeding toddlers whisky in their milk?

'I'll make some coffee,' she said, as I stood, stuck for a reply, staring down at her from halfway up the stairs. 'Go and have your shower.'

I was still there, halfway up the stairs, when Pam came out of the kitchen, heading for the front door with a face like a squashed prune.

'You know what? You're probably right,' I told her departing back. 'My life's a mess. I seem to have lost the plot.'

But I didn't need *her* to tell me that. My own family obviously agreed.

KATE

I Hear Thunder, I Hear Thunder, Hark Don't You?

It's surprising what shock tactics will do. By the time I'd showered, dressed, and gone back downstairs, the kitchen was clean, tidy and free of the smell of bacon, the wash load Pam had put on was finished and hanging on the line, and everyone seemed to be busy.

Jackie was keeping Freddie amused, and thereby seemed to have lumbered herself with the other little ones too, playing a game of *The Farmer's in his Den* which seemed to be going on forever with very little hope of any of them apart from Izzie having much idea what they were doing. Steph and Jo had apparently compiled a shopping list between them, and the men had gone off together to Tesco's. Emilie had gone upstairs to tidy the bedrooms, and Toby was in the garden with Clément, wiping down the garden table, getting extra chairs out of the shed and cleaning the barbecue.

'Thank you,' I said to Jackie. 'I'm so sorry about all that.'

'Don't be silly.' She smiled, and then added with an anxious shrug, 'I just wish we knew where Bob was.'

'Me too.'

'Are you OK now?' she asked quietly. 'If I'd been you, I'd have sent the family packing. You've had enough on your plate already.'

'I know. But that's not their fault. And I *did* forget.'

A wave of guilt washed over me again. *Forgot* Danielle's children coming. *Forgot* the family coming for lunch. *Wasn't there* when Steph needed me.

'Don't blame yourself,' Jackie said, as if she could read my mind. 'You do so much for them. It won't hurt them to get stuck in and help.'

'Will you stay for the lunch? Please?'

'Thanks, Kate, but no. I'll stay for a bit longer to give you a hand, but then I ought to get back. Keith is beginning to think I've got a secret lover.'

'God, yes. I keep forgetting you've got a husband.'

'Damned nuisance, aren't they.' She laughed. 'But I'll hang onto him while he's still so good in bed.'

Steph, who had come over to ask if either of us wanted a coffee, almost recoiled in horror at overhearing the last few words.

'Don't worry,' I told her, laughing too now. 'She's joking.'

'Yes, of course I am,' Jackie said. 'He's not *that* good!'

'Honestly, Mum,' said Stephanie, predictably, watching as Jackie gathered all the kids together again and started *Ring a Ring of Roses*. 'I'm really not sure about her. The things she says! And the things she *wears*.'

'Don't be such a snob,' I told her lightly, giving her a quick hug. 'She's been a good friend and a great help. Now then: where are those guys, with the shopping?'

The guys, when they eventually returned, had been to the pub on the way back from Tesco's, a fact which annoyed Stephanie and Jo far more than it did me.

'I only had a half pint of lager!' Michael said, sounding aggrieved. 'I was driving.'

'And I suppose *you'll* want *me* to drive home later now,' Steph said crossly to Ben, who was doing the inane grinning of someone who's managed to down a few pints very quickly. 'Even though I've been ill, in hospital.'

'You keep saying you're fine now!' he protested with a shrug. 'And you're not drinking anyway.'

'No, I'm not, because I'm feeding your baby, in case you'd forgotten.' Isaac, as if on cue, woke up and started grizzling, and she picked him up, elbowing Ben out of the way. 'I'm in a permanent state of exhaustion, and you can't even be trusted not to go to the pub.'

'Once! Just once, I fancy a couple of beers with my brother-in-law ...'

'While we're all waiting for our food,' Jo joins in, giving Michael a look.

'All right, everyone, calm down, the food won't take long,' I said with a sigh. It was one thing having them all here – another thing if they were going to start bickering. 'Anyway, *I* haven't even had breakfast.'

'You did refuse a plate of bacon and eggs,' Toby reminded me, 'even though it was almost forced on you.'

He gave me a quick grin, having apparently worked out by now why Pam upset me, and I smiled back at him. He'd grown up into a really nice young man – mature, sensible, handsome and intelligent. I wondered, briefly, whether his real father ever thought about Toby: what he looked like, how he'd turned out. What he'd missed, all those years, not being there as his dad.

But then I put it out of my mind. Fathers, paternity issues – I didn't want to think about that right now.

'Have you got a drink?' I asked him. 'We'll start cooking in a minute.'

'I'm fine, thanks, Nan.' The English endearment almost brought tears to my eyes. It was hard, having these grandchildren living abroad, growing up in a different culture, speaking a different language. Hardly ever seeing them. He put an arm round my shoulders. 'I'm sorry, but I'll have to leave soon. I won't stay for lunch. I have work tomorrow.' Again, he gave me the little quick grin, and squeezed my arm like he knew what I was thinking. 'I'll try to stay longer next time. I'm ... sorry I haven't come more often.'

'Don't be silly.' I blinked back the tears. 'I know how busy you all are. You have your own lives to lead. I'm just pleased to see you whenever you can manage it.'

Saying all those things we're supposed to say, while of course, I didn't mean a word of it. I really wanted to say I wished he and his brother and sister lived closer, that they could just get a bus to come and see me instead of booking a ferry. That they could find the time to come more often. And then I felt guilty for thinking it, because I knew *I* should have made more effort to see them, too, if it wasn't for all the other demands on my time, from the rest of the family. I hadn't even remembered they were coming. If I was honest, I hadn't even been looking forward to it – it had felt like a nuisance, like an imposition, being asked to mind the two teenagers. What sort of a grandmother was I?

'Cheer up,' he said gently, watching my face. 'We do know it's hard for you too, Nan. The others – the little ones – they need you more, for now.'

I didn't even bother, this time, to wipe away the tears as we hugged.

'I'll drive you to the station,' I said when I'd managed to compose myself. 'Just let me know when you're ready.'

'No! You're busy. I'll call a taxi, it's no problem.'

'I can give you a lift, Toby,' Jackie offered. She was sprawled on the grass, having just performed '*We all fall down!*' with the children for the third time in a row, and had now announced that she was knackered. 'I'll be going soon too, and I have to pass the station.'

So with two of the company preparing to leave, everyone seemed to be settling down. Isaac, fed and changed, had been put down on a rug to kick his legs in the sunshine, and Stephanie and Jo had given up nagging their husbands and gone into the kitchen to start preparing salad. The twins, and Freddie, were all looking ready for a nap before lunch, while Izzie had brought her doll's pram out into the garden and was happily occupied with an imaginary game of 'taking my baby to the park'. Clément and Emilie were watching the men trying to get the barbecue alight. We were *almost* the picture of a happy family occasion.

Then two things happened.

First, there was an ominous rumble of thunder ... and within minutes, the sky had turned from blue to black, the first few big fat raindrops were splattering on our heads ... and then all hell let loose. In the sudden downpour, Stephanie ran into the garden to grab the baby, the children all began to shriek with excitement and tear around the lawn getting soaking wet, the barbecue, having just sparked into life, was immediately extinguished, leading to much swearing from the men and laughter from the teenagers. Steph, her breathing aggravated by the abrupt change of weather and the way she'd dashed to rescue Isaac from the rain, began to wheeze and cough while I rummaged in her bag for her asthma inhaler. Michael rounded up the children, Jo stripped off their wet things and wrapped them in towels, Ben ran round the house closing doors and windows as the rain continued to beat down in torrents, while Jackie and Toby gauged the distance to Jackie's car outside and agreed they'd wait for the worst to pass before they made their departure.

And then ... then the second thing happened.

Bob turned up.

JACKIE

This Old Man Came Rolling Home

He was there at the front door, with the thunder crashing all around him and the rain dripping off his head and off his soaking wet clothes, and as we all gathered in the hall to see why Kate had shrieked in surprise, he swayed a little on his feet, held onto the door frame and asked, in a really weak, tired voice: 'Can I come in?'

Kate grabbed hold of his arm, like she was afraid he was going to fall over (and actually, it did look quite likely), and pulled him into the house.

'Come and sit down, quickly. Someone put the kettle on. Bob, you need to get out of those wet things. Emilie, can you go and get my dressing-gown from my bedroom, please? It'll have to do for now, Bob, while we dry off your clothes. How about a nice hot shower? Or a whisky? Would you like a whisky? You look as if you need one.'

Bob had allowed Kate to help him into the kitchen and sit him down at the table.

'I just ... I ... j... just ...' he stammered, and then, taking a deep breath, looked straight back at Kate and said: 'I just came for Freddie. I came straight here. I'm so sorry, Kate ... so sorry about it all.'

'Ssh, never mind that now.' Kate had become business-like in her concern for Bob. She glanced at me, her eyebrows raised, before fibbing to him: 'Freddie's having a nap just now, so let's get you warm and dry first and you can see him when he wakes up.'

Taking the cue, I hurried into the lounge, where Freddie was sitting on the sofa with the twins, all of them half asleep with thumbs or dummies in their mouths, being read a *Gruffalo* story by Jo.

'What's going on?' she mouthed to me over their heads.

'Freddie needs to have his nap upstairs,' I said quietly. 'Come on, Freddie – upstairs with Jackie, yes? You can have the rest of the story later.'

Fortunately he was too sleepy to protest. I carried him quickly up to Kate's spare bedroom and put him in one of the twins' cots.

'Have a nice sleep,' I said, giving him a kiss before I drew the curtains and tiptoed out. For a second I felt a strange kind of sadness, wondering when I'd be seeing him again, now that his granddad was back. I'd spent quite a bit of time with him over those couple of days, and I'd got fond of the kid. Yeah, me of all people. Must have been going soft in the head.

'Has he told you where he's been?' I whispered to Kate. She was making Bob a hot cup of tea while he was in the downstairs toilet, getting out of his wet clothes.

'Not yet. That's not the priority at the moment,' she said. 'Have you seen the state of him? He looks ill. He looks like he hasn't slept all weekend.'

'I know. But even so ...'

'And he must have walked all the way from the station. He can hardly stand up, poor man.'

I nodded. I admired Kate for putting Bob's wellbeing first, but if I'd been her, I'd have felt like shaking him. I'd have been interrogating him about why he went to Ipswich, why he dumped poor Freddie on her without asking her permission, what the hell he'd been doing up there since Friday afternoon. After all, she'd had all the stress and worry of it, (and so had I, come to that, rushing her up to Ipswich and back, spending the entire afternoon and half the evening feeding treats to a hyped-up child, not that I minded, of course).

'As soon as he's dried off and rested a bit, I'll see what I can find out,' she added.

We were both distracted for a few minutes, then, by various members of the family coming in and demanding to know what was happening, and who was the guy who'd turned up on the doorstep looking like a tramp and was now sitting in the lounge looking ridiculous in Kate's fluffy cream dressing-gown, and was there any point waiting for the rain to stop or should they instead just cook the food in the oven, and When Is Lunch Nanny, I Am Very Hungry? (That last, from Izzie of course).

'Give the rain another five minutes!' Kate ordered them all, shooing them out of the kitchen. 'It's easing up a bit and the thunder's not so loud. There's still plenty of time to try the barbecue again. Izzie, ask Mummy if you can have a biscuit. But only if you stop whining.'

I had to hand it to her. From the moment Bob arrived, she seemed to have switched from Exhausted and Emotional to Charged and Capable, just like that.

'Would you take that cup of tea in to Bob, please?' she asked me, handing me the steaming mug. 'And give him a couple of biscuits to keep him going. Tell him I'll make him a sandwich or some hot toast in a minute.'

'But ...'

'He probably hasn't eaten today,' she said firmly. 'He can't be expected to wait until we decide what to do about lunch.'

I put the mug of tea down on the coffee-table next to Bob, with two biscuits next to it, and he picked one up immediately, eating it in two mouthfuls, watched by an open-mouthed Izzie. Perhaps Kate was right. The second biscuit disappeared just as quickly.

'He's had *two*,' Izzie said to her mother, her lower lip wobbling when she was promptly told to be quiet.

'Kate said she'll make you a sandwich in a minute. Or some toast,' I told Bob. 'How are you feeling now?'

'Better, thank you, Jackie. So sorry to cause all this fuss. And with Kate's family all here, too,' he added to me in a whisper, looking mortified. 'Seeing me ... like this.'

'Don't worry, it suits you,' I tried to joke, but when he started to run his hands over his two-day growth of stubble and his lank, unwashed thinning hair, I realised he wasn't just referring to the dressing-gown. 'Never mind, I don't suppose you've had a chance to ... wash, or shave, or whatever, during the last couple of days,' I said, hoping this would serve as a hint. Didn't he *realise* we were desperate to know what it had all been about?

But I didn't get a chance to find out whether he was going to answer or not. Kate burst back into the room, looking worried, searching all around her like she'd lost something.

'What's up?' I said.

She went to the fireplace and ran her hand along it, moving ornaments, looking behind framed pictures of the children. Came over to the coffee-table and lifted Bob's cup, feeling over the arms of the sofa, lifting cushions and shaking them.

'What have you lost, Mum?' Stephanie asked, looking up from a conversation with Jo.

'My watch.' Kate was kneeling to look under the sofa now. 'I've only just realised I didn't put it on this morning. It must be in here somewhere. Don't worry, I'll find it later.'

'Not your gold watch?' Stephanie said, looking suddenly severe. 'The one we bought you for your sixtieth?'

'Yes, of course the gold watch, it's the only one I've got,' she retorted, sounding flustered now. 'I'm sure it must be ...'

'Well, it'll be in your bedroom, won't it? If you didn't put it on this morning,' Jo said.

'No, because I slept down here last night, on the sofa. I remember taking it off. I put it ...' She frowned. 'I think I put it on the coffee-table here, next to the sofa, but it's not here now.' She was doing another sweep of the table as she spoke, frowning, looking puzzled.

'Maybe you left it in the bathroom,' Ben suggested.

'Shall we help you look, Mémée?' Emilie, who'd been hanging around with her brother by the patio doors, watching the rain, was looking at her nan sympathetically. 'Don't worry, it will be found, it must not have walked away.' The girl's English was so almost-perfect that her occasional minor slips were kind of quaint, rather than just wrong.

'Not unless it walked away to the same place as the phone, the keys, and the diary,' Michael said – and there was an immediate hush, everyone looking at him with distaste like he'd farted during the National Anthem.

'Of course it hasn't *walked*,' Kate said, but I could see in her eyes that she was shaken, and I didn't blame her. She'd told me her children thought she was losing her marbles because her things had all started to go missing. She hadn't needed Michael to remind her that none of the other things had turned up yet.

'Please don't wake Freddie up!' she called, as the two teenagers disappeared upstairs to begin their search of the bathroom and bedrooms.

'Perhaps you should get your friend here to check his pockets,' Michael said, and this time the silence reverberated, heavy with shock, like static in the air.

'*What* did you say?' Kate turned on him, her voice taut and sharp.

'You thought you left the watch over there, on the table. I'm just pointing out the obvious. He's sitting the nearest.'

'Michael,' Stephanie warned him, but her eyes didn't leave Kate's face. 'I don't think that's ...'

'I'm sorry, Mum, but let's face it, we're all pussy-footing around here, but the fact of the matter is, you've got people coming and going here who we don't know from Adam. I mean, sorry, mate, but who exactly are you? We're all here for a family lunch with my mother, and you just turn up, out of the blue, off the street by the look of you, and no-one asks any questions, you just get fed and watered and dressed in my mother's clothes ...'

I had an inappropriate urge to snigger at this, but managed to stifle it.

' ... and you don't even bother to introduce us, Mum. Are you surprised we all wonder who the hell he is and what he's doing here?'

'Bob is my friend,' Kate said, standing up straight and looking back at Michael with a glare that could have cut through ice. 'That's all you need to know, and I'd be grateful if you'd treat him the way *I* would treat any of *your* friends. With respect. Thank you.'

Silence. She went to turn away, but Bob reached up and touched her arm.

'It's all right, Kate. I'll go. I'll take Freddie, and leave you to it.'

'You're not leaving!' she said. 'I'm not having you made to feel unwelcome in my house, Bob.'

'Honestly, it's fine. I'm feeling better now. I just needed a sit down and ... thank you for the tea ... I'll get my clothes.'

I'd put them in the tumble-dryer. I went out to get them, but even from the kitchen I could hear Kate's voice.

'But we need to talk! About what happened – why you went to Ipswich – why you ended up in hospital! Have you heard from the police? They've got your wallet!'

I came back in with his clothes and handed them over to him in a bundle, not really wanting to look at his underwear. Especially if he'd been wearing them for three days.

'How did you know I'd lost my wallet? How did you even know I'd been to Ipswich?' he was asking Kate, looking at her in surprise.

'It was bloody lucky we found out!' I interrupted angrily. 'We went up there after you! Kate was beside herself with worry! We've *both* been worried sick! What on earth did you expect? Sorry,' I added to Kate. 'But it had to be said.'

He got to his feet, shakily, the dressing-gown hanging ridiculously short above his knees. I averted my eyes, dreading that it might come open.

'I didn't realise,' he said. 'I am so very sorry. I wouldn't have troubled you, obviously, if I'd known how it was going to turn out. I know it was asking a lot. I need to explain.' He looked around the room – at Michael glaring at him, at Stephanie, Ben and Jo all frowning with disapproval and suspicion, at Toby who was looking out of the window and pretending not to be listening, and little Izzie watching him with rapt concentration. Probably wondering, like me, about the security of the dressing-gown. 'But now is probably not the time.'

'No,' Kate agreed. 'You're right. Let's talk later, Bob. As long as you're all right, that's the main thing.'

The woman was a saint. I still wanted to strangle him.

'I'm fine now,' he said again, and holding the dressing-gown together, he tottered out of the room with his bundle of clothes.

'I still say you should check his pockets,' Michael said again as soon as the door of the downstairs loo had closed behind him. 'Was he here when the other things went missing?'

'Oh, for God's sake!' Kate said. She shook her head and flounced out of the room and up the stairs. After a few minutes I heard her, in the hall, handing little Freddie over to Bob and saying goodbye.

'OK, Toby,' I suggested to her eldest grandson as the whole room had once again fallen silent. 'It's hardly raining now. Shall we make a move?'

I didn't know about him, but I wasn't too sorry to go. The storm might have been over, but the atmosphere in that house had turned pretty bloody nasty.

KATE

Going to the Zoo, Zoo, Zoo

The weather cleared up, the barbecue was salvaged, everybody ate and drank, and enjoyed the sunshine in the garden again while the kids played with their toys. I'd like to say the day turned out to be a success, but although I did my best to play the part, I just couldn't get myself into the party mood. I was upset about Bob – seeing him in such a tired and dishevelled state had been a shock, and to be honest I was a little anxious about just handing Freddie back to him, even though the child's place was obviously with his granddad rather than with me. But I wasn't convinced Bob was feeling completely OK. And also, I was upset about losing my watch, on top of the other things. And I was annoyed with Michael about the hostile accusations he'd made about it to Bob, although there was no way I was going to bring that up again and start a proper argument, not in front of all the children.

I called Bob that evening, after everyone had gone home (apart from Clem and Em of course, who were glued to the TV).

'Are you OK?' I asked him.

'Yes, of course. I was just tired, Kate – I'm fine now. And I can't tell you how grateful I am to you, but I've been so worried ...'

'That makes two of us,' I said. 'We had no idea what had happened to you.'

'I know. You must have thought I'd abandoned him. I was supposed to be coming straight back, but it all went wrong.'

'So it seems,' I said. I sighed. No point being angry –
he'd obviously had a rough time of it, what with being in
hospital, and losing his wallet. 'What happened, Bob?'

'It's a long story,' he said.

'OK, well let's just take one thing at a time. I heard you
were taken to hospital. By ambulance.'

'Yes. It was all a bit of a fuss about nothing, really. I
passed out, on the train, and I must have fallen off the seat
and hit my head. Everyone else was more worried about it
than I was.'

'Well, naturally they'd be worried, Bob! A head injury
is always a cause for concern, and they'd want to check
why you passed out in the first place.'

'Yes, that's what they said. They kept me in overnight,
and then they decided I was fine and could go.'

'Go *where*?' I asked, pointedly. 'To see Craig? Was
that the plan?'

'Yes.'

I waited. This was surely where he was supposed to
explain himself. Why all the bloody secrecy, why the need
to smuggle himself off without asking my permission to
leave his grandson with me. Why he couldn't take Freddie
with him. Why he'd behaved so strangely, so completely
out of character. Why he'd caused me and Jackie so much
bloody aggravation.

'I … wanted to have a chat with him,' he said.

'A chat? For God's sake, Bob!'

'I know how it must sound. I know I took the most
appalling liberty, leaving Freddie …'

'That's beside the point. To be quite honest, I'm
worried you've lost the plot. All that sneaking around and
bother, just for a *chat* with your *son*?'

'Well, that was the plan. But with one thing and another
…'

'You lost your wallet. Did you get it back? Did the
police manage to find you?'

'Yes. They called Craig. His number was in my wallet but he'd missed all the previous calls, from the hospital, because he had his own problems, you see.'

To be frank I couldn't really give a monkey's about Craig's problems. I had enough of my own.

'Well, I'm glad you got it back. What a mix-up. Did they tell you – the chap who found it was in hospital, and they thought he was you?'

'Yes, I heard. Look, Kate, I'm sorry but I'll have to call you back. I'd just got Freddie to bed when you called, and he's still not asleep. He's started crying.'

'You've still got him with you? Hasn't Nathan been to pick him up? I thought he was supposed to ...'

'I'll explain later – it's a long story.'

So he kept saying. I was wondering whether we'd ever get to the end of it.

'OK, we'll catch up again tomorrow,' I suggested. 'I just wanted to apologise again for my son being so rude to you earlier.'

'Well, fair enough, he doesn't know me, and I did kind of force myself on you and your family today. But obviously, I have no idea about your watch, I'm afraid.'

'Of course you don't. I've probably just put it down somewhere. I'm getting so absent-minded. Look, how about I come to you tomorrow? I don't normally have any of the children on Mondays. Oh ... hang on – my grandchildren from France are here and I promised to take them somewhere. Can we make it afternoon – probably latish?'

'That'll be fine. See you tomorrow then, Kate. And thank you again. You've been a real friend. I couldn't have blamed you if you'd never spoken to me again.'

It was true. I wouldn't have blamed *myself* if I'd never wanted to speak to him again. But although he'd given me – and Jackie – such a lot of grief, I was quite sure he hadn't intended to. I just couldn't believe it had all been his fault.

Bob was basically a nice, sincere person and I had no intention of taking any notice of my son's nasty slurs against his character. What was more – and I hadn't told anyone this, not even Jackie – I still had that tiny suspicion that he liked me. I mean, not just as a friend. It was just the way he looked and smiled at me sometimes. I can't say I was comfortable with the idea, and I wasn't sure what I was going to do about it, in terms of dissuading him. But it did make me even more certain that he wouldn't have done anything deliberately to upset me.

Clément and Emilie had asked me to take them to the zoo in Colchester. I was somewhat surprised – the zoo was normally my fail-safe day out with Izzie, or even the twins. While they were arguably a bit young for it and sometimes got more excited about being bought an ice-cream or cake from the café there than about the animals, I'd have thought the teenagers were well past being impressed by such things.

'But there is no zoo where we live!' Emilie explained. 'I love to see the animals!'

'We haven't been to a zoo since last time we stayed with you,' Clément said. 'It's too far, at home.'

It was true, they lived in the back of beyond. The nearest town of any size was, in character, more like a village, and it was probably half a day's drive to anywhere teenagers might like to go. Not for the first time, I wondered why the hell Danielle and Marcel had decided to settle somewhere so remote. I felt sorry for the kids. And because I was conscious of the fact that I'd already let them down and started off their week badly, I'd agreed readily: the zoo would be fun. It would give me a break from worrying about everything else. And rather than do it on a day when I had the twins, and would have to take them along with us too, we might as well go on Monday.

We were in luck: we woke up to a beautiful morning and made an early start. The tickets cost me an arm and a leg but I was happy to treat them. Clem and Em had been so good, so uncomplaining about the strange goings-on at my house since their arrival (in fact I think they'd found it all quite exciting), and I was infused with warmth for them both, feeling quite guilty about my reluctance to host them. It was unfair of me, I told myself as I led them through the turnstiles into the zoo, to cast all teenagers in the same light. These two had turned out to be nice kids, and in fact I was wondering now why I'd insisted on only having them for a week. No wonder Danielle thought I was mean. Perhaps I'd call her tonight and suggest keeping them for a bit longer. Two weeks wouldn't kill me, would it, or maybe even three. It'd give her a break, and save Toby coming back for them quite so soon.

And then I looked round, and they'd both gone.

It took me some time to grasp the fact that they'd actually buggered off – that they hadn't just gone briefly out of sight in the crowd. I waited, peering behind people, stepping to the side of the path, expecting at any minute to see them catching me up. Then I walked on a little way, not particularly rushing, thinking they'd passed me somehow and I'd meet them coming back to find me. When I still couldn't see them, I decided it'd be best to wait for them by the entrance. Being the school holiday, the zoo was already busy and it wouldn't make any sense for me to wander off in search of them. They couldn't have gone far, I reasoned, before they realised they'd lost me. It didn't cross my mind at that point that 'losing' me was exactly what they'd planned to do.

So there I stood, close enough to the entrance to spot them when (I thought) they'd surely come back looking for me. I checked my watch. Roughly ten minutes since I'd noticed they were missing. Fifteen minutes. Twenty.

Thirty. By now, I was getting cross. What was the matter with them? Surely, even if they'd got lost, they were old enough and sensible enough to ask someone to direct them back to the entrance – it was pretty obvious that was where I'd wait. Once again I cursed my stupidity for having lost my mobile. I really must get myself a new one – this was *just* the kind of occasion when it would have helped.

After forty minutes, I was fed up with standing around waiting for them, but still not particularly worried. They weren't toddlers, after all. It'd be ridiculous to start a search for 'missing children', at their age. I put my irritation to one side and started trying to decide where else they might have chosen to go and wait for me to find them. Surely not back to the car? No – I'd been watching the turnstiles. I'd have seen them going out. Would they be daft enough to just stroll round the zoo on their own, looking at the animals, thinking we'd somehow bump into each other by chance? It suddenly occurred to me, perhaps a little belatedly, that perhaps I *should* be more concerned. OK, they weren't little children, but they *were* still kids. They shouldn't be left to wander around here on their own – it was a big zoo, and it was crowded, and who knew what kind of people hung around here, looking for innocent young teenagers fresh off the boat from rural France? And supposing Clem and Em had been split up – lost each other as well as me in the crowd? Would either of them be stupid enough, naïve enough, to be lured away … perhaps with an offer of a Coke or an ice-cream?

Coke! Ice-cream! Why didn't I think of that? The natural place any teenager would head for if they didn't know where else to go would be the café. I was so relieved to have thought of it, to finally have somewhere to go, something positive to try other than standing here waiting for a glimpse of either of them, that I almost ran to the nearest signpost, and from there, in the direction of the café, arriving so out of breath that I fell through the door gasping. People looked up, staring at me, as I stood clutching the back of a chair, getting my breath back as I looked around the room, from table to table, and finally realised my grandchildren weren't there.

'Excuse me,' I said urgently to one of the women serving behind the counter. 'Have you seen two teenagers in here this morning?' I stopped. How ridiculous. There were teenagers everywhere. 'Have you served any kids with French accents?' I tried again.

She looked back at me impassively. 'I sorry. I not understand. I serve kids, yes?'

Polish, or maybe Slovakian – she wouldn't know a French accent in English if it came with bells and whistles attached.

'Never mind.' I turned to go back out. Nothing else for it, I'd have to speak to someone official – find out if there was a place for lost children – get an announcement made, or something. I *was* worried now. How the hell had they disappeared so suddenly?

And then, as I walked back out of the café door, I saw them.

They were sitting at one of the tables on the patio area outside. I'd hurtled into the café so fast I hadn't even noticed there was an outside eating area – it was slightly to the side of the building. They were with three other teenagers. Clément was tipping his chair back on two legs, laughing loudly and holding – was that a *cigarette*? – in one hand, and a bottle of Coke in the other. And Emilie … Emilie was sitting very close to one of the boys. And he had his arm round her.

I didn't stop to think. I didn't stop to give them a chance to notice me, to put down the cigarette, shake the boy's arm off, sit up straight, perhaps look abashed or apologetic. I marched straight over to them, thumped both hands down on the table, making them all jump and making Clément almost fall off his chair as it righted itself onto four legs and wobbled so that his Coke and his cigarette both looked in danger, for a second, of being dropped.

'What the *hell* do you think you're doing?' I demanded.

He was frantically putting out the cigarette, waving the smoke away from his mouth as if it would make any difference. He blinked, he stuttered, he mumbled, a mixture of French and English, none of it comprehensible. He hadn't yet looked me in the eye.

'And *you*!' I turned to Emilie, who was now sitting bolt upright, her eyes wide, staring straight ahead of her. 'Do you even *know* this boy?'

'We have been talking,' she said. 'They are from Romford.' She rolled the 'R' of Romford, making it sound a hell of a lot more exotic than it deserved.

'I don't care if they're from Buckingham Palace!' I said. 'You don't know them! Clear off!' I added to the three boys. 'I'm their grandmother – they're with me.'

'We were here first,' protested the boy who'd been fondling my granddaughter. 'They came and sat with us. The kid asked me to get his smokes for him.'

He looked about seventeen. I wanted to slap his stupid face.

'Clément, Emilie, get up, we're going home,' I said, in a tone that brooked no argument. I gave the three Romford boys a final withering glare and, taking my two charges by their arms, not caring how much I humiliated them, I marched them back towards the exit.

'Are we not going to see the animals?' Emilie asked tearfully.

'No, you are not. And if you don't want me to report back to your mother about this, you'd better both stop complaining.'

Not that Clément had yet uttered a single word.

In silence we returned to the car. In silence they climbed into the back seat. In silence I started the engine and headed back to the main road. After a mile or two, when I'd calmed down enough, I glanced in the mirror, to see the pair of them looking out of opposite windows, studiously ignoring each other.

'Well,' I said, '*That* was a waste of my time and money.'

'Sorry,' Emilie whispered.

'We were only meeting some English people,' Clément argued. 'That's why we come to England, isn't it? To practise our English?'

'Don't give me that, Clément. You sneaked away from me – don't pretend you got lost, I waited for you for nearly an hour! Nearly an hour, waiting, worrying about you ...'

'Sorry,' Emilie whispered again.

'And as for you!' I retorted, catching her eye in the mirror. 'Snuggling up to that lout! A complete stranger! Did he touch you, for God's sake?' Anything could have happened. I shivered. God, it didn't bear thinking about.

'Of course not!' she said, tearfully. 'Connor was a nice boy!'

'*Connor* had no business putting his arm round you, Emilie – you're only thirteen and you didn't even know him. I hope this isn't how you behave with boys back at home?'

'No! They are all boring! None of them are as nice as Connor.' She sniffed into a tissue. Any minute now, she'd be telling me she loved him and she couldn't help it.

'Grand-maman's right, Emilie,' Clément told her. 'You shouldn't have let him cuddle you. I should have stopped him. I should have been protecting you.'

'Yes,' I agreed. 'You should have.'

'It was your fault anyway!' Emilie retorted. '*He* made me go to the café, Grand-maman! I wanted to come back to you!'

'No you did not! You wanted to come to the café too!'

'Tu mens, cochon! Tais-toi, imbécile!'

The argument immediately degenerated into an exchange of quick-fire French insults, until finally I shouted at them both to shut up, and added in my sternest possible voice:

'You've both disappointed me today, and that's all there is to it. Now there'll be no outing to the zoo, and if we go anywhere else this week, you'll have to stay with me and be watched the whole time, like I would with Izzie.'

'You won't tell our parents?' Clément asked sulkily.

'I suppose they don't know about your smoking?'

I glanced in the mirror and was pleased to see he'd had the grace to blush.

'No,' he admitted quietly. 'But I've only tried a few times.'

'Then now would be a good time to *stop* trying it. Before you find you can't. And before you ruin your health.'

'Oui, c'est vrai, Clément,' said Emilie primly. 'I have told you. Smoking is dirty and stupid, isn't it, Grand-maman.'

'Ferme la bouche, stupide!'

'OK! Enough! Smoking is stupid, cuddling up to strange boys is stupid, wandering off from me in a busy place and leaving me to worry about you is just plain bad manners and bad behaviour. Now, that's *it*! I don't want to hear any more from either of you about it. Understood?'

Yes was muttered by both of them as they continued to stare out of their own windows.

We were home in time for a sulky lunch together. Needless to say, I'd changed my mind about offering to have them for an extra week – what the hell had I been thinking of? Had I *completely* lost my mind? Or forgotten how bloody difficult and annoying teenagers could be?

226

Well, I wasn't going to let these two out of my sight any more if I could help it. I called Bob and told him we'd have to shelve our get-together for now. Much as I wanted to find out what *his* story was, this time I definitely had to put my responsibility to my own family first. Whether they liked it or not!

KATE

We All Fall Down

The next day, Tuesday, I had the twins as usual. There was no playgroup, it being the school holiday, so apart from a trip to the shops (with Clément and Emilie trailing along with us, at my insistence), we spent the day mainly in the garden. The twins played with their toys and in the paddling pool, and chased each other round in circles, while the teenagers stretched out in the sun reading on their iPads and we all gradually got over the previous day's hostilities. By the time I'd given them their tea – fish fingers again, as there was little else the twins would eat at that point – I was feeling tired. It hadn't been a particularly difficult day, but with everything else that had been going on recently, I was ready for a break. I found myself looking at the clock and hoping Michael wouldn't be too late picking the children up. I was pleased to see his car pull up outside at six o'clock on the dot, and when I opened the front door to him, there were shouts of joy from the twins. But Michael himself looked anything but happy.

'I need to talk to you,' he said, sitting down heavily on the sofa.

'That sounds ominous.'

'Well.' He scratched his head, pulled at his tie. 'I should probably just come straight out and say it. I expect you'll be relieved, anyway. Jo and I have made a decision, Mum. We've found a childminder.'

'What for?' I looked at him in confusion. 'You don't need to – I'll be around – I'm not going to France, am I.'

I'd almost forgotten the conversation I'd had with him a few weeks back. I'd mentioned that Danielle had been trying to persuade me to go to France during the summer.

There had been a very half-hearted suggestion that I might agree to go over for a week, and that Mike and Jo would make alternative arrangements for the twins.

'I didn't mean just for that, Mum. I meant permanently.'

'Oh.' The word came out of my mouth on a sharp expiration of breath, as if I'd been winded. I sat down opposite him, my legs suddenly feeling weak. 'Why?'

'Well, let's face it,' he began, almost aggressively, making me sit back in my chair in surprise, 'It's too much for you, isn't it. Having these two for three days every week.'

'No, it isn't. I've never said it is, have I?'

'Not in so many words. But it's obvious. You're not as young as you were ...'

'You say the nicest things,' I tried to joke, but he didn't smile.

'You should be living your own life. Not having the grandkids inflicted on you all the time.'

'Michael, they *are* my life. A big part of it, anyway. I enjoy having them – I keep telling you that! Why on earth would you want to fork out for a childminder?' I paused, suddenly worried. 'Is it something I've done wrong? You would tell me, wouldn't you? I mean, I know I'm old-fashioned, but I do try to keep to the rules. I don't give them too many sweets or biscuits. I've never smacked them or anything like that.'

'Of course you haven't,' he soothed, sounding suddenly less hostile. 'Mum, of course you haven't done anything wrong – you couldn't if you tried. You've been amazing, having the kids every week. They've loved coming here. Honestly, we couldn't be more grateful.'

'But now you think I'm too old. All of a sudden. What is it – you're worried I might drop one of them on their heads? Or maybe you really do think I'm losing my marbles, just because I've mislaid a few things recently?

You think I'm going to leave the children somewhere, in a shop or playgroup or whatever, and come home without them? Is that it?' I demanded, my voice wobbling slightly.

Michael just shook his head, looking down at the twins, who were playing on the floor at his feet. And in the silence, I suddenly thought I understood.

'It's all this nonsense about my friends, isn't it! I can't believe you're serious ...'

'Not just that,' Michael said quietly, lifting his eyes to meet mine now. 'Not the friends so much, actually, although it did convince us we'd made the right decision – that performance here on Sunday with that old guy turning up uninvited.'

'His name's Bob!' I said, exasperated now beyond measure. 'And you were horribly rude to him, actually – accusing him of stealing my watch!'

'Well, have you found it yet?' he retorted, fixing me with a challenging look.

'No. I haven't, and I haven't found the phone either, or the car keys, or the diary. I've been a bit too busy, that's all.'

'You see! *That's* what we're all saying. Those things are important, Mum. It's serious that they've gone missing. If you're too busy even to look for them, then obviously everything's got too much for you.'

'What's all this *we*? *We're all* saying?' I interrupted. 'You wouldn't be referring to your sisters, by any chance?'

'Well.' He looked slightly awkward. 'Yes, OK, Steph's been saying for a while that it's got too much for you, having the twins. And Danielle's been saying for ages,' he ploughed on, ignoring my protests, 'that it isn't right.'

'I see.'

'What? Mum, I've argued with them both about this ever since the twins were born, but you know what? I'm sick of it, sick of everyone telling me I'm taking liberties by letting you look after them.'

'You're *not* taking liberties. It's got nothing to do with Danielle or Stephanie. *We* agreed this between us, and I'm happy with it, so as long as *you're* happy with it, what's the problem?'

He sighed. 'The thing is, I'm not happy with it anymore. It's not your fault,' he added quickly. 'It's been great. But it's time for a change.'

'I see,' I said stiffly. 'Well, I'm sorry if you think I'm not capable of looking after your children anymore.'

'It's not that. Please, don't be like this about it. You can still see them – weekends, whatever, it's not like we're, I don't know, moving to America or anything.'

'That's not even remotely funny,' I said.

Michael got up and crossed the room to sit next to me.

'Please don't make this harder for me,' he said quietly.

'Don't do it, then! There's no reason! It's just Danielle, bloody well interfering. Just Steph being hormonal.'

'No. It's me, and Jo, deciding to do the right thing. To stop *putting* on you, Mum, and start organising our own childcare, like responsible parents. Like you brought us up to be.'

'And you can afford it, can you? This childminder?'

'Yes.' He looked away, looking slightly shifty. Obviously it was going to cost an arm and a leg. I sighed with exasperation. This was ridiculous.

'Right, I'm going to speak to them both – Stephanie and Danielle – and tell them to mind their own business. I'll sort it out, OK?'

'No, Mum. You'd just make things worse. Don't get involved. Just leave it, please.' He paused. 'The twins are starting with the childminder next week. It's all arranged.'

'I see.' I swallowed. 'So I'm still allowed to have them for the rest of this week?' I asked with heavy sarcasm. 'You think I can cope?'

'Unless you ... don't want to, in the circumstances. I'll take a couple of days off, if necessary.'

'Don't be absurd. Of course I'll have them. And there's still time to just cancel that childminder.'

'Sorry, Mum. That's not going to happen.' He leaned down to kiss me. 'Come on, kids. Say bye-bye to Nanny.'

Say bye-bye to Nanny. Such an innocuous phrase, but suddenly it made me feel like crying.

It was a warm night and I slept badly, throwing off the duvet, tossing and turning as I went over and over the conversation with Michael in my head. I'd decided not to phone either of my daughters until the following day. I needed to calm down first. By the time morning came, it was raining. No playing in the garden today. The sky was grey and everything looked dark and miserable, matching my mood exactly.

What was it all about? I couldn't stop thinking about it, couldn't concentrate on reading the twins their stories or discussing with Clément and Emilie the urgent question of whether, in light of their good behaviour since Monday, I could now give them a reprieve of sentence and allow them at least to walk to the shops and back on their own.

'We'll take the twins with us!' Emilie suggested brightly. 'To give you a rest, yes?'

'No, absolutely not!' I retorted, my full attention immediately restored. 'It's hard enough for me to trust the two of you on your own after what happened at the zoo. I certainly wouldn't trust you with the children.'

And then I remembered that apparently I wasn't to be trusted with them anymore myself. Had I really been so very unreliable lately? I mean, OK, there had been a couple of incidences of forgetfulness, but surely not enough to merit a complete ban on me having the twins? It *must* be, as Michael implied, more about the criticism from his sisters. The sooner I had it out with them both, the better.

'OK, Clément,' I said, somewhat reluctantly. 'To the shops and straight back. You look after Emilie, you don't talk to any strangers, you don't attempt to buy cigarettes.' He'd never get away with it anyway. He looked even younger than his fifteen years.

'Of course not!' he said, as if such things had never crossed his mind before.

'I'm giving you half an hour,' I warned him. 'You have your mobiles on you? Good – keep them turned on. If you're not back by ten-thirty, you're in trouble. Understand?'

'Yes.' He frowned. 'I'm fifteen, Grand-maman, not five.'

I nodded, deciding it wouldn't help to remind him once again *why* he and his sister were being treated like five year olds. Perhaps if they'd learnt their lesson and proved it now, I could ease up a bit on them. It wasn't much fun for any of us, having them sulking around the house.

I sat the twins in front of the TV watching *CBeebies* – without feeling the slightest twinge of guilt about it – and phoned Stephanie first.

'What have you been saying to Michael?' I demanded as soon as she answered the phone.

'Sorry? What do you mean?' She sounded taken aback, and no wonder – I hadn't even said hello or asked how they all were.

'You know what I mean. That same old tired story about how I shouldn't be looking after the twins. It's obviously finally got to him. He's stopping me from having them.'

'Oh.' There was a silence. And then: 'Yes, I know.'

'You *know*? Why didn't you tell me?'

'Well, sorry, Mum, but I didn't think it was my place to say anything to you. It's their decision, isn't it. I don't know why you seem to think it's my fault.'

'Really, Stephanie?' I sighed with irritation. 'You've been nagging him and Jo about it for months! It was none of your business!'

'That's not why they decided to stop sending the twins to you, Mum,' she said quietly. 'If he told you that, he was just trying to make you feel better.'

'How's that supposed to make me feel better? I love having the twins! I love having *all* the children, you know that. I suppose you'll be telling me next you don't want me to look after Izzie, ever again!'

There was a horrible moment of complete silence before she said, quickly: 'Of course I'm not saying that. But you've got to admit, Mum …'

'What? I've got to admit what?' The moment of silence had unnerved me. Had Steph actually considered it? Stopping asking me to look after Izzie? What was going on here? What had I done?

'You don't seem to be coping as well as usual,' she said. 'I mean, if it was just one or two things, fair enough, we'd put it down to your age. But well, quite honestly, we've all been worried about you. You're losing things, forgetting things …'

'OK, so I've been a bit busy! I've had one or two things going on! But I'm still perfectly capable of looking after the children, for God's sake!'

I turned round to glance at the twins as I spoke, just in time to see Amelia, who'd apparently got bored with *CBeebies*, picking up the wastepaper bin and emptying it over Alfie's head. Alfie immediately started to cry and getting to his feet, covered in bits of rubbish, tissues and used wet-wipes, pushed his sister backwards so that she landed flat on her back and started yelling too. As I broke off from the conversation with Stephanie to tell them to shush, that I'd be with them in a moment, the doorbell rang and I could hear Clément and Emilie outside on the step, arguing fiercely in French.

'I'm going to have to go,' I said wearily. 'All hell's breaking loose here, as usual.'

It was just a turn of phrase. It's just something you say, isn't it – it doesn't actually mean anything. It didn't mean the kids were in mortal danger or that the house was about to fall down around us. But the way Stephanie simply said '*I see*', and the tone she said it in, made my heart sink. I seemed to have got myself marked down now as completely incompetent – a grandmother who couldn't be trusted to care for her grandchildren without some disaster befalling them. And I had no idea how I was going to convince everybody otherwise.

PAM

Three, Four, Knock on the Door

It seemed to me that the more I did to help Kate, to try to make up for my previous lapses of politeness and be a good friend to her, the less thanks I got. I mean, I'd apologised, hadn't I, and although I did understand that she'd find it difficult to forgive my rudeness on those couple of occasions, I thought I'd done more than enough since then to show I wasn't normally like that.

The thing was, I really did enjoy being part of it all. It had been such a pleasure, getting to know the French teenagers, helping Kate out by babysitting for that little boy Freddie and then cooking breakfast for everyone on the Sunday morning. I'd felt … like I was part of the family. I was so happy, having people around me who needed me and appreciated me. All of them apart from Kate herself, it seemed, and yet she was the one who needed the most help! Why couldn't she see that? Surely most people who were as completely disorganised as she was would have welcomed the support of someone like me who could take charge and smooth things over for her?

The most irritating thing was that she seemed to prefer having that Jackie woman around, and yet you only had to look at her to realise she was as hopeless as Kate herself. At least Kate, despite her obvious faults, was a natural, loving grandmother. Anyone could see how much she adored those children – she was just so forgetful and shambolic about everything. Whereas Jackie really didn't seem to have a clue. How she managed to cope with that little granddaughter of hers (Autumn! I'd never heard of such a name!), and how anyone trusted her with the child, I had no idea. Apart from anything else, she tried to dress like a teenager and spoke like a navvy.

I didn't see any of them on the Monday or Tuesday, but on the Wednesday I was at the shops when I heard someone speaking very loudly in French and sure enough, it was Clément and Emilie, arguing over some money.

'Hello!' I called to them. 'Are you all right?'

'Hello.' They both answered me politely, still looking disgruntled with each other. That's teenagers for you – I know. I had more than enough dealings with them when I was teaching. 'How are you?'

'I'm fine, thank you. But do you need some help with your money?' I asked kindly, thinking that perhaps they hadn't quite got to grips with the English coins. I blamed the Euro, actually. Before that was introduced, everyone in Europe had to cope with various different currencies, but now they all had it easy and it had made them lazy.

'No, we're OK,' Clément said. 'We're used to it. We come to England every year.'

'And every year,' Emilie said, pouting at him, 'you *patronise* me.' She said the word with a delightful French inflection, making me smile. 'You think I'm still a child who can't count!'

'No, Emilie, that isn't true. I don't patronise you. But Grand-maman told me I have to look after you, and you know she wouldn't want you to spend all your money on trashy magazines.'

'Ces magazines ne sont pas *trashy*!' she retorted, hands on hips, eyes blazing at her brother as she swung wildly between languages. 'They're about ... celebrities ... les célébrités britanniques – they help me to learn the *culture*!'

'Shall I settle the argument?' I offered. Diplomacy was called for, you see. 'Perhaps if you just buy *one* magazine for now, Emilie, and show your grandma, then if she agrees that it's not a waste of your money you can buy another one tomorrow?'

'That's fair, isn't it, Emilie?' Clément said.

'No, not if you consider how *you* spend *your* money when Grand-maman isn't looking,' she said. 'Getting someone to buy you cigarettes! And now the packet is hidden in your room, Clément – don't think I didn't know! Would you like Grand-maman to know about that, and tell Maman?'

There was immediately another angry exchange in French between the two of them, the gist of which I was able to interpret as meaning Emilie was a nasty tell-tale and Clément was a fat pig.

'Well, this isn't helping, is it,' I pointed out when they'd both run out of insults.

'No, and we have to get back. We're only allowed half an hour,' Clément said. 'So hurry up and buy your one magazine, Emilie. It's the best solution.'

She huffed and puffed and marched into the newsagent's, while he watched her, shaking his head.

'Half an hour?' I asked him. I know it was none of my business, but it seemed very odd, Kate giving them such a short time limit, as if they were little children.

'Yes, since Monday when Emilie got us both into trouble by being found with a boy.' He tutted and raised his eyes. 'He was older than her, and a stranger.'

'Oh, my goodness.' I felt quite alarmed. I didn't like to ask exactly what had been happening with this boy. Emilie hadn't seemed that kind of girl to me, but then again, from my experience with teenagers I was well aware that their hormones could lead them into all kinds of unsavoury situations. 'Where was your grandmother when this was going on?'

'Looking for us,' he said, and gave a short laugh. 'We were at the zoo.'

Before he could tell me any more, Emilie returned, carrying a copy of one of the worst examples of sensationalist gutter journalism. I managed to hide my distaste. Surely Kate wouldn't allow her to buy any more like *that*. But then again, who knew what Kate was letting them get up to? By the sound of things, Clément was not only smoking but hiding cigarettes in his room, and Emilie … well, I hardly liked to imagine what Emilie had been doing while Kate was 'looking for them' at the zoo. How had she managed to lose them in the first place? She really was hopeless. If only she'd asked me to go with them! I'd have so enjoyed having a day out with these two kids. All they needed was a bit of proper adult guidance. And it didn't seem as if they were getting any of *that* – not this week, anyway.

'Shall I walk back with you?' I asked them now. 'Have you finished your shopping, Clément?'

'Yes, thank you.'

'He's bought *sweets*,' Emilie said derisively. 'Such a waste of money.'

'I bought them for the twins,' he retorted. 'And for Grand-maman. To make up for … what happened on Monday.'

'Huh,' was all Emilie said.

But I was thinking – what a nice young man. If he'd bought more cigarettes, of course, I'd have gone back to the shop with him and told the shop assistant in no uncertain terms that I would report them for serving cigarettes to a young person under the age of eighteen. Kate might believe in being lenient about such matters but I didn't agree. It needs to be taken seriously.

'I hope you *aren't* smoking, Clément,' I said calmly as we started to walk back. 'I know some people think it looks *cool*, but all it actually does is destroy your health.'

'I told you,' Emilie said rather smugly in French, and Clément looked like he wanted to kick her.

'I know about the risks,' he said. 'I'm not stupid. I just tried *one*.'

'Huh!' went Emilie again, and I thought it might be better to leave the subject alone. In fact the best thing, I decided suddenly, might be to have a discreet word about it with Kate. If she was any kind of grandmother at all, she couldn't possibly take offence at *that*, could she. She'd surely have to be grateful to me for bringing it to her attention.

The two teenagers were still arguing when we arrived at Kate's house. She apparently hadn't trusted them with a door key (which in my view might have encouraged a sense of responsibility) so we had to wait on the doorstep in the rain while from inside, we could hear the sound of the twins crying.

'I wonder what's wrong with the little ones,' Emilie said, trying to peer through the glass in the front door.

Probably Kate having some kind of disaster again, I thought to myself – and at that moment the door was flung open.

'Sorry, I was on the phone,' she said. And then, seeing me, 'What do *you* want?'

Which I thought was unnecessarily rude, really, considering how much I'd done for her already. She was holding Amelia in her arms, jiggling her and trying to quieten her screams, while Alfie, whose hair seemed inexplicably to be covered in bits of paper and disgusting used tissues, was clinging to her legs and grizzling.

'I presume it's another bad day?' I said.

And believe it or not, she burst into tears.

I ushered Clément and Emilie into the house, took Amelia out of Kate's arms, passing her to a very willing Emilie, and told Kate to go and sit down while I cleaned Alfie up the best I could. I really would have liked to wash his hair. God only knew what bacteria were lurking in those tissues – but perhaps I'd manage to do that later.

'Put the kettle on, please, Clément,' I called. 'I'll make your grandmother a good strong cup of coffee.'

It was quite obvious that things were going from bad to worse. She couldn't cope. I needed to have a serious talk with her, pointing out (without any suggestion of blame, of course) the way her problems seemed to be escalating, and outlining a proposal for how I could help. I doubted very much whether she'd resist the offer this time. She certainly wouldn't want things to reach the point where she had to tell her children she couldn't manage to look after the grandkids anymore. I'd suggest that to begin with, I'd come in every day to help out. Make lunch, perhaps take the children out for a while to give her a break, that kind of thing. I'd say that we could always stop the arrangement if she seemed to be managing better. But somehow I didn't think that was going to happen. She was going to need me. I was sure of it.

'Kate,' I began, putting the mug of coffee down on the table next to her. She had her head back against the cushions now, her eyes closed as if she was exhausted. 'How are you feeling now?'

'Sorry,' she said at once, her eyes flying open. 'Just being silly. Feeling a bit tired ... didn't sleep very well. I'll be fine now.'

Not even a *thank you*, even though I'd got the twins sitting nicely and quietly now with a biscuit each and fresh cups of water and I'd persuaded the older two to start emptying the dishwasher and taking the clean washing out of the machine. But I overlooked the lack of gratitude. She wasn't feeling herself.

'To be honest, I'm *not* sure you will be fine, Kate,' I said gently. She gave me a frown of surprise but I carried straight on. It had to be said. 'I appreciate that you're probably suffering from some kind of depression ...'

'What!' She was sitting up straight now, the surprise on her face giving way to annoyance. But I ploughed on. Nobody with depression likes to admit it, I know that.

'I understand how difficult it is, looking after children, and especially with the added burden of having teenagers in the house,' I said. 'I do have a lot of experience with teenagers – I was a teacher at a comprehensive school, you see. And actually, what I *intended* to talk to you about today was the issue of Clément's smoking. Did you *know* he had cigarettes hidden in his room? Were you aware that he's putting his health at great risk by ...'

'What the hell?' she said, looking like she was about to get up and hit me. 'Who the hell asked you to stick your nose into it?'

'It's OK, I've had a talk to him, but I guessed you might not know it was going on,' I said quickly. 'And I'm sorry to have to say, he also told me there was an incident on Monday with Emilie and a boy. I don't know exactly how far things went, it's rather a delicate situation but obviously we need, between us, to ...'

'*What*?' she said again, red in the face now. '*We* need to ...? *We* don't need to do anything! *You* just need to get the hell out of my house and stop interfering! How many times do I have to say this? It's unbelievable!'

'All right, all right, calm down now,' I said, wishing I'd had the sense to leave those more important issues for a better time. 'I know you're under stress. More to the point, Kate, I think you know, don't you ... you've reached the point where you've got to accept that you need some help. Take just now, for instance. Both the twins crying, mess all over the place – nobody's blaming you! But an extra pair of hands would make all the difference. Come on, now, admit it. You really do need me to help you, don't you.'

She got slowly to her feet. For a minute she didn't say a word, just stood there, looking at me, her face like thunder. I wasn't sure whether she was going to shout at me or start crying again. But when she did finally speak, it was in this strange, flat voice as if she'd just given up caring.

'It might interest you to know,' she said, 'as you seem to be obsessed with every detail of my sodding life …' I flinched at the ugly word but allowed her to finish. She was obviously totally out of control. 'After tomorrow I won't be looking after the twins anymore. My son apparently agrees with you, and it seems my daughters do too. I'm no longer considered fit to take care of the children. So no, I don't need your help, or your bloody interference, and if you think I'm depressed, it's because I'm absolutely sick of you turning up on my doorstep making me feel even worse than I do already.'

I must say, I didn't see *that* coming. Although I shouldn't really have been surprised. Let's face it, her children weren't wrong! But it was a shame I hadn't had a chance to help her out with the twins before it came to this.

'Well, let's see. Would your son perhaps give you another chance if you told him I was going to give you some help?' I suggested.

'NO!' she yelled. 'No, no, no! Can't you get the message? I don't want your help! How many times do I have to ask you to clear off and leave me alone?'

I was beginning to think it was actually something worse than depression. She'd sounded completely delusional there, for a moment. Anyone would think I was being a nuisance to her.

KATE

This is the Way we Wave Goodbye, Wave Goodbye, Wave Goodbye

I didn't even have words to describe how astounding her impertinence was. Where did she get off, coming to my house yet *again*, despite being told more than enough times now that she wasn't welcome, sticking her oar in, criticising me, talking as if my grandkids were somehow her responsibility! It was unbelievable. But to be honest, I was far more concerned with the situation in my own family than anything else at that point in time. I'd even practically forgotten about poor Bob, almost forgotten any of that stuff had ever happened. I just couldn't believe I was being 'sacked' as the carer of my own grandchildren.

Having got nowhere with my conversation with Stephanie, I tried several times that day, and again during the evening, to speak to Danielle. I knew my eldest daughter well. If anyone had been stirring it, playing on her brother's conscience about me having the twins, it'd be her. But I couldn't get hold of her. Maybe she and Marcel were taking the opportunity to go out gallivanting somewhere out of mobile range while their children were with me. Or maybe she knew exactly why I was calling her and didn't want to pick up.

The next day, Thursday, Michael brought the twins round instead of Jo. He was carrying a bouquet of flowers, and the twins were clutching a piece of coloured paper each, covered with crayon scribbles and with 'Thank You Nanny' printed on the top in Jo's writing. I felt like a teacher on the last day of the school year, saying goodbye to my favourite pupils.

244

'It doesn't have to be like this,' I whispered to him after thanking them all. 'I don't see the need.'

'It's all decided, Mum,' he said calmly. 'Have a nice day.'

Well, I had to, didn't I, for the children's sake. For their sake, I couldn't argue the point any further, and I couldn't be anything other than my usual cheerful self with them. I wished it wasn't the summer holiday. What I'd really like to have done was to take the twins to the music group; it would have taken my mind off everything. Thinking about this gave me an idea. I still couldn't quite face seeing Bob today. I'd had to mentally shelve his problems for now and if I saw him, I'd naturally be thrown back into trying to get to the bottom of all that business again. I felt bad about it, but it'd have to wait. However, Thursday was Jackie's day off – the day she looked after little Autumn. I phoned her and asked if she'd like to come round for the day 'as there's no music group on.'

She appeared to hesitate. 'Just me? Or have you asked Bob too?'

'No.' I frowned. 'I know it sounds bad, but I can't quite face talking to Bob about his problems at the minute. I'm feeling a bit down, myself. I'll explain when you get here.'

Having confiscated the remainder of Clément's cigarettes and given him and Emilie more dire warnings about their behaviour, I relented a little further and allowed them to spend the morning in town, with various conditions attached about coming back on time, phones being switched on, and the promise that if they stuck to my rules I'd take them somewhere more interesting the following day when I didn't have the twins. Not that I'd have *that* to think about in future.

'What's up?' Jackie asked as soon as she'd arrived and settled Autumn to sit on the floor watching the twins play. 'You sounded a bit upset on the phone. Is it about Bob?'

'No.' I sighed. 'Oh God, you must think I'm so selfish. I've completely shelved Bob at the moment.'

'Why?' she intercepted quickly. 'What's he said to you?'

'Nothing!' I looked at her in surprise. 'What d'you mean?'

She dropped her eyes. 'Oh, well, you said on the phone earlier that you couldn't face speaking to him, so I thought ...' She tailed off. 'I don't know what I thought.'

'No.' I frowned. What was she getting at? 'No, it's just that I'm a bit caught up with family things at the moment.'

'Are Clément and Emilie being difficult?' Jackie had heard the tail end of my list of instructions to them as I saw them off at the front door just as she arrived.

'No more than you'd expect, I suppose, considering their ages.' I shrugged. 'I lost my cool with them the other day because they gave me the slip at the zoo and I found them misbehaving with a gang of boys from Romford. But I think we're back on track. No, it's my son,' I added quietly. 'He doesn't want me to look after the twins anymore. He's sending them to a childminder, starting next week.'

'Oh.' She looked at me with her head on one side. 'That's a bit sudden, isn't it? What, has he decided you need a rest?'

I tried to laugh but it didn't come out right. 'Huh. Something like that. Something like he's decided I'm losing my marbles as well as losing half my possessions. No, the truth of the matter is that his sisters have been nagging him about it and I think he's just had enough. I can't seem to talk him out of it. He's only told me now, when they're due to start with the childminder next week. So it's a fait accompli.'

'Have you spoken to your daughters?'

'Only Steph, so far, and needless to say she denies it's anything to do with her. According to her it actually *is* because I've lost a couple of things and forgotten a couple of things. I mean, I know I've been a bit busy lately, but would *you* say I'm incapable of looking after the children?'

'Of course not,' she said at once. 'Don't be ridiculous. You're far better at all this stuff than I am. I'd leave Autumn with you any time, at a drop of a hat.' She laughed, and then added, 'But of course, it's different for me. I'd be only too happy if my daughter didn't want me to look after Autumn anymore. I'd probably be down the pub having a drink to celebrate!'

'I don't believe you.' I managed a smile. 'OK, you grumble about it, but you love having Autumn really.'

'I *love* her, of course I do. But I don't really enjoy the responsibility, and the whole business of keeping her occupied. And that's just one day a week!' She shook her head. 'You're amazing, the way you cope with all your lot. Oh! Sorry! Now I've made you cry!'

I shook my head, wiping my eyes. 'No, I'm just feeling stupidly emotional about it. Silly really – it's not like I'm never going to see the twins again, obviously. But it's the end of my time as their *carer*. They've grown up so close to me.'

'Of course they have. Three days every week – no wonder you've got such a bond with them. Oh God, I'm making it worse, aren't I! Look, maybe your son will change his mind. When he's paid the childminder's fees for a couple of months, he might start to realise what a good thing he had with you. And in the meantime, I bet you end up having Izzie more often! Stephanie will probably take the opportunity to slot her into your free days!'

'I wouldn't be so sure. Even *she* sounded like she thought it might be a good idea not to trust me in future.'

'Never. I don't believe it. Come on, cheer up. Let me make us both a cup of coffee and then how about we take the kids out to the park while the sun's shining? Can you call those errant teenagers of yours and get them to come and meet us there? We could all have lunch out together, unless they'd think it was too un-cool to be seen with us?'

I laughed. 'They might, but let's do it anyway.'

But although I made an effort, for everyone's sake, the day still felt all wrong. It felt, somehow, like we were celebrating the twins' last day with me. And as far as I was concerned, it was no cause for celebration.

Michael arrived early to collect the children, almost as if he'd decided to deliberately cut short my last day of looking after them.

'Please change your mind, Mike,' I tried again. 'This is so silly.'

But he shook his head. 'Let's not get upset about it,' he said. 'You'll still be able to see them.'

'Well, it won't exactly be easy, will it! If they're with the childminder.'

'But you can come round to visit them sometimes, on the days Jo doesn't work.'

Visiting them. It would never be the same. But I realised there was no point making any more fuss. It would do no good to be seen as the one making difficulties, being awkward. It was true, after all – I could visit every week. It wasn't as if I was being denied access to the children – God forbid – like Bob was afraid might happen to him.

'Right. Yes, of course I'll do that. Maybe I'll give Jo a ring then, and arrange something for next week.'

Michael looked slightly alarmed now.

'Well, I'm not saying ... I mean, maybe not straight away, Mum. Jo tends to make plans, you know, for her days off. She normally sees friends on Mondays, and takes the twins to a playgroup on Fridays. But I'm sure at some point she'll have a free day. Yeah, give her a ring some time.'

'Or perhaps it'd be better if I popped round over the weekend? Or how about you all come for Sunday dinner again? Clément and Emilie will have gone back by then and ... I promise I won't forget about it this time!' I gave a little laugh to show I was taking it all with a good grace – my reputation for forgetfulness and unreliability.

'Well, you know how it is.' He gave a fleeting, awkward smile, looking at a point somewhere over my shoulder. 'We're always pretty busy at weekends. But yes, of course, we'll see if we can fit that in before too long.'

'That would be lovely,' I said, trying not to sound too desperate. How the hell had it come to this? Up till now I'd been in constant demand, and yet suddenly I seemed to be reduced to begging to see the family. But as Michael and I carried the twins out to the car between us, as I bent to kiss them goodbye once they'd been strapped into their car seats, I made sure I kept my smile bright and my voice cheerful for their benefit.

'See you soon, my darlings.' I turned to Michael. 'Alfie's still having trouble with that tooth coming through. He had some Calpol at about half past two.'

'OK. Thanks Mum.' He kissed my cheek. 'For everything.'

I got straight on the phone to try Danielle again – and this time she answered.

'I hope you're satisfied!' I snapped as soon as we'd said hello. 'Michael and Jo have stopped me having the twins.'

'And about time too,' she responded calmly. 'I've been telling them for ages ...'

'You've been *interfering* for ages, you mean, and it was never any of your damned business! Why can't you just get on with your own life and let your brother and sister get on with theirs?'

'Calm down, Mum! God! What's got into you? Had a bad day or something?'

'Yes, you could say that. I've just said goodbye to Alfie and Amelia, with no idea when I'll be seeing them next.'

'So be grateful for the rest!' Danielle laughed. 'Come on, Mum, it was ridiculous, the way they were expecting you to have their kids all the time. You'll be able to do what you like now.'

'You really have no idea, do you?' I said. 'We were all perfectly happy with the arrangement before you stuck your oar in. Are you jealous, Danielle – is that what it's all about? Well, I'm sorry, but you *chose* to live in France! What was I supposed to do – get on a Cross Channel ferry every week to babysit for you?'

'Of course not. I'm not jealous!' Danielle sounded indignant now. 'And I'm grateful you're having *my* kids this week, even if ...' She paused. I waited.

'Even if what? I forgot they were coming on Saturday? I know, I know it was awful but I've explained, it was an emergency, unfortunately. I'm sorry, but the kids were fine.'

'I was actually going to say, even if you did manage to lose them both at the zoo – God knows how.'

I gasped. 'They've told you *that*? I didn't *lose* them, Danielle! They deliberately did a runner when my back was turned!'

'Well, I know they're not babies but it would have been nice if you could have kept more of an eye on them, that's all I'm saying. I mean, they're in a foreign country and they're not used to crowds.'

'I can't believe I'm hearing this! I'm not even going to tell you what they were getting up to when I found them! I'm afraid I've had to restrict their freedom since it happened.'

'Restrict their freedom? Mum, they're only kids. It's supposed to be their holiday.'

I bit my lip. I'd promised Clem and Em I wouldn't tell their mother the details of their escapade on Monday as long as they behaved themselves the rest of the week. But I was irritated that they'd given her a version of the story that was edited in their favour. Let's face it, you just couldn't win with teenagers!

'I know it's their holiday, and if you ask them, I'm sure they'll tell you they're having a good time,' I said, thinking of the slap-up lunch and ice-creams I'd bought them today, to say nothing of the trip to the London museums we'd planned for the next day. 'So please don't start thinking they're being neglected.'

'I wouldn't dream of it,' she responded, sounding offended. 'I know you've always given them a good time when they come over. I said I was grateful, didn't I? *I'm* not the one who takes liberties.'

I gave up. To be honest I just couldn't face arguing anymore. No doubt my comments would soon be reported to the rest of the family anyway, probably giving them even more reason to think I was too tired, too old, too cranky to be left in charge of any of their children. Maybe Jackie was right after all. Maybe I should just accept it and be glad I was going to have more free time in future.

But the strange thing was, all I could think about as I watched TV with Clément and Emilie that evening was Pam, and how miserable her life seemed to be. How soon before *having more free time* became a curse of boredom rather than a gift of freedom? And how soon before *not* seeing my grandchildren turned me into a nasty, vindictive piece of work like her?

KATE

Curly Locks, Curly Locks, Will You be Mine?

For the next few days I was kept busy. As promised, I took Clem and Em up to London on the Friday, and the Science Museum and Natural History Museum lived up to expectations, making the day without doubt the highlight of their holiday. On the Saturday afternoon, Toby arrived, this time in a battered black Mini with go-faster stripes, instead of coming on the ferry and the train.

'Borrowed it from one of my friends,' he said, laughing at his brother's excited reaction. 'You might have to sit on your rucksack on the way home, though – the boot's not that big.'

He bundled both kids into the car and drove them into town to shop for some presents for their parents, and to my surprise arrived back with a present for me too – a nice plant for the garden and a bottle of red wine. I was touched. In the end, despite everything, I'd enjoyed having them and would miss them when they'd gone.

Toby stayed overnight again and on the Sunday, Steph and Ben came over with the children for a quick early lunch with us before it was time for the French kids to leave. If Michael, Jo and the twins were conspicuous by their absence from this occasion, nobody seemed to want to comment on it, and I tried not to think about it.

And so it was Monday morning before I finally got round to speaking to Bob again, and by then I was very conscious of the fact that over a week had passed since he'd been home, and I still hadn't found out what had happened.

'Sorry. I've been tied up with family stuff,' I explained. 'How are you?'

'Fine, Kate, thank you.'

'I presume Freddie's gone home now?'

'Um … yes. Yes, he has.'

I frowned at the hesitation there, but no doubt I'd find out in due course what was going on.

'Have you got time for a proper chat today, Kate?' he went on. 'I realise I still owe you an explanation about what happened the other week. You don't have the twins today, do you?'

'No. Nor *any* day, now.' I took a deep breath. 'I'll tell you when I see you. Yes, let's meet up for coffee, Bob – say half an hour's time?'

We arranged to meet at a café not too far from him, and I took a slow walk into town, arriving before Bob. At only half past ten on a Monday, the place was empty, but I chose a table in a corner anyway so that we could talk privately if it got busier later.

'So, tell me how you and Jackie found out I'd gone to Ipswich.' he said after we'd got past the pleasantries.

I felt a flicker of irritation. In the circumstances, it surely should have been *me* asking all the questions first!

'Coincidence,' I said with a shrug. 'My very nosy and not very pleasant neighbour saw you leave my house and go off in the taxi, and then watched Jackie and I running around the street looking for you.'

He had the grace to look abashed. 'I'm so sorry. I didn't think about how much anxiety I'd be causing.'

'Obviously not. Well, this same neighbour then just happened to go to the station at the same time as you, and apparently bought your train ticket for you. Return to Ipswich.'

'Oh. Yes, of course, I remember. I was feeling a little bit shaky. There was a queue, and this very kind lady offered ...'

'Kind lady?' I snorted. 'She just wanted to find out where you were going, so she could report back to me. But

I must admit, for once in her life she was useful.' I took a sip of my coffee and continued: 'And then you phoned for help – from the hospital.'

'Oh dear. I knew I'd made a mess of that call. I was rushing to get my words out, you see, before the money ran out. No, I wasn't at the hospital anymore when I called you. I'd been discharged, and been taken to Craig's house by taxi, but that was when I discovered my wallet was missing. I only had a handful of change in my pocket. I called you from a phone box in Craig's road, just to apologise and ask if you could possibly help by having Freddie for a little longer.'

'It was a bit late to ask, by then!'

'I know. I'm sorry.'

I shook my head. It was pointless, really, for him to keep on apologising now.

'I just want to know what it was all about, Bob. You said you were going to see your son for a *chat* – but it was obviously more than that!'

'Yes.' He sighed. 'Well, it was late before I even managed to see him – Craig. He wasn't in, and nor was the new boyfriend.'

'They weren't expecting you?'

'No. The whole thing was supposed to be … you could say a surprise visit. So I was going to let myself in, but – and I know this sounds really silly – but my key to Craig's house was in my wallet.'

'Which you'd lost. Oh God, it gets worse. So how did you get in?'

'I didn't. Couldn't. I went round the back way, sat on the doorstep and waited for him to come home.'

'Poor you,' I said, deciding to put everything else to one side for now. 'What an ordeal you had, one way and another.'

'Well, it sounds ridiculous now,' he said. 'But at the time, it just felt like the only thing I could do.'

I was silent, thinking about the timescale. While he'd been sitting on his son's doorstep all that Saturday, Jackie and I had been to the hospital and back. I'd seen the stranger in the bed who wasn't Bob, taken Freddie back home with me again, found out about my French grandchildren turning up, and rushed to another hospital because of Stephanie's asthma attack – to say nothing of finding Pam practically running my household for me. Neither of us had exactly had the best days of our lives.

'I think I must have fallen asleep out there,' Bob was saying. 'It was dark by the time Craig came home. He opened the back door and I actually fell in at his feet. Scared him half to death.'

'I can imagine! So, once he'd picked you up off the floor, you managed to have your little *chat*, I suppose?'

Bob shook his head and I noticed his hand was shaking as he took a mouthful of his coffee. I laid my hand on his arm, but instead of going on with his story he put down his cup and looked – just sat there looking – at my hand on his arm, until I suddenly felt really awkward about it and moved it away. It was a few moments before he looked away, coughed, and said:

'Um, no. In fact we didn't get very far with what I'd gone up there to chat about, because it turned out something terrible had happened.'

'Something terrible?' I said, my mind filling with all sorts of possibilities. 'What …?'

'It was Nathan.' Bob stopped again, put a hand to his head and sighed, and I remembered again that he was elderly, and frail, had been poorly and seemed to have gone through a pretty nerve-racking time. No wonder he was struggling to get the story out.

'Craig's ex? Freddie's … father?' I encouraged him.

'Yes.' He shook his head. 'Poor chap. I've felt so much sympathy for him, Kate, as you know. Through all of this, he was the innocent party, as far as I could see. I always liked him, too.'

'I know. I know you were angry with your son about the way he dumped Nathan.'

'Yes. Exactly. Well, where was I? As you can probably imagine, it took Craig a few minutes to get over the shock of me falling into his kitchen like that, and then he made us both a cup of tea, and then of course he had to introduce me to Andrew – that's the new boyfriend – and I had to try to be polite although it was difficult, in the circumstances.'

I kept quiet, trying to be patient. I wanted to know what had happened to Nathan, not how they'd had a cup of tea and tried to be polite.

'And I suddenly noticed how pale and shaken my son looked,' he said. 'Like he'd had a terrible shock. Worse than me falling in through the door, I mean. I asked him what was up, and … oh, Kate. He just buried his head in his hands and started crying. Sobbing, like a child. I kept asking what was wrong, what I could do to help, but he couldn't even speak to me. In the end, it was Andrew who had to tell me.'

'Tell you what?'

'Nathan had tried to commit suicide.'

'Oh, God!' I gasped. 'That's awful!'

'Yes. They'd had the phone call that morning. He'd taken a whole load of tablets, but then thank God, changed his mind – only because of Freddie, he said – and he managed to make himself sick and then called an ambulance. He's going to be fine.'

'Thank God for that. What a horrible shock for Craig, though – and for you.'

I started to put a hand on his arm again, and then thought better of it. I didn't want him giving my hand that strange look again.

'Yes, it was. But … I'm sure it's made Craig think, you know. Stupid boy, he'd obviously been so carried away with this affair with *Andrew*, he really hadn't taken in how badly he'd hurt Nathan. How much Nathan still cared about him, you know?'

'Do you think he might still have feelings for Nathan, after all?'

'I'm hoping so, Kate.' He sniffed. 'I can't say I thought much of the new chap. He was very off-hand with me, and not particularly gentle with Craig, either, considering how upset he obviously was.'

'Probably jealous – seeing Craig upset about Nathan. Worried Craig was going to change his mind and go back to him.'

'Yes. Well, let's keep our fingers crossed.' Bob was looking exhausted by now, just talking about it. 'Anyway, you see, it was very late by then, so I obviously stayed overnight with them, and got the train back on the Sunday morning. And as you know, I came straight to you, to get Freddie back. Craig asked me to hang on to Freddie for a few days until Nathan was completely better.' To my horror, his poor tired eyes filled with tears. 'Oh, Kate, I can't tell you how sorry I am about all this. It's been the most awful strain – all of it – coming on top of all the worry about Craig, and Freddie. I thought I was losing my mind. To be honest I've felt so guilty for what I did to you, running out on you like that and leaving Freddie with you, not coming back or even being able to contact you! I was afraid you wouldn't want anything to do with me anymore.'

'Don't be silly,' I told him gently. 'Of course I *was* worried, and a bit annoyed at the time, to be honest. But you've obviously been through a horrible experience, and at the end of the day, Freddie was fine with us and you knew I'd look after him for you.'

I was feeling so sorry for him, and was so busy reassuring him that he was forgiven, and that we were still friends, it didn't even occur to me until later that he hadn't actually even told me yet why he did it – why he went to Ipswich to see Craig in the first place, and why the *little chat* they were going to have was such a big secret, why he couldn't take Freddie, why he couldn't even tell me he was going. Afterwards, I couldn't quite understand how we'd still failed to cover that part of the story.

But at the time, there was a very good reason for it. As we sat there in that quiet cosy corner of the café, Bob dripping apologies along with his tears, me gushing on about how much I sympathised with his ordeal and would do anything to help him, something suddenly changed between us. Something I'd been suspecting, and half dreading. Something I should have been much more wary of when I kept touching his hands and arms so sympathetically and calling him my dear friend.

'Kate,' he said abruptly, just as I'd finished going on about how all that mattered to me was that he was safe and that everything was going to be all right, 'You do know, don't you. You do know how I feel about you?'

'Oh,' I said. How inadequate. How totally, totally rubbish. 'Oh. Right.'

'You're my dearest, dearest friend. I'd be lost without you.'

I must have said something flippant. Trying to treat it lightly – *yes, of course we're friends, I'd be lost without you too, ha ha.* But it didn't work. He grasped both my hands across the table and fixed me with a look that made me want to get up, turn around and run out of that café like all the hounds of hell were chasing me.

'I mean I think you're wonderful, Kate. I mean ... you must know! I love you.'

'Oh,' I said again, and I could hear my voice shaking. 'Look, I'm sorry, Bob, but I've just realised the time. I've got to ... um ... go and do something. I'm expecting someone ... a delivery. I'll talk to you soon, OK? Take care.'

Ridiculously, having made such a terrible, God-awful hash of my reaction to the poor man's declaration, I then nearly kissed him goodbye. It was probably made even worse because I just stopped myself in the act of bending down to plant one on his cheek.

'Bye!' I said quickly, fumbling with my bag, throwing down some money for the bill, nearly sending my chair flying as I jumped up and turned to go. At the last minute, as I was *about* to run out of the café like all those hounds were after me, I caught sight of his face and realised how badly I was handling it. I stood stock still, looking back at him. 'I'm so sorry,' I said very quietly, with the dignity (finally) that he deserved.

'Don't be,' he said. 'It's my fault. I shouldn't have said ...'

'It's OK. I just can't ... I'm sorry. I wasn't expecting ...'

I shook my head. He gave me a little sad smile. We did a silly little wave to each other. And that was how we left it.

And I went home wondering how the hell we were going to manage to still be friends, after that.

BOB

She Loves Me, She Loves Me Not

What a stupid, stupid old fool. Why did I have to go and say that? What did I think I was – a hero out of some Victorian romantic novel? I mean, look at me! Old and decrepit and as daft as a brush. How on earth could I imagine any woman being interested in me, never mind such a lovely woman as Kate? What had got into me? Now I'd ruined everything. Embarrassed her, probably offended her – I doubted whether she'd want to see me anymore.

The stupidest thing of all was that I'd already talked to Jackie about it, and she'd warned me not to say anything to Kate. Poor Jackie, I'd probably embarrassed the hell out of her, too. I didn't mean to say anything, but it just sort of came up in conversation. I'd bumped into her in town early one morning – it must have been Thursday, I think that's her only day off work. I hadn't slept well so I'd got up early and gone for a stroll to get a paper. She had the little girl for the day and said she'd popped out to get some more milk.

'How are *you* now?' she asked me pointedly, and I replied that I was fine, but still feeling bad about the way I'd put upon Kate and herself over that weekend and caused them so much worry.

'Well, I can't really comment. I haven't seen Kate since Sunday,' she said, 'so I haven't heard the full story.'

'I haven't seen her myself since then, either,' I admitted. 'She's had her hands full, with her grandchildren from France. I've promised to explain everything, just as soon as she has time to talk to me. In fact, I owe you an explanation too, don't I,' I added. 'From what Kate said, you went with her to Ipswich and helped her with Freddie.'

I was aware that Jackie seemed a little less forgiving about the whole thing than Kate. Fair enough, she hadn't known me for long and probably thought I'd behaved atrociously.

'It's OK. Just talk to Kate about it, Bob. I'm in a bit of a hurry to get the milk and get back home – Autumn hasn't even had breakfast yet.' She glanced at me as she was about to move on with her pushchair. 'I don't know what it was all about, but I'm sure Kate will forgive you.'

It felt like she'd handed me a straw, and I promptly clutched it. I'd been so worried, ever since leaving her house on Sunday, that Kate would be angry with me – because of the way I'd interrupted her family barbecue, quite apart from all the rest of it.

'Do you really think so?' I said, perhaps a little too eagerly. 'I did *hope* she'd forgive me, but ...'

'Well, yeah, course she will. She's your friend, isn't she. She thinks a lot of you.'

'Does she?' I couldn't help it – my heart was soaring. 'Is that what she says? Has she told you that?'

Jackie gave me a funny look. 'Well, not in so many words. Just – you know, it's obvious she likes you.'

As I've said already, I'm a silly old man. I took this completely the wrong way. I was so relieved to hear that she wasn't likely to bear a grudge for the episode at the weekend, I chose to read too much into it. I was probably grinning like a maniac. Jackie must have been getting worried.

'I'll let you into a secret,' I told her, like a stupid lovesick schoolboy. 'I feel the same way about her. I think she's wonderful. Do you think she might be interested in me – you know, as we're both on our own?' I didn't get any further, because by now Jackie's face was a picture of horror.

'I just meant that she likes you as a *friend*,' she said, very fast, her face now a bit pink. 'I mean, I really don't think … well, I have no idea … but that wasn't what I was implying. I'm sorry. I didn't mean to make you think …'

'Oh. Right.' We both coughed a bit and looked around us. I don't know which of us felt more awkward. 'Sorry. You must think me very foolish. The thing is, I've always wondered, you see, but I never liked to say anything. Perhaps I lacked the courage. Do you think, at least, it might be worth me having a word with her … in that respect?'

'Oh, Bob, I really don't know. Look, I'm sorry – as I said, I'm in a bit of a hurry. But please, don't rush into anything, saying anything to Kate that you might regret. You're such good friends, but if you were to, well, if you came on a bit too strong to her, it might put her off. Do you understand what I'm saying?'

'Yes. Yes, of course. Thank you, Jackie. I'm sorry if I've spoken out of turn. Silly old fool, getting carried away.'

We said goodbye and she rushed off, still looking quite perturbed. And I hobbled off home, feeling somewhat chastened. She was right, of course. If I *was* ever going to tell Kate how I felt about her, I'd have to wait for some sort of sign that she felt the same way about me. I'd hate to embarrass her and ruin our friendship.

But that was before we had coffee together. Before she listened to me so kindly, so sympathetically, saying she'd do anything to help me, calling me her dear friend. Before she touched my arm and looked at me with such concern and tenderness. Before I realised, looking into her lovely eyes, how much she really meant to me, how devastated I'd be if I couldn't see her. How much I loved her.

Before I made such an almighty prat of myself by telling her.

KATE

See How They Run

I phoned Jackie that evening, after she'd got home from work. Well, I had to talk to somebody about it, didn't I. I still didn't know whether to laugh or cry. Poor Bob. I felt so bad about it – but surely I hadn't done anything to encourage him?

'Of course you haven't,' Jackie tried to soothe me. 'In fact, Kate, I'm sorry but in a way I think it's my fault.'

She told me she'd seen Bob at the shops, on Thursday morning before I called her to come round and have coffee with me.

'I *thought* you sounded a bit odd when you asked me if he'd spoken to me,' I said. 'What happened?'

'I was just trying to reassure him that you'd forgive him, you know, for the whole *Ipswich* situation last weekend, once he'd managed to explain it to you. I probably said something about you being good friends, and for some bizarre reason, he took it all wrong and started going off on one, about whether you might be *interested* in him. I was so shocked, I had no idea what to say. I don't know which of us was more embarrassed.' She paused. 'You *don't* fancy him, do you?'

'No!' I said, and promptly felt guilty for being so vehement about it. 'Look, he's a really nice man, and to be honest I probably gave him the wrong impression this morning. He was telling me what happened in Ipswich – how he was ill on the train, lost his wallet, and then when he finally got to see his son, it turned out the ex – Freddie's father – had attempted suicide. Craig had just got back from seeing him.'

'Oh God. Poor guy.'

'Yes. So the whole episode was a dreadful experience for Bob, too.'

'It must have been. So was that why he dashed up to Ipswich in the first place?'

I paused. 'No. It had only just happened that day. He never actually did get to explain that bit,' I realised.

'Before his declaration of love?'

'Ooooow! Don't say it like that. It's making me squirm. I still feel really horrible about it. As I said, it was just listening to what he'd gone through, feeling sorry for him, I must have somehow conveyed the impression I felt – you know. Something more than sympathy. Now I've probably gone and upset him.'

'Broken his heart. You cruel woman.'

'Jackie, honestly, I don't think it's funny. He's quite vulnerable, really, and lonely. I'd never want to hurt him. But how can I see him as a friend now? It'll be excruciating for both of us.'

'Come on, he'll get over it.' She definitely wasn't taking this as seriously as I was! 'I must say, Kate, if I was getting all this attention from a man friend, I'd feel pretty chuffed about it. You seductress, you!'

'For God's sake! I'm sixty-two and he's over seventy! It's ridiculous. And a bit sad.'

'Sorry. I suppose it *is* sad, really. As you say, he's probably just lonely, and still misses his wife – she died, didn't she?' Then she spoilt it by sniggering and adding, 'I've got to hand it to you, though. I hope I'm still capable of pulling the blokes when I'm sixty-two!'

'Oh, I might have known it'd be pointless talking to you about it!' I said, pretending to be annoyed.

But after we'd hung up, I went and looked at myself in the mirror. *A seductress? Still pulling the blokes?* No, it was no good kidding myself. I was just a very plain woman past her prime, going grey and in need of losing a stone or two. It was absolutely bloody ridiculous. The poor man was obviously suffering from stress.

If nothing else, because I wasn't having the twins for now – (I kept telling myself it was only a temporary thing, that Michael would change his mind when the reality of the childminder's costs kicked in) – at least I had time to do a proper, thorough search of the house for the things that had gone missing. I was going through the kitchen drawers when Steph called round on the Wednesday morning with Izzie and baby Isaac.

'What's all this?' she said, looking at the kitchen table. It was covered with the contents of my least tidy kitchen drawer – the one where everything that didn't really belong anywhere else got dumped – and the drawer itself was upside down on the floor.

'I'm having a sort out,' I said.

'I see.' She sat down and watched me for a minute. 'Well, I'm pleased you're making good use of your extra time. Not sitting around moping, you know, about not having the twins.'

'I'm not *making good use* of the time,' I said, feeling irritated. 'This isn't something I wanted to do – I'd much rather be playing with Amelia and Alfie. I'm looking for my phone, and my car keys.'

'Oh. And your diary. And your watch.'

'Yes, exactly. I've obviously put them somewhere safe, so I'm going to look through all the places I haven't checked yet.'

'Well, they weren't in *that* drawer, were they,' she pointed out. 'You've emptied it now.'

'I know.' Why was she making me act so defensive? Yet again? 'So while I've got everything out of it, I'm going to sort through it all and tidy it up.'

'OK. Well, don't stop on our account. I only called round to make sure you were all right. Not moping.'

'Thanks.' I sighed. 'Oh, put the kettle on, then. Might as well stop for a cuppa.'

'Can *I* help you look, Nanny?' Izzie said. 'Shall we tip another drawer upside down?'

'I've got a better idea,' I told her, pouring her out a tumbler of milk and getting the biscuit tin down from the shelf. 'When we've had our drinks, shall we go to the park for a little while? It's too nice a day to be stuck indoors, really, isn't it.'

'No, I need to go to Tesco,' Stephanie said as Izzie started jumping up and down and singing about the park, and her scooter, and the slide, and the swings. 'Sorry. I'm out of milk and I need eggs and cereals.'

'That's OK.' I smiled. 'Mummy can go and do the shopping, can't she, Izzie, while we go to the park. Shall we feed the ducks? I'll take Isaac, too, Steph, if you like. Has he been fed? Have you got his pram?'

'Oh. Well, thanks, Mum, but it's OK, I shouldn't be very long at the supermarket and then we'll need to go home and have a quick lunch because ...'

'All right, but still, you'll get done quicker if you leave the children with me. You can all have lunch here. I'll get it ready while you're shopping. Izzie can help.'

'I want to go to the park, Mummy! I want to ride my scooter! I want to feed the ducks!'

'Well, you can't.' Stephanie gave me a black look. 'There isn't time.'

OK, perhaps I shouldn't have mentioned the damned park. 'We can do something else instead while Mummy's gone,' I tried to soothe Izzie. 'Play in the garden?'

'No, they're coming to Tesco with me,' Steph insisted. 'Izzie, you're going to play with Surya this afternoon, remember? We need to get the shopping, go home, have an early lunch and get you round to Surya's house. Anyway, Nanny's busy.'

'I'm not,' I tried to protest, but I could see I'd already started World War Three so I changed tactics quickly. 'But Mummy's right, Izzie. You want to be ready in time to go and play with your friend, don't you.'

'No. I don't want to go and play with Surya anymore. I want to play with Nanny. I want to go to the park.' The volume was increasing and the lower lip was wobbling. Oh, damn. Me and my big mouth. 'I WANT TO FEED THE DUCKS!'

'Right, that's it! Get in the car – we're going to Tesco right NOW, and if you don't stop yelling and start behaving yourself, you WON'T go to Surya's or anywhere else today!' Grabbing the sobbing child by the arm and picking up baby Isaac, miraculously still asleep in his car seat, with the other hand, Stephanie marched to the front door with them both. 'Sorry about this,' she said. 'But I wish you hadn't ...'

'I know. My fault.' Although I'd only tried to help, hadn't I? Tried, failed. 'I'm sure she'll settle down in a minute.'

'Hmm.' She glanced back at me after strapping both children into the back of the car. 'Good luck with finding your things,' she called above Izzie's crying. And she was behind the wheel, starting the engine, before I could even respond.

Never even drank her cup of tea.

Would it *really* have upset the day's schedule if the children had stayed with me while she did the shopping? Wouldn't Izzie still have been on time for her play date if they'd had lunch with me? Maybe I was being a bit over-sensitive. But it felt ominously like Stephanie was now as reluctant to leave her children with me as Michael was.

I spent the rest of the day turning out more drawers, more cupboards, stripping cushions off chairs and reaching behind wardrobes and bookshelves. Nothing. No phone, no car keys, no diary, no watch. It was the watch that bothered me the most. As my children had pointed out, it had been my sixtieth birthday present from them and was probably expensive as well as being special. As I cooked my dinner that evening I went back, in my mind, to the occasions when each of the items had vanished. Was there any common denominator to those days? It was hard, now, to remember exactly what had been going on when I discovered the first couple of things missing, but the watch had definitely gone the previous Sunday, that disastrous day of the family barbecue when Bob had turned up. *Surely* to God, my son wasn't right? It was just ridiculous to imagine Bob had anything to do with it.

I sat down with my dinner on a tray on my lap, trying to think. Now, in the light of Bob's embarrassing declaration, could I imagine the possibility of him taking something like my watch as a – yuck, I didn't even know what to call it – a *keepsake*? I forced myself to think back, to try to recall the previous thing, the diary. Bloody hell. Would someone who secretly had feelings for a person want to steal their diary, to snoop through it and see what that person was up to? And take their phone for the same reason – to read their text messages and see who they were calling? Yikes! This was a truly scary thought. Maybe I *should* be seriously considering it?

No! I shook my head at my own silliness. Bob might have got a bit ... emotionally dependent on me, whatever. But he wasn't, could never be, a thief. No way. He was such a *gentleman*, so old-fashioned *polite*. It just didn't add up. I didn't care what Michael or anyone else thought, Bob would never have taken anything from me, or anyone else.

But it was looking, horribly, like *someone* had. And the more I thought about the occasions when I'd noticed the things missing, the more my suspicions in another direction became much more likely.

I was going to have to go and have a word with my least favourite neighbour.

KATE

The Wicked Witch

I did it the following day. It was only going to get harder if I put it off, and I was already dreading the confrontation. Let's face it, however much I disliked the woman, it wasn't going to help if I steamed in accusing her of being a thief. I had to handle this carefully.

Needless to say, she looked pretty shocked when she opened the door to me.

'Kate!' she said. 'Well! This is a surprise. Would you like to come in? No children today?'

'Thank you.' Better to be inside, than having this conversation on the doorstep. 'No, no children.' I didn't elaborate. I'd already told her about the twins going to a childminder, and it was none of her business anyway.

She led me through to the lounge, pointing to an armchair like I was an honoured guest.

'Tea or coffee?' she asked, smiling. 'I've got some fruit cake if you ...'

'No, thanks. I don't think this will take long. I just need to ask you something.'

'Of course.' She sat down opposite me, looking expectant. Hopeful. 'Is there something I can help with? Something with one of the grandchildren, perhaps?'

'No. It's nothing like that.' I took a deep breath. 'Pam, you know ... you've heard me saying I've had a few things go missing.'

'Yes.' She frowned at me. 'Have you had any luck finding them?'

'No. That's what I've come to ...'

'Dear me. It's been too long, Kate. And your watch! That must be quite valuable.'

'Exactly. So I wanted to ask you ...'

'Would you like me to help? I'd be more than happy to. I think the best way is to take one room at a time, emptying it completely, in a really methodical way, and then move on to the next room, and eventually you'll have done a thorough search of the whole house.' She smiled again. 'I know how busy you are. So how about you just let me come in and do the whole thing? It'll save you having to worry.'

'I've done it already. That's not what I was going to ask you.'

'Oh.' She frowned, looking disappointed, and it came to me that perhaps she'd taken the things *precisely* so that she could involve herself in doing this whole-house search, eventually pretending to find the items for me and thus (ha ha) making herself invaluable to me. This thought gave me the encouragement I needed to tell her straight:

'What I wanted to ask you was whether *you* might have picked them up.'

'Picked them up?' she echoed, looking at me as if I'd spoken a foreign language. 'What do you mean?'

'Taken them. Maybe even by accident,' I added quickly, although it didn't exactly come out right. 'I don't know, maybe just picked them up with something of yours, by mistake, when you were in my house.'

There was a silence. She stared at me. I tried not to flinch.

'You think I stole them, don't you,' she said eventually, very quietly.

'Look, that's not what I'm saying, exactly, but the fact is ...'

'You think I'd do that? *Steal* things from you? I can't believe you'd think that!'

To my horror, she suddenly started to cry. Really cry – not just a few tears welling up in her eyes, but gulping and sniffing, working up very quickly to full-on, noisy, messy

271

crying out loud like one of the grandchildren having a tantrum. To say it wasn't what I'd expected would be an understatement. I'd fully anticipated anger. I'd imagined her screaming abuse at me, throwing me out of her house, never wanting to speak to me again. I'd even thought it might be worth it, to get her off my back.

'All I've ever done is try to help you!' she was saying in between her sobs and her gasps. Her nose was running. It was bloody awful. 'Tried to be your friend! Might have spoken out of turn a couple of times ... tried to apologise ... tried to make amends! Wanted to be part of the family! Loved all your grandchildren like they were my own! Never thought ... never *dreamt* you'd think that of me – that I'd *steal* from you, Kate! Never! Never!'

And there she sat, rocking back and forth in distress, going *Never! Never!* like a clockwork toy that had got stuck, while her tears flowed and her voice grew hoarse and I ... despite all my intentions, all my resolve, to say nothing of my avowed and *deserved* dislike of her ... I felt terrible.

'OK,' I said eventually. 'OK, look, I didn't mean it like that.'

She kept rocking. She kept crying.

'I just meant, maybe you'd picked them up by mistake, right? I just thought maybe you could have a look, for me. That's all. OK?'

She grabbed a tissue from up her sleeve, blew her nose, carried on crying.

'All right – for God's sake – I'm *sorry*! Please, stop crying.' I hesitated. 'Let's have that cup of coffee, then. We can talk about it, at least, can't we?'

It took another few minutes of persuasion to get her to stop. Part of me was cross with myself. But I couldn't stand it, seeing her bawling like that. OK, so she'd spent the last few weeks doing everything possible to annoy me, I didn't like her, didn't even trust her, but I'm only human, and I'm not normally a vindictive person. She was genuinely upset. So instead of getting any further in the search for my missing stuff, I was in her kitchen, finding mugs, making coffee, cutting up her bloody fruit cake, bringing it all back to the lounge on a tray and encouraging her to eat some cake, it'd make her feel better. The irony wasn't lost on me. I was taking over, taking charge in *her* house in exactly the way I'd hated her doing in mine.

'Lovely cake,' I said as she began to calm down a bit.

'Thank you.' She nodded and blew her nose. 'I enjoy baking. Although I don't know why I bother. Usually there's nobody to share it with.'

We sat there awkwardly with our plates on our laps. I didn't want to raise the subject of theft again and start her off on another crying fit. What I'd really like to have done was to knock back my coffee, get up and just go. But I couldn't. I felt obliged to say something else.

'You make cakes for your … um … for the children I suppose. When they come.'

Her eyes filled with tears again and she put the plate down on the coffee table with a clatter. Oh God. Wrong thing to say.

'Yes. I make cakes, I buy sweets and biscuits and all the other treats – I make sure I've always got things for the children in case they come. But they hardly ever do, anymore.'

Perhaps it touched a nerve with me because I was feeling sensitive about not having the twins, about Steph not wanting to leave Izzie and Isaac with me. Or perhaps I just did feel quite bad about thinking her a thief. Maybe she wasn't. Maybe I'd jumped unfairly to conclusions. Either way, I actually felt a bit sorry for her.

'That must be hard for you,' I said. We both sipped our coffee and she blinked back her tears. 'So did you *used* to see the children more often?' I added.

'Yes,' she said very quietly. 'When Colin was alive, they were round here all the time.'

'Colin was your husband?' She'd never mentioned him to me before. Not that I'd really ever given her the opportunity.

'Yes. Well, I called him my husband, of course, although .... we never actually married. That's the trouble.'

I watched her, holding her mug, taking little sips from it, looking down at the carpet, and I hesitated. I knew I was on the brink of something here. She was about to confide in me – tell me what it was all about, the whole business with those children and why she was so bloody miserable. I wasn't sure I wanted to hear it. Why would I want her confidences? I didn't exactly want her as a friend! I could just go, get out of here now, before she went any further. Or I could be … generous. Forgiving. And just take a few minutes to listen.

'The trouble?' I said.

'When he died ...' She gave a little shudder, as if the word, the fact of it, still haunted her, then she looked away, shaking her head. It was obvious she couldn't go on.

'I'm so sorry.' If Pam had been a friend – a close friend, a nice friend – I'd have hugged her. But neither of us were ready for that. 'How long ago did he pass away?'

'Two years,' she managed to choke out. 'I'm all right, you know. I just ... it's so silly, but I still find it rather hard to actually *say* it. So silly.'

'I don't think so.' We were both silent for a moment. 'It must have been an awful time for you.'

'Yes. It was a heart attack, you see – so sudden. No warning.' Pam shook her head. 'Sometimes I still find it quite difficult to believe that he's really gone. Even now.'

'Of course. You must do.'

'And the worst of it is –' Her voice dropped to a whisper, as if she couldn't bear saying it out loud, 'They hate me, you see.'

'Who? Who hates you?'

'His son. Russell, Colin's son by his ... his wife. Russell and Tania – that's the daughter-in-law – they always blamed me, of course, for breaking up the marriage.' She seemed to be on a roll now, the words suddenly spilling out as if a dam had been broken. 'It's true, I'm afraid. I was the Other Woman. Colin left his wife for me, and unfortunately, they never divorced. He wanted to, she refused, he thought if he left it for a while, she'd eventually agree. He felt so guilty, you see, about hurting her, that he didn't want to push it. And it just never happened. So she, Diana, she's the poor widow, the one everyone feels sorry for, and I'm just the wicked witch.'

'But life's never quite that black and white, is it.'

'Life according to Russell is *exactly* that – black and white, and I'm the black.'

'Is that why they don't let you see the children very often?' I asked her.

'Yes. While Colin was alive it was different, you see? It's funny how they never blamed *him*, for leaving Diana. The whole thing was apparently my fault. I must have amazing powers of seduction I didn't even know about,' she added with sarcasm. 'I somehow persuaded this middle-aged man against his will to fall in love with me.'

'Children can be so unfair about their parents' relationships. So blind. It couldn't have been a very happy marriage, after all.'

'Oh, but apparently it was! Apparently everything was sweetness and light until I came along.' She shook her head. 'No, of course not. Colin told me they barely spoke to each other. They didn't argue, so Russell seriously seemed to believe it was perfectly fine. Anyway, Colin was the children's granddad, so they didn't mind *him* seeing them. They managed to ignore me, like I was part of the furniture, whenever they came round. I didn't care. I fell in love with the children, just as if they were ... *my own.*' She whispered the last two words, looking like she was going to cry again.

'You never *had* children of your own?' I said, although it was obvious.

'No. I'd actually given up on the whole idea, you know – meeting someone, getting married, having a family. I was in my late forties when I met Colin. I had my career – we were both teachers – I had my own home, my own life, I was *settled*. Then Colin came along, joined our school from an inner-city comprehensive, and, well, there was something *instantaneous* between us. Scary. But wonderful.'

'At least you had that. Those years together.'

'Yes, of course. I wouldn't change anything. I wasn't happy about breaking up his family, but you know, Diana wasn't really surprised. She wasn't devastated. Colin was far more worried about it than he needed to be. But Russell – as I say, he just never forgave me.'

'But they still do let the children come to you occasionally?'

'Only when it suits them. When they don't seem to have any other option for a childminder.'

'Then they've got a bloody cheek, if you don't mind me saying so.'

'I know. But I put up with it, you see, because I love the children. And they're all I've got. I took early retirement from teaching. Colin and I were going to enjoy our free time together. My friends at the school all turned against me right from the beginning. They disapproved of me seeing Colin. Almost as much as his son did!'

'That's tough. You must have been so hurt.'

'Well, at the time I didn't care too much. I had Colin, you see? You know what it's like when you first fall in love with someone – you don't think you need anyone else. But now, now he's gone ...'

'You're lonely.' And now, to be fair, I could understand why.

'Yes. Sometimes.' She swallowed, took a breath, and admitted quietly, 'Most of the time.'

I picked up my last bit of cake, absent-mindedly, and put it back down again.

'I do understand that,' I said.

'I doubt it,' Pam retorted, and then added: 'Sorry. But you have so much in your life.'

'Yes, you're right – my family. They're lovely, of course, and they … well, up till now, they've kept me busy.'

I was going on to say more. To remind her about the twins going to a childminder, tell her about my children being strange with me. I was even going to have a whinge about the fact that – apart from Bob, and now Jackie – I didn't actually have any friends myself. That somehow, since I stopped working, since the grandkids started coming along, I'd been too busy to keep hold of my old friends. I hadn't made enough effort. I'd ignored invitations to coffee mornings, girls' nights out, things like that, and eventually people gave up on you, you couldn't blame them. I was going to say that anyway, several of those friends were never really *mine* – they were the wives of Dennis's friends. Friends we used to see when we were a couple, during the early years, the better years. They tend to drop away after you get divorced, especially if you're the one doing the divorcing.

But I didn't say any of that. Because looking at Pam now, and having listened to her baring her soul to me, I could see that she was far more lonely, far more unhappy, than I'd ever been. I was still wary of her moods, but I supposed I could understand them a little better.

'I didn't steal anything from you, Kate,' she said, finally looking me in the eyes. Her voice, now, after all the whispering and tearfulness, was surprisingly firm. 'I promise I have no idea where your phone and watch and things are. I know I've upset you, and I can't seem to put that right, however hard I try. But I would never do that. Never.'

'I believe you,' I said. 'I'm sorry I even suggested it.'

'Well.' She gave a little quick smile. 'I suppose I can understand it. I've been in your house a lot. More than I should have been. I *was* trying to be helpful, but I can see that it was probably coming across as interference. I shan't do it anymore.'

And there it was. The perfect opportunity for me to be rid of her. To agree, to say yes, it would be a good idea if she stayed out of my hair in future and stopped poking her nose into my family's business.

'Don't be silly,' I said instead. 'You're welcome any time, Pam.'

Damn. Soft touch, or what?

JACKIE

When They Were Down, They Were Down

Poor Kate. She was really missing the twins. I called on her again on my day off, the Thursday afternoon, to find her looking fed up and miserable, not like her at all. I was quite concerned.

'How's it been, this week?' I asked.

She shrugged. 'Not exactly a barrel of laughs. What with Bob ...'

'Oh yes. The grand proclamation of love!' Mistake. She wasn't amused. 'Sorry. I know it must have been really embarrassing.'

'Yes, but also I'm worried, now, that it'll be awkward between us. I want to still be friends with him, but I can't bring myself to phone him. I won't know how to speak to him.'

'Well, let me do it, then. Maybe I can have a ... discreet little word with him. About you.'

'Oh God. No, please don't. I just want to pretend it didn't happen.' She sighed. 'Anyway, I've got other things on my mind.'

'I know. I've been thinking of you. But you *will* see the twins again soon, I'm sure you will.'

'It isn't just the twins. Stephanie refused to leave Izzie and Isaac with me yesterday, just for an hour or so while she went shopping. There was quite a scene – no, not between me and Steph!' she added quickly. 'With Izzie. My fault. I shouldn't have offered without checking with her mum.'

'Oh, I'm sure it was just that she needed to take them with her for some reason.'

'That's what she was trying to pretend. But it didn't ring true. She doesn't want to leave me in charge of them, Jackie. None of them trust me anymore.'

I sat down next to her and gave her a hug. 'Come on, this isn't like you. You're just upset about Michael and the twins – you're reading too much into everything. It'll all come out with the wash.'

'I hope you're right.' She smiled at me. 'Sorry, I really am being a misery, aren't I. It's lovely to see you, and Autumn,' she added, giving my little one a quick kiss as she toddled past. 'But the other thing that's made me feel a bit sad is – I went to see Pam this morning.'

'Oh God. No wonder you're miserable.'

'No, listen. I actually went round there to accuse her of stealing my things – my phone and my watch and ...'

'You think she did it?' Bloody hell. This was a turn-up for the books. With a bit of luck she could get the old witch arrested.

'I *did* wonder about it. Just thinking that she might have been in the house whenever something went missing – it was hard to remember exactly, but I thought it was possible. But now I'm positive she had nothing to do with it. I actually feel sorry for her.'

She told me how Pam had burst into tears, and then told Kate her entire life history, by the sound of it, including the fact that she'd nicked some woman's husband, would you believe? And apparently that was why his kids didn't like her seeing the grandchildren.

'Bloody hell,' I said when she'd finished telling me. 'I'd never have had Pam down as a man-eater.'

Kate shrugged. I could see she'd completely changed her tune about the woman.

'They fell in love. His marriage wasn't working, and his wife didn't seem to care much. It's the son who's never forgiven her. I just think it's so sad.' She looked like she was about to cry, herself. 'Life's too short for all this bitterness, Jackie. I'm going to try again to get along with her. She's so lonely.'

'Well, good for you,' I said. 'Although if it was me, I'm sorry but I don't think I could forgive the things she's said to you.'

'I didn't say it would be easy,' she admitted with a little smile.

I felt a bit sad and worried myself after I left her. I might not have known her for too long, but I'd got used to Kate as a strong, cheerful, no-nonsense type of person, and I didn't like seeing her looking so down. She'd told me how she'd had the whole house upside down this week, searching again for the things she'd lost. It was the watch that upset her the most because her children had bought it for her.

'I think they're hurt that I've been careless enough to lose it,' she said. 'That's probably not helping the situation.'

'I'm sure there is no *situation*,' I tried to reassure her. 'It's just Michael reacting to the criticism from his sisters, like you suspected.'

'Perhaps,' was all she said.

I'd already made up my mind what I was going to do when I got home. I had Bob's number in my phone from when all that Ipswich stuff kicked off.

'Kate doesn't know I'm calling,' I said as soon as he answered. 'She wouldn't like it, so please don't tell her.'

'Right.' It was obvious he felt extremely uncomfortable. 'Is she … I hope she's OK?'

'Not really,' I said, coming straight to the point. 'For one thing, she's worried about her family. Her son's stopped her having the twins.'

'Oh, yes, she did say something about that. I didn't realise it was permanent.'

'Well, I hope it isn't, but it's still upsetting for Kate. Her children seem to think she's getting forgetful, because she's been losing things. Bob, please don't take this the wrong way, but ...' I swallowed. 'I've got to ask you. You wouldn't – of course you wouldn't – have *borrowed* anything of Kate's, would you? Just to, I don't know, *remind* you of her? Something like that?'

'What? *Borrowed* anything? What on earth do you mean? You don't mean the dressing-gown, do you? She only lent it to me because my clothes were wet, and I gave it straight back.'

'I actually meant her phone. Or her diary. Or her car keys. Or her watch.'

There was a silence. Then:

'The watch she lost on the Sunday. When I was there. You think her son was right, do you, Jackie? You want to blame me for that too? And even the other things – things that went missing when I wasn't even there?'

He sounded ... not angry, not disgusted or shocked ... just *wounded*. Weary, as if this was just one more blow in a series of many.

'I'm sorry. But I had to ask, Bob. I didn't for a minute believe it, but ... well, in light of the fact that you've told me how *fond* you are of Kate, I just wondered.'

'You thought I'd behave like some demented stalker, taking things of Kate's to keep at home and gloat over?' He sighed. 'You've got me wrong, Jackie. I may have been a stupid old fool, speaking out of turn, making poor Kate feel upset and awkward – you needn't think I haven't been angry enough with myself for that. But I would never, *ever*, do anything to hurt her.'

'Of course not. No. I knew that really,' I said quickly. 'I just had to check, all right? I mean, you might even have picked the things up, meaning to put them down again – it could just have been an accident.'

'I haven't touched them, any of them. But I suppose I should be glad you're trying to help her. I don't suppose she'll be in a hurry to see *me* again.'

'She'll see you, of course she will. You just need to give her a little time. You unnerved her a bit.'

'Yes. I should have listened to you, shouldn't I. You did warn me not to say anything to her.'

Poor guy. He sounded desolate. But what could I say? Like he said, I'd warned him. I couldn't believe he'd still gone and blabbed to her about being in love with her. For God's sake! At his age!

'It's just that she was being so kind to me,' he was going on. 'I suppose I mistook it for … something more. But she's just a kind person, isn't she – kind to everyone. Now she probably thinks I'm disgusting.'

'No she doesn't,' I tried to soothe him. 'She just likes you as a *friend*, Bob. You'll have to get your head around that, if you want to still see her.'

'Yes. I know.'

'So anyway.' More to the point. 'Kate says you never did explain what you were actually doing the other week. Why you went to Ipswich.'

'Didn't I? Oh. I thought I did. I was going to see Craig. Well, that was the intention, anyway. But of course, it turned out he wasn't at home, because he'd gone to see Nathan, because Nathan had tried to commit suicide.'

'Yes, I heard about that – I'm really sorry. But why was it such a big mystery, Bob, if you were just going to see your son? Why didn't you tell us where you were going? And why didn't you take Freddie with you?'

'Oh. Well. The thing is, Jackie – I didn't want to tell Kate because I thought she'd try to talk me out of it. And I couldn't take Freddie because that was the whole point. I was keeping him.'

'*Keeping* him?' I frowned. 'What do you mean?'

'I went up there to have a serious talk with Craig. To deliver an *ultimatum* to him. I'd decided that, unless he came to his senses, left that other chap and sorted things out with Nathan – unless the pair of them got back together for Freddie's sake, I wasn't going to let *either* of them have him. I was going to keep him myself. It would be better for him, that's what I'd decided. Better than being passed back and forth between them, used as … as some kind of *pawn* in their disputes with each other. I don't want that for him, you see? It's not fair. He'd be better off with *me.*'

'Bob. You know you can't do that,' I said, fairly gently. I wasn't taking him seriously, to be honest. 'You'd just be made to hand him back – you know that. They'd get the police and the Social Services involved if necessary.'

'They'd have a job!' he retorted – and suddenly there was a new, hard edge to his voice. I sat up in my chair. Bloody hell, surely he didn't actually mean it? 'They'd have to find me first.'

'They know where you live, mate. Come on – nice try, Bob, but it wasn't going to happen, was it.'

'Oh yes it was,' he said. 'I wasn't going to be hanging around at home with the boy, I'm not that daft. I was taking him abroad. I'd already got hold of his passport without anyone noticing. I had it all worked out. I got the idea from listening to Kate talking about her daughter – how isolated it is where she lives. I was planning to take Freddie to France, Jackie. And I'll tell you what: if all this hadn't happened with poor Nathan, and if Craig refused to listen to me, I'd have done it.'

'Don't be silly, Bob,' I told him. 'I can understand how you felt, but I think you're letting your imagination run away with you.'

'I don't expect you to understand,' he said. 'But if it had come to the crunch, I'm sure *Kate* would have helped me.'

I didn't see the point in arguing. He was being ridiculous. But I knew for a fact that there was *no way* Kate would have got involved in helping him out with such a crazy scheme. And even if she'd have considered it once upon a time, she certainly wouldn't now! Running off to France with his grandson? No way. Privately, I was beginning to think the guy was off his head.

KATE

How I Wonder What You Are

I'd never heard anything so ridiculous in all my life. When Jackie called me to tell me, I agreed with her that Bob must be losing his mind. That'd explain a lot. I tried to call him, twice, but he wasn't picking up. I didn't know whether he had caller display, but if he did, he seemed to be avoiding talking to me. I didn't bother to try again. I really couldn't take it seriously.

But only a couple of days later, I had to reassess my opinion. Danielle called from France, and she sounded quite put out.

'What's all this about some random man friend of yours wanting to come over to France with his grandchild?' she demanded.

'Oh, God. Please don't tell me he's somehow got in touch with *you*? I thought he was making it up.'

'Well, I don't know whether it's some kind of *joke* or not, but apparently he told Clément, when the kids were over with you, that he was coming over. Actually, *you* talk to Clément. Clément!' she yelled. 'Come and explain to your nan how you invited this person to come over to France.'

There was a pause, some muttering, and then Clément came on the phone.

'Hello Grand-maman,' he said in a sulky voice. 'I did *not* invite him. It's not my fault.'

'Well, whose fault is it, then?' I heard his mother exclaiming.

'What happened, Clem?' I asked him. 'When did Bob talk to you?'

'That Sunday, at your house, when it rained. When he turned up and borrowed your dressing-gown,' he said.

'OK. But I don't remember you having any conversation with him?'

'It was outside. Afterwards, when he was leaving. I'd gone outside by the garage to … um …' He dropped his voice. 'I don't want to say why,' he whispered.

'Oh. I see. For a smoke – am I right?' The cheeky bugger must have already had some cigarettes on him, even before the ones he acquired on the trip to the zoo.

'Yes,' he whispered. I could imagine Danielle breathing down his neck. To be honest, I hoped she was going to find out – if she didn't already suspect – about his smoking. But that was a matter for another time.

'And while you were out there, you saw Bob leaving, and he talked to you?' I prompted.

'Well, I was just saying goodbye to the little boy – Freddie. And I said to his granddad that Freddie was a cute little kid. I was just being polite.'

'Fine. And?'

'Well, we said goodbye, and then – the granddad suddenly looked around, to see if anyone would see us talking together, but of course, we were by the garage, out of sight. And then he said this very strange thing to me. He said: *'I was thinking maybe I'd bring Freddie to France for a holiday. Somewhere quiet. I hear it's quiet where you live?'* And he asked me the name of our village.'

'Oh, he did, did he?' I said.

'So you didn't know, Grand-maman?' Clément said. 'He didn't mention it to you?'

'No. And why am I only just being told about this?'

'I didn't think much about it at the time. But since I've come home, I've been worried about it. He seemed very *secretive* about it. I didn't like to think he might be planning to … um … *steal* his grandson?'

287

'*Abscond* with him, I think that's the expression you need.'

'*Abscond.* Yes. So I thought I should tell *Maman.* She thinks it's my fault!' he added indignantly. 'It's not my fault, is it, Grand-maman?'

'No, Clem.'

'You think perhaps it was a joke?'

'Well, I think Bob has been feeling a little bit wrong in the head,' I said, and then wished I'd phrased it better. 'A bit upset – OK? Because of some issues – some things happening in his family. But I'm going to talk to him. Don't worry, it definitely wasn't your fault. Now, pass me back to your mum, please, Clem.'

'So what's going on?' Danielle demanded instantly. 'Who is this person?'

'A friend of mine who's been going through some problems. It's OK, he won't turn up on your doorstep.'

'Well, from what Clem says, he sounded like he was planning to run away with his grandchild. Did you know about it?'

'No.' I sighed. 'As I've just explained to Clément, I didn't even know they'd had a conversation. Don't worry, I'm sure he *wouldn't* have done anything silly.'

Actually, I wasn't sure about that at all. Not anymore.

'Well, I'd be grateful if you'd talk to him, Mum, whoever he is. I'm not at all happy about strange men asking my son where he lives. It's really quite sinister. It makes me wonder what the hell was going on while the children were staying with you.'

'Oh, for heaven's sake, nothing was going on, Danielle.' Nothing apart from your son getting cigarettes bought for him and your daughter cuddling up to strange boys from Romford. 'Everything was absolutely fine and normal. This is a problem between me and my friend. He might have an overactive imagination, but there's nothing at all sinister about it, I promise you.'

'If you say so,' she said, not sounding convinced. And then, abruptly changing the subject: 'Anyway, I hear the twins are with their childminder now. Probably best all round, isn't it.'

So the evidence against me was mounting. Not only was I forgetful and incapable of looking after the children, I also had friendships with sinister men who dropped hints about absconding to France with little children. I tried yet again to call Bob, as soon as I'd hung up from Danielle, and when I still got no response I simply set off to walk round there.

'What on earth did you think you were doing?' I demanded as soon as he opened the door.

Despite my anger, I couldn't help but notice the way his eyes lit up when he saw me, and then clouded over again. He looked away, obviously still too embarrassed to talk to me, but I pressed on regardless.

'What made you even *think* about going to France with Freddie, you idiot, never mind talking to my grandson about it – putting that anxiety on him – he's just a kid! Have you gone completely mad, Bob?'

He held the door open for me and finally met my gaze again.

'Yes,' he said quietly. 'I think so.'

Over coffee in his little sitting room, I calmed down a bit. But only a bit. I listened to him confessing that he'd been in such a terrible state when he found out he might never see Freddie again, he now accepted he wasn't behaving rationally. He didn't know why he'd told Clément about it, it was just that he seemed such a nice boy, he was kind to him and was being sweet to Freddie. Apparently he'd managed to convince himself – and I had the uncomfortable impression he still *was* convinced – that I'd somehow help him if it ever came to the crunch and he decided to make a run for it to France with the child.

And all through this, I simply couldn't stop thinking that this was the man whose welfare I'd put before my own family, dashing up to Ipswich, forgetting about the kids coming from France, not even getting as cross as I should have done about the imposition of having Freddie dumped on me without even being asked. I'd defended him to Jackie, and against accusations from my own children. I'd listened to him and worried myself sick about him. And now it seemed he was just another person who took me for granted, treated my generosity in the most appallingly off-hand and ungrateful fashion.

'Oh!' he said, looking at me in alarm. 'Please, Kate – please don't *cry*. I couldn't bear to think I'd made you cry.'

'I'm not,' I retorted, wiping the tears away crossly.

I was just so *disappointed*. All that stuff the previous week about loving me – it was rubbish. He'd *used* me, and he thought he could do it again if necessary. I looked up at him with a sudden realisation: it was the other way around! *I* had actually loved *him*! If loving someone meant caring about them, then that's what I'd done: I'd cared about him, I'd have done anything to help him. And, as usual, as I should have learned from past experience, loving someone had ended up making me feel let-down and bitter.

'I'm sorry,' he said now, dropping his eyes. 'I realise I must have worried your grandson by talking to him about it. But at the time, well, I'd just got back from Ipswich and I hardly knew where I was or what I was doing. I was so exhausted. So much had happened.'

I sighed. It was true – he'd been ill, knocked himself out, been taken to hospital with concussion, lost his wallet, found out his son's ex partner had tried to commit suicide …

'I know,' I said, finally swallowing back my own hurt feelings. 'I know you'd had a rough time. But …'

'But that doesn't excuse the way I behaved, does it. I can't ask you to understand, because the honest truth is, I don't understand it myself. I think I *did* go a little mad. The thought of losing Freddie … it just tore me apart.'

'But you told me you were coming to terms with it, Bob!'

He gave a snort of laughter. 'I was a good actor, wasn't I. I didn't want anyone to see how I was really feeling, what I was thinking … planning to do. I just had to have a plan, you see. Something I could do, if Craig wouldn't see sense, if he refused to listen to me. I'd have done anything, Kate, anything rather than let Freddie be fought over and passed back and forth between them like a parcel. Anything rather than never see him again.'

I closed my eyes and nodded slowly. Of course. He was right. I mean, what he *did*, what he supposedly planned to do, was completely crazy, but he was right to say that in those circumstances he'd have done anything. I'd been so lucky, seeing so much of my grandchildren – up till recently I'd taken it completely for granted. And now, just because I wasn't having the twins regularly anymore, just because Steph hadn't wanted to leave Izzie and the baby with me on one single occasion, I was already starting to panic. If I couldn't imagine now what Bob had been going through, couldn't sympathise with how desperately – and yes, *crazily* – his situation had made him behave, then all my years of loving my grandkids had taught me nothing.

I got up and went over to him, put my arms round him and quite deliberately kissed him on the cheek.

'It's OK,' I said. 'I understand.'

Well. I was *trying* to understand, anyway. That was a start.

KATE

The Big Bad Wolf

I stayed with Bob for most of the day. There was a lot to catch up on. We talked about the twins going to a childminder, about the fact that my missing things hadn't turned up, that I'd accused Pam of taking them and ended up feeling sorry for her. And he told me something even more interesting.

'The endpoint of all that's happened, Kate, is that Craig's thrown Andrew out.'

'Oh! Oh my God. Is he getting back together with Nathan?'

'It's too early to say, but I certainly hope so. Apparently he saw Andrew in his true colours after Nathan's suicide attempt. Would you believe, he got angry with Craig for being so upset about it! He kept sulking and reminding Craig that Nathan was his ex and that *he* was the one Craig should be concentrating on now. Like a spoilt child! In the end Craig told him that he'd been with Nathan for a long time and they had a child together, and if Andrew couldn't accept that it meant he'd always have some feelings for him, he'd better clear off.'

'And is Nathan OK now?'

'Yes, according to Craig he's made a full recovery. I feel sorry for the poor chap. He was completely devastated by the break-up with Craig, you know. All right, I know he started being difficult about Craig's access to Freddie – after we found out Nathan was the biological father. But to be honest, now I've calmed down about it all, I can't say I blame him, really. Why should he be reasonable? Craig had treated him appallingly, throwing him out and moving another man in.'

'Well, I suppose there's always blame on both sides when people break up.'

Bob looked at me sheepishly and sighed. 'None of us have come out of this very well – me included. But even if they *don't* get back together, I think things are going to be settled more amicably now between Craig and Nathan, regarding Freddie. They've both had a shock, and presumably done a bit of thinking about … you know. Things younger people don't often think about.'

'How short life is? How pointless it is to waste time being angry and hurting each other?'

'Something like that, yes. I hope.'

I took a deep breath. 'Well, I agree. I must admit I came here feeling cross and upset with *you* today, Bob.'

'I don't blame you,' he admitted quietly.

'But let's draw a line under all that now, shall we? Go back to how things were?'

He looked at me for a moment. I knew he understood what I was saying. No more talk of love and stuff. It was taken for granted that we cared about each other. We didn't have to embarrass each other and make things uncomfortable.

'Friends again?' he said hopefully.

'Friends again,' I agreed firmly. 'Of course.'

I felt happy, almost carefree, as I walked home a little later. It was such a relief that everything seemed to be working out OK for Bob and his family. Compared with the stuff he'd been through, I had absolutely nothing to complain about. The twins going to a childminder? So be it. As Jackie had pointed out – some grandparents would sigh with relief. Steph not leaving the children with me? I'd just read too much into it. I was being silly. I should appreciate my luck that I saw the grandkids at all. Just imagine how it must feel to be like Pam, sitting there waiting for the odd occasion when her husband's nasty son deigned to let her see the children.

I turned the corner into our road, still thinking about Pam and promising myself I'd make an effort in future to be more tolerant of her moods. And there, outside her house, was a large shiny black car. Inside the car was a disgruntled looking woman, and leaning on the car door, staring up and down the street, was a very cross looking man. And in the back seat – two children. The little girl was a similar age to Izzie and I recognised her immediately as the child I'd seen very occasionally with Pam. This was them! These were the son and daughter-in-law who'd been giving Pam so much grief. I glanced at him as I passed. He scowled. *What* a charmer.

'Can I help you?' I said. I can't think what possessed me. 'Are you looking for Pam? I'm her friend.'

Well, that was something of an exaggeration. But he didn't need to know that.

'Are you really?' he said, looking down at me like I was something unpleasant that had crawled out of the gutter. I didn't like him. I wouldn't have liked him even if Pam *hadn't* told me about the way he treated her. But she had, so I liked him even less. And I sure as hell wasn't going to let him talk to *me* in that tone.

'Yes, I am. My name's Kate. And you are?' I said, pretending not to know, forcing him to introduce himself.

'Russell Haynes,' he said, imperiously. 'Your *friend* looks after my children.'

'Does she, indeed?' I wanted to slap him. He made Pam sound like a paid childminder.

'I'm rather surprised to find that she's out.' He looked at his watch. 'I don't suppose you have any idea where she might be?'

'I'm afraid not.'

'Well, that's very bloody inconvenient. We've come to leave the children with her,' he said. 'We're supposed to be going out tonight. '

'She couldn't have been expecting to have them,' I retorted. 'She'd have made sure she was here, I know she would.'

'Well it's a real bloody nuisance.'

'It's our own fault, Russell.' His wife had got out of the car now and come up behind us. 'Pam didn't know about this,' she explained, turning to me. 'We only tried calling her earlier today. We kept trying, and when she didn't answer we thought there might be something wrong with her phone, so we've just brought the kids round anyway in the hope it'd be all right.'

'Well, there you go, then,' I said. 'Unfortunately, it's not all right, is it. She's gone out. She has got a life of her own, you know. I happen to know how much she loves your children and enjoys looking after them. But she can't just sit here every day doing nothing on the off-chance that you might send them round.'

'Well, it's very inconvenient,' Russell repeated, having obviously taken no notice of this whatsoever. 'It's completely letting us down – we've got tickets for a concert, and a restaurant booked.'

'Hang on a minute,' I said, 'She hasn't let you down, has she, if she didn't even know about it.' I should have shut up and minded my own business. But I was really cross now. The bloody cheek of him! 'You're out of luck this time, I'm afraid – you've had a wasted journey.'

'I can't believe this! Those tickets were bloody expensive,' he said, sighing. Then he turned back to me, looking me up and down again, like he was trying to work out whether I was suitable, and added: 'I don't suppose *you're* available to look after the kids tonight?'

'What?' I said, aghast. 'You don't even know me!'

'Russell,' Tania warned him, a hand on his arm. But I was already squaring up to him.

'Look after your children? No way, Sunshine. Pam would have done it willingly. Perhaps you should ask her more often. Meanwhile if you're so worried about how much money you've wasted, perhaps you'd better go and stand outside the theatre and try flogging your tickets half-price!'

And with that, feeling thoroughly satisfied, I turned away and walked off home.

But of course, the feeling didn't last. As soon as I'd shut the front door behind me, I started to have regrets. It would be awful if I'd made things worse for Pam. Once again: me and my big mouth. I'd need to apologise. And the sooner the better.

PAM

Oh Why Are You A-Weeping, A-Weeping, A-Weeping

I'd been up to London again. It hadn't been a very good trip. I wasn't feeling at my best when I got home. To be honest, I went straight indoors and laid down on the sofa. I thought about making myself a cup of tea, or maybe even heating up some soup – I hadn't had anything to eat. I thought about putting on the TV, or just the radio, or picking up my library book, to take my mind off things. But the next thing I knew, I heard the door bell ringing, and realised I must have gone right off to sleep. It took me a while to come round – I felt completely disorientated. Then the door bell rang again. Somebody was getting impatient. So I got to my feet and staggered to the front door.

It was Kate, and she was looking at me with a shocked expression that swiftly changed to one of concern.

'Pam, are you all right?' she said.

I didn't realise I looked that bad.

'Yes, thank you, I'm absolutely ...' I began. But I couldn't finish. I couldn't say it – couldn't get the words out. What was the point? What was the point of continuing to tell people I was *absolutely fine* when I *absolutely wasn't*? 'Actually, I'm not feeling too good,' I admitted very quietly.

It felt so defeatist to be admitting it. For months I'd been pretending everything was going to be OK, that if I kept denying anything was wrong, I'd be able to get through it. It wouldn't get to me. It wouldn't *kill* me. But now, suddenly, I was beyond pretending, even to myself. And it might have been defeatist, but on the other hand, in some ways it was a relief to let go, give in, and ... OK, wallow in it.

'What's wrong?' Kate was asking, and I realised I was seeing her through floods of tears.

'Sorry.' I didn't seem to be able to talk properly. The word just kept bubbling out of me, along with the tears. 'Sorry ... so sorry ... sorry ...'

'Is there anything I can do?' she asked. 'Shall I make you a cup of tea, at least?'

I held the door open for her and she went straight through to the kitchen.

'Go and sit down,' she said, and I went back to the sofa, fell against the cushions, left her to get on with it. Everything seemed completely unreal. It was so unlike me. Letting Kate, of all people, see me in a state like this *again* – as if it wasn't bad enough that I'd cried my eyes out when she came round to accuse me of stealing her stuff! But I felt too weak to care.

'Here you are,' she said eventually, bringing me a hot mug of tea. 'Would you like something to eat too?'

'Maybe just a biscuit,' I managed to get out, now I'd stopped blubbing. 'They're in a tin in the cupboard over the ...' She was back with them within seconds. 'I'm so sorry,' I said yet again.

'Don't be silly. Do you want to talk about whatever's happened, or would you prefer it if I left you in peace?'

I took a deep breath. It would be so tempting to share it with someone. I just didn't know whether Kate would be the right person. Let's face it, she and I had had a somewhat up-and-down relationship.

'Is it about the children?' she asked gently. 'Only if it is, there's something I need to tell you.'

Apparently they'd been here. Russell and Tania, with the kids. Kate was watching me carefully as she described what happened, probably worried I was going to start crying again.

'I recognised the little girl – Lily, isn't it. She – the woman ...'

'Tania.'

'She was in the car with the children. He ...'

'Russell.'

'Yes. He was obviously looking for you. That's what I came to tell you.'

'Did they speak to you?' I asked in surprise.

Kate looked a little embarrassed. 'Well, actually, I spoke to *him*. I probably shouldn't have done. I asked if I could help him, and he ... kind of *demanded* to know where you were.'

'Wanted me to do an emergency babysit, I suppose,' I said ruefully.

'Yes! Exactly!' Kate sighed and shook her head. 'I'm really sorry, Pam, but I'm afraid I was quite rude to him. Knowing what you'd told me about the way they take advantage of you – and the way he spoke to me! – it was just too much.'

'It doesn't surprise me,' I said. 'Tell me what happened.'

Kate sat down next to me. 'Well,' she said, 'I explained that I didn't actually know where you were, and he did all this huffing and puffing, looking put out, as if it was my fault, and saying they'd been expecting you to have the children tonight.'

'He didn't even ask me!' I protested. 'I'd have been here, obviously, if he had.'

'Of course you would,' she agreed, 'And I told him that. He didn't like it. But I must say *she* – Tania – seemed a lot less hostile than him.'

'Yes. She normally is.'

'She admitted they'd only tried to call you about it earlier today, and when you didn't reply they just thought they'd bring the kids round anyway. Are they for real? What's the matter with them? Do they think you just sit here day after day, never going out, waiting for them to call?'

I sighed. 'The trouble is, Kate, that is exactly what I normally do. But today I had an appointment ...' I'd been about to tell her. To spill it out. But she cut in quickly, crossly:

'It doesn't matter why you were out, Pam! The point is, you're entitled to a life!'

'Well ...'

'I'm sorry, I know I shouldn't have interfered, but he made me so cross – going on about you letting them down, and what a bloody nuisance it was because they'd got tickets for a concert and a restaurant booked! I told him you loved having the kids and if you'd been *asked* about it you'd have made sure you were there, but as it was, he was out of luck.'

'What did he say to *that*?' I asked. I could just imagine.

'Muttered on about the bloody theatre tickets being expensive.' Kate looked at me. 'Is he always such an arse?'

'Yes.'

'He actually asked me whether *I* was available to look after the children!'

'Oh, God.' I looked at Kate's indignant face and suddenly, ridiculously, I had an urge to laugh. It must have been a kind of hysteria – wanting to cry and laugh at the same time. 'I'm so sorry,' I said, swallowing it back. 'What did you say?'

She coughed and looked down. 'I'm afraid I said no. In fact, to be entirely truthful, I said '*No way, Sunshine*'. I do feel bad about it now – I mean, *you've* helped me out, several times, haven't you – and I would have done it for *you*. But I'm sorry, there was no way I was helping that unpleasant couple, especially him. I don't know how he had the nerve to ask! I told him ... I hope I haven't made things any more difficult for you, Pam. I hate telling you this now, while you're so upset. But I told him he'd better go and flog his tickets outside the theatre.'

At that, I couldn't hold it back anymore. I burst out with such a shrill shout of laughter that Kate actually jumped in her chair. She must have thought I'd lost my mind. Well, maybe I had.

'Good for you, Kate,' I said, wiping my eyes. Yes, laughing and crying at the same time – it obviously was hysteria.

'You're not upset with me?' she asked warily. 'I mean, if I've made things worse, I'll speak to him again and apologise.'

'Don't you dare. He had it coming to him. As you say, he's a thoroughly unpleasant man and if it wasn't for the children I'd have had nothing to do with him since Colin passed away.'

'But now you need to keep on the right side of him.'

'I thought I did, Kate. But, well, sometimes things happen that make you reappraise everything. You realise life is so precious, so fragile, it's just ... just plain silly to waste it waiting for other people to change, when they clearly aren't going to. I've spent too long waiting around for Russell and Tania, dancing to their whims, taking everything they threw at me, thinking I had no option. I've wasted so much of my life, and now it's too late.'

She shook her head at me. 'Don't say that. *Talk* to them, Pam. Lay it on the line – tell them you won't put up with being used anymore. Tell them they should be letting you see the children for *their* sake – for Lily's and George's sake, not just because they sometimes need a babysitter. Talk to Tania, if Russell won't listen.'

'You're quite right, that's what I should have done. I should have done it years ago. But it *is* too late now. I won't be able to look after the children anymore. I'm not going to be well enough.' I swallowed, took a deep breath, and finally said it out loud for the first time. 'I've got cancer, Kate. I've known about it for a while, but today ... today I've just been told that it's inoperable.'

KATE

He'll Come Back and Marry Me ...

I'd never felt quite so stunned in my life. It was just appalling to think that this woman, whose moods I'd been complaining about ever since I met her, had been hiding a serious illness all along.

'Why didn't you tell me?' I said – which was hardly fair, as I hadn't exactly been a warm and welcoming friend to her. Until a few days earlier, when she'd told me the whole story about her partner dying and how his son had been treating her, I'd actively disliked and discouraged her.

'I didn't want to talk about it,' she said with a shrug. 'I suppose I was in denial. Hoping it would just go away if I kept it to myself.'

It turned out that the day she'd seen Bob at the station – when she'd bought his ticket to Ipswich for him – was the first time she'd been to see the specialist at one of the London hospitals with the diagnosis of pancreatic cancer. At this second appointment, she'd been given the results of further tests – and the devastating news that the cancer was inoperable, as the tumour was too close to an artery.

'There's *nothing* they can do?' I asked, aghast.

'They're going to try radiotherapy and chemotherapy,' she said, sounding strangely matter-of-fact about it now that the crying and laughing and hysteria had abated. 'Sometimes, apparently, these sort of tumours can be shrunk and then they *can* operate.'

'So it's not a ... definite ...'

'It's possible it might *not* kill me.' She nodded, tried to smile. 'I didn't want to ask what the odds were.'

'Oh, God, Pam. I'm so sorry. Look – if there's *anything* I can do ... I mean, while you're having the treatment, while you're not well – I'm sure you're going to need some help. I'll do whatever I can.'

'That's kind of you, Kate. But I know how busy you are, with the grandchildren.'

'I'm not, anymore.'

And I realised I'd been right all along. Sometimes my friends *did* need me just as much, or more, than my family did, and I shouldn't have had to apologise for that. I'd always been there for my children, for my grandchildren, and I always would be – but sometimes they'd have to join the queue. And for the foreseeable future, I was going to put Pam at the front of that queue whenever she needed me.

'We're going to beat that bloody cancer,' I told her, blinking back my own tears. 'You and me together – we're going to fight the damned thing and beat it – OK?'

And finally, I gave her a hug.

'God. I'm really sorry to hear that,' Jackie said when I'd finally finished telling her the news. There was a silence. Then: 'I realise how this is going to sound, Kate. But you know, you don't have to *like* someone just because they have cancer. You can help her, of course, and feel sorry for her, but …'

'I know what you're saying.' I managed a laugh. 'And you're right – I didn't like her, at all. It's hard to say how I feel about her now. I suppose it is just sympathy, but I think she needs some, and deserves some. Poor cow – the way she's been treated since her partner died, and now this.'

'Absolutely. I agree. But it didn't give her the right to be so bloody rude to you.'

'No. I do understand it a bit better now, though. She says she realises it was a bad idea, keeping everything locked up inside her. Things fester, don't they, when you do that.'

'I guess so. Ha! I love the way you spoke to the horrible stepson and his wife, though!'

'Russell? Yes, I couldn't help myself. He was so obnoxious. Actually Tania seemed a little less aggressive. She looked quite embarrassed, like she didn't agree with the way he was carrying on. It made me wonder whether things would be different if it was up to her.'

'It's a pity she doesn't stand up to him and say so, then!'

'Well, yes. But I suppose Colin was *his* father so she probably feels like it's not her call. Or else she's scared of him. It wouldn't surprise me, he seemed such a bully of a man.'

'I just don't understand why women put up with blokes like that,' Jackie retorted impatiently. 'Especially when they've got kids. What sort of an environment is that for children to grow up in? Nobody needs to tolerate a rotten marriage, these days.'

'No.' I sighed. 'You're probably right.'

I'd tolerated mine for longer than I should have done. But then, Dennis was never exactly a bully. Just a waste of space.

As the weeks passed, I became more used to not having the twins every week and hardly ever being asked to look after Izzie. I wasn't sure whether it was because I'd begun to accept the situation, or whether I was just too busy to worry about it. Pam started her radiotherapy sessions, and I drove her to appointments, sat with her in waiting rooms, and stayed with her at home when she felt too poorly to do anything for herself. I had a lot of time to talk to her, and a lot of time for reflection. Since she'd opened up to me about the situation with the children, and her cancer, she seemed so much calmer and even more cheerful, despite the seriousness of her illness.

'I've realised crying and railing against it won't help,' she told me fairly early on during her treatment. 'I'll give myself a better chance of recovery if I try to stay positive.'

I felt humbled by her attitude, to be honest, and decided it wouldn't hurt to adopt a similar principle to everything in my own life. It had done me some good to realise that nothing I complained about was quite so grim, by comparison with what Pam was going through.

There were some good things going on too, though. At the beginning of September, Izzie started school and after the first day, phoned me herself to say:

'Nanny, guess what I found out today?'

I smiled, reasoning that it could have been almost anything. The width and depth of what a four year-old has to learn during her first couple of years at school is quite awe-inspiring.

'What, darling?'

'I have to go to school *every day*! And not just half days like pre-school, Nanny, but the *whole* day, *every single day of my life*!'

'Well,' I said, laughing, 'you don't have to go on Saturdays or Sundays. Or in the school holidays.'

'Oh.' There was a note of disappointment now. 'I thought it was every day.'

'Did you want to go every day, then, Izzie?'

'Yes! I love school! I wish I could *live* there, Nanny!'

Stephanie took over the phone from her and told me in a slightly offended tone:

'Four years of non-stop love and care, and she turns round and says she wants to live at school!'

'You should be grateful she likes it so much,' I said, still laughing. 'She's so little. I was worried about her starting so early, Steph.'

'I know. It's the same for all the kids with summer birthdays. Well, I guess you're right, it's a relief she got on so well today. Let's hope it lasts!'

I wanted to offer to pick her up from school sometimes. To share in it – the newness, the excitement. Or offer to have the baby occasionally, now Izzie would be at school every day, so that Steph could have a proper rest. But I didn't. If she wanted my help, she'd ask. If she didn't ask, she obviously still didn't need me.

Bob and I had spoken on the phone a couple of times. He'd been very sympathetic about Pam, but because I'd been busy looking after her, I hadn't seen him for a while. It was quite a shock when he called to remind me that because the new school term had started, so had the Mini Music Maker sessions. I'd completely forgotten about them. They wouldn't be a part of my life now anyway.

'No point me coming, without the twins,' I said, trying not to sound maudlin about it.

'No, I suppose not.' Bob paused. 'But you'll still come and meet us at the café afterwards, won't you? Jackie and me?'

I thought about it – about the convivial chats we used to enjoy over coffee and cakes while the children played. Ridiculously, it seemed like a lifetime ago but it had only been six weeks. Such a lot had happened during that time. I realised I was missing it – the routine of having those sessions to look forward to every Thursday, catching up with my friends regularly instead of having snatched conversations on the phone when I wasn't busy with Pam. But Pam had become quite dependent on me since her treatment had been making her feel poorly, and I couldn't let her down.

'You could bring your friend along, couldn't you?' Bob said, as if he'd heard what I was thinking.

'I don't know. She's quite weak, but I suppose I could drive her. It might cheer her up, give her a change of scenery.'

'I hope you can, Kate. It would be so nice to see you.' He sounded quite excited about it. I hoped he wasn't getting silly ideas about me again. I really didn't feel up to dealing with that. But then he added quickly: 'All of you, I mean – Jackie, and your friend Pam too.'

'In that case,' I said, 'I'll definitely try to get there.'

As it happened, the following Thursday Pam was having quite a good day.

'I think that would be rather nice,' she said when I suggested the outing. 'If you're sure you don't mind taking me, Kate?'

'Of course not. I think it'll do you good.'

'And you. You've been spending far too much time with me, and neglecting your other friends, and family.'

I didn't respond to this, but it brought a lump to my throat, thinking how much nicer and less selfish Pam seemed these days. I just hoped the change hadn't come too late.

We were the last to arrive at the usual café. Bob and Jackie were already there with Freddie and Autumn.

'It's so nice to see you!' Bob exclaimed when we'd got settled. He was grinning from ear to ear. He seemed even more excitable than he'd sounded on the phone. 'Thank God you're here. I've been bursting to tell Jackie my good news, but I wanted to share it with all of you together.'

'Go on, then!' I said, laughing. 'We could all do with some good news, Bob. What is it?'

'My son. He's back with Nathan.'

'Oh, that really *is* good news!'

'Yes. Craig says he realises now that the affair with the other chap was just a fling. Whatever that's supposed to mean,' Bob added with a note of disgust. 'He says he should never have finished with Nathan – the suicide attempt was all his fault, and he'll never forgive himself. Of course, it was already over with Andrew, and a good job too, but I'm *so* happy Craig and Nathan are back together.'

'So will everything go back to how it was before? Freddie will be back with them both?'

'Yes. So I won't have to worry anymore about anyone stopping me seeing him. Unless Craig ever decides to do something stupid like that again.'

'Well, let's hope not,' Jackie said. 'It sounds like he's come to his senses.'

'Yes, it does.' Bob smiled broadly again. 'They're getting married in April!'

'Oh!' I squealed again – and this time I got up and hugged him. So did Jackie. And I think Pam would have done, too, if she'd had the strength. 'That's the best news of all! I think we should all have chocolate muffins to celebrate!'

'And you're *all* going to be invited to the wedding!' Bob said, laughing with pleasure. 'Craig says he'd like me to bring my closest friends. He wants to meet you.'

'In that case, I wouldn't miss it for the world,' I said.

'Me neither,' Jackie agreed. 'How kind of him.'

Pam just smiled. I glanced at her, and had to look away again. I knew exactly what she must be thinking.

'There's only one problem with April,' Jackie said after Bob had gone and bought cakes for us all and we'd managed to calm down a bit.

'Oh – what?' I said, teasing her. 'You've got a better offer already?'

'Well, in a way, yes. But I just hope the dates won't clash.'

'What is it?' I asked her. I suddenly noticed she was looking pretty excited herself. 'You're not pregnant, are you?'

'What? No I'm bloody not, Kate, for God's sake – I'm past that anyway, thank God! But my daughter is. She's expecting in April.'

'Oh!' I looked at her in surprise. 'Autumn's going to have a little brother or sister, then?'

'Half-brother, or half-sister, yes. Erin's got herself a new man, and he's lovely, thank the Lord – not a nasty bastard like Autumn's father, whoever the hell he was and wherever the hell he's gone. Sean, the new boyfriend, has got a good job and it seems Erin will be able to stop work when the new baby's due – and perhaps work from home afterwards. It'll be so much less stress for her.'

'That's great, Jackie,' I said. 'You must be so happy for her.'

'Yes, of course. And yours isn't the only family with a wedding coming up, Bob! But they're going to wait till after the baby's born. And of course, as soon as I know the date, I'll let you all know. I'll want my friends there, obviously, and I'm sure Erin and Sean will agree.'

'Oh, *another* wedding!' I squealed. 'I'm going to have to buy a dress. And some shoes!'

We all laughed. Even Pam, although she still wasn't saying anything.

'So – are you going to be looking after *two* grandchildren next year, Jackie?' I asked, to change the subject slightly.

'Oh, bloody hell, I hope not! I was rather hoping I could give up this lark, once she stops work.' She looked over at the toy corner, where little Autumn was giggling at Freddie as he ran around her. I watched Jackie's expression soften. 'Although I suppose,' she added quietly with a little smile, 'there could be worse ways of spending my day off ... couldn't there?'

KATE

Leave Them Alone, and They'll Come Home

I'd pretty much given up worrying about my missing things, although I still felt a pang of regret and sadness when I looked at the cheap new watch I'd bought myself to replace the sixtieth birthday one. I'd got a new phone, had another spare key cut for the car, and seemed to be managing OK without a diary now that I didn't have any babysitting dates to remember. I'd begun to adapt to seeing less of the children. Their parents had kept their promise about including me in family events, although these didn't seem to happen too often. But during the first week of October it was the twins' second birthday and I was invited to their little party on the Sunday afternoon.

Jo greeted me at the front door with a curiously sheepish look. She didn't seem to be able to meet my eyes.

'Come in, Kate. The children are looking forward to seeing you.'

They ran down the hallway at me, yelling. 'Nanny, Nanny, Nanny!' they screamed together as they flung themselves at my legs, nearly sending me flying. They both seemed to have grown since I last saw them. Amelia was talking in sentences and Alfie had had his hair cut. I was almost overwhelmed with the pleasure of seeing them, of holding their soft, pudgy little hands and sitting with them on my lap. I spent so long hugging and kissing them both that I almost forgot to get their birthday presents out of my bag – and then we had another round of squealing and hugging as they unwrapped the Peppa Pig house and the Fisher Price garage. And finally, as they ran off again to chase their little friends round the house in an orgy of over-excitement, there was a sudden silence in the lounge and then Michael coughed and said, avoiding my eyes in much the same way as Jo had done:

'Mum, I need to talk to you.'

'Fire away, then,' I said. What now? There wasn't anyone else I could be banned from looking after, was there?

'It might actually be easier if I show you. Come up to the children's bedroom for a minute.'

Now completely intrigued, I followed Michael as he silently led the way upstairs and into the brightly painted bedroom the twins shared, where we both stepped awkwardly over discarded toys towards the miniature white wardrobe with its frieze of red elephants and yellow giraffes. Michael opened the wardrobe door and reached in to take something out, finally turning to me with an unreadable expression on his face.

'We … *I* … owe you an apology, Mum,' he said very quietly. And he held out the object he'd taken out of the children's wardrobe.

It was a bag – the kind of miniature vanity case in shiny pink plastic that little girls love to carry their treasures around in. I recognised it as the one Amelia sometimes used to bring round when she came to me for the day.

'It's Amelia's, isn't it,' I said, wondering what I was supposed to do with it.

'Yes. She hasn't played with it for a while.' He swallowed. 'I suppose it got pushed to the back of the toy cupboard. We bought them new bags when they started … to go to the new childminder. Little rucksacks with animal faces on, you know the kind of thing?'

'Yes. I know.' And the point was … ?

'The other day the childminder wanted us to send their swimming things round with them. There wasn't room in their bags, with all the usual stuff, you know, the spare nappies and everything. Amelia must have heard Jo say she needed another bag for their stuff, and she ran upstairs and came back down with this little case. Jo laughed at her – said it wasn't going to be big enough for their swimming costumes and towels, she'd need a carrier bag …'

'OK.' I sat down on one of the twins' little low beds. 'Michael, what's this got to do with me?'

He held out the little pink case again.

'Look inside, Mum,' he said.

I opened the clasp and lifted the lid. There, amongst an assortment of sparkly bracelets, a tiny toy camera that had probably come free with a comic, a plastic whistle and a sheet of Peppa Pig stickers, was my mobile phone. I gasped, lifted it out of the bag and beneath it was my diary. In the little side pocket of the case, along with two pink hair slides adorned with daisies and a broken seashell, were my car keys. And right at the bottom of the case, wrapped up in a doll's dress, was my gold watch.

'Oh!' I said. I shook my head. I just didn't know what else to say. It was such a complete surprise. 'Oh – my things.'

'I'm so sorry.' Michael looked wretched. 'We're both – Jo and I – we're both so sorry, Mum. After everything we said about you being careless.'

'Not to mention accusing my friends of stealing from me.' I said it gently, quietly, but I felt it needed to be said.

I watched my son struggle with his face.

'Yes. You're right. I should never have said that. And at the end of the day, it was Amelia who was stealing from you.'

'No, Michael!' I sat up, alarmed by this. 'Of course she wasn't *stealing*! She's too young to understand that concept. She was just *collecting* things! I hope you weren't angry with her?'

'No, not exactly angry, but we did tell her it was wrong to take things away from anyone's house, obviously.'

'Fair enough.'

'It was our fault for not looking in the bag when she brought it home.'

'Well, it wouldn't have occurred to you, would it. It's not as if it's the bag where we kept the nappies and things. You'd only have expected her to have her toys and treasures in it. I remember she went through a phase, for a few weeks, of bringing it with her every time she came, and then, of course, she got fed up with it and started bringing something else.' I smiled. 'That's just what kids do.'

'You're taking this awfully well,' he said. 'I wouldn't have blamed you if you'd been cross.'

'I'm just glad to have these things back. Especially the watch. The others didn't really matter, although it was a bit of a mystery and it's good to get to the bottom of it.' I looked up at him and smiled again. 'I'm not cross, Mike. Please don't worry about it. Life's too short.'

'Thanks.' He gave me a hug. I felt relieved, and somehow vindicated. Perhaps now I wouldn't be thought of anymore as the silly old bat who was losing her marbles.

'How's it going with the new childminder, anyway?' I asked as we went back downstairs.

'Yeah – OK.'

I glanced at him, wondering why the response had sounded a little abrupt, but his face had closed up again. Perhaps the twins were having difficulty settling down. I hoped not. It would be awkward now for Michael and Jo to lose face by admitting it. I wondered why I was suddenly feeling so magnanimous and seeing everything from their point of view.

It wasn't until the birthday party was over, and I was on my way home, that I also wondered why a childminder would be taking the children swimming. It seemed an unusual set-up. I frowned to myself and made a mental note to ask Michael about it next time we spoke. But as it happened, I didn't have to wait that long.

When I thought about it afterwards, I was surprised I hadn't found out sooner. I didn't realise my family were so good at keeping secrets. I marvelled at the fact that none of them had slipped up and mentioned it to me. In the event, it was Danielle who found out – Danielle who, like me, had been excluded from the knowledge of what was going on behind my back.

It was a Thursday, the week after the twins' birthday, and I was running very late for meeting Bob and Jackie after the music group because I'd been over the road with Pam, who was having a bad day. I was just looking at the time, and deciding I might as well call Jackie now and apologise for missing it, as they'd probably be on their way home by now anyway, when the phone rang.

'Oh my GOD, Mum,' shouted Danielle as soon as I answered. Her voice was shaking. 'It's him. They haven't told you that, have they. It's *him.*'

'What? What's who? Calm down, Dannie – what's the matter?'

She took a long, shuddering breath, like a sob. 'This so-called *childminder* they're sending the twins to. You have to do something, Mum – they won't listen to me! They have absolutely no idea! They don't remember. They were too young. They think I'm making it up.'

'What?' I said, my legs suddenly going weak, my head spinning with panic. 'What are you saying? Who …?'

'*Dad*! They've been back in touch with him. They didn't want to tell you. For God's sake, Mum, they're letting *Dad* look after their children!'

I didn't even hang up the phone – I just dropped it. I could hear Danielle shouting 'Hello? Hello? Mum?' as I grabbed my car keys and ran down the hallway.

For the past twenty-two years, my ex-husband had been living in the next town from me. For twenty-two years, as far as I possibly could, I'd avoided seeing him, speaking to him, coming into any sort of contact with him. But now, for the first time, I was going to his house. I ran out of my front door as if the devil himself was chasing me. And trying, as I fumbled with the car keys, to stop the memories flooding back, the memories of the sort of father he'd been. The sort of grandfather – the sort of *childminder* – he'd surely still be. It just couldn't be happening. I couldn't let it. I had to stop it, right *now*.

KATE: 24 YEARS EARLIER

Where is the Boy who Looks After the Sheep? He's Under the Haystack, Fast Asleep

It had been another difficult day. My boss had given me an urgent report to type just as I'd been hoping to start clearing up ready to go home. I tried to rush it, but was making slow progress, one eye on the clock, half my mind on what would be happening, or *should* be happening, at home. Danielle and Michael should have been picked up from school; Stephanie should have been given her tea. I jumped every time the office phone rang, half expecting it to be the secretary at Michael's school, calling yet again to ask why nobody had come for him, or Danielle saying she was going home on her own but hadn't got enough money for the bus.

If only, I thought for the thousandth time, we hadn't moved away from my parents when we got married. If only I had a sister, a cousin, a close friend living nearby who I could ask to help with the children while I was at work. There were neighbours, but how could I admit the scale of the problem to the elderly couple next door, or to the people the other side who had four immaculately turned-out children themselves? More than anything, if only I didn't have to work full-time to provide for the family. If only I had a husband who could do it instead, or failing that, could at least play his part and be trusted to look after the children!

It was dark by the time I finally got home. Dark outside, and dark in the house. I let myself in, snapping on the hall light with increasing irritation and anxiety.

'Hello?' I called. 'I'm home. Sorry I'm late. Why are you all in darkness?'

No answer. I walked through to the kitchen, calling again, and finally to the lounge, turning on the lights as I went. The TV was blaring, a news programme, and Dennis was on the sofa, flat out on his back, snoring, an empty bottle and several cans on the floor by his side. I ran upstairs, two at a time, calling the children.

'Dannie? Michael? Are you up here? Stephanie?'

My heart was hammering. Steph was only three. Danielle, unfortunately, was used to having to look after her, but if she wasn't here – if she and Michael hadn't got home from school – little Stephanie must be here somewhere on her own. Or as good as on her own.

'Where are you, children?' I called again, beginning to panic.

I ran back downstairs, grabbed Dennis roughly by the shoulders, shaking him, getting no response other than a grunt, a moan, more snoring. I was just taking hold of his arm to give him another, harder shake, just taking a breath ready to scream in his ear, when the doorbell rang. It was my next door neighbour, Evelyn, the one with the four children. She was carrying Stephanie in her arms, and was followed by Michael, who was crying, and Danielle, who was trying not to.

'Oh my God.' I ran to take hold of Steph. 'What happened? What the hell happened?'

'She had an asthma attack.' Evelyn said. She glanced in the direction of the sofa, and I couldn't have missed the look of disgust that passed over her face. 'Danielle did the right thing, bringing her in to me. She's all right now, love, don't worry. Just a bit exhausted, poor little pet.'

'We were frightened,' Michael said, wiping his eyes. 'She was going a funny colour.'

'I got her to use her puffer, but she wasn't getting any better,' Danielle said. 'I was really scared, Mum. I thought maybe she'd have to go to the hospital.'

'So did I, at first, to be honest,' Evelyn agreed. 'But I helped her use the inhaler again and, well, her breathing's back to normal now.'

I laid Stephanie down gently in the armchair, and put my arms round my older two children.

'You were very sensible – well done,' I said. 'And thank you so much,' I added shakily to Evelyn. I really didn't know what else to say. The smell of alcohol in the room was overpowering, the evidence of Dennis's neglect all too obvious.

'You're welcome. I'd better get back, though – mine are all indoors watching TV,' she said. She headed for the door, turned back to glance towards the sofa again, and hesitated for a moment, looking as if she was going to say something, but obviously thought better of it.

'I think she ate peanut butter,' Danielle said as soon as the front door closed behind her.

'What?!'

'Yes, she did,' Michael said, nodding. 'The jar was open on the table and she had some on a piece of bread when I got home.'

'You got home? Dad didn't collect you?'

'No.' He shrugged. 'I walked home with Sam and his mum.'

'And I got the bus,' Danielle said. She gave me a very direct look. 'I always make sure I've got enough money for the fare now, Mum. He hardly ever comes to pick me up. By the time I came in, Stephie was already wheezing, Michael had gone upstairs to get her inhaler, and Dad was … asleep.'

'I see.' I was having to take deep breaths to control my rage. Peanut butter? How the *hell* could Dennis have let her have that? He knew as well as I did that she was allergic to peanuts.

'Why did you eat the peanut butter, sweetheart?' I asked Stephanie gently, kneeling down beside her and stroking her hair back from her face. 'Didn't you remember that it makes you very poorly?'

'Sorry, Mummy. I was very hungry,' she said. 'I couldn't wake Daddy up. I just ate what was on the table.'

I looked through the open door to the kitchen. The table was still cluttered with the remains of the family's breakfast – cereal bowls, spoons, plates, half of a sliced loaf and sure enough, the open jar of peanut butter. I felt as though my heart would break. My little girl – my baby – hadn't been fed all day. She'd been so hungry, she'd climbed onto a chair and helped herself to something that could have killed her. Thank God she had presumably not managed to spread very much of it on the bread.

I didn't wake Dennis up. I couldn't even bear to look at him. I shepherded all three children into the kitchen, closed the door, and Dannie helped me clear up the mess and prepare a meal for us. I listened to their stories about their days at school, helped them with their homework, fed them their favourite dinner, treated them to ice cream, lemonade and biscuits, fussed over them and did everything I possibly could to shower them with double the love, to make up for their father's neglect, although I knew it could never be enough.

By the time he woke up, the younger two were in bed, and Danielle was in her room listening to her music. It wasn't until several years later that she admitted she'd heard what I'd said to him, what I'd called him, as he staggered blindly outside to be sick. I'd known for a long time that he was a drunk, who cared more about the contents of the next bottle than his own children. He'd always liked a drink, but the alcoholism had only really got a grip on him when he was made redundant. At first I'd made excuses for him – his self belief had taken a battering and he didn't have the confidence or the energy to stir himself from the couch to get out and look for another job. And then I'd gradually become too weary, too exhausted from working and trying to fill the gaps in his supposed childcare, to face up to what was happening or do anything about it. But that day something changed inside me. He wasn't just neglecting my children, he was a danger to them. I was never going to put them at risk again.

It was another two years before we actually divorced. The decree absolute came through just as Stephanie started school. I'd needed that time to fight and struggle and plead my way to a promotion at work, that would pay me a decent salary to provide for a childminder after school hours, and pay Danielle a small allowance for looking after the younger two during the holidays. But from the day of the peanut butter episode until I could afford to separate from him, I never again left Dennis in charge of the children. The very next morning, before going to work, I went to see Evelyn next door and opened my heart to her. It was humiliating, but necessary, and of course, none of it surprised her. Her older three children were all at school and she had a little boy a few months younger than Stephanie. I threw myself on her mercy, asking her if she could possibly look after Steph for me until I was in a position to pay someone.

'I'll make it up to you,' I promised. 'But if I'm honest, at the moment I just don't know how.'

'Would Michael like to walk the dog for me every afternoon?' she suggested after a moment's thought. 'It'd be a great help.'

I never forgot her kindness – not only in having Stephanie for me every day, when I couldn't afford to pay her, but in suggesting such a simple little thing to supposedly repay the debt, when we both knew it never could. When things got better, long after the divorce, long after we'd moved to the new house and the children had grown up, I bought her extravagant presents every year for Christmas and her birthday to show how grateful I was.

'You don't need to do that, Kate,' she would say with a gentle smile. 'I was just glad to keep the poor mite away from that brute.'

As I say, he wasn't actually a brute. He was just a pathetic, useless, drunk. But given a choice between a brute and a drunk, when it came to looking after young children, I didn't think there was much to choose between them.

BOB

Rapping on the Windows, Crying through the Locks

Kate didn't turn up to the café that Thursday. I was a little concerned – she'd said she was going to be there.

'Probably just changed her mind. Got busy with something, or perhaps her daughter came round with the baby,' Jackie said, shrugging.

'I don't know. It's not like her.' I picked up my cake and put it down again. I couldn't settle. I'd been looking forward to seeing her.

'Would you like me to call her?' Jackie asked, giving me a smile. 'Will it put your mind at rest?'

'Oh, thank you. If you wouldn't mind. She's got her old mobile back again now, you know.'

'Yes, I know.'

Jackie tried Kate's home number, and then her mobile, and finally shook her head at me.

'Not answering, Bob. Sorry. I reckon perhaps her friend Pam's taken a turn for the worse and Kate's too busy looking after her to bother with the phone.'

'Yes, you're probably right.' Kate had been such a wonderful friend to Pam, especially when you considered how badly the woman used to behave to her. I sighed. She'd been a wonderful friend to me, too, and I didn't like the uneasy feeling I had now, that something must be wrong, if she hadn't even had time to phone Jackie or me to let us know she wasn't coming.

As we were leaving the café afterwards, I suddenly made a decision.

'I'm going to go round and see her, Jackie. I know I'm probably being silly, but I've just got a funny feeling about it. I want to make sure she's OK.'

Jackie looked at me and sighed.

'OK, Bob, if it makes you feel better, but let *me* go instead. I've got the car. I'd offer to drive you, but I've only got one baby seat in the car.'

'Thanks, but I'll be fine. My knees aren't too bad today.' I smiled and said goodbye to her.

'Let me know, won't you,' she called as I walked off with Freddie in the pushchair. 'Give me a call later to let me know she's OK.'

I was a bit out of puff by the time I reached Kate's road. I slowed down, not sure whether to be relieved or not to see her car on the drive. Jackie was probably right, she'd just stayed at home because of her friend Pam, or because her daughter had visited. But as I approached the house, her front door suddenly flew open and Kate came tearing out, pulling a cardigan on as she ran to the car.

'Kate!' I called, hurrying the last few yards up the road. She turned round and saw me just as she was getting into the driver's seat.

'Bob! What are you doing here?' She was putting the key into the ignition, not waiting for an answer. 'Look, I'm sorry – I can't stop – it's urgent.'

Now I was standing beside the car, I could see she was in a state. Her face was flushed, she was breathing fast, and her hands were trembling so much she seemed to be having trouble starting the car.

'What's happened?' I said. 'Can I help? Let me help!'

'No, I've got to go! Oh, *shit*!' she swore, and I blinked in surprise. 'I can't get this bloody key in.'

'Kate, please, calm down! Whatever's happened, you can't drive in this state! Tell me what's happened. There must be something I can do.'

'There isn't, Bob, not unless you've suddenly got a driving licence.' She took a deep breath and added, 'Sorry. I'm sorry, you're right, I've got to calm down. Right.

Right, that's better,' she said as she finally turned on the ignition. 'Thanks, Bob, but it's really urgent, I have to go. I have to rescue the twins.' She suddenly started shaking again. 'They're with my ex. I've just found out.'

'Rescue ...?' I stared at her. And then, for the second time in half an hour, I made a sudden decision. Kate still had two child seats in the back of her car from when she'd looked after the twins. 'Wait!' I said. 'Take some deep breaths!' I threw open the back door of her car, and as she gabbled at me in confusion about what the hell I was doing, I unstrapped Freddie from his buggy, fastened him into one of the car seats faster than I'd ever managed the manoeuvre before, and with a speed and efficiency that surprised me even more than it must have done Kate, I folded the buggy and put it in her boot.

'I'm coming with you,' I announced, panting from the effort as I finally got into the passenger seat, 'whether you like it or not.'

'I don't need you to ...' she began, but I stopped her, putting one hand over hers that was trembling on the handbrake.

'I don't know what it's all about – you can tell me on the way,' I said. 'It's obviously a very upsetting situation, and if I *could* drive you, I would. But the least I can do is be with you, to support you. I won't say a word unless you want me to. Now, take some more deep breaths, and then let's go. Slowly.'

She swallowed, wiped her face, shook her head, and then sat up straight and let off the brake.

'Thank you, Bob,' she muttered as we pulled out onto the road. 'You interfering old sod.'

'You're welcome,' I said.

By the time we'd driven the short distance to Braintree, where her ex lived, she'd given me a brief explanation of the situation. Kate had never really talked to me about

Dennis before, but he certainly did sound like – as she put it – a waste of space, and I was pretty shocked to hear that her children had been in touch with him behind her back.

'I can't trust him with those babies,' she said, her voice beginning to shake again. 'I've got to get them away from him.'

I wanted to ask why she hadn't simply called her son or daughter-in-law about it, but I guessed this option simply seemed more immediate, as they'd both be at work. And anyway, there wasn't time to say any more before we arrived at the house where her ex apparently lived. I can't deny I felt a bit nervous. I mean, it was rather impetuous of me to insist on getting involved. I hoped the guy wasn't going to turn nasty.

'Wait in the car, Bob,' Kate said.

'But ...'

'I appreciate you coming with me. I promise I'll shout if I need you.' She shrugged. 'Don't worry. He was never violent. But there'll probably be a row.'

I watched as she went up to the front door and rang the bell. Rang it again. Looked through the glass – looked all around – and rang it a third time, banging on the door with the other hand. I opened the car door, wondering if I should point out the obvious – that he'd taken the children out – when a neighbour appeared on her doorstep, staring at us both.

'No need for all that racket. Dennis has gone out. Told me he was taking the two little ones swimming.'

'*Swimming?*' Kate said, putting her hand to her mouth and seeming to sway for a moment.

'Yes, to the local pool. He took them the other day, too – says they love it. Nice of him, isn't it? Not every grandfather would do that, not with two of them, and they're quite a handful too.'

'Which pool?' Kate interrupted. 'Quickly!'

Looking offended, the woman gave her directions and turned to go back indoors, as Kate ran back to the car and started the engine again, looking grim.

'I should have guessed,' she said as we roared off down the road. 'I should have realised. Michael said the childminder had started taking them swimming! Oh, God, please don't let him be drunk.'

'Surely he wouldn't be,' I tried to reassure her. 'Surely, if he's taken them swimming ...'

'He did it once with Michael and Stephanie,' she said. 'Steph was only about the twins' age. He took them in the main pool and forgot to put Steph's arm-bands on. If the lifeguard hadn't been watching ...' She shuddered. 'I told him if he ever took them anywhere near water again without me being there, I'd leave him and he'd never see the children again. I was a coward. I should have just done it, not talked about it. He nearly *drowned* her.'

'But he didn't. The lifeguard was there,' I said. 'And you weren't a coward. You were just trying to survive.'

'Trying to protect myself, my marriage!' she retorted bitterly. 'It was my children I should have been protecting. I should have got them away from him sooner than I did, Bob. I've always known it. I've always blamed myself. If this is history repeating itself ...'

'Don't think like that.' I looked at her taut, anxious face and I just wanted to make it all better for her. 'Nothing bad is going to happen this time. You're making sure of it.'

We parked at the swimming pool and, ignoring Kate's suggestion that I wait in the car again, I followed after her as quickly as I could, carrying Freddie, as she raced into the building and, frustrated by a barrier with a turnstile, waited impatiently at the reception desk for someone who was paying for a water workout (whatever that is).

'We're not swimming,' Kate said when it was finally our turn. 'We just need to go through and meet someone.'

'Meet someone at the café?' said the receptionist.

'No. At the pool.'

'You can't go to the pool without paying for a swim.'

'But we're not swimming,' I protested. 'We just need to see someone who's brought two children here.'

'You won't be allowed on the poolside in outdoor clothes and shoes,' the receptionist said, looking from me to Kate with irritation as if we were being awkward.

'We'll take them off, then!' Kate exclaimed. 'Here –' She got out her purse. 'For God's sake, I'll just pay for a swim, then – how much is it?' She threw a ten pound note on the desk. 'Just give us the tickets and let us through, *please.*'

The transaction was conducted in silence, with more truculent looks at both of us. I half expected the woman to call the manager to get us thrown out before we'd even got through the turnstile. Kate was sighing and gasping with impatience.

'OK,' I was trying to reassure her as we followed the signs through the changing area to the pools. 'We're here now. Let's try the learner pool first, he'll surely be in there with them. Take your shoes off, Kate, or we'll get thrown ...'

'No time!' she started to say.

And then, there they were.

'Nanny!' shouted Amelia, running towards us along the edge of the pool.

'Don't run, Amelia!' called a tall, bearded man who was following her, holding Alfie's hand. So this was Dennis. He didn't *look* drunk. And I noticed both the twins were wearing armbands. That was something, at least.

'Nanny!' Alfie joined in, letting go of his grandfather's hand and starting to run too, before being held back by Dennis – who was staring at us as if he'd seen a ghost.

'Kate?' he said, and his face creased into a worried frown. 'What are you doing here? Is something wrong? Is there a problem with Michael? Jo?'

'*Wrong?*' she said – the word came out on a long, trembling exhalation of breath, and she repeated it, more loudly, more angrily: '*Wrong?* I'll tell you what's *wrong*, Dennis! *This* is! This whole set-up, this whole secret so-called childminding set-up that nobody wanted to tell me about. And no wonder – no bloody wonder, is it? How *dare* you take my grandchildren away from me? How *dare* you, after everything that happened with our own children?'

'Let's not do this in front of the kids, Kate,' he said, quietly. Amelia and Alfie had both stopped dead, looking at her in surprise.

'Whassa matter, Nanny?' Amelia said. Both the children were wet and shivering.

'I need to get them dried and dressed,' Dennis went on.

'No you don't,' Kate snapped. 'I do. *I* will.'

'Kate, this is ridiculous. I ...'

'It's not ridiculous, actually,' I said, stepping forward so that I was eyeball to eyeball with him. 'You have no idea what Kate's been through, worrying about these children. She's quite right – in the circumstances, it would be much better if she takes the children to get them dressed, while you ...' I glanced down at his dripping swimming shorts, 'You might like to get yourself changed. Then it'll be easier to have a proper conversation.'

Dennis stared at me. He was younger than me, taller than me and had at least twice as much muscle bulk. I felt an idiot for not keeping my mouth shut. But then I saw the look of gratitude Kate was giving me, and I felt something altogether different.

'And you are ...?' Dennis demanded, looking me up and down.

I pulled myself up to my full height, such as it was.

'I,' I said, lifting my chin, smiling back at him, 'am Kate's boyfriend.'

KATE

I'll Huff and I'll Puff and I'll Blow Your House Down

It was actually the best thing he could have said, even if it wasn't actually true. Despite everything, I couldn't help smiling as the shock registered on Dennis's face.

'Is that right?' he demanded.

'Yes. He's my boyfriend.' I took hold of Amelia's and Alfie's hands and led them towards the changing rooms. 'Where are their clothes?'

Dennis followed me, handing me a key on a band that he'd taken off his wrist.

'In the locker. It's number seventy-two, down that aisle there.' He gave Bob another black look. '*He's* not dressing my grandchildren. I don't know him from Adam.'

'I'll take Freddie to the café and wait for you there,' Bob said at once. He smiled at me and, turning his back on Dennis, gave me a wink and then a quick peck on the cheek. Dennis was looking indignant.

'He's a bit old for you, isn't he?' he muttered as Bob walked away.

'You've got a bloody cheek,' I retorted, not amused anymore. 'He's a lovely man who happens to care about me – and I care about him,' I added, realising how true it was.

'In that case,' Dennis said, to my surprise, as he turned his back on me and went to get his own clothes out of another locker, 'good for you.'

'I swimmed, Nanny!' Amelia babbled with excitement as I stripped off her armbands and wet costume and wrapped her in her towel. 'I swimmed a lot!'

'Swim, swim!' echoed Alfie.

'I jumped in!' Amelia jumped up and down on the floor of the changing cubicle to demonstrate. 'Jump! Jump! In the water!'

'Did you?' I looked at her anxiously. 'Were you wearing your armbands? Was Granddad holding your hands when you jumped?'

'Granddad holded me,' she confirmed. 'Alfie jumped too.'

'Dump! Dump!' agreed Alfie, demonstrating with a slightly wobbly hop and a skip.

I tried, while I was towelling them both dry and helping them into dry nappies and clothes, to take some deep breaths. OK, the main thing, the most important thing, was that they both seemed fine. Dennis didn't appear to have had a drink. It was strange to realise that I couldn't actually remember when I'd last seen him sober. Since the divorce, I'd only seen him a handful of times, at a distance, and I'd had no idea, or any interest come to that, whether he'd been drunk or not. But he'd certainly been drinking throughout most of our marriage. He looked older now, of course, but also ... somewhat different, being sober. Better, obviously. Fitter. But to be honest, who cared? Today might have been a one-off. He might be drunk again tomorrow, for all I knew, and I sure as hell wasn't going to take that chance. As far as I was concerned, he wouldn't be bringing the twins – or any of the grandchildren – swimming again, because he wouldn't be looking after them.

'If Michael and Jo don't want me to look after them, I'll pay for them to get a proper childminder,' I told him when we were all assembled in the café. 'This is *not* going to happen anymore.'

He frowned. 'Why would they not want *you* to look after the twins?'

'You tell *me*!' I retorted. 'Did they tell you I was too forgetful? Or too busy with my friends? Or did they say it was because Danielle was nagging them?'

'I don't know what you're talking about. I was under the impression you couldn't look after them anymore for some reason of your own.'

I stared at him. 'I don't believe you. You're saying they didn't even tell you they'd stopped me from having the twins? I'd been looking after them three days a week for the past eighteen months. They told me they'd found a childminder. If I'd known it was *you*, inveigling your way into their lives, stealing my grandchildren from me ...!'

Dennis held up both hands, shaking his head at me.

'Kate, I promise you, it wasn't like that! It was no secret, not as far as I was concerned, anyway. I presumed you knew I was seeing Michael, and Stephanie.'

'You really think I would have stood for it?' I snapped.

'Sorry, but it wasn't your decision to make. They're grown-ups, it was up to them to decide whether they wanted to be in contact with me or not.'

'Alfie and Amelia aren't grown-ups, though, are they. They didn't get any say in this! They were happy with me. And more to the point, they were *safe* with me.'

'What's that supposed to mean?' He narrowed his eyes at me. 'They're perfectly safe with me too.'

'Are they? What, just until you have the next drink? The one that takes you over the edge?' I lowered my voice, glancing at the twins, who were tucking into juice and biscuits. 'Like when you took Stephanie swimming and nearly drowned her,' I added in an angry whisper. 'Or when she had a bad asthma attack – *your* fault – and you slept through it? Slept through your daughter having an almost-fatal allergic reaction, Dennis!'

He dropped his eyes. There was silence for a moment.

'Nanny?' Amelia began, looking from one of us to the other.

'Children, if you've finished your drinks, why don't we go and look at the little train over there?' Bob suggested. I nodded my thanks at him as they jumped up eagerly and ran with Freddie to the coin-operated children's ride in the corner of the café.

'You're right. I deserve everything you can say about me, the way I was back then,' Dennis admitted quietly. 'But I can't do anything to change the past, Kate. God knows I've spent every day of my life since the divorce, regretting all those things. I know it doesn't help,' he added quickly. 'But it did have one good outcome. After you divorced me, I gave up the drink.'

'Oh, yes, sure. For how long? A day? Two days?'

'For good.' He frowned again. 'I thought you realised that? I told you at the time I was going to join AA.'

'Yes, you probably did, but you'd said it before, and you'll probably say it again.'

'Kate, I meant it. I did join AA. I stopped drinking. I haven't had a drink since.' He gave a little wry smile. 'I'm one of their most successful graduates. I help mentor the new recruits now. I mean it, I'm sober, Kate. Not just today, not just this week. I don't drink anymore. I learned my lesson.'

'Did you.' I felt tears come to my eyes. 'Did you really. Well, thanks. It was too bloody late.'

'I know. I'm sorry.' We looked at each other, and I could actually see the bare honesty in his eyes. But then he added, 'I thought, by getting in touch with the children again, by trying somehow to make up to them for everything ...'

'They didn't even remember! They were too young to understand how bad it was! I presume *Danielle* didn't rush to be reunited with you?'

'No.' He looked away. 'Sadly, not. I presumed it was too awkward for her – living in France.'

'No, Dennis – face facts! She's still too angry with you! She had to help me bring up her brother and sister because you were too *pissed* to take any part in their childhoods. She had to watch me clearing up after you – throwing out your empties, clearing up your sick, opening the windows to get rid of the constant *stink* ...'

'I know. I know. I'm sorry.' He spread his hands. 'What do you want me to say?'

'Did you think it'd make you feel better, getting back in touch with the other two – was that it? You thought it'd be nice to start all over again with them now, wipe the slate clean? That just isn't fair!'

'No. That wasn't it. I haven't done this just to make *myself* feel better. I thought they'd tell *you* I was seeing them again. I thought if you heard I was sober, that I was being a better father now ...' He stopped, seeing the look on my face. 'But I see I was wrong. As you say, it's too late.'

'You were hoping for ... what? A reconciliation?' I said incredulously. 'Are you *joking*?'

'Well, obviously it's out of the question anyway. Apparently you're with someone else now.'

'Yes! Yes I am! Bob and I are very happy together!' I lied smoothly. 'But that's beside the point. You've tricked Michael and Jo into letting you look after the twins.'

'No tricks! They asked me. They said they were stuck, that you couldn't do it, and I agreed.'

'But they didn't know about your drinking. Michael's forgotten, or he'd never have let you have his children, even for a day, even for a minute!'

'I told them.'

'You what?'

'I told them, of course I did.' He shrugged. 'It was only right to be honest about it. They know the whole story now. They're just pleased at how I've turned my life around. They say I deserve another chance.'

I gasped. 'Oh, *do* they!'

'Yes, Kate, they do. They trusted me with their children, and I can't tell you how much that means to me.'

I looked over at where Bob was lifting Alfie into the little train next to Amelia. Their shiny blond heads touching, their sweet baby faces beaming, they were squealing and laughing with excitement, and I loved them so much it made my heart lurch.

'And I can't tell *you*,' I said stonily, 'how much it hurts me.'

Bob and I followed him back to his house. I watched the back of his car all the way, imagining the twins in their car seats in the back, resenting every extra minute they were spending with him.

'Do you want to come in?' he asked as we pulled up behind his car.

'No thank you. I'm going to phone Michael. We'll go from there.'

'Fair enough.' He unstrapped the twins from their seats and took them inside, closing the door behind them. I swallowed, but the lump in my throat wouldn't go down.

'Are you sure you don't want to ...?' Bob asked gently.

'Not yet. I'll wait for Michael.'

'I know about it,' I told him as soon as he answered the phone. 'I know about your father. I'm at his house.'

'Oh God. Mum, I'm sorry. I was going to tell you.'

'Were you?'

'Yes! Yes, of course I was. I mean, it would have come out sooner or later, we knew that.'

'Yes. Probably as soon as Amelia could manage to say the word *Granddad*,' I said. 'No wonder you weren't inviting me round too often, Michael. You must have been worried she was going to manage to tell me about it herself any time now.'

'Mum, that's not how it was. Honestly, listen ...'

'No – *you* listen! Have you got any idea how much this has hurt me? Stopping me from seeing the twins and sending them to *him*? Can you imagine how I felt when I found out? He was a *drunk*, Mike – a hopeless, stinking, drunk. He nearly killed Stephanie. He ...'

'*What*?'

I stopped. 'He said he told you.'

'He told me he'd had a drink problem,' he said, shakily. 'But what are you saying about Steph?'

'We need to talk.' I stared out of the car window, at the house where my lying, selfish, ex-husband was robbing me of the company of my grandchildren. 'I'll wait for you here.'

He got away from work early. He pulled up on the opposite side of the road, with a screech of tyres and a look of real anxiety. Bob, who seemed to have been emboldened by pretending to be my boyfriend, gave me another kiss on the cheek as he got out of the car.

'I'll take Freddie for a little walk for five minutes,' he said, 'and give the two of you some space.'

'So tell me,' said Michael as he slid into the passenger seat.

And I did. I didn't spare him. I didn't leave out any details.

'I don't remember,' he said, his voice wavering. 'I didn't realise it was quite so ...'

'Dreadful,' I filled in for him. 'It was dreadful. Did you think I'd have left him, if it wasn't?'

He swallowed. 'He's different now, though.'

'Yes. So I understand.'

'But you can't forgive him. I suppose I don't blame you,' he added quickly.

'No, I can't forgive him. I'm glad he's got himself off the drink. But he's manipulated you, and Steph, and it's not right that he's looking after the kids. Even if he is different now. It's not ... it's just not ...'

'Fair.' Michael looked at me and nodded. 'I'm sorry, Mum. We honestly thought it was for the best at the time. I know Danielle made us feel guilty, but we thought she was right, we thought it was for the best for *your* sake. We thought it was too much for you and you were getting stressed out – we seriously believed that was why you were losing things. Jo and I have felt really bad about it since we found out it was Amelia who took them.' He sighed. 'We've been going over and over it every evening, discussing how to tell you it was Dad looking after the twins, and whether to change our minds and ask you to have them back again.'

'Yes! Please, yes, I'd love to have them back.'

'But you're so busy now! You're looking after your friend who has the cancer. Don't get me wrong, I think it's great that you're doing that. And then there's ...' He nodded to the pavement outside the car, where Bob had returned and was now talking to little Freddie sitting in his buggy. 'There's Bob,' he said. 'I gather you two are an item now.'

'What? No, we're not an item! Who told you that?'

'Nobody. I just thought – from the way he's come with you today, and he seemed to be so, well, protective of you. And the way he looks at you, and everything,' he added, looking a bit awkward. 'I just assumed.'

I looked out at Bob again. It was true. He'd come with me – insisted on it – listened to me and comforted me, stood up to Dennis for me and even declared himself to be my *boyfriend.* In my head, I'd treated it as a bit of a joke, but I was being unfair. He'd already told me he loved me; I'd already explained that I only loved him as a friend.

'We're very fond of each other,' I told Michael now, without taking my eyes off Bob. 'He's a lovely man. He'll always want whatever's best for me.'

'Then that's good. I'm pleased.' He coughed. 'Look, Mum, I've got a suggestion. Jo's friend Sally has recommended a childminder – a real one this time,' he added with an apologetic smile. 'We'd like to give her a try – it'll be good for the twins, too, as there'll be other children there for them to play with. We're just going to start off with one day a week, though. So we'll only need childcare on two other days in future. How about you and Dad share it? One day a week each?'

'No, Michael. He shouldn't have the twins at all. I'll have them both days. I can fit it around Pam. It'll be fine.'

He was quiet for a moment, chewing his lip.

'You don't think he has the right to see his grandchildren at all?'

'The right?' I scoffed. 'No, I do not. He hasn't earned any rights. And anyway, wasn't it you who found out for me about grandparents' rights? We don't have any! You told me that yourself! If I don't have any rights, he *certainly* doesn't.'

'That's true. I did think it was sad, though, when I found that out – about grandparents' rights. I wonder how many grandparents are having to live with that situation, and can't do anything about it.'

I looked out at Bob again, and thought, with a pang, about what he went through, to say nothing of the lengths he'd been prepared to go to, when he thought he might be stopped from seeing Freddie. I thought about Pam, spending her lonely days sitting at home longing for the occasional chance to see those kids she thought of as her own grandchildren. As I watched him, Bob turned and looked back at me. He opened the car door.

'Everything all right?' he asked cautiously. 'Shall I go for another walk round the block?'

'No.' I smiled at him. 'We're just finishing talking. Thanks, Bob. You've been such a help today.'

'It's nothing compared with the help you gave me a while back,' he said, leaning awkwardly down to talk to me around the car door. He glanced at Michael and added with a little shake of his head, 'It's hard, you see, lad. Hard for us grandparents, if we think we're losing our grandchildren. We've got no rights, as you know. Even when we're helping you out, doing you a favour by looking after them, we're actually relying on ... your *generosity*.'

'I know,' Michael said quietly. 'I can see that.'

'OK,' I decided suddenly. 'You're right, it's the best way forward.'

'You'll have the twins again, one day a week, for us? We'd be so grateful, Mum.' He pulled me into a hug and kissed me. 'And you don't mind about Dad doing the other day?'

'It's not my decision, is it. *I* don't like it, but if you and Jo are quite satisfied that he's a reformed character, quite sure he'll never do anything to put the twins at risk ...'

'We have to be. I understand how you can't forgive him, Mum, but – it's made me happy to have my dad back in my life again, and in my children's lives.'

'Well, what can I say to that? I just wish I had your faith.'

'Tell him we'll be doing spot checks on him,' Bob said. I looked up at him, and the expression on his face was so earnest, I wanted to jump out of the car and kiss him.

'That's not a bad idea, actually,' Michael said, laughing.

'I wasn't joking,' Bob said. 'If it stops Kate from worrying, we'll come round here every week and see what he's up to. You can tell him that from me.'

'OK, you're on. I will,' agreed Michael. 'I'm glad Mum's got you to fight her corner, Bob. And thank you both. I'm sorry you had such a shock today, Mum. Sorry about all of it.'

He got out of the car to go and collect the twins.

'You can get back in the car now,' I told Bob, smiling up at him.

And when he did, I kissed him.

KATE

If You're Happy and You Know It

If anything, Stephanie was even more shocked than Michael when I told her the truth about her father.

'He took me in the pool without armbands and let go of me?' she whispered. She glanced at Izzie, who was playing with her toys on the floor. 'And I was only ... how old?'

'About two.'

She swallowed.

'The lifeguard ran round and got you. They phoned me, from the pool, to come and pick you and Michael up. The shock of being yelled at by the lifeguard had almost sobered your father up by then. Almost.'

'You could have got him arrested, couldn't you? Surely, it was neglect – even more than the other times.' I'd already finished telling her about the peanut butter, the lack of food, the asthma attack. As well as several other incidents, almost as bad.

'Why do you think I'm still so angry about it?' I said. 'Why do you think I can't get over it, even if he has completely changed?'

'Because you can't forgive him, obviously.'

'Because I can't forgive myself either.' I turned away and tried to swallow back the tears, but she was beside me in an instant, putting her arms round me. 'It was my fault too,' I finally admitted as my daughter held me. 'I should have left him much sooner – as soon as there was the slightest inkling he'd put any of you in danger. I was too afraid of being on my own with three children. Looking back, it's just ridiculous. He was never there for us anyway! What kind of mother was I, putting up with that sort of a life, when I should have taken you away from it?'

'What kind of mother? A frightened one, obviously,' she said softly against my hair. 'And one who deserved so much better.'

'I can't understand Michael and Jo,' Danielle said on the phone. 'What the hell's wrong with them? They're *still* letting him have the twins? Even now they know what he's like?'

'What he *was* like,' I said wearily. 'Look, I don't particularly like it either, but if I start kicking off about it, there's going to be more animosity and in the long run, it'll be the children who are affected.'

'They'll be affected if he starts getting pissed again and neglects them, Mum!'

I sighed. I didn't blame her. Like me, she was never going to get over the way Dennis used to be.

'He's not drinking now. I know there's no absolute guarantee that he won't start again, but at least now Michael knows exactly how bad he was back then, he'll be watching him like a hawk. So will I.'

'But you trust him. You're trusting him with those children?'

'I'm not sure I'll ever be able to trust him again, not one hundred percent. But I do believe him – he's sober, he's different. Too late, from my point of view. But maybe not too late to have a relationship with his grandchildren.' I paused. 'I happen to think it's important , that relationship. I've realised, recently, how lucky I've been.'

'Not lucky!' she retorted. 'You've been taken for granted!'

'No, Dannie, I haven't been. We've been through this before, but you really do need to understand – I love all the grandchildren equally. That includes yours, and yes, I wish I could see them more often. And you! But that's the way it is. You know, I was terribly hurt when Michael said I wouldn't be looking after the twins anymore.' I felt the wobble in my voice. 'It was a misunderstanding, but you didn't help, by constantly getting on at him about me having them too much.'

'I was only thinking of you,' she said a little sulkily.

'Well, thank you, but trust me – I can make my own decisions about what I've got the time and energy to do with my life. I'm not totally incapacitated yet.'

We both laughed and it took the edge off things slightly.

'So, now we've got this new agreement about sharing the childcare,' I went on, 'I want it to work. I don't want any of you bitching at each other about what you do – or what I do.'

'OK,' she said quietly. 'Understood. So what about Steph? Is she up for all this forgiving and forgetting too?'

'Well, as you know, she's been seeing your father recently too, but she's not sure now whether she wants to anymore. She needs time to process what I've told her about him. If she does get over it, and wants him to go on seeing Izzie and the baby … well, if I can put my personal feelings to one side, I think you should do the same.'

'I suppose so. But he needn't think *I'm* ever going to start having jolly little visits to him, and nor are my children.'

'Nor am I,' I assured her. 'But you know, Dannie, your kids will have to make their own minds up.'

There was a silence. I could picture her, over in her house in France, grappling with the truth I'd had to take on board myself. The fact that even if we stop our children from seeing their fathers, our grandchildren from seeing their grandparents, they might decide to do it anyway when they're old enough.

'I've already told them what he was like,' she said. 'They've never wanted anything to do with him. They've got too much loyalty to *you*. And so have I, Mum,' she added.

'That's nice to hear. Thank you.' I smiled to myself. 'And I do appreciate that you want what's best for me, and for your brother and sister. But please don't worry. Everything's under control over here. As I said, we'll all be watching your father so closely he won't dare put a foot wrong. Even Bob is on the case.'

'You and Bob,' she said. 'It sounds like you're getting very friendly?'

'Yes, we are,' I said, and left it at that.

None of her business!

Actually, it would have been hard to give much more of a response, because I didn't really have the words to describe where our relationship was at. It was true that since the day he came with me to confront Dennis, things had changed. We were seeing more of each other, and we were more comfortable with each other. I think we were both aware that his chivalry that day, to say nothing of the kiss in the car afterwards, had melted away the awkwardness that had hung between us ever since the mortifying day he'd told me he loved me. Nothing had been said, by either of us, but if we walked together we'd link arms, and on a couple of occasions when we'd watched a film on TV together at one or other of our homes, we cuddled up on the sofa. We kissed goodnight, but it was … tender, rather than passionate.

'I've got to say this,' I told him eventually, determined to overcome my embarrassment and get it out of the way. 'If you're thinking … well, if you're hoping …' I looked away from him and took a deep breath. 'I don't want anything physical, Bob. I'm sorry. I've been so long on my own. It's so long since I've had any interest in … '

'Thank God for that!' he said immediately. 'I was terrified you might be expecting me to try to perform. I'd have to have gone and bought some of those pills,

346

whatever they're called – and probably got a book out of the library to remind me how to go about it!'

And we both laughed so hard, it was a good ten minutes before I could get up off the sofa to make our cocoa.

JACKIE

And They All Lived Happily Ever After

I was a bit surprised at first. Kate had been so horrified when he'd come out with all that crap about being in love with her, hadn't she! But after a while, when I got used to seeing them together, holding hands and joking together like an old married couple, I started to get it. They just *liked* each other. They cared about each other. They looked out for each other. They were comfortable together and company for each other. I guess, in the end, that's a kind of love too, and probably a lot less bloody hassle than the kind where you want to rip each other's clothes off one minute, and tear each other's throats out the next.

And the other thing, of course, was that they'd both been through some crap, one way or another, and helped each other through it. They both understood the whole *grandparent* thing – they had that in common. And OK, when I first met them, it was true I thought they were both nuts, the way they seemed to think it was such fantastic fun having their grandkids. Looking after little Autumn – back then, as far as I was concerned it was a duty, not a pleasure. Who'd have thought I'd be looking forward to the next grandchild as much as I was now? To be totally honest, I was glad my daughter wasn't going to be working after the baby arrived. I wasn't too sure I could face looking after two of them at the same time. But of course, I knew I'd go round there like a shot if she needed me. I was even planning to take a couple of weeks off work, just so I could get a chance to bond with the kid. I wasn't very good at that kind of stuff. But I was going to try.

It was good to have Kate back at Mini Music Makers on Thursdays with the twins. It hadn't felt right without her there.

'That's a bit of luck, you getting a Thursday!' I said, as I knew she was only having the twins one day a week now.

'No luck involved,' she shot back. 'I told Dennis I was doing Thursdays so if he wanted to do anything, it would have to be Tuesdays. If he didn't like it, he could go to hell.'

I liked her new attitude to her ex. Before, she never used to talk about him. It was like he was a nasty secret she was keeping locked away. Now it was all out in the open and so were her feelings about him. I thought it was better – healthier. She said she was never going to start liking him, but she'd got to accept that he was part of her kids' and grandkids' lives now if it was what they wanted. I admired her for that.

There was something else I admired too – the way she was looking after Pam. I'm afraid that woman had got right up my nose from the start, and I wasn't at all sure that if I'd been Kate, I'd have been able to get past that, even despite the cancer situation. Pam was certainly different now, in fact it was hard to believe it was the same woman, but I put that down to her being ill, and weak, and not having the strength to be so nasty.

And then, everything changed.

It was the last session of Music Makers before the Christmas break, and the kids had had a brilliant time. Someone's granddad had dressed up as Father Christmas and the children had all got a little present, and a cake, and played games and sung Christmassy songs. Afterwards, Kate had promised us coffee and sandwiches back at her house instead of going to the café.

'We'll make it our own little Christmas party,' she'd said, adding that she wanted to include Pam. 'She's been feeling a lot better recently,' she said. 'I think she's turning a corner, with this treatment.'

Of course, I was glad to hear that, and we were all pleased to see Pam looking brighter, better, and happier. She'd dressed up a bit, put on some Christmassy earrings, and was looking like she was really in a party mood.

'You're looking really well,' I said. 'Are they pleased with you at the hospital?'

'Yes.' She nodded and exchanged a look with Kate, who smiled back at her. 'In fact, Kate took me for an appointment yesterday – and to cut a long story short, it's very good news. The tumour has shrunk. They're going to operate in the new year.'

'That's terrific news!' Bob shouted, struggling to his feet and going to hug her. 'Kate, you didn't tell me.'

'I wanted Pam to have her moment,' she said. 'Isn't it marvellous?'

'It's not necessarily going to work, you know,' Pam warned her. 'There's still a long way to go, a lot of *ifs* and *buts.*'

'But it's looking more hopeful?' I suggested.

'Definitely.' She smiled round at us all. 'I'm focusing on those weddings coming up. I want to be here for them! And your daughter's new baby, Jackie – I've got to hang on to see whether it's a boy or a girl.'

'Don't talk like that,' Kate said quickly. 'You *will* be here.'

'Well, at one time it didn't look too likely, but now there's a chance, at least. And obviously, I have *you* to thank for much of that – all the TLC you've been giving me. So I've bought you a little something for Christmas, Kate, to show my appreciation of you for being such a good friend.'

We all cheered, even as Kate tried to shrug it off, and say all the usual stuff about having done nothing at all, really it was nothing, it was only what anybody would do –

and all the time Pam was holding out this little gift-wrapped box and pushing it into her hands until Kate was forced to take it and unwrap it. It was a gorgeous silver and jade bracelet, which she put on straight away, making a joke about not leaving it lying around while Amelia was there in case it got taken home in her bag, and we all laughed.

'You didn't need to do that,' she told Pam quietly.

'Well, I wanted to. I'm well aware of how I behaved to you, earlier on.'

'That's all in the past. And I understand. You had your reasons.'

'Reasons, perhaps, but no excuses. And now ...' She smiled around at us again. 'Now, things have changed.'

'Yes, thank God,' Kate began, but Pam stopped her.

'I'm not just talking about my health. Things have changed with my family. I mean, Colin's family.'

'Oh?' I knew what the set-up there was, of course. And I'd loved hearing about the episode where the horrible son and his wife had turned up, expecting a babysitter, and Kate had given them a piece of her mind – that was brilliant! 'What's happened?'

'She's left him!' Pam looked like she wanted to jump up and down, she was so delighted. 'Tania's left Russell! Apparently he's moving to America – wanted her and the kids to go with him – but she finally put her foot down. She said he'd been a controlling bully all through their marriage, never allowing her any opinions of her own or to have a life of her own, and when he told her these plans he'd made for relocating to America, without having even consulted her about any of it, she suddenly realised she'd had enough. She told him she wasn't going, the children weren't going, and by the way, she didn't even want to be married to him anymore.'

'Oh my God!' This was all apparently news to Kate as well as to me and Bob. 'What did he say?'

'She said at first he looked as if the shock might kill him. But when he realised she was serious, it was almost like she was a servant who'd overstepped the mark so he wanted rid of her as soon as possible. And as for the children – he thinks if he has them out to stay with him in the States every school holiday, that'll be 'quality time' for them all. He actually thinks they're going to look forward to it.'

'Well ...' Kate put her head on one side. 'Well, maybe they will. Maybe it's good that they'll still see their father.'

She'd changed her tune, you see. Since she found out two of her own kids had been secretly meeting up with their dad, it had made her think. She'd already said as much to me.

Pam shrugged. 'Perhaps you're right. Or perhaps he'll find someone else out there to farm them off to when it becomes inconvenient to look after them.' Then she smiled again. 'But the good news, from my point of view, is that Tania's told me I'm welcome to see George and Lily as often as I want, whenever I want. She says I'm welcome at their house, that she'll bring them over to see me as often as she possibly can, that she's sorry, really sorry, about the way things have been ...'

She couldn't go on – she was overcome. Kate and Bob were both on their feet, hugging her again, and I felt like I should follow suit, but I guess I'll always be the cynic of the bunch. I couldn't help thinking: *Yeah, she's sorry now, she's happy to welcome Pam into their family now – well, there's a surprise. She's going to need all the help she can get now she'll be a single parent!*

'I know she might just be using me again,' Pam said eventually, blowing her nose, and I felt guilty, as if I'd spoken out loud. 'I don't think it's *just* that, though. I always did think Tania would be different with me, if it wasn't for Russell. And anyway, to be honest ...' She paused, seeming to struggle for the right words.

'You don't care, do you?' Kate suggested. 'At the end of the day, you're going to be seeing much more of the children. That's all that matters.'

'Exactly,' she said. 'That's it, exactly, Kate. I love them, and I think – I *know* – they want to see me, too.'

'It's a special relationship, isn't it,' Kate said, glancing at Bob, and he put his arm around her as they both smiled at each other. 'Grandparents and children – it's something very special. We can't afford to be too picky about it. We just need to be happy that we have it.'

Just at that moment, my little Autumn came tearing into the lounge, from where they'd been playing with their toys in the other room, chased by Freddie and closely followed by the twins, all of them shrieking at the tops of their voices, laughing and excited and just being happy, normal children. And I thought about the new baby coming, and how Autumn was going to love being a big sister, and how much better I'd be this time around at changing nappies and folding up buggies and all the other stuff I'd struggled with – and I realised they were right. I *got* it, after all. I might have been the last to do it, but I got up and gave Pam a hug too, then, and I have to say I felt quite warm and fuzzy and happy inside. But then again, it was Christmas, and I'd probably got a sugar high from all the cakes and mince pies.

'There's something else special, too,' I said. Perhaps I was actually drunk, although I'd only had a coffee. 'Us four. *We're* special, aren't we? Grandparents United, that's what we are! Mess with one of us, you mess with us all!'

'You're right there,' Kate said, giving Bob a special kind of smile that made my warm fuzzy feeling go slightly quivery at the edges. 'Grandparents United, that's us.'

'What's *Grandparents?*' We hadn't noticed little Freddie had been listening.

'We are,' Bob told him. 'All of us nannies and granddads. We're called *grandparents.*'

'Because you're grand?' he said, and we all laughed.

'Yes, that's right, we're *grand*,' Kate said. 'Like the *Grand Old Duke of York*, Freddie!' She got to her feet, yelling at the kids that she was going to make their lunch, and if anyone didn't want cheese or Marmite they'd better shout *now*. And all four of them scuttled back out of the room, Freddie and Amelia competing with each other to shout *Cheese!* and *Marmite!* the loudest

And as they all went out of earshot, she turned back to us and added with a smile, 'And, talking of *Grandparents United*, if I ever want the ex-husband bumped off in the middle of the night, I'll count on you three to give me a hand – right?'

'Right!' we all chorused.

I actually thought it sounded like a bloody *grand* idea. But then, let's be honest – I would, wouldn't I.

Printed in Great Britain
by Amazon

62908351R00201